SONGS OF THE LOST ISLANDS

SONGS
OF THE
LOST ISLANDS

Part Three
THE VALLEY OF
NARGROND

SACD Catalogue record: 000178361 – 28/04/2016

Book's cover and portraits:
Virginie Carquin - Brussels, Belgium

Heraldry, genealogy and maps:
Sylvain Sauvage - La Tour-de-Peilz, Switzerland

Editorial correction:
Thomas Bailey - Oxford, UK

Editorial review:
Laurent Chasseau - Paris, France
Eric Train - Biarritz, France

Songs of the Lost Islands existing publications

· An Act of Faith – May 2019

· The Lonely Seeker – June 2019

· The Valley of Nargrond – July 2019

Forthcoming publication

· Two Winged Lions (2021)

Biography

C. A. Oliver was born in 1971 and spent his youth between Oxford and Bordeaux. From an early age, he was an avid reader of both the English and French canons, and it was J.R.R. Tolkien and Maurice Druon who would come to influence his writing above all others.

In his teenage years, Oliver and four friends began a tabletop role-playing game. Fifteen years later, after 3,500 hours of discussion, imagination and strategy, what began as a game had developed into an entire universe. As gamemaster, Oliver documented the gargantuan campaign's progress.

This fantasy world lay dormant for several years. Then, in 2014, after witnessing uncanny parallels with real-world politics, Oliver began to forge Songs of the Lost Islands, a 12-part fantasy series that draws heavily on the fifteen-year campaign. He started writing the first trilogy at Sandfield Road in Oxford, the very street on which Tolkien once lived. It was concluded at Rue Alexandre Dumas in Saint-Germain-en-Laye, where Dumas composed The Three Musketeers.

C. A. Oliver now lives between Paris and Rio de Janeiro, having married a Brazilian academic. Songs of the Lost Islands has been above all inspired by what Oliver knows best: the ever-changing winds of global politics, the depth and scope of English fantasy; and the fragile, incomprehensible beauty of his wife's homeland.

ISBN: 9781081491420
Legal deposit: July 2019

Acknowledgements

It has taken me five years to write the first three instalments of Songs of the Lost Islands. But developing the world that is the basis for these books was an even longer process.

It is now thirty years since I first joined forces with four of my closest friends to devise the world of the series. It began in the summer of 1989 with the creation of an RPG wargame campaign, in which different Elvin civilizations fought for the control of a distant archipelago. The arrival of Curwë and his companions in Llafal, an Elvin port on the island of Nyn Llyvary, marked the starting point of a story that would go on to last decades.

For the first twenty-three years, we had no intention of sharing these myths, legends and adventures with anyone outside our tight-knit group. It was a secret garden, or perhaps rather a dragon's lair, rich with treasures built up over 3,500 hours of gameplay. No intruder ever broke their way into our various dungeons: the garage of 37 Domaine de Hontane, near Bordeaux; a cramped bedroom in Oxford; and a flat in Arcachon, with a beautiful sea view we never found time to enjoy.

After the campaign had drawn to a close, the years went by and I found that I was missing the thrill of those night-time gatherings: the smell of smoke, the taste of wine and, above all, the noise of the rolling dice.

I therefore eventually gathered the material accumulated over all those years of frenetic creativity, and soon realized that I possessed enough content for twelve books. The distinctive nature of this story lies in its genesis: characters, embodied by players, interacting with plots and settings developed by the game master. Outcomes were decided by applying a set of specific wargame rules, the authority of which was unquestionable.

The result was quite stunning: a fifteen-year long campaign made up of dozens of characters, whose destinies were determined by both the roll of the multifaceted dice and the choices made by the players.

Much to my surprise, the first readers of An Act of Faith were very enthusiastic in their responses, and eager to discover what would follow. Some were fascinated by Roquen or Curwë, others resonated naturally with the more reckless Irawenti, while the more aesthetically minded readers were attracted to the Llewenti.

My mind was made up. I embarked on a quest to complete the twelve-book series.

When I started, I had no idea how complex it would be to forge Songs of the Lost Islands from all the material I had before me. I now look in utter fascination at the copies of An Act of Faith, The Lonely Seeker and The Valley of Nargrond sitting on my desk and feel relatively confident that the remaining tomes will follow. The debts of gratitude that I owe are therefore very significant.

Firstly, I must thank my beloved family: Mathilde, Marion and Agatha, who probably think me mad, but who nevertheless continue to provide their unwavering support.

I am enormously grateful to the scholars who have helped me negotiate the pitfalls of writing fantasy: Eric Train and Laurent Chasseau read the first drafts of the Songs and provided me with their insightful responses and suggestions. Their feedback was invaluable, not least because their passion for the Lost Islands dates all the way back to 1989.

The series could not have been written without Thomas Bailey, a gifted poet who studied at Oxford University, whose expertise and enthusiasm turned a manuscript into the finished article.

I am also extremely grateful to Virginie Carquin and Sylvain Sauvage for wonderfully designing and illustrating the Lost Islands, that last refuge of the Elves. Their prodigious efforts gave me the strength to push ahead, at a time when I was finally waking up to the full scale of the challenge before me.

Virginie is illustrating all twelve books of Songs of the Lost Islands. She has produced a series of twenty-three portraits of characters in the novels. Her work also features on the covers of the collectors' editions.

Sylvain has served as chief concept designer for the Lost Islands' world. His achievements include creating the maps of Oron, the genealogy of the clans and houses, and all their emblems and insignia. His overall contribution to the project is even more far-reaching; it includes, among many other things, designing the series' website.

Lastly, I must thank the readers of Songs of the Lost Islands, for already making it through more than a thousand pages of stories and legends about the Elves. As Feïwal dyn puts it:

"The quest for the Lost Islands is a journey that cannot offer any hope of return. It is a leap in the unknown. It is an act of faith."

TABLE OF CONTENTS

CHAPTER 1: Mynar dyl

2716, Season of Eïwele Llyi, 101st day, Nyn Llyvary, Llafal

"Stop at once! This is painful."

Though Mynar dyl spoke softly, all those who stood within the great edifice could feel his discontent. He shook his head sadly, a look of poignant regret upon his face. The fair warlord of clan Ernaly seemed upset by his troupe's poor performance. They were hardly living up to the grandiose spectacle he had envisioned.

Although they knew their director was unhappy, most of the dancers and musicians gathered in the central part of Eïwele Llyi's temple had missed what he had said. Like apprentice actors struggling to appreciate some nuance in Llewenti pronunciation, all those assembled leaned forward and strained their ears. Silence descended like a rapid gust of wind across the nave. Tension in the rehearsal reached its peak, as the troupe's collective attention focussed on Mynar dyl. It felt as if all the heroic characters, whose images decorated the numerous stained-glass windows above the nave, were holding their breath along with the performers below.

Within the spacious white temple of Llafal, Mynar dyl's voice rose.

"This shrine will soon host the music festival of Llafal. When the time comes, this very stage, at the heart of the temple, will become the centre of the Lost Islands."

Mynar dyl allowed a little time to pass before continuing, so that all could measure the importance of what would follow. He was dressed with elegance. Three white feathers hung from a dark green cloth tied around his blond hair, and his dance costume was a beautiful sapphire blue. Fierce beauty radiated from his features. The warlord continued.

"Our troupe has been chosen by Matriarch Nyriele to open the festival. I am sure you can all understand her reasoning. I believe she wants her temple to remain the greatest place on the Islands to worship artistic creation and sovereign beauty. Our sole purpose is to honour her ambition. This is the task which was appointed to us by the high priestess of Eïwele Llyi."

Reaching the centre of the nave, Mynar dyl stopped in front the temple's main altar, taking a moment to contemplate it. This unique sculptural masterpiece was made entirely of black marble, except for its base and decorative moulding.

From his high position in the temple's chancel near the altar, Mynar dyl looked down at the brightly coloured throng of dancers and musicians who formed his troupe. His hawk-like eyes admired the drawings and paintings displayed across the stage. Over fifty days of artistic devotion had gone into setting the impressive scene before him.

Seeing the anxiety he was instilling in his troupe, Mynar dyl glowed with pleasure. before continuing his speech with his usual professorial tone, going back to the genesis of his musical composition. He enjoyed the thrill of his power.

"The beginning of this year was marked by a major disaster, a tragedy unseen for several centuries. From the chaotic surge of the Sea of Llyoriane emerged a tidal wave, which devastated the lower city of Gwarystan, killing hundreds, if not thousands, and destroying entire boroughs near the harbour where mostly Men dwell. Elves in the richest parts of the great city were left unharmed. But among the traumatised victims who had witnessed the devastation, rumours circulated of gigantic waves repeatedly hitting the walls of the upper city, as though Gweïwal Uleydon himself had come to challenge the might of King Norelin's great stronghold."

The evocation of the recent tragedy provoked a deep silence. A growing malaise could be felt among the audience. Though they, as Elves of Llymar, would all be considered rebels by the king, none of them saw the inhabitants of his capital city as their enemies. No true Llewenti would ever wish such evil upon another Elf, even a Hawenti of Gwarystan.

"Victims of the natural disaster are still struggling to cope with the trauma of losing their homes and livelihoods. They witnessed first-hand what happens when the full force of nature is unleashed. It should remind us all the overwhelming power of the God of all Seas...
Faced with the tragedy that has ravaged Gwarystan, the Elves of the Islands should call upon Gweïwal Uleydon to seek his clemency. This is what we are trying to achieve with this grandiose ballet today: to pay homage to the Master of the Oceans and thus proclaim that we, the ancient Llewenti clans, remain his devoted servants," insisted Mynar dyl.

All Elves present nodded in agreement.

Ever since their coming to the Archipelago, the Llewenti had exclusively worshipped the deities of the Islands, and they did so with fervour. But they also understood the influences of other Gods. Though they did not worship them, they feared them, as one fears a threat on the distant horizon.
The God of Seas and Waters was an exception, due to his realm's proximity to their Islands. The Llewenti would often offer Gweïwal Uleydon sacrifices in the hope of appeasing his wrath.

Now that Mynar dyl was sure he commanded the full attention of his troupe, he elaborated further on the origins of his work.

"This ballet recounts the battle of Ruby and Winds... It depicts the great confrontation between the deity of winds and storms, Eïwal Ffeyn, and the fleet which carried Lormelin the Conqueror and his armies to our shores."

Mynar dyl looked fixedly towards an imaginary horizon, as if he were contemplating the infinity of the Austral Ocean's grandeur. His tone became more delicate. He seemed about to unveil an intimate secret.
A few dancers chose to sit down.

"You may be wondering why I decided to base this ballet upon events that occurred over 2200 years ago. I chose this decisive moment because it was the turning point in Llewenti history. This year's terrible events in Gwarystan somehow resonate with that long-forgotten past... when Gweïwal Uleydon roamed our waters.
I believe this piece has the power to evoke those heroic times when history became legend. I am eager to see your standard of performance start to meet those expectations."

Mynar dyl looked in the direction of a tall dancer, perched on narrow, six-foot stilts, dressed in the garments of the God of all waters. Gweïwal Uleydon was represented as being almost naked, barely covered by a toga made of shellfish. The towering dancer bore a harpoon and a casting net, the traditional weapons associated with the Master of Oceans. Painted across the upstage floor was a palace of coral and aquamarine. A beautiful backdrop depicted the Sunrise Gates, the entrance to Gweïwal Uleydon's marine domain. Emblazoned upon the dancer's crown was the god of waters' symbol, a casting net creating a tidal wave.
Now turning fully towards the tall dancer, Mynar dyl continued, his masterful tone now tainted with irony.

"My dear Ollayu, it is painfully evident from your performance that you have not yet sufficiently imagined what being a God would mean. Have you even considered the burden of your responsibilities towards Oron and its inhabitants?" he asked, like someone who had.
"When I see you crossing that stage, I am afraid. I feel utterly terrified. You're dancing in a way that looks like you're about to unleash a tidal wave against the entire Archipelago. You will know from your history and indeed from the very fact that we are standing here today, that nothing of the sort happened at the battle of Ruby and Winds..."

Mynar dyl abruptly mimicked some of the character's body movements in an exaggerated, grotesque way, mocking the dancer's substandard performance. A few Elves laughed, but the majority chose to remain silent. Any one of them could be the next target of Mynar dyl's ire.

Indifferent to his audience's mixed reaction, the warlord turned to other ancient myths to hammer his point home.

"After the genesis of Oron, each Gweïwal received his own realm to rule. After millennia of devastation, the chaos was ended. Since that time, the Greater Gods have avoided openly influencing the fate of the world."

Many of the dancers and musicians looked to the various marble statues which adorned the temple's nave, as if their frozen expressions could verify what Mynar dyl was saying. The statues all showed legendary figures from the Islands' history.

"Hence my humble request, my dear Ollayu! I do not want to see Gweïwal Uleydon stomp across that stage as though he were about to bring down the walls of the white temple with all his wrath."

Humiliated in front of his peers, Ollayu looked awkward, almost ridiculous in his supposed divine attire. Mynar dyl ignored his dismay.

"Music!" he ordered with a commanding tone.

"Mynar dyl will dance," announced the conductor of the symphony orchestra as he tapped his staff on the stand before him.

Soon a servant, who stood inside one of the numerous alcoves of the white temple, emerged from the shadows and brought forth a wooden box subtly carved from a reddish wood. The young Elf drew from the box a pair of fine sandals. Silver lace adorned the precious shoes, and hawk feathers had been set on their sides. The servant kneeled to put these dancing shoes on his master's feet.

The troupe's silence was so deep that nothing was heard but the careful fitting of the sandals. Then, Mynar dyl stood and, like a dancing king, sovereign of his realm, began gracefully stretching out his limbs, before rolling his head and torso down towards his feet to release tension throughout his body. Finally, the warlord performed three slight gestures of his hands, each possessing a magic of its own.

"Asna[1]," Mynar dyl uttered, and he thrust his hand forward in a commanding way.

"Eyu[2]," he said, his right foot tracing an elegant wave above an imaginary ocean.

"Ron[3]," the warlord concluded, as he mimed the God of all waters launching his mighty harpoon.

The music began to play.
Like an astonishing, gravity-defying acrobat, Mynar dyl began a true dance of waters, a sea ballet, the likes of which had rarely been seen.
After several passes, he stopped and addressed an imaginary public, like a Master of Dance would a lay audience.

"Gweïwal Uleydon is one of the chief architects of the world. He comes third in majesty among the Greater Gods, after Zenwon, the Air, and Agadeon, the Earth, but before Narkon, the Fire. Gweïwal Uleydon ensures the fluidity of all water upon Oron, blending with air to form clouds, freezing it into ice, running it down rivers and mixing in with all aspects of life. All bodies of water are under his government: lakes, bays, rivers... and even the streams under the earth, for his influence runs through the very veins of the world..."

Mynar dyl improvised a few dance steps, as light as the foam which floats above cresting waves, to illustrate the God of all waters' fluidity of movement. Catching his breath, he went on for the benefit of his troupe.

---

1 Asna: 'Power' in lingua Llewenti

2 Eyu: 'Water' in lingua Llewenti

3 Ron: 'Attack' in lingua Llewenti

"The audience needs to understand the reason for Gweïwal Uleydon's presence in the Austral Ocean on that dramatic day. It was no accident but his secret bond to the Elves that drove him to those latitudes, as the great Irawenti fleet travelled the high seas with King Lormelin's army onboard..."

Fully absorbed by what he described, like a seer experiencing an intense vision, Mynar dyl recited an entire passage of an ancient text by heart. The warlord possessed a gift for recounting tales. Acting came to him naturally.

"Afterward, with the glorious Dawn of Spring, those majestic Vessels were primed to set Sail, towards the lost Archipelago where the Star had fallen. Flying atop the Ships' Masts, billowing in the morning Wind, were the Colours of the noble Houses: the royal Red of the Dor Princes, the dark Green of the House of Dol Nos-Loscin, the midnight Blue of the House of Dol Etrond, along with many other prestigious Insignia, which all signified the Challenge that this Fleet did issue to the Austral Ocean, and their Ambition to conquer a new World."

Silence followed. The troupe's attention had been completely captured by the melody of the prose. Mynar dyl continued his explanation, like one enflamed with a mission. He wanted his artists to acquire a full comprehension of the tale, so that they could share his vision of the story. The warlord worked to inspire his listeners.

"You need to imagine the vastness of the Austral Ocean covered in the sails of the Irawenti ships. You need to see hundreds of their naves sailing south, their ship-decks bustling with High Elves in their thousands, their masts displaying the colours of the prestigious houses. The migration of an entire nation across the ocean: this is what I want you to contemplate..."

Mynar dyl looked down at a dozen Elves who were covered in wood and canvas. Positioned at regular intervals across the stage, they were meant to represent the Irawenti naves. His voice still melodious, he went on.

"Gweïwal Uleydon is escorting this great fleet of Elves secretly. He does not wish to be seen. Do you understand? Of course, he is the protector of all seafarers, but most of all he is the chief god of the Irawenti clans. Imagine him as he is represented in most Elvin traditions: a lawful power with a benign influence, a god who takes great care to preserve the world's harmony. Gweïwal Uleydon is offering calm seas to facilitate the migration of the children of Ö, as he calls his beloved Elves.

He remains their secret protector. Imagine that, on that historic day, the God of all waters is peacefully swimming in the wake of the Irawenti ships he so cherishes."

To illustrate his words, Mynar dyl performed in a few elegant steps amid the performers representing the Irawenti naves. Then he stopped, as if caught in sudden fright. None could understand the source of his fear, but all Elves present looked up to the temple's ceiling, where the warlord was pointing.

"Eïwal Ffeyn has come!" he cried out. "The deity of storms will sink Lormelin's fleet! The divine rebel will not let the High Elf king reach the shores of the Lost Islands!"

Answering his cry, numerous acrobats jumped from the shadows of the wooden beams that held up the white temple roof. Clad in grey garments, their silhouettes arced along great curving trajectories above. Thin, almost invisible ropes held them to the temple's roof. The acrobats, mimicking the flight of Eïwal Ffeyn's eerie servants, crossed the central nave's large space like as many priests of the deity of winds atop griffons and hippogriffs. They began a frantic battle against the Irawenti naves. The eyes of those fantastic creatures shone like the sun. Their golden colours glittered, as if their brightness could drive away the harmful invaders from the Islands.

"But the evil has not yet passed! The battle of Ruby and Winds begins!" cried Mynar dyl, as the music of the heroic symphony intensified.

A moment later, Mynar dyl stopped the ballet once again to give his own interpretation of the drama to the ensemble. From the humiliated Ollayu's hands, he seized a brightly coloured stone meant to represent a rich jewel with azure shades. Dancers and acrobats, musicians and actors, all stopped again to listen to his words.

"It was at this very moment, just as the celestial cohorts of Eïwal Ffeyn threatened to sink the fleet of the High Elves and the fury of the deity of winds could not be held back any longer, that Gweïwal Uleydon chose to offer the 'Aquamarine Pearl' to King Lormelin.
The God of all waters was forever changing the fate of he who would become the conqueror of the Archipelago. He had intervened in the destiny of the Hawenti nation... and therefore that of the Llewenti.
At this precise moment, I want the music to stop. I want only the sound of silence then: a long, very long and deep silence... as deep as the Austral Ocean itself. The public must understand that History was changed forever."

Brandishing the fake bluish stone above his head, as though it were the legendary jewel of Gweïwal Uleydon, Mynar dyl returned to the role, his eyes set ablaze by the passion that inhabited him.

"The Lenra Pearl!" he exclaimed like one possessed. "Gweïwal Uleydon has given the purest Aquamarine jewel to the king of the High Elves! Do you know what this means?"

Like enraptured children entranced by a powerful wizard, the troupe remained motionless and silent.

"Legends tell us that Lenra was a gem cut by Leïwal Vauis, the God of crafts, from the very essence of the Inner Sea. When the Pearl was offered to Gweïwal Uleydon, it was among the most prized of all the wonders crafted by the Gods and was coveted by many of them. It was said that the power of the Aquamarine Flow was woven through it...
Do you understand now? Lormelin took the Lenra Pearl. He used its power to defeat Eïwal Ffeyn.
The deity of storms and his celestial army were cast out of the Archipelago to their doom, incarcerated in the vast expanse of the Sea of Cyclones..."

Mynar dyl let a moment pass before concluding.

"The defeat of Eïwal Ffeyn will be the final act of our ballet. I will perform the role of the deity of storms when he understands that his fate has been sealed."

All looked at him in awe, already impatient to learn about the performance he had secretly prepared for the day of the spectacle. Such was the appeal that Mynar dyl could generate; he was a sufficiently complex artist to evoke a compelling mixture of fascination and repulsion.

★

Since the beginning of Mynar dyl's discourse, a clan Ernaly guard had been waiting in the shadows of the temple's colonnade, never quite daring to interrupt his chief. Seeing that Mynar dyl was now finished, he rushed forward, eager to deliver his message.

"Noble Warlord!" the guard of clan Ernaly called.
"What is it?"
"He... He is in Llafal!" The Elf pronounced, his trembling voice betraying a keen emotion.

Mynar dyl remained stolid, apparently unconcerned by the news. Nevertheless, with a quick gesture of his hand, he indicated to one of his servants his intention to change clothes. Water, soap and towels were brought to him, along with a fresh tunic and his favourite weapon, a long javelin decorated with hawk feathers. He washed his body thoroughly and replaced his dancer's outfit with his usual attire. Mynar dyl quickly finished dressing in his resplendent clothes, fitting for an Elf of his position. His long cloak, robes and boots, all a tasteful mixture of brown and green hues, were embellished with silver markings. A rich ermine fur was wrapped around his neck. He completed his gear with two shining long swords. Finally, he placed on his head the diadem of Tios Halabron, symbol of his authority upon the city of Eïwaloni.[4]

---

4 Eïwaloni: 'Divine trees' in lingua Llewenti

"Are you sure of this?" he responded at last, with a tone of cold authority.

"Noble Warlord, the Renegade was seen near the port, disguised as an Irawenti sailor," started the guard of clan Ernaly, visibly under pressure.

"How do we know it is him?"

"Well," the messenger hesitated, "by accident, I would almost say. He came across Sarady, who saluted him according to the Blue Elves' custom. Sarady, as you know, has become fluent in lingua Irawenti since dealing with the community of Mentollà."

"And?"

"This supposed sailor failed to answer in his own tongue. Sarady suspected something was amiss. There are signs that never lie. After the Renegade's initial mistake, Sarady became sure that his sailor's clothes were merely a disguise. He went with discretion to Naloy with his suspicions, who immediately ordered his troops to surround the west boundaries of the port, where the Renegade was seen last. He sent me to warn you straight away."

"This is fascinating! The Renegade is being hunted throughout the Archipelago, yet he chooses to come to Llafal, under my very nose... what can he be up to? Now, lead me to him, we must capture him immediately. We can leave nothing to chance," concluded Mynar dyl.

The pace of his speech and his striking appearance made his determination very explicit.

The two Elves began to leave the temple of Eïwele Llyi. They took the passage of gigantic fluted columns that led north from the main sanctuary. In the antechamber at the end of the majestic hallway was a fountain, its water continuously running out from six ancient pools of marble. A dozen clan Ernaly guards, fully armed, were stationed in the courtyard. With a simple nod from their warlord, they were hurrying on his heels. The messenger continued his report as they sped through the temple grounds.

"He is unarmed, posing as one of the port's workers, carrying bags in and out of the storage buildings."

"Unarmed? Are you sure he left his glaive behind?" checked Mynar dyl.

"No one has seen his sword, noble Warlord, but it is possible he has hidden it nearby."

"Then time is of essence. This is an unexpected opportunity."

In the glare of the early summer sun, the clan Ernaly unit left the quiet pathways of the temple's garden. The low, steady beat of their footsteps echoed like a band of faraway battle drums, detracting from the beauty of the place which was covered in vines and shrubs. They rushed through the shadows of the trees and along its vibrant flowerbeds.

The group soon reached Temple Square, which looked out over the Halwyfal Basin. The entire city could be seen from the esplanade. Layers of terraces had been built into the slopes above the shores of the great basin below, and from afar they resembled a crescent moon caressing the expanse of green water.

Mynar dyl looked out across the city, seizing a moment of respite to clarify his thoughts and shape a plan of action.

Dense woodland covered much of Llafal's surroundings. Beyond the high hills encircling the city of clan Llyvary was the forest of Llymar, a green sea of evergreen pines. It was an area of thick undergrowth and tangled passages. Apart from the occasional game trail, only a few paths led out of the city.

"Have we secured all escape routes out of Llafal?" checked Mynar dyl.

The messenger nodded to confirm. "Naloy immediately dispatched guards to each gate. We are checking everyone who enters and exits the city. We have not yet involved clan Llyvary in any of the steps we have taken. We have been discreet."

The clan Ernaly Elves descended the temple steps, passing the House of Essawylor, a large wooden construction which stood slightly downhill on the outskirts of the city.

Marching in single file behind Mynar dyl, the retinue hastened down streets, lined with tall wooden houses and slender pines. The lower expanses of the city surrounding the harbour were hidden in the shadow of Eïwal Ffeyn's hill. Under the afternoon sun, Llafal could be fully admired in all its beauty, like an amorphous mosaic of green and pearl.

The passages were lively and vibrant. It was as if the inhabitants had all decided to leave the shelter of their homes to celebrate the impending Season of Eïwele Llya.[5]

After continuing down through several different neighbourhoods, the clan Ernaly Elves finally reached a promenade that bordered the Llafal docks. Opposite the water, colourful paintings of dolphins decorated the ports' warehouses. Streams flowed from several marble fountains. Mynar dyl paused, taking the entire scene in with his ever-discerning gaze.

In a few hours' time, the sun's orb would disappear completely behind the treetops of Llafal's rugged coastline, and the small fishing boats would return to port. But, for now, the sailors of the clan Llyvary were nowhere to be seen. In contrast with the city, which was bustling with life as its inhabitants went about their business with their usual enthusiasm, the harbour of Llafal was almost empty. Only a small fishing boat could be seen gently drifting away on the calm waters of the Halwyfal. It was the time of the clans' sailing regattas, and the entire fleet of Llafal swanships had set sail for Penlla, the other harbour city of Llymar Forest.

Mynar dyl decided to stand at the top of the steps to the Llafal sailor's guild. From there, he could oversee the movement of his fighters as they spread around the area, closing in their encirclement of the warehouses.

Mynar dyl called upon his second-in-command, a veteran fighter of the clan Ernaly, known for his blind obedience and fierce nature. Naloy's leadership skills were in no way comparable to those of Voryn dyl, Mynar dyl's younger brother, who had gone missing a few years before. Nevertheless, Naloy was considered a capable commander. But on this occasion, a kind of excitement had pervaded his mind, like an inexperienced hunter impatient to snare a much-desired prey.

---

5 The Season of Eïwele Llya: Period from July to October in the Llewenti calendar

"We are ready for the catch, noble Warlord," he proudly announced, his eye as murderous as that of a hawk ready to dive for a kill.

"Prepare your fighters for a deadly confrontation. This prey will not surrender," Mynar dyl replied bluntly.

Oddly enough, however, Mynar dyl's eye was fixed on the sea's horizon, as though he were more interested in the drifting of that lonely fishing boat than by the final manoeuvres of his troops.

"I remember a small path," he said unexpectedly, "leading from the bottom of these warehouses down to the beach of Eïwele Llyi. I don't suppose that this path is currently being watched, Naloy?"

The veteran fighter was visibly caught off guard by the question. "That path is a dead end," he replied, his voice strained with a new tension , "bordered by cliffs as steep as Gwarystan's walls. It leads only to a small sandy beach. Getting to that beach would be difficult."

Mynar dyl had a grim smile, yet somehow looked deeply disappointed.

"Getting to that beach would be difficult... You are not wrong," he murmured, with an almighty effort to restrain himself. "And there is a good reason for it!" he added, now looking furious.

Mynar dyl breathed heavily, trying to gain control of himself. Naloy was puzzled, unable to understand what his warlord meant and the reason for his sudden anger.

After a while, Mynar dyl managed to calm his raging emotions. Most unexpectedly, he started to relate legends of the love affair between the deities Eïwal Ffeyn and Eïwele Llyi. It was as if time were no longer a priority, and that Mynar dyl had forgotten about the capture of the most wanted renegade on the Islands. His tale told how the deity of winds had established the site for the very city of Llafal. Eïwal Ffeyn used his extraordinary powers to carve a gorgeous bay at that precise point on the

Halwyfal's shores, to create a beautiful port for Eïwele Llyi. His magnificent gift had earned him a passionate kiss from his muse.

"It was no mistake that Eïwal Ffeyn made access to the beach of Eïwele Llyi difficult. Can you imagine why?" Mynar dyl asked.

After a time, the now abashed clan Ernaly commander responded.

"...No."

"The reason is simple. The deity of winds, may the Gods protect us from his wrath, did not want anyone to witness what he was planning to do with his beloved Eïwele Llyi after she had given him that passionate kiss."

"Ahh!"

"Legends has it that he had his way with her over the course of many moons, savagely possessing her like a storm unleashed upon an isolated island, until she finally managed to flee his grasp... swimming into the Halwyfal... towards the sea, Naloy..."

Mynar dyl's eye was now calm, still focused on that small white sail still drifting away on the horizon.
Naloy looked from his warlord to the fishing boat, back and forth, several times until he reached the conclusion in panic.

"You mean to say that the Renegade is fleeing on that small nave? We must call upon clan Llyvary and send their swanships to stop him."

"Swanships?" Mynar dyl wondered , "What swanships? They all left days ago for Penlla to participate to those ridiculous regattas Leyen dyl Llyvary has organized. I am afraid, Naloy, that there are no vessels for you to command. Besides, our fugitive seems to have organized his departure with great care. If my calculations are correct, his small sailing boat will reach the passes of the Halwyfal just in time, before the change of the tide. It means he planned his escape very carefully and made sure no pursuing ship would follow him into the open sea."

With an impatient gesture of the hand, Mynar dyl pointed at the warehouses, without even looking at Naloy, his mind already racing to answer another riddle.

"You may begin the attack! Do let me know the outcome. I am heading back to the House of Essawylor. There is something I must clarify."

Without even a salute for his second in command, Mynar dyl walked away, leaving Llafal's port and retracing his steps towards Temple Square. Alone, without the support of his guards, he did not hesitate to push his way through the crowd gathering around the Daly Nièn.[6] Many Elves were exchanging goods and news around the great fountain square of the city. This was the very heart of Llafal, where the growers and artisans ran stalls. The Elves of Daly Nièn watched him pass through, but they could tell Mynar dyl was preoccupied. His reputation was that of a cranky, impatient noble, known for being quick to anger. Indifferent to the unfriendly reactions of the crowd, Mynar dyl crossed the great fountain square of Llafal with his usual arrogant gait, visibly lost in his thoughts.
Earlier, on his way to the port, he had noticed something odd, something that looked out of place amid the vibrant and lively upper parts of the city.

Mynar dyl's steps led him back to the House of Essawylor, that recently built edifice, which resembled a large, upturned ship. The warlord carefully examined the great wooden hall. He cast his gaze, full of disdain, from the centre of the structure to the many sides of the building, which jutted out like the oars of a powerful rowboat. From the look on his face, Mynar dyl seemed moved beyond words by what he saw: to revulsion, anger and, most of all, a deep, aching distaste for the work of the House of Essawylor's architects. His artist's soul suffered at the sight of what he considered to be an insult to the harmony of the beautiful dwellings of Llafal that surrounded it. Such an obtuse intrusion of Irawenti style into the city of swans hurt him deeply.

The House of Essawylor was a place of entertainment and recreation. It had rapidly become Llafal's most popular venue, for it regularly staged musical performances. In preparation

6   Daly Nièn: 'The fountain square' in lingua Llewenti

for the great festival of music, gatherings of Irawenti bards had been programmed every day. The full city of Llafal was teeming with excitement. Rumour had it that Curwë, the House of Essawylor's master and a renowned artist, was preparing a spectacle of rare originality. Clan Ernaly sources said that the bard from Essawylor hoped to win the entire contest with a Muswab[7] performance that would combine the exotic notes of Irawenti music with the more classical art of Llewenti dancing. On that day, however, in front of the House of Essawylor's doors, there was no cheerful crowd eager to capture a glimpse of the build-up to the festival. In fact, there was no one at all, and all its doors and windows were closed.

"My dear Curwë, where is your army of partygoers, that rabble you get drunk enough to applaud your supposed art?" Mynar dyl wondered aloud.

Still looking at the great wooden hall, the warlord took a few steps back and reached the shade of a dense grove of apple trees and pines. A light sea breeze carried the bewitching perfume of plant essences. Mynar dyl was suddenly overwhelmed with a sense of well-being and cleanliness.

'Today's hunt might prove successful after all,' he thought.

Mynar dyl drew a potion from his pocket, pulling the cork out of the small phial. A pleasant smell of roses surrounded him. That sweet flower's fragrance soon attracted the birds of the grove. Mynar dyl identified a small one. It resembled the ruby-throated hummingbird, except that the bird's gorget was a deep violet with a slow gradient to black. The exact pedigree, though, was of little importance. The small bird was no bigger than a large insect. That is what mattered. Mynar dyl captured it with a rapid and effective gesture of his hand. Making sure not to harm it, he drew the small bird up to his face, to share a conversation. Soon, a joyful twittering confirmed to Mynar dyl that the hummingbird understood what was expected of it.

7   Muswab: 'warm musical spell' in lingua Irawenti. This genre comes from Essawylor.

After sitting down on the grass and tipping his head down, Mynar dyl released the small bird. Like a colourful butterfly breaking free from its chrysalis, the hummingbird flew towards the House of Essawylor.

Meanwhile, Mynar dyl had covered his face with his hood. He was muttering strange words and his eyes had turned white. The warlord was concentrating hard. He had taken control of the small bird's senses. His own breathing had ceased. The hummingbird quickly made its way into the House of Essawylor, disappearing through a small gap that it found between the supporting beams of wood and the soil.

Mynar dyl managed to maintain his mental control upon the small bird for a relatively long time. The House of Essawylor was a large building that, beyond its main hall of festivities, was made up of many other smaller rooms. The hummingbird explored each of them like a scavenger ranging a canyon to find food. At last, Mynar dyl broke out of his highly concentrated spell and into a coughing fit, gasping desperately for air.

"May the deities of the Islands be praised!" he proclaimed aloud once he had recovered from his effort.

Visibly overwhelmed with excitement by what he had discovered, Mynar dyl felt compelled to address a silent prayer to the Mother of the Islands, his most favoured divinity.

'I thank Eïwele Llya for her constant support, and for instilling the faith in my heart to serve her work!'

★

An hour later, the House of Essawylor was discreetly surrounded by clan Ernaly fighters. Mynar dyl had called upon each of his guards present in the city that day. The warlord of Tios Halabron possessed no authority in Llafal, which was one of clan Llyvary's fiefs. He needed to act with caution, for this initiative violated the laws of Llymar Forest.

Two entire units, led by their commanders, more than fifty Elves in total, were waiting on Mynar dyl's orders. The clan Ernaly's insignia, the grey falcon, was woven into their hair along with their many hawk feathers.

The Elves of the clan Ernaly were hiding amidst the vegetation of the area, creeping between trees and behind houses. They had positioned themselves at regular intervals in a circle around the great hall. A dozen fighters, armed with javelins and short swords, were standing close to one of the House of Essawylor's windows at the very back of the Halls, ready to storm the place. Four archers supported them. Their short bows were raised, and their quivers were heavy with arrows. The rest of the clan Ernaly's troops guarded all other escape routes from the great hall.

Mynar dyl noticed a few passers-by looking with suspicion in the direction of his hidden fighters. Although, once they spotted the warlord of Tios Halabron, no one dared enquire further, the strange looks in their eyes indicated that the alarm would soon be raised, and that clan Llyvary's troops would imminently be mustered. Llafal was a quiet city populated by Elves who enjoyed their tranquil lives. Any disturbance of the peace would not go unnoticed for long. Rumour of this concentration of clan Ernaly troops would spread fast. The matriarchs of the city would soon be alerted.

Mynar dyl started incanting words of power. The hinge-pins that were used to hang the shutters of the window started to melt, as if heated in an invisible blacksmith's forge. Just as the metal began to glow red-hot under Mynar dyl's spell, the hinges broke apart. The searing heat also set the wood on fire, causing further damage. The shutters finally fell to the ground, leaving the back window unprotected.

Naloy ordered the attack. The commander of the assault rushed in, smashing the glass of the window. He rolled inside the room, closely followed by his fighters, their javelins in hand. In an instant, a dozen clan Ernaly guards were inside the House of Essawylor. They positioned themselves to secure the room.

Finally, Mynar dyl could follow. He found himself in Curwë's study. The House of Essawylor's master had set up his private quarters where his former associate Aewöl used to dwell. The room's interior had changed little since the days of the one-eyed Elf. Reaching up to this vast chamber's high ceiling were enough species of plants to fill a wild forest. The room was furnished with precious furniture and refined tapestries, giving the place a luxurious atmosphere. Musical instruments, ranging from different types of lyres to a huge array of drums, were strewn across the fine wooden floor. Bookcases were crammed with manuscripts and works of literature. The chaos that reigned amidst the elegant design of the room conferred the place with the air of an exotic bazaar.

Curwë was sat in a comfortable armchair with numerous ancient-looking scrolls laid out in front of him. An empty crystal vial was also placed on his desk, next to a skilfully crafted glaive that was propping up an unfurled map.
It seemed as if Curwë had not yet recovered from the surprise of the sudden intrusion in his dwellings. His gaze was lost, darting from the broken window, to the blade of Naloy pressed against his neck, to the other clan Ernaly fighters threatening him with their javelins and bows. He seemed utterly amazed by the situation. The violence of the attack had shocked him into a state of wordless disbelief.

Stepping inside the room, like a victorious warlord strolling across a conquered battlefield, Mynar dyl reached for Curwë's desk and seized the unsheathed broad sword. The brightest emeralds adorned its shining blade. Mynar dyl examined it carefully, like a jeweller would a precious diamond.

"This is the legendary Rymsing," he finally said with a radiant smile , "the Blade of the West, which brings hope to the Elves, the sword of the fabled Seekers... and the Secret Vale's property... Is it not?"

Curwë remained paralysed.

"My dear Curwë, I am most surprised, you seem to be taking the day off! I would have expected to find you with your head down, busily preparing for the upcoming music contest.

A little bird told me you have been harbouring the greatest ambitions for this year's festival. Rumour has it, you have been mouthing off in public about how you will outclass the ballet I have created. Yes, that's right, I also heard you like boasting about your art above all before Nyriele dyl Llyvary. I know you spend a lot of time with her, telling her wonderful stories of faraway Essawylor, singing the songs of the legendary heroes of the High Elves and whispering into her hear. These innocent games have been going on for some time now. By all accounts, you entertain her well, some even say passionately so. I do not doubt you have a certain ability to make her eyes shine.

Perhaps you have dreamt of seducing her. Perhaps you imagined she would offer you her heart, overwhelmed by your pretty green eyes and curly hair.

You have chosen a difficult path, Curwë.

I am not saying this to diminish your merits, however. The truth is, I sincerely believe that you have set such an unattainable goal only to glorify yourself. After all, despite your curly hair and green eyes, beneath it all you are a true High Elf. One of the worst kinds, in fact: one who does not know his rightful place on Oron, and who will wreak chaos until he has managed to disturb the harmony that the deities have granted us.

But here we are. Or rather, here you are, caught reading the secret scrolls of the Dyoreni and in possession of the sword Rymsing, the stolen blade sought by the powerful Arkys across all the Islands...

Isn't it funny how, in the space of a single day, one's life can change so completely?"

Curwë now understood the desperate position he was in. As Mynar dyl's cynical words cut into him, he sensed an unfamiliar feeling growing inside him, called kunumi in lingua Irawenti, or 'a great anger'.

"You are a miserable Elf, Mynar dyl!" he replied bluntly, failing to control his disdain. "You are a snake whose venom poisons all around him."

"These are the words of a defeated coward, worthy of a lowly thief caught in the act. I would have expected better of you."

Determined to see this battle through to the end, Curwë threw all his forces into the fight.

"You do realize that, if the scrolls of the Dyoreni and the sword Rymsing have been found in my possession, it is because they were willingly given to me. Dyoren wanted them in safe custody before he set off on another perilous journey to fulfil his quest. He is heading to the valley of Nargrond, on the trail of the lost sword Lynsing. Dyoren may, at this very moment, be marching to his own death."

A sly smile had drawn itself across Mynar dyl's face. His manner and expression signalled his utter disinterest, for his elder brother's fate.

"Perhaps Dyoren the Seventh," he replied sardonically , "appointed 'Curwë the First' to be the next Seeker? Perhaps Dyoren the Seventh, in the true spirit of his rebellious order, chose his successor himself? That would make perfectly sense. Or rather, it might make perfect sense in the deeply troubled mind of a renegade Elf who defies the Secret Vale's orders. I can only guess at the kind of madness an Elf like that might dream up. Perhaps Dyoren the Seventh believes the Arkys of the Secret Vale are imposters, unbelievers who do nothing but preach empty words. Perhaps he now sees himself as the deities' true messenger on these Islands, responsible for delivering their holy words?"

Curwë spat back a counterattack. "Perhaps it is you, Mynar dyl, who plotted against him, so that you would be entrusted with his sacred glaive? Dyoren once told me you wanted Rymsing for yourself. You have always craved its power; you have always dreamt of wielding a sword whose blade could harm the Gods themselves. Will you deny it?"

After a moment of surprise, Mynar dyl openly laughed at the accusation.

"My foolish brother thought I wanted to become the next Seeker? Did he really make you believe that?
No, my dear Curwë, choosing a life of sacrifice and abstinence for the benefit of the Islands' Elves has absolutely no appeal to me. On the contrary, I am very ambitious indeed for the

earthly things a Seeker must forego. A knight of the Dyoreni must denounce worldly power, noble titles and all pleasures of the flesh, as things that will never give him peace of mind or wellbeing of spirit. They happen to be things I rather like. I look around me, and I seize the best of what life has to offer. This is who I am, Mynar dyl, a great poet but nevertheless a physical being, subject to all kinds of temptations. I run after the pleasures of this world, including the carnal ones. I see it as my right to caress the softest of skins..."

Mynar dyl's voice had true musicality. The rhythm of his words syncopated like notes on a musical score. He was a master of subjugating the mind. Curwë remained silent, like one temporarily defeated. He was looking at his opponent with fascination. His fearful gaze fixed upon the finely drawn mouth and hawk-like eyes of the warlord.

Mynar dyl closely examined the shining glaive he was holding in his left hand. He seemed to be weighing up whether he would trade his current life for the duties that came with the Sword of the West. Would he take that path for the sake of the greater good of the Islands? As he thought, he started licking the sharp blade of Rymsing.

"No, definitely not," he concluded with a grim smile , "I would much rather be the father to Nyriele's children."

Blind with rage, Curwë rushed forward. But his attempt was immediately stopped by Naloy's short sword. The blade cut deeply into the flesh of Curwë's shoulder. At the same time, one of the archers released an arrow, which buried itself into the wood of his chair, pinning down the sleeve of Curwë's tunic and forcing him to remain seated.
There was nonetheless a palpable threat of a bloody fight breaking out, such was Curwë's fury. His past actions in battle undeniably demonstrated he had little regard for the odds when his honour was at stake.

A sudden noise outside interrupted Curwë's imminent execution. Heavy footsteps could be heard. The loud cries of clan Llyvary guards, eager to understand the cause of the turmoil, filled the street. A moment later, fighters were inside the House of Essawylor. Their progress through the great hall could be heard distinctly, for the echoes of their aggressive exchanges with the clan Ernaly guards soon filled the study. There were many of them, and they sounded impatient to put an end to the clan Ernaly's actions.

Realizing that he had little time before losing control of the situation, Mynar dyl brought his face very close to Curwë's. An idea had dawned upon the warlord of Tios Halabron. He placed his hands upon the armrests of the Curwë's chair. His breath was calm. He drew from his pocket a fine piece of jewellery, the colour of emerald. The rune of clan Ernaly was nestled inside the pendant, along with several small pearls.

"My dear Curwë," whispered Mynar dyl , "you now have a choice to make. Either you leave Llafal today as a free Elf, never to reappear in front of Nyriele again... and swear that what I have discovered is true..."
"Never..." Curwë fought back , "never will I swear anything for you, miserable Elf."
"Or... or you proclaim yourself to be the new Seeker, the honourable wielder of Rymsing, the greatest rebel of our times and... you will have to face the Secret Vale's justice."

Heavy steps were heard coming down the corridor. The guards of clan Llyvary were approaching.
Curwë, in a last desperate effort, tried to find a way out of Mynar dyl's ultimatum.

"An oath obtained through coercion or force has no value. You know this, Mynar dyl."
"If you are stupid enough to believe that, you know nothing of the rune of Ernaly's powers. Swear, if you want to live!" commanded the warlord of Tios Halabron.

The guards of clan Llyvary were right behind the door. The scraping of their metallic armour could now be heard distinctly.

"I will leave Llafal... I swear..." said Curwë finally, almost breathless.
"And?" insisted Mynar dyl, more threatening than ever.
"I... will not appear before... Matriarch Nyriele... again..."

"Swear it on the rune of Ernaly, cursed Hawenti, or be lost!" Mynar dyl murmured, his tone insistent but his voice low.

"I swear," Curwë finally committed. But he spat on the greenish pendant as Mynar dyl brought it to his lips. The emeralds of the Ernaly rune glittered brightly as the Llewenti warlord applied it to Curwë's cheek, like an ointment rubbed into infected skin.

"There, your fate is sealed," said Mynar dyl with an air of triumph. While the fire of victory burnt in his eye, Curwë's face grew despondent in resignation.

The clan Llyvary's guards appeared at the study's entrance. They commanded the clan Ernaly fighters to drop their weapons immediately. Tyar dyl Llyvary, the warlord of Llafal, walked through the door.
His tan-leather coat, weapons and helmet were all adorned with the white swan of Nyn Llyvary. He was armed with a long sword, and an oval shield hung at his side. On his back, his cloak was the light green of his clan.
With a very polite tone, Mynar dyl admitted the old Elf inside the study, declaring emphatically that he was most welcome.

Tyar dyl moved forward slowly, as wanting to witness for himself what had happened in this room now that all noise had ceased around him. The warlord of Llafal looked for a long time at the faces of those present in the room, as if Eïwele Llyo, the deity of foresight, wanted him to learn the truth from their features: the calm of Mynar dyl; the satisfaction of Naloy; the coldness of the clan Ernaly's fighters; and the lost gaze of Curwë.

"What happened here, Master Curwë?" Tyar dyl asked in a laconic tone, his gaze fixed steadily upon the owner of the house.

Mynar dyl did not give him a chance to respond, cutting him off by dropping Rymsing on Curwë's desk as if by accident. The fine broadsword slowly fell onto the wooden surface with a metallic thud.
All looked at its shining blade with fascination. The silence was deafening.

After observing the fabled glaive for some time, Mynar dyl finally spoke.

"The Blade of the West and the scrolls of Dyoreni are recovered, noble Tyar dyl... Clan Ernaly had to rescue Master Curwë in his own dwellings after he was taken hostage by Dyoren. It appears the Renegade was ready to use all available means to push Curwë into revealing precious information, information that he did not even have... I regret to inform you the Renegade managed to flee. But we took his precious sword from him, and he has also left behind the scrolls of the Dyoreni. These spoils offer me some comfort. It is a great achievement to have these items in our possession, and will no doubt fill our matriarchs' hearts with joy."

Still standing in the middle of the study, Tyar dyl remained impassive, like an old bird perched on a branch, his head to one side, watching the scene with both mistrust and disinterest. Perhaps he was waiting for Curwë to confirm the warlord of Tios Halabron's tale, but the bard remained silent, his eyes empty, still in utter shock. Once again, it was Mynar dyl who provided an explanation.

"Master Curwë was very affected by the events, as you can well understand in someone threatened with death. He has been held hostage for some time, and was perhaps tortured, by a mad Elf desperate for information. You must imagine Curwë's distress, for he would never have been able to satisfy the requests of such a troubled mind. His captor was obsessed with the testament of Rowë and the lost Swords of Nargrond Valley. He used potent sorcery to make him talk and keep in place.
Curwë's liberation was fast, but it came late...
He expressed his wish to return to Mentollà as soon as possible, where his friends will be of some support. He has asked me to be of assistance."
Mynar dyl looked to Curwë. He held out his hand in a gesture of friendship. For a moment, it seemed as if the mark on Curwë's left cheek glimmered with a greenish glow. At last, Curwë spoke out, his voice weak.

"I shall go back to Mentollà... now... I have nothing more to say."

Curwë then left his study under the watchful protection of the clan Ernaly guards. He passed by the ranks of the clan Llyvary fighters, who showed him signs of compassion. Through the maze of the House of Essawylor's rooms, he walked like a bewitched Elf, and was finally guided into his bedchamber. Instructions were given to prepare his gear. Curwë would depart for Mentollà the next morning.

★

The sun was already setting behind the high pine trees of the Halwyfal's shores when Mynar dyl finished his account of the day's events. He had explained in detail what had occurred that afternoon in the streets of Llafal; from Dyoren's flight at the harbour to the final scene in the House of Essawylor.

"The deities of the Islands have favoured us once again, noble Gal dyl..." the warlord of Tios Halabron concluded. "It is nothing short of miraculous that we have recovered both the Blade of the West and the scrolls of Dyoreni in one fell swoop... Imagine... After one of my guards saw through Dyoren's disguise, the Renegade had no time to go back to the House of Essawylor. May the deities be praised; he could neither recover his belongings nor finish off his hostage. Instead, he chose to flee..."

Nyriele and her father stood before him, bewildered at such unexpected news. After leaving the House of Essawylor, Mynar dyl had decided to inform the young matriarch without delay. Tyar dyl and his retinue had escorted him, along with the Seeker's precious possessions, to her private quarters at Temple Square. The 'Old Bird' had been surprised by Mynar dyl's initiative. For his part, Tyar dyl insisted that they immediately report to Matriarch Lyrine, who had legitimate authority over such matters. But the warlord of Tios Halabron would not be moved.

Incidentally, when the two commanders arrived to meet with Nyriele, they found Gal dyl there with her. The Protector of the Forest and his daughter were playing a harp and flute beneath the arcades of the matriarchs' compound. Their easy attitude demonstrated the profound affection of a father for his daughter. But Mynar dyl's account had visibly taken them aback.

After a moment, Gal dyl spoke. "So, the Renegade managed to escape once again."

"He did," confirmed Mynar dyl. "Dyoren used a small boat to leave Llafal before the tide changed. By now, he will have crossed the passes of the Halwyfal."

Nyriele looked relieved to hear of his escape. "Father, I think it is better this way. We have already recovered the sword of the Seeker and the precious scrolls of his knighthood's order. This is all that matters to the Secret Vale. Dyoren's fate is not ours to decide."

Surprisingly, Mynar dyl agreed with her. "You speak wisely, Nyriele. To tell you the truth, I chose to let Dyoren go... He is my elder brother, the last of my kin. He chose the wrong path in the end, but who amongst us can guess at what burden he had to bear?"

Mynar dyl knew that Nyriele held Dyoren in the highest regard and knew how she always defended him fiercely since his degradation. He was choosing to support her. Eventually, Gal dyl seemed to accept their point of view.

"You are capable of showing mercy, Mynar dyl, and it gladdens my heart. May you be praised for what you accomplished today!
In truth, to become a Seeker is to be deprived of one's life. I can understand what Dyoren must have felt. For a Protector of the Forest who wields the Spear of Aonyn knows it too..."

The last dyn Avrony paused for a moment. Mynar dyl almost recoiled at what he saw as an indulgent display of self-pity. But Nyriele put her delicate hand on her father's arm.

"How is Curwë?" she asked.

The young matriarch could not help showing her deep concern for the House of Essawylor's master. It was common knowledge in Llafal that Curwë had become Nyriele's closest friend. She would dedicate time to any of his initiatives. The two Elves could often be seen together, either participating in some artistic event or coordinating the work of various guilds and communities. In truth, the House of Essawylor had become another temple dedicated to the deities of creation and art, such was the energy its master put into pleasing the beautiful high priestess of Eïwele Llyi.

Mynar dyl had expected this question to come. He answered in a calm voice. His tone expressed a benevolent sympathy for Curwë.

"Curwë is shocked, for he suffered greatly at the hands of the Renegade. He was the victim of potent sorcery. Fortunately, he has survived the ordeal. I believe that he will one day recover from this distress. He asked me to organize his return to Mentollà. I hope that the bonds of friendship with his original community will help him through this difficult time. Curwë is a High Elf, different from us, stronger and less susceptible to the dangers of this world. Do not worry, Nyriele, he will recover. I know how close you are to him," confided Mynar dyl in a mild tone.

His spies had reported the two Elves were occasional lovers. This news had hurt him very deeply. For one thing, such a relationship interfered with his own plans but also, and perhaps more importantly, it offended his core principles. Mynar dyl secretly believed the only seeds of Llyoriane were the Llewenti, rightful owners of the Islands and the only children of the deities. He considered all High Elves as evil and dangerous, cursed scions of the Gods, whose race was plagued by the lust for riches and power.

But Mynar dyl had been wise enough to hide his great disappointment. He knew that any matriarch of the Llewenti was free to choose whoever she wished to be her lover. It had been so since the dawn of time, since the reign of Llyoriane, the queen who had, among her many admirers, picked some of the deities of the Islands themselves.

Meanwhile, Gal dyl frowned. He felt hurt and irritated by Mynar dyl's last words, which referred to his daughter's relationship with Curwë. Gal dyl did not seem to share the same compassionate feelings for the bard from Essawylor.

"It is right that Curwë should go back to Mentollà; that is where he truly belongs. I believe he has more in common with the wild Irawenti than with us."

It was not the first time that, as a father, he had expressed his dislike of some of his daughter's friends. But not all of Gal dyl's questions had yet been answered.

"Now, I wonder why Dyoren would risk his life to question Curwë. What valuable secret could the bard possess to justify such bold act?"

"This is a just remark, and I must admit that it also amazed me," answered Mynar dyl.

He paused for a moment and frowned, as if still puzzling over the unresolved question of Dyoren's motivations.

"Though I cannot be sure," Mynar dyl eventually confided, with a secretive tone , "I believe Dyoren wanted to question Curwë about the testament of Rowë."

"But why would he do that now? Why would Dyoren take such a desperate risk, after such a long time? The Nyn Ernaly campaign and the fight for the testament of Rowë goes back almost four years," wondered Gal dyl.

"Perhaps the story of Curwë and Rowë's testament only just reached Dyoren's ears. The Renegade interpreted it in his own way. He probably thought that Aewöl had not been the only one who had read the forbidden contents of Rowë's will. Perhaps he thought that Curwë had also absorbed precious information, potentially about the Swords of Nargrond Valley and where they were now."

Gal dyl remained unbelieving. "This would make little sense. The testament of Rowë cannot be read, we now know this, the lord of the House of Dol Nargrond made sure that its contents could be known only once. Besides, I personally addressed the matter of Aewöl. I made him pay for his sacrilegious act."

"This is true enough, and you acted well on that day, Protector of the Forest. But who knows what goes on inside a troubled mind? Dyoren has spent his entire life seeking the lost Swords of Nargrond Valley. It is his sole obsession. I believe he would stop at nothing to obtain information that could help him on his quest," argued Mynar dyl.

Gal dyl seemed to consider this last point as a fair argument.

"Maybe you are right, Mynar dyl, that would go some way to explaining his actions. Dyoren was not in the hall of sails when the Daughter of the Islands enlightened us about the true nature of the testament of Rowë. But Curwë was, as was his sacrilegious companion Aewöl. I heard the two were close friends. Isn't that true, Nyriele?"

Gal dyl turned to his daughter with a disapproving look. Nyriele's blue eyes expressed a sudden malaise. With an effort, she forced herself to smile and, suddenly, her face was blessed with unreal beauty. The young matriarch looked like the finest creature ever conceived, an Elf blessed by Eïwele Llyi with overwhelming beauty. She stroked her golden hair with grace. The two warlords immediately fell under her spell. There was no way to resist her charm.
A knock at the door interrupted the scene. Nyriele rose, tall and slender. She crossed the arcades' hallway to answer the door.

Nyriele wore a delicate beige gown which greatly enhanced her elegant silhouette. It felt natural for her to display her beauty for, among the priestesses of Eïwele Llyi, it was not considered vain. Mynar dyl looked at the soft curves of her body, his imagination set ablaze.
Mayile, one of the apprentices at Eïwele Llyi's temple, was on duty that day. As she entered the matriarchs' compound, her blue eyes expressed excitement.

"Matriarch Nyriele," the maiden started , "the noble Tyar dyl has returned with the guards of the stronghold. He has confirmed the secure recovery of the Seeker's treasures. Matriarch Lyrine awaits the Protector of the Forest and the warlord of Tios Halabron.

"The noble Tyar dyl stressed that she is waiting," Mayile added with a touch more urgency.

Gal dyl immediately stood, suddenly tense. He was wearing fine robes in the mahogany and beige colours of his clan, which gave him a look of true nobility, like an authentic heir to the bloodline of Eïwal Vars. Yet, in that instant, his worried look betrayed a certain apprehension for the impending meeting with the most powerful of Llymar's matriarchs.
Sorrow and pain had inflicted their worst upon the last surviving dyl of the clan Avrony, and despite his tall stature and powerful build, his gaze sometimes failed to conceal his anxiety. He hastily bid farewell to his daughter, like a warlord departing for a difficult campaign.

Meanwhile, Mynar dyl had gathered his possessions. In turn, he drew near and bowed before Nyriele. The shadows of the arcades masked his facial expression as he murmured in her ear.

"The time for you to bear children will soon come, Nyriele, you must know this."

Their eyes met for what seemed like an eternity. There was a long silence as his burning gaze showed how much he desired to be the father of those future children. His blonde hair was as radiant as ever. In that moment, to Nyriele's eyes, Mynar dyl was the very embodiment of carnal attraction, like a stag of the forest who had just defeated the last of his competitors. His body and mind were almost completely overcome with desire. Nyriele trembled.

Quickly regaining his composure, Mynar dyl turned to Gal dyl and nodded that he was ready to leave.

CHAPTER 2: Fendrya

The green-tinted moonlight danced upon the surface of the bay's waters. As its illuminating glow spread to the coastline, the contours of a wooden hut emerged from the night's mist. Butterflies were swarming around it: an odd phenomenon, given the hour. It was still before dawn and they visited the isolated hut's only inhabitant.

Inside, more chrysalis slowly began to brush the light clothes of an Irawenti lady who was lying on the ground. Fendrya dyn Feli was resting peacefully on an improvised bed sheet made of leaves and sand. Eventually, the butterflies reached her long dark hair, gently coaxing her away from her dreams. The young lady opened her eyes and got quickly to her feet, like an animal of the forest awoken by a strange noise.

Fendrya watched the night ballet of the chrysalis with haggard eyes. She slowly remembered she was being woken up early for a reason.

Once finished with her morning rituals, Fendrya stepped out of the hut. It stood on a beach, south of Mentollà, a wild coastal area along the bay of Gloren. She could feel the strong sea breeze in her hair and could hear the waves breaking. The waters bordering the woods of Sognen Tausy were hazardous, owing to strong currents. Fully exposed to the Austral Ocean's wrath, the dangers of this coast made it a notorious graveyard for sailors. Looking at the multitude of stars sparkling in the night sky, a happy realisation passed through her mind.

'This will be a cloudless day. The very best time to explore the sea's riches.'

The woods of Sognen Tausy had a changeable, oceanic climate, much like her homeland of Essawylor. It often rained, but sunny days were also very common. Summer was drawing near, and she knew that in the coming weeks temperatures in the region of Mentollà would soar.

Fendrya examined her surroundings. A few tents had been set up close to her hut, on the edges of the forest. Several small boats were beached on a reef in the creek. She was not travelling through this wild area alone; her armed escort was never far away. The Irawenti liked living according to ways that dated back to the early days, long before they dwelt in the Lost Islands or even in Essawylor. They were nomads who made their home on the sea's shores. Adventurous and inquisitive about the outside world, the Irawenti were used to travelling vast territories and adapting to the changing natural resources available to them. The proximity of the sea meant that they were always protected; if the need arose, they could quickly load all their possessions into their canoes and escape at any moment.

Fendrya began her day with a rich meal. Seafood formed the basis of her diet. She enhanced her breakfast with fruits, berries, wild grains and various tree syrups. Once she had eaten, she wandered along the beach towards a pile of rocks worn down by the sea. Fendrya expertly hopped from one slippery boulder to the next, until she reached the top of the largest one. From this precarious lookout, Fendrya could watch over a small creek, shining with crystalline water.
The priestess felt inspired by her protective divinity to celebrate the beauty of this place through prayer. Soon after coming to Llafal, Fendrya had embraced the vision and values of the deity of arts and love. Developing a philosophy of beauty, which was now her duty as a cleric of Eïwele Llyi, corresponded naturally to her own instinctive beliefs and core commitments. Fendrya began her devotional chanting.

Eïwele Llyi's beauty is all around me, and for this I give thanks. Its radiance lights up my life and nurtures my soul. I shall find beauty wherever it takes root, and I shall help that beauty flourish, so that all may partake in the joy and happiness it brings. I shall always give shelter to Eïwele Llyi's creations, for her teachings guide the course of my life.

Without a moment's hesitation, she dived into the sea from the top of the great rock.

Once below the surface of the water, the young lady swam towards the depths where light was dim. Her senses were keen, especially hearing. Like baleen whales who navigate immense oceans by listening for the echoes of little clicking sounds, she had no difficulty finding her way among the many crevasses of the rocky shore. The seabed teemed with swaying algae and a wide array of anemones.

Fendrya also possessed the ability to hold her breath for a long time and was quite happy roaming with the crabs and clams.

These rocky shores guaranteed food and provided shelter for a diverse multitude of sea life. Fendrya marvelled at the bright colours and distinctive shapes bobbing around her. The bay's species had adapted to its sandy seabed, and many could change colour to blend into their environment.

Suddenly, Fendrya spotted an octopus. She had almost missed its eight tentacles and well-developed eyes, as the ingenious mollusc had made itself almost invisible, camouflaged and twisted into a gap in the coral below. The octopus, sensing danger, sprung to life an attempt to escape her grasp. But the young lady was faster still. As quick as any reef shark, she seized her prey with both hands. The creature tried to defend itself with a long-spiked tentacle, but its attempt was of no avail, and soon it found its way into her netted bag.

Every morning, Fendrya spent many hours seeking oysters: not to eat them, but as part of the painstaking process of culturing sea pearls. The young lady was an expert in this field: one of very few Elves who knew precisely where to insert the bead from one oyster into the tissue of another. After this insertion, it would take several years for this second oyster to begin producing the gem. Influencing the colour of the pearls required an entirely different set of rare skills. Fendrya alone possessed the knowledge that ensured the oyster would produce the finest nacre.

The clan of Filweni had named her 'Keeper of Pearls' in Mentollà, responsible for distributing the clan's pearls among the most valued members of the community.
Sea pearls, believed to be gifts that came directly from Gweïwal Uleydon, were the Irawenti's most prized possessions. No currency was used among the Blue Elves, as barter was the norm.
Members of the clan of Filweni were only permitted to wear their sea pearls on special occasions, such as feasts and gatherings. They relied on the Keeper of Pearls to find resolutions to any disputes that arose out of their bargaining. Fendrya therefore exerted an undeniable authority within her community.

Fendrya's task that morning was to collect one of these precious natural gems. Since her arrival in Mentollà, she had been farming oysters every day in the hope of creating lustrous pearls. Their brightness ranged from shining white to almost jet-black, and every shade could hold undertones and overtones of green, pink, blue, silver and yellow.
The most valuable were the Piwada Marfewa[8], due to the uniqueness of their naturally dark tones. This rare sea pearl derived its name from where it was primarily cultivated: the blue lagoons around the islands of Essaweryl Bay. It was believed they had the power to absorb the light of Cim, the holy star of the sea depths, and hold some of its power.

At last, Fendrya made a conscious effort to pull herself out of the water. The sun was already high, the sovereign ruler of a cloudless sky. She crossed the beach with her octopus prey in her bag and one of the precious Piwada Marfewa in her hand. After greeting the other Elves on the beach with a customary Irawenti hug, she retreated to her private quarters inside the wooden hut.

---

8 Piwada Marfewa: 'Pearl from Marfewi' in lingua Irawenti

For the next two hours, the young lady carefully studied the remains of the octopus, using a sharp scalpel to dissect and extract some of its most peculiar parts. Fendrya was skilled with her hands and had a natural aptitude for any task that required both patience and perseverance.
She then used a phial of azure glass to mix the mollusc's remains with source water.

The next step in preparing the decoction involved the black pearl. Fendrya handled the Piwada Marfewa with great care. The Blue Elves prized them highly for their aphrodisiac properties. Seers even held they were a key component for any good love potion. Fendrya marvelled at the sight of her creation.

'A true black pearl is rare in these waters,' she thought. 'It is a gift from Gweïwal Uleydon. Its effects will cure the soul.'

The young lady started by delicately slicing the black pearl with a small knife, its handle beautifully incrusted with fragments of aquamarine. Using three separate measuring cups, she blended the ingredients, without getting so much as a speck of the liquid on her clothes. At last, she deemed her work for the day to be complete. Fendrya spoke to herself out loud out of sheer joy.

"Siw![9] This potion would cure any ailing soul in a flash."

Reaching into a large pinewood chest, she picked out a set of colourful earrings and bracelets from Essawylor. She then dressed herself in simple white robes. The thin cloth proudly displayed the fullness of her form.

Less tall and elegant than her cousin Arwela, Fendrya was slenderer, with a wiry and muscular agile body. Her skin was darker, tanned because of her preference for living outdoors. Against her dull skin, her eyes were light blue, and azure reflections emanated from her long black hair. Fendrya considered herself naturally handsome and, unlike other ladies, she did not feel the need for excessive jewellery. Her clothing was worn for decoration and modesty rather than practicality, because the Irawenti tended to prove highly resistant to the extremes of hot and cold weather conditions. She chose a light

9   Siw: Interjection meaning 'Holy star' in lingua Irawenti.

dress on that day. This was unusual, for the Keeper of Pearls generally favoured a long white toga in all aspects of community life.

Fendrya looked in her mirror. She felt satisfied with her appearance; after a hard morning's dive, she had now brought the sensuality of her feminine beauty to life.

With a happy heart, she could now rest still in her hammock until the arrival of the patrol from Mentollà.

★

A few hours later, a unit of Irawenti fighters reached the small beach. They arrived triumphantly, amid applause and shouts of joy, as companions were reunited.

Their cheering became louder until it rang in Fendrya's ears and she could sense the laughing and playing all around her. The noise woke her from her slumber. An instant later and she was on her feet.

When she came out of her wooden hut, Fendrya witnessed a most unexpected scene. The newcomers were bathing in the sea. Their armour and weapons were strewn across the sand in utter chaos, waves lapping at the discarded helmets and chain mail.

The only items that had been stored with any care were their short bows and quivers, which were neatly leant against the wall of the wooden hut. These fighters were, first and foremost, renowned as expert archers, and the short bow was their most valued possession.

Fendrya recognized the newcomers. They were part of Mentollà's elite unit. The community operated a conscription system, whereby all Elves of the fortress had to undergo specialised training in the rudiments of warfare. This group of fighters were the most skilled with the broad sword and the bow.

In that moment, however, it was difficult to believe that they were some of the bravest soldiers on the Islands. They were splashing around in the shallow waters with a dolphin, playing gleefully like children with a pet.

Without asking permission, a first Elf had dived into the sea, and was soon followed by many of his companions. Dolphins were sacred in their eyes. Given their reckless and adventurous nature, the Irawenti did not bow to authority readily, and on this occasion their commander had not even tried to intervene.

A tall Elf, clad in a dazzling armour, came to greet Fendrya. She immediately recognized Roquendagor.

"My lady," the knight began with laughter in his voice , "you are lucky enough to witness Mentollà's elite troops, those fearless warriors we trust to defend our community!"

Despite the irony in his words and his friendly attitude, Fendrya saluted him with great respect, bowing ceremoniously. The commander of Mentollà stepped towards her with determination, like entering a battlefield. Clad in his plate armour, the fearsome knight was armed for war. From the look of his garments, one might think that the armies of the Dragon Warriors were drawing near.

Fendrya was surprised by the kindness of Roquendagor's tone. She smiled back confidently, thinking that her sustained efforts to please him had not been fruitless. The look in her eyes was one of friendship and charm.
Fendrya decided to switch to lingua Irawenti. She could also have spoken the language of the High Elves, but she knew her exotic accent would colour her pronunciation, and somehow it made her feel inferior. Her mother tongue was her favoured idiom, for it was both rich and subtle.

"Siw!" she replied with a smirk. "Trust them? I don't find that very reassuring... I think I'd rather be protected by the commander of that elite unit. Some say he is both wise and strong..."

Fendrya carefully contemplated her interlocutor. She saw only benevolence and kindness in his face. His body language showed some signs of embarrassment, as though he were not entirely indifferent to her compliment.

Fendrya liked to tease the proud knight. She found him charming and entertaining. Roquendagor had confessed he had known very little of the Irawenti during his time in Essawylor. Despite living by their side for over a century, he had never showed any curiosity for their culture or customs. Sometimes, Fendrya could not believe her ears. Some of Roquendagor's genuine reactions to what she told him were unexpected and sounded odd coming from a great lord of the High Elves. His quizzical looks had made her laugh on several occasions.

Roquendagor now seemed to be looking forward to spending some time conversing with Fendrya. It was an opportunity to demonstrate his newly acquired knowledge of Irawenti culture to the beautiful priestess. Unexpectedly, Roquendagor recalled an old memory from his days in Essawylor.

"One of my most striking memories," he began assuredly , "is when I was back in Ystanlewin, riding my horse along the banks of the Siàwy Lenpi[10] on a summer's morning. I came across a lonely Elf, who was busy launching a small boat into the river. I remember how old he looked, which was so unusual for an Irawenti. He had grown weary of the world, and it showed. I asked him what his destination was but could not understand what he meant by his reply. He told me that he was sea-bound, that he was heading to the Gates of Sunrise. I knew nothing about those gates, though I remember thinking that they certainly sounded a long way off. For a start, Ystanlewin was nowhere near the sea. I wondered why the old Elf would embark upon such a long journey without equipment or supplies. Before setting off, he said that where he meant to go, neither the size of his boat or the treasures it carried would be of any avail. At the time, I thought that the old Elf was mad, and I paid no further attention to his fate.
Only recently did I learn the significance of his words. Arwela kindly explained them to me."
Fendrya was pleased. "Siw! This is a touching story. I am glad you sought the answer to that riddle. It is true those Irawenti who reach an advanced age will one day hear the 'call of the sea'. From that time forth, they will become increasingly obsessed with their last journey. When the time comes, they set

10   Siàwy Lenpi: 'the fifth river' in lingua Irawenti. It refers to one of the main rivers of Essawylor.

out in a small boat, sailing their way down the rivers, eventually reaching the sea. As the old Elf told you, their purpose is to reach the Gates of Sunrise, the entrance to Gweïwal Uleydon's realm. Their fate beyond that is unknown. It is commonly believed that the Greater God of Oceans reincarnates them into dolphins."

"So Arwela said. You must understand, to me these superstitions... apologies, I mean these beliefs, are somewhat esoteric. The Irawenti faith in the God of Oceans is so... different, if not contradictory, to what Hawenti Mythology tells us..."

"Perhaps it's time to reconsider what you were taught," Fendrya suggested with a smile.

During his days in Essawylor, Roquendagor had been raised according to the strict principles of a high-born Dol education. He used to consider Irawenti, for the most part, as mere Wenti, 'Free Elves' or even 'Simple Elves,' a joyful and adventurous people. They lived shorter lives than their Hawenti brethren, usually less than five centuries. Due to their carefree nature, they did not age in appearance, always looking like beautiful, careless youths. To his High Elf eyes, this essential difference contributed to an inevitable distancing between the two races.

"There is truth in your words, Fendrya..." Roquendagor acknowledged, nevertheless.

Since his arrival in the Archipelago, his dealings with the Irawenti had become common, and through this frequent contact the tall knight's haughty views had already somewhat changed. It was now his firm belief that the Irawenti possessed a wisdom of their own. There was a lot to learn from them. They were at their most skilful when aboard ships, and Roquendagor truly admired that courage.

"You should know that I have made considerable progress," Roquendagor resumed, eager to make his point very clear. "Since we moved to Mentollà, I have had the honour of commanding Irawenti troops directly. I now fully understand how important it is to take the beliefs of those who fight under my command into consideration. I have always felt responsible for the lives of my fighters, even now that I know our arrival on the Archipelago's shores serves a higher purpose."

Roquendagor's gaze was fixed on the horizon. The knight was inspired with a sense of duty to others and a love for his new community. Fendrya was deeply impressed.
In the distance, his troops were demonstrating their exceptional connection with the sea. They were swimming out and back again with surprising speed, diving from the rocks, and leaping out of the water: they were enjoying all the pleasures the beach had to offer. Indifferent to this apparent lack of discipline, the two Elves continued their conversation.

"Siw! Your words are full of wisdom, Roquendagor, and do you much honour. Allow me to offer you some further advice.
Make sure you respect the customs of your fighters! Do only this, and they will remain loyal to your standard to the last. You must observe their funeral rites, for the Irawenti belief in the afterlife is profound. Even the souls of those who suffer a violent death will be summoned by Gweïwal Uleydon.
Make sure the bodies of the fallen are returned to rivers or the sea and perform the appropriate offerings. The Greater God of all Waters will call them to the depths of the Eastern Ocean, beyond the Gates of Sunrise. Gweïwal Uleydon will transform the dead fighters into marine spirits. Cil, Cim, Cir! [11] they will thereafter roam the oceans at his service."

An incredulous Roquendagor stared at her, smiling confusedly. Fendrya could not help laughing. Although he must have thought these beliefs naïve, she did detect a certain amount of curiosity on his part. She feared that, despite his current friendliness and innate kindness, his smile betrayed a certain irony. Roquendagor must have thought that the Irawenti were no more than a collection of idealistic nomads: simple fishers and gatherers, of no interest whatsoever to a great knight.

Fendrya decided to challenge Roquendagor. Not only did the High Elves had all kinds of preconceptions about her people, they also had arrogant beliefs about themselves. Despite sharing

---

11   Cil Cim Cir: 'With the stars' favour', oral expression in lingua Irawenti.

a destiny for several centuries in the kingdom of Essawylor, she knew the relationships between Hawenti and Irawenti had always been mired in ignorance, mistrust and prejudice.

"You smile, but what do you know about the history of my nation?" Fendrya asked with a challenging tone.

Roquendagor's reaction was defiant. "I know a lot, young lady, more than you might expect..."

Fendrya remained silent and impassive, waiting for what would come next. When the haughty knight began to speak, he was like a respectful student before his master.

"The Irawenti were nomads, who used to roam the plains of the Mainland, until the chaos of the early First Age forced them to flee..." started Roquendagor.

"Forced us to flee?" she asked, failing to properly convey her sense of outrage at the statement. "You mean that my forefathers fought their way bravely up to the high valleys of the Ivory region, away from the turmoil of the Mainland."

Roquendagor faltered, feeling suddenly embarrassed. "Indeed, that is what I meant..." he corrected before continuing. "Then, for more than two millennia, the Irawenti lived peacefully in their haven. They extended their realm into remote vales, under the protection of their high mountains' peaks. They became ever closer to the Llewenti, who had settled in Essawylor, and the two races developed trade and alliances. The culture and craft of your forefathers benefited greatly from these contacts."

"The Llewenti also benefited a lot from the knowledge of the Irawenti," Fendrya could not help but add.

"Indeed, they did," agreed the complacent knight. "This very long period of prosperity ended when a large horde of Men attacked Essawylor's western borders, marking the beginning of a long war, called the 'Wrath of the Trees'."

"We were sworn allies of the Llewenti clans and we honoured our pledge," reminded Fendrya, her tone insistent.

Roquendagor nodded in agreement. "I know your ancestors did, and they fought the horde of Men ruthlessly. However, after countless battles, they finally withdrew behind the protection of their mountains. The Irawenti realized that their Llewenti allies had become obsessed with the legend of the Fallen Star, and that their clans were organizing expeditions across the Austral Ocean to find the last refuge of the Elves."

"The Llewenti decided to abandon Essawylor. Why would the Irawenti keep fighting for a realm that was not theirs?" asked Fendrya.

"Forgive me, I am not implying that it was wrong or dishonest. I simply learnt at the Diamond College that, for over four centuries, the Irawenti stayed in the refuge behind the high-mountain passes, until they finally resolved to hunt down the Desert Horde from the woods of Five Rivers.

At last, the Irawenti clans marched on Essawylor and routed the human invaders, driving them off into the confines of the desert."

Fendrya looked surprised that Roquendagor's account of her forefathers' long history had ended so abruptly. Her next question was almost vindictive.

"How can you not mention King Iraw, the great hero who led my people to victory and reconquered Essawylor?"

"Iraw? That name rings a bell... but I must admit I cannot recall his feats. I suppose praising the only king the Irawenti crowned was not the Diamond College's priority. It was mostly Hawenti scholars who attended those history classes, and few were interested in the legends of your people," admitted Roquendagor, somewhat tactlessly.

Fendrya felt offended. "Cil, Cim, Cir! This is precisely why your account also omitted Azuw, the first guide of my nation, the wisest of rulers. Azuw participated in the council of the Elder Kings. He decided not to accept the gift of immortality offered by the Gods. Thus, the Irawenti came to be counted among the seven Elvin tribes who chose to remain free, unlike the so-called High Elves."

Immortality, that cursed gift of the Gods, irremediably segregated the High Elves from the other Wenti. Fendrya had mentioned it because she was angry and, on some level, wanted to punish him. Roquendagor felt disappointed and a shadow passed over his expression.

Fendrya realized she had gone too far. The priestess pushed ahead with her lesson with passion, to distract Roquendagor from the sudden anguish which had seized him.

"Siw! King Iraw was a distant heir of our first guide, Azuw. Iraw had been captured and tortured by the Men of the Desert Horde after a skirmish at our border. Divine intervention freed him of his bonds. Gweïwal Uleydon manifested himself to him. The Lord of all Waters blessed Iraw with his protection. He returned to the Ivory Mountains wearing the insignia of his new charge as messenger of Gweïwal Uleydon. The hero was then crowned king of all the clans. Possessed by his new faith, he convinced his people to worship the God of Seas and to free the shores of the Austral Ocean from the presence of the repugnant Men of the desert.
The Irawenti pledged their souls to the service of Gweïwal Uleydon, in exchange for victory in the war against the horde. This is how our clans finally prevailed.
After the conflict, my people settled in the tropical forests of Essawylor.
Siw! At that time, our borders encompassed considerable lands, from the shores of the Austral Ocean to the peaks and vales of the Ivory Mountains. King Iraw recognized twenty-nine children from relationships with his many lovers. These numerous heirs formed the nobility of the Irawenti, those we call dyn[12]. After the death of King Iraw, my people divided their realm among those twenty-nine clans."

Roquendagor was enthralled by this tale.

"I would like to learn more about these legends. Is there any book that tells your ancient hero's story?" he asked.
"There are three collections of poetry: Newy, the Stream, Rywë, the River and Rya, the Sea."
"Ah yes," Roquendagor recalled , "I know the names of those ancient works. Queen Aranaele prohibited the distribution of the manuscripts."
"No wonder," replied Fendrya. "The queen of Essawylor felt that the message within those works was a direct threat to her authority over the twenty-nine clans, her vassals."

---

12 dyn: 'Descendant of' in lingua Irawenti. The word is used to identify a Blue Elf of noble blood.

"Did you have access to these forbidden texts?" asked Roquendagor.

"Of course, I did. My noble bloodline can be traced back to King Iraw. I belong to the clan of Feli," proudly declared Fendrya, her rebellious eye burning with the flame of freedom. "Newy, Rywë and Rya are the central religious texts of the Irawenti; we believe them to be the word of Gweïwal Uleydon. It is regarded as the finest work in our literary canon. The three poems are structured into verses, which we call suwi, and each suwi is made up of a certain number of lines, which we call awi. The fact that we have the Newy, Rywë and Rya manuscripts in our possession is the most important of Iraw's miracles: they are proof of his legitimacy. According to the traditional narrative, several scholars, companions of our king, served as scribes. They were responsible for writing down his revelations."

"From what you are telling me, I can now understand why the masters of the Diamond College chose not to cover King Iraw's feats in their classes," said Roquendagor.

Fendrya felt encouraged by the knight's understanding tone.

"I read the first pages of Newy in my early youth," she confided. "I can still perfectly remember the moment I opened the book. I was in my parents' tent, near Essaweryl Bay, barely a few hundred yards from the beach where King Iraw had recited his revelations. Before that, my cousin Arwela had entrusted me with a secret I will never forget.

'First read Newy, second read Rywë, and only then can you start studying Rya, the greatest poem of all time. You will need to read it several times before you can truly measure the magnificence of that work...' Arwela spoke with such reverence, like a truly devoted scholar. It felt like I was about to unveil the secret of creation.

One cannot enter the world of Gweïwal Uleydon without immersing oneself totally. It takes a certain amount of time to become familiar with all the concepts and allegories. The narrative frame enables you to enter this legendary world, but only after a demanding and sustained effort.

The three poems of Iraw need to be reread rather than read. Anyone who wants to properly understand them must first be ready to study his poetry repeatedly.

I personally discovered the depth of Iraw's spirit only after long walks along the edge the world. I would pour over the manuscripts as I followed in the footsteps of my king along the paths of Essaweryl Bay. His wisdom was in every page of those ancient writings."

Roquendagor looked at the beautiful priestess with admiration. The way she spoke betrayed the intense passion that inspired her. He let her continue her stories and explanations about the customs and beliefs of her nation, as though time had no influence.

Eventually, however, his troops tired of splashing about in the shallow waves and began to show signs of impatience; a long journey was still ahead of them. This unit was heading towards the mountains of the Arob Tiude, where the sentries needed to be relieved. The community of Mentollà kept a permanent watch over the barbarian tribes who lived west of Nyn Llyvary, and sentinels were positioned above each path to control routes from the valleys of Men. Roquendagor reluctantly realized it was time to conclude this highly enjoyable exchange.

"My dear Fendrya, it was a pleasure meeting you again. It is important to make the most of these rare, pleasant moments after the dark days which followed the battle of Mentollà. Our community endured cruel trials...

I must now be on my way. A long journey awaits my unit. We will travel the paths of the Arob Tiude for several days. There are six mountain passes to cross, forty leagues to walk and a total of twenty thousand feet of hill to climb."

"Cil, Cim, Cir!" she exclaimed, feeling pity for Roquendagor. "Reaching those heights must be tiring... not to mention dangerous."

"Not if you are well trained and mentally prepared, like we all are," replied Roquendagor with dignity. "We have a duty towards our community. It is vital that we watch over the western passes if we want to ensure Mentollà's safety. In fact, walking along the tracks of the Arob Tiude is now a passion of mine. There is no better challenge. The rough terrain of the mountains builds character as well as the body, preparing you for whatever life may throw at you in the future.

This time, I must be back in Mentollà before summer arrives. We are awaiting the return of Nelwiri. As soon as your cousin comes back from Nyn Llorely aboard the Alqualinquë, we will set sail for Gwa Nyn. I do not anticipate seeing you again before we return from the main island."

Fendrya looked sad. "So, I heard. Feïwal dyn has decided to explore Gwa Nyn. I wish you a safe journey... and I have prepared you a gift. It is a potion, like those I have already given you. It will fortify your heart during the trials you will face."

Roquendagor took the little flask and murmured a few words of thanks to Fendrya before bidding her farewell. He was soon on his way, ordering his troops at the top of his lungs to form ranks. The commander of Mentollà was thus ensuring their cohesion. He made sure the fighters he was responsible for were always ready to snap into an organized formation. Now running in a single file, the unit disappeared rapidly into the shadows of the woodlands.

Fendrya remained on the beach, listening as the light echoes of their footsteps faded into the distance. In that moment, she was overwhelmed with a sense of fulfilment. The young lady liked her new, constantly active life on the Islands. She shared her time between Mentollà and the cities of Llafal and Penlla, where she had taken on responsibilities at the temples of Eïwele Llyi. Her current existence was full of surprise, and perhaps this friendly relationship with the former lord of House Dol Lewin was the most bewildering aspect of it all. Moral standards were liberal among the Irawenti, and both males and females were free to choose their partners according to their feelings. The duration of these relationships varied, but there were certainly plenty of examples of love lasting centuries.

However, though occasional flirtations between Irawenti and High Elves were common enough, lasting relationships were unheard of. Without really grasping the significance of her repeated expressions of interest in Roquendagor, Fendrya was unconsciously setting out into unchartered territory. She was applying the principles of Eïwele Llyi's teachings to new horizons. Feeling rather thrilled by what the future might hold, she decided to go swimming.

She stopped when she saw her guards in a tight huddle on the shoreline. Fendrya moved closer to find out what had drawn their attention.

The carcass of a drowned bird had been washed ashore. An arrow had pierced its heart. Though the wood of the missile was decaying, the distinctive colour of its fletching was still visible.

Fendrya immediately recognized the dead bird as a 'white goose', a unique species of waterfowl most often found in Essaweryl Bay, beyond the Austral Ocean. She knew many different types of waterfowls: general grey geese, black geese and more distantly related members of the species, such as the many kinds of ducks. But the white goose was remarkable; it was as big as a large swan, though it could not fly. Back in Essawylor, this rare bird was considered blessed by the divine light, and indeed the only place she had ever seen one was in the temple of Cim, in Queen Aranaele's courtyard.

White geese were said to possess a direct bond with Cim, the star of the deep sea, which shone from the depths of Essaweryl Bay. The sacred birds of the temple of Cim were famous for doing their part in the fight for the safety of Essawylor. On several occasions, the white geese had alerted Queen Aranaele of approaching enemy ships in the bay by squawking and flapping their wings.

Fendrya had to fight her way through her assembled guards as she waded through the shallow waves. She reached the dead bird with difficulty; her companions were staring at the body in utter confusion, too stunned to step aside and form a path for her. Their attention was focused on the arrow. Their solemn murmurs invariably alluded to the Men of the Desert Horde.

Fendrya held the dead white goose in her hands. A sacred bird of the temple of Cim had been killed by a barbarian arrow. How could this have happened? How could the Austral Ocean have carried the corpse to this beach of northern Nyn Llyvary, more than two thousand leagues away from Essawylor?

Fendrya needed to find answers. With an unusual commanding tone, she dismissed her guards and took refuge in her small wooden hut. She immediately began to study the dead bird.

She took some surgical scissors and sliced its flesh down to the bone; in this way, she could understand the basic pattern of its physical structure without undertaking a full dissection.

"There can be no doubt," she concluded aloud after some effort. "This bird is a sacred goose from the temple of Cim. It was killed by an arrow of the Desert Horde. The ocean has brought it to our shores. I must go immediately to Arwela. She'll know how to interpret this phenomenon."

★★

Nyn Llyvary, Mentollà, one day later

Feïwal dyn Filweni was standing out in the open, perched on the edge of Mentollà's highest parapet. He was looking uneasily towards Gloren's Bay as mist was gathering above its emerald waters. His long, dark hair was covering the left side of his face. The silvery feathers and natural vines that were woven into his dark locks were fluttering in the wind. The guide of the clan of Filweni remained silent as he looked out. He seemed unsettled, even upset.

Arwela stood a few yards from him, but at a safer distance from the void. Her manners betrayed nothing but calm. She was oblivious to her brother's state of mind; her attention was focused on the third participant of this meeting, her cousin Fendrya.

"Cil, Cim, Cir! You already knew? Didn't you?" Fendrya repeated, with an accusatory tone.

She leaned against the keep's wall, her eyes blazing with anger. Her long, dark-azure hair reflected the glow of the late afternoon sun. Her inquisitive gaze was fixed upon her cousin. Unexpectedly, Arwela provided the answer to her question. She had so far ignored the hostile, inquisitive attitude of her cousin.

"This is not the first dead bird that has come ashore near our home," Arwela acknowledged.

A diadem of pearls adorned her head. The light robe she wore was of beautiful design. Its shimmering white and azure tones gave the seer of the clan of Filweni an exotic beauty, like that of some nymph from the tropical seas.

"You owe me the truth," insisted Fendrya. "Did I not follow you aboard the Alwïryan to cross the Austral Ocean? Have I not left my family and my clan behind to assist you in your endeavour? I remember your words, Feïwal dyn. 'The quest for the Lost Islands is a journey that cannot offer any hope of return. It is a leap into the unknown. It is an act of faith.' Well, I performed that act of faith, and I survived. I believe that I now deserve better."

There was open dissent in her words, bordering on rebellion. Feïwal felt the need to take immediate action. Irawenti hierarchy was strictly patriarchal and the guide of the clan was the undisputed leader. He only relied on the noble 'dyn' for counsel when he judged it appropriate. With a voice full of authority, Feïwal warned his cousin.

"Siw! Watch your language, Fendrya, and show some respect! Remember where you stand!"

The Irawenti did not build places of worship to serve their different cults. Instead, priests celebrated their faith in natural surroundings. The sentry's walk at the top of Mentollà's keep was one of these dedicated places.

"Fendrya, there is purpose behind each of my actions," Feïwal continued. "Every breath I take, every word I say, every decision I make serves a purpose. I have only one goal: the safety of my people.
When I granted the Council of the Forest's request to build the Great Swanship the Llewenti so desired, it served that purpose.
When I authorized Nelwyri to sail the seas of the Islands to expand the trade routes of our guild, Alcalinquë, so that Curwë and Aewöl could accumulate riches, it served that purpose.
When I asked you to join with the temple of Eïwele Llyi as a spy among the Llewenti, it also served that purpose."

Feïwal's wavy hair was masking his left eye, but the determination in his gaze could be felt all the same. His clothes, so light they were almost floating, gave him a mystical aura. His manners betrayed nothing but authority.
Fendrya felt the need to apologize.

"Pardon me, Feïwal dyn, for my inappropriate remarks. It is just, Siw! I am so concerned for our people. I examined the womb of that bird. If I am proved right, if that goose does come from the temple of Cim and was slaughtered by the barbarians of the Desert Horde, it could mean the capital city of Essawylor has been plundered."

Feïwal did not reply, visibly impatient. He preferred to look beyond the vast sea, which lay at his feet and stretched out for many miles. Arwela looked at him like she needed his approval before talking. The guide of the clan of Filweni generally listened to the wise advice of his elder sister. She was well versed in the lore of the three stars. With a simple gesture of his hand, Feïwal allowed Arwela to speak.

"What you read in the womb of that dead bird is true. The barbarians have killed the sacred geese of the temple of Cim. Essawylor is at war. In all likelihood, after the fall of the northern province a few years ago, the Desert Horde then succeeded in invading the wood of the Five Rivers. Ystanlewin controlled the roads of the North. When it fell and the House of Dol Lewin was destroyed, that city became the key to the kingdom, which the Men of the desert then seized. From that great fortress, an army can launch attacks southward, even to the great shrine of Queen Aranaele."

"So, the temple of Cim was conquered and Essawylor is at war," said Fendrya, still failing to figure out what it implied for the clan of Feli and her own family.

"We believe so," confirmed Arwela.

"But for how long have you been hiding these events from me... hiding it from the rest of the clan?" wondered Fendrya, still upset at having been ignored.

"It was earlier this year," Arwela replied , "that Feïwal dyn discovered the first dead bird on the beach of Mentollà, during the days of early spring. Since then, other dead birds have reached our shores."

"Siw! What you are saying, Arwela, is that dead birds washed up on Mentollà beach, in our own creek, as though..."

"...as though the invisible hand of Gweïwal Uleydon had brought the corpses of the sacred geese to our shores," concluded the seer of the clan of Filweni.

Fendrya looked at Feïwal in awe. She could now begin to understand what he must have suffered since the beginning of spring. The guide of the clan of Filweni had always taken responsibility for the fate of his kin, even those who did not belong to his own clan.

Fendrya believed that he was blessed with the ability to interpret the Flow of the Islands, this raw and chaotic magical energy which provided him with a significant and wide-ranging power over his environment.

Fendrya remembered the night when, from the top of the ruined tower, Feïwal had acted as a focal point for the gusts of power that blew across the peninsula from the Austral Ocean. Drifting energies had been drawn to him, forming a vortex like water in a whirlpool.

As Fendrya looked at him now, she could feel how his abilities had developed. Feïwal was closing his eyes as if concentrating on the sounds and smells of the sea and the caress of the maritime breeze. The waters of Gloren Bay were teeming with mystical energy which drifted the unsteady winds of the Islands Flow towards Mentollà. Surely, Feïwal knew how to interpret the signs sent by the Gods.

"Have you tried to return to Essawylor?" Fendrya enquired, now with a more respectful tone.

Feïwal remained impassive, his eyes still closed.

"Of course, you did…" Fendrya guessed, answering her own question. "I was surprised when you decided to sail the Great Swanship into the open sea. Winter was not completely gone, and I wondered why you would take such a risk. The ocean is dangerous beyond the calm waters of Penlla Bay. Several sailors were lost during that journey, and the Great Swanship came back to Llafal's harbour after having suffered considerable damage. I remember how you explained to the Council of the Forest that you needed to test the new vessel. But that was untrue.

In fact, relying only on a small crew, you attempted to make another crossing of the Austral Ocean… but this time you failed to cross the Sea of Cyclones. The passage was not granted to you."

The guide of the clan of Filweni did not utter a word to confirm this assumption, but his elder sister did.

"This is true, Fendrya. We could not inform you of this initiative. Do you understand? Your presence at Matriarch Nyriele's side at the temple of Eïwele Llyi could have jeopardized Feïwal dyn's plan. Everything you know, everything you may think, might well be figured out by the matriarchs. I do not perceive to what extent my powers can conceal your mind from their suspicions. The wiser course is to keep you in the dark, for you to better exploit your strategic position in Llafal and Penlla. The Llewenti clans were deliberately kept away from our project. Imagine their reaction if they had learnt that Feïwal was about to risk the Great Swanship to cross the Austral Ocean again. The clan warlords of Llymar have waited a long time for this powerful vessel to be at their disposal. They would never have agreed to risk it. To tell you the truth, we do not believe the Council of the Forest would support any attempt to rescue our people. The prospect of welcoming tens of thousands of new refugees would have appealed to them little. It would give the clan of Filweni the collective strength to shift the power balance in the Islands."

"Siw! I understand. I do understand. Once again, Feïwal dyn has demonstrated courage and tenacity beyond words. I deeply apologise for my misconduct towards you, my cousin. Can you forgive me?" Fendrya almost begged, feeling deeply sorry.

Feïwal did not reply, but Arwela approached her cousin and held her hand with true kindness. She reassured her.

"Do not feel troubled, Fendrya. Feïwal is the guide of the Filweni but also the shepherd of the Irawenti who came in service to bring hope to our people. He was blessed by the divinities who protect us. You must trust him with all your soul..."

Arwela did not terminate her sentence but Fendrya could feel what was at stake. After a pause, the seer of the clan of Filweni resumed.

"I am assisting him in his task as best I can. The only thing you should know is that we, the dyn Filweni, will deploy all available means to protect our nation, whatever it takes. You hear me... whatever it takes."

Fendrya considered Arwela's eyes in that instant. What she saw frightened her and she felt a tremor. There was, in the clan of Filweni, an indomitable resolution that was scary. No wonder the first sailors who had managed to cross the unfathomable ocean were from that bloodline, she thought.
Driven by a mysterious force, Fendrya felt the need to bow respectfully before her guide. Thus, she was renewing her oath of fealty.
Feïwal came close to her.

"Rise, Fendrya, you have my blessing..." he said before recalling a memory aloud. "My father, Fadalwy dyn, told me this once:
'Do not challenge the deities of the Lost Islands. Rather, if you are seeking enlightenment, beg them for peace and security of passage. And if you do end up setting foot on the Archipelago, then show endurance, for the gates to transcendent knowledge lie in the shadows of their dungeons. Yourselves, and perhaps later generations, will benefit.'
Today, his words ring true."

Fendrya did not understand Feïwal's augury. Her mind was still singularly focussed on the consequences of the war against the Desert Horde. She needed to know more.

"Feïwal dyn, what do you think is the situation in Essawylor? Is there still hope for our clans?" she asked, looking for reassurance.

The guide of the clan of Filweni made a special effort to accommodate her concerns.

"We do not know anything for sure, but what we can guess is that the war against the Desert Horde will be long. Despite the laws Queen Aranaele introduced in the kingdom, the clan is still the basis of the Irawenti' organisation in Essawylor. I expect that the other twenty-eight guides have organized the defence of their territories according to the ancient tactics. If war is raging within the woods of Five Rivers, they would have renounced their loyalty to the four remaining houses of the High Elves. I believe they avoided direct confrontation with the Men of the Desert. They must have fled to the Ivory mountains. This is what our people has always done in the past when it was threatened."

"But the clans rarely deal with each other," argued Fendrya. "I have never seen them collaborate, except when forging trade agreements."

"Rest assured they will come together when making such crucial decisions," Arwela reassured her.

"After Ystanlewin fell and the House of Dol Lewin was destroyed, I sat at a war council summoned by Queen Aranaele," Feïwal confirmed. "All Elves underwent weapons training and all those who were skilled at hunting were mustered. Because there was no formal army in Essawylor, the High Elves needed to call upon the clans' guides and the noble dyn to provide fighters for the defence of the kingdom.
The queen's sole power is to coordinate the efforts of the guides. Note that the armies of the Dol houses directly serving Aranaele operate on their own, without comingling with their allies. Thus, the defence of Essawylor is based upon a disciplined, heavily armed Hawenti block, surrounded by many mobile Irawenti units able to strike at any moment before retreating as fast as they came."

Arwela added to her brother's reasoning. "We think the armies of the four remaining Dol houses defended the temple of Cim. But we believe our clans fled and survived. They would never get trapped in a helpless siege.
As we speak, the banners of the great houses of Dol Linden, Dol Amrol, Dol Morlin and Dol Armin, have most probably been removed from the temple's bannisters and replaced by the red snake, the vile standard of the Desert Horde."

Fendrya felt less overwhelmed with worry now that she was no longer in the dark. Seeing her calm restored, Feïwal and Arwela saluted her with a bow and resumed their walk along the parapet, leaving her alone.

Fendrya looked around admiringly at the shores of the Sognen Tausy woods. From this high viewpoint, she could see the coastline, a series of peninsulas and bays radiating out from a centre dominated by the Arob Tiude hills. The Llewenti suggested that its shape stuck out of the west coast of northern Nyn Llyvary like a lobster's claw ready to snap. Everything on that coastline was subject to the sounds, smells and spray of the sea.

At last, Fendrya's gaze lingered on the parapet's wall behind her. Paintings represented Eïwal Ffeyn as a winged Elf, wandering the vast, stormy ocean, with only his long blue hair to protect his modesty. His flag was a trident struck by lightning upon a dark azure background. The deity of winds, divinity of freedom and rebellion, was viewed by most Irawenti as a distant threat, a source of destruction and wreckage that inspired dread in the hearts of sailors. He had claimed the life of many Elves over the years.
Fendrya remembered the songs she had heard in Llafal, legends that claimed Eïwal Ffeyn had been confined to the Sea of Cyclones by the power of the High Elves. Feïwal knew the fate of the deity of storms. He had sworn before his clan that his mind and soul would henceforth be fully devoted to Eïwal Ffeyn.

*

Fendrya had already taken her leave when she remembered the reason, she had returned to Mentollà in the first place. The succession of events the day before had completely destabilized her. Instead of using the tower's stairs to descend to the courtyard, she retraced her steps along the narrow parapet. She struggled against an intense sense of vertigo. The keep sat atop three huge stone arches, that interconnected to form this wide, fortified walkway. She walked by the many ballistae which threatened any vessel seeking refuge in the creek below. Finally, she reached the platform of catapults, whose heavy projectiles could crush any attackers from land. Feïwal and Arwela still stood there, in the open, conversing quietly despite the strong sea breeze. Fendrya faced her two cousins once again. Her tone was somewhat embarrassed.

"Siw! I forgot the reason I came back to Mentollà in the first place."

Feïwal and Arwela looked at her with interest, eager to know more.

"I have spent the last few weeks in Llafal," Fendrya began , "rather than Penlla, as the city is bustling with activity ahead of the music festival. The shrine of Eïwele Llyi is very much in the public eye, for the main celebrations and performances will take place in the white temple."

"I have heard that Curwë is preparing a Muswab of rare originality. Many of our musicians and dancers have left Mentollà to take part. The Irawenti will undoubtedly win," rejoiced the delighted Arwela.

Fendrya tempered her enthusiasm. "I am not so sure. The truth is that Mynar dyl's ballet is receiving much more public attention, and rightly so, for many guilds of the city have been involved in preparing the scenery and costumes."

"I doubt that you returned to Mentollà," Feïwal intervened , "to update us on the odds of who will be crowned at the music festival."

"No, you are right," Fendrya agreed. "Though what I must tell you is closely related. You know I have certain duties at the shrine of Eïwele Llyi. I have been assisting the other priestesses in their preparations for the music festival. One night, as the white temple was emptying, I overheard a conversation between Mynar dyl and Gal dyl. I was drawn to them because their voices were raised; it seemed that the two clan warlords were having some kind of altercation. Many were those Elves who kept their distance. I did the opposite. I managed to sneak into an alcove where I could listen to their dispute without being seen. Much of their conversation was lost to me, including the initial reason for their quarrel."

"What did you hear, Fendrya?" Feïwal asked with impatience. "This might be of considerable importance in the events to come. We need to understand which side the Protector of the Forest favours: Curubor and the house of Dol Etrond, or Mynar dyl and the clan Ernaly. There are currently two main currents of thought at the Council of the Forest, each in direct opposition to the other: one is expansionist, which favours the integration of the repentant houses from Gwarystan into Llymar; the other is far more isolationist."

"I was only within earshot at the end of their conversation, once the two warlords thought they were alone in the shrine. Things had calmed down by then. I happened to hear the terms of a very special bargain... a bargain that sounded rather like blackmail to my ears..."

"What do you mean?" Feïwal insisted.

"Mynar dyl said he would return a small, ancient scroll to Gal dyl, apparently the 'least important' of a number of texts he mentioned, which used to belong to an old priest of Eïwal Vars."

"What was the contents of this message?" Arwela suddenly asked. "I know priests of Eïwal Vars play a specific role in the army of Llymar, due to their special affinity with animals, and particularly with small birds. The Llewenti commanders use them to convey messages of confidence between their units."

"I do not know what the message said," confessed Fendrya. "But it must have been very important, for Gal dyl looked terrified at the prospect of Mynar dyl making it public. This small, ancient scroll, the 'least of messages' as Mynar dyl put it, must have been something that would threaten the integrity of the Protector of the Forest. I would not be surprised if Mynar dyl had proof compromising enough to send Gal dyl before the Council of the Matriarchs."

Feïwal approached his cousin nervously and kissed her forehead.

"Fendrya, you do not realize how crucial this piece of information might prove. May you be praised for what you have done, may you be saved from the wrath of Eïwal Ffeyn! May you be blessed by Gweïwal Uleydon!"

Visibly the guide of the clan of Filweni lacked the words to congratulate her for her findings.

"That is not all,", confided Fendrya with a smile. "I heard what Mynar dyl demanded of Gal dyl in exchange."

"What was it?" asked Arwela and her brother at the same time.

"Mynar dyl solemnly promised that he would return the precious scroll only once Matriarch Nyriele is pregnant with his child…"

There was a long silence, which Feïwal eventually broke.

"May the wrath of Eïwal Ffeyn descend upon Mynar dyl for his evil deed. He blackmails the father to gain access to the daughter's bed. What a vile act!"

Arwela was looking out at Cil, a bright star that had begun to appear in the western sky as darkness slowly fell around them.

"Mynar dyl is looking to unite the three bloodlines of the true Llewenti," the seer of clan Filweni assessed , "those clans who have always remained faithful to the Islands' deities and never bowed in front of invaders. He knows Matriarch Nyriele's child could become the ruler of the Llyvary, the Avrony and the Ernaly. He probably sees himself as the regent of this future realm. But his treacherous course has no guarantee of success. The matriarchs are sole mistresses of their destiny. No matter what influence Gal dyl may possess over his daughter, no matter what means he uses to persuade her, in the end the choice will rest with Nyriele."

*

Fendrya finally exited the ruined tower. She walked through its door, an immense iron structure covered in pentacles, with two guards of the Unicorn in their purple garb stationed on either side.

When the young lady emerged from the great keep, she felt the need to watch life as it went by, slowly, under the murmur of the ever-present parrots from Essawylor. It was still spring time, and at sunset one could often see mist emerging from the Bay of Gloren. The sunshine of the late afternoon had nevertheless brought a comfortable warmth. Summer was getting closer. Large coastal trees bathed the ancestral stones of Mentollà in purple shadows, as the light streamed down through their greening leaves. The Elves' existence was quiet in Mentollà, bathed by the waters of the tower's creek.

Amid the rolling hills of this Sognen Tausy plateau, interspersed with small vales and countless streams, it seemed that time had slowed to nature's pace. The Elves of Mentollà appeared to lead their lives in an ordinary manner, conducting their seasonal occupations with serenity. Such was the nature of all Elves. They were perfectly able to while away their time simply enjoying the beauty of their environment, without ever becoming restless.

Over not so many years, things had changed considerably. After the war Mentollà had faced, the threats of barbarian raids and the fear of retaliation from the king of Gwarystan had kept up a significant pressure on the small community. These adverse times had demanded a prodigious effort. The resolution and perseverance they all had demonstrated could not have been matched. The community had completed the restoration of Mentollà's buildings and ramparts. The fortress walls had been rebuilt, thanks to the masonry skills of the Unicorn guards. The compound had been fortified and its defences strengthened. Heavy ammunition had been stored in case of a siege. All possible protective measures had been implemented to safeguard the security of the refugees from Essawylor. A serene atmosphere now prevailed among the community of Mentollà.

So, to enjoy that evening's beauty, Fendrya decided to sit quietly on the steps which led from the keep to the creek. From her high viewpoint, she could peacefully watch the gentle spectacle offered by the Elves within the compound and beyond.

The sailors of the clan of Filweni were regrouping their small vessels behind the protection of the creek's rocks. Teams of rowers drove narrow, lightweight boats into Mentollà's safe harbour. They were bringing home plenty of supplies. Their canoes were full of shellfish and oysters, which could be found in abundance along the shores of Gloren's bay.

Other Irawenti were returning to the fortress after roaming the trails of the Sognen Tausy woods in search of wild fruit and game. It looked as if their hunting trips had been successful; numerous partridges and other wild birds now promised to find their way onto the small community's plates that night.

Fendrya took a few deep breaths, concentrating on what she valued most. This breathing technique helped her reduce the tension of the previous days and allowed her mind and body to feel more at one. Freshly cut grass, the burgeoning flowers of spring and the salty tang of the sea wafted through the air, letting her know that she was safe. There was something distinctly fortifying about the scents of home, this feeling of comfort, and having family and friends close by.

Above her loomed the keep, a tower of a hundred and fifty feet, its round stone walls broken only by arrow slits. The top of the tower still resembled a mouth opened towards the heavens, like an ancient giant bearing the wounds caused by the wrathful deities of the Islands.

Mentollà's courtyard, however, was a fine sight, equalling the richest of Llafal's gardens in majesty. The Irawenti had introduced exotic plants from Essawylor into the grounds of the fortress compound. Nutmeg and cinnamon had been planted alongside date palms and magnolia. Each season of Eïwele Llyi, the tropical trees' scents reminded the small community of their days in Essawylor. Six stone buildings with majestic arches occupied the courtyard's centre. They had been rebuilt with granite from the Arob Tiude Mountains. Their chimneys and ceilings were now repaired.

Suddenly, Fendrya's eye was caught by a group of unexpected guests emerging from the shadows of the woods on the other side of the creek, two hundred yards in front of where she sat. She immediately identified the newcomers as guards from the clan Ernaly. Their clothes were dark green and hawk feathers were woven into their hair. They were escorted by Irawenti sentries, who were keeping a respectable distance.

The clan Ernaly unit cautiously approached the outer walls from the creek's beach. They seemed to be on high alert, scanning their surroundings at every step, as if they expected some mischief from the Elves of Mentollà who surrounded them. Finally, the Llewenti reached the fortress' moat on the other side of the beach and stopped there. They did not ask to be allowed inside but instead opened their closed ranks to provide passage for an Elf who seemed to have been their prisoner. Several bags, including a luxurious travel case, were dropped on the sand. The clan Ernaly guards did not remain much longer and, despite the approaching darkness of night, they were quickly on their way, as if a pack of wolves were after them. Their green cloaks soon disappeared into the darkness of the woodlands; in the same direction they had come.

The Elf they had escorted stood alone on the beach. He looked strangely familiar to Fendrya. A moonbeam took on silvery reflections as it danced upon the surface of the creek's waters. The light of the rising moon spread gradually to the beach. Then she recognized Curwë.

The unexpected arrival of the bard left Fendrya intrigued. Immediately, she stood up and retraced her steps towards the fortress' courtyard. The young lady moved quickly, using her staff to clear a route through the wild grass of the creek's path. Further away, on the other side of Mentollà, the ocean roared while she walked along the slippery path. Even the surrounding noise of the sea failed to distract Fendrya from her thoughts.

'What is Curwë doing in Mentollà a few days before the festival in Llafal? And why has he been escorted by clan Ernaly guards?' she worried.

★

It took Fendrya but a few moments to reach the fortress' gates. Sailors, hunters, guards and artisans alike had all gathered around Curwë to welcome him and help carry his belongings. All the Elves of Mentollà had developed the deepest sympathy for the Elf with green eyes. Curwë was considered a hero, a flamboyant character and a prodigious bard who had the talent to enchant his audience with his unparalleled way of playing the Muswab, the music from Essawylor.

Fendrya immediately saw that Curwë was not looking his usual self, as if some serious incident had occurred. The bard was trying his utmost to hide his distress, giving special thanks to some of his companions, complimenting others with warmth. But the young lady could not be fooled by his unconvincing attempt to mask his state of mind.

Using her authority among the community, she requested that they be left alone, claiming the bard needed to rest after his long journey from Llafal. Fendrya was Curwë's friend and one he trusted. They had grown even closer since they both had been living in Llafal. The House of Essawylor, where Curwë dwelt, had become the Irawenti priestess' second home over the last few years.

Curwë agreed to be taken to the garden of Cil, a small orchard of mango trees where they could talk in peace. Once they were quietly seated on the elegant bench of the grove, away from prying eyes, Fendrya called upon their special friendship to get to the bottom of what had happened.

"Tell me why your heart is troubled. I see an infinite pain in your gaze. What has happened to the flamboyant Curwë?" Fendrya asked, trying to show as much compassion as she could.
The bard sang the first line of one of his songs. "I ignore sadness, the Muswab will chase it away..." but the tone of his voice was not convincing.

After a while, he agreed to explain his sudden arrival.

"Feïwal dyn has called me. He is meant to travel to Gwa Nyn this summer. I have decided to go with him."
Fendrya looked surprised. "I thought you did not wish to join him and had chosen to stay in Llafal. Feïwal dyn was angry for several days after you refused his call for aid. I heard him say you were changed and no longer recognized your true friends. He blamed the new life you enjoy in Llafal, your close relationships with the Llewenti and your taste for the finer things in life..."
"Well, I've changed my mind after all, and decided to honour my vows to the warlord of Mentollà. In fact, I came here to apologize. I will be the first one at Feïwal dyn's side for this expedition to Gwa Nyn. Look, my personal belongings are already packed," insisted Curwë, visibly eager to maintain his secret despite the evidence.

Fendrya still could not believe his story. None of it rang true.

"But Nelwiri dyn has not yet returned from Nyn Llorely. The Alqualinquë is not expected before the beginning of summer. "

"Then I will wait here," cut in Curwë, before adding with a disenchanted look , "the air of Mentollà will do me much good."

"But you had plenty of time to take part in the festival in Llafal before departing. Many were those who thought you could have been rewarded with the gifts of Eïwele Llyi. Your victory would have had a considerable echo throughout the Islands. It would have made us proud. Curwë, do not pretend you came back to Mentollà willingly. I simply cannot believe it. Will you tell me the truth? I am sure I can help you," pressed Fendrya.

Her facial expression, her upturned nose and the sparkle in her eyes expressed the most candid and genuine feelings of compassion. Curwë could not resist such kindness for long.

"Well, you will learn what happened sooner or later, so I might as well explain it to you now. Maybe being relieved of this burden will do me some good..." the bard said.
Breathing deeply, like easing an unseen pain, Curwë began.
"I was humiliated, Fendrya, or perhaps worse: my honour and dignity have been severely wounded. This is the reason I have withdrawn to Mentollà. I was wrongfully degraded by... Mynar dyl."

"Cil, Cim, Cir!" Fendrya reacted.   "What happened?"
"Dyoren returned to Llafal."
"Dyoren, the Renegade!" the young lady exclaimed.
"Dyoren the Seeker, the knight of the Secret Vale. He came to ask for my help," specified Curwë.
Fendrya was shocked. "But all the Llewenti clans are after Dyoren. They want to capture him. The matriarchs of Llymar have condemned him for rebellion."

"That is true, but Dyoren is nevertheless a great knight, an Elf of valour, worthy of our admiration. He means a lot to me. I consider him to be something of a mentor," confided Curwë.

"How can this be? You barely know him." Fendrya was lost.

"More than you think. To tell you the truth, Dyoren believes we were meant to meet. Something to do with my unusual green eyes is what he told me. A dream he had repeatedly, which he believes is inspired by his legendary sword. Whatever sorcery is behind it, there is a strange bond between us, and, since that day I saved Rymsing from the barbarians, our paths keep crossing. What I am trying to tell you, Fendrya, is that Dyoren wanted me to become his heir."

Curwë's expression was full of pain, as if he could still hear the words which Dyoren had spoken to him, lashing at his soul.

"What did you do?" Fendrya enquired, now deeply concerned.

"I helped him, as was my duty. I chose that path because it was dictated by my honour."

"And you got caught by Mynar dyl?"

"In a way, Fendrya, but Dyoren escaped, and that is what matters. The clans of Llymar took back his possessions, the Blade of the West and the scrolls of the Dyoreni, but they failed to capture him...

As for me, Mynar dyl pressured me into leaving Llafal and returning to Mentollà if I wished to avoid confronting the Council of Matriarchs. So here I am, defeated and humiliated. The rage inside me hurts, Fendrya, like never before. I know now what Lord Roquen must have felt when he was ignominiously degraded by Queen Aranaele."

"Siw!" Fendrya replied. "I know all too well how your temper can burst into flames. I have seen it happen. But you should calm down now and rejoice that the worst did not come to pass. I am glad Mynar dyl acted this way, giving you a chance to make amends. By letting you go, he proved wiser than I would have thought. After Aewöl's exile, new accusations against our community would have been disastrous. These are hard times indeed. Everything seems to be falling apart."

"I will not accept this fate, Fendrya!" insisted Curwë in a fleeting fit of anger.

"Of course you will accept it! Within any Elvin realm, conflict will exist. They can be of many different natures, from power struggles to family rivalries. These disputes can lead to grave consequences, such as treason or even murder. But generally, wise rulers prevent their emergence and avoid their destructive effects with the power of law. Resolving disputes is one of the many responsibilities of those who command our common fate. This is the duty of the Council of Matriarchs in Llymar, and we owe them our allegience. Siw, Curwë! What you are telling me is dangerous. Confronting Mynar dyl as you did was a deadly mistake. All his actions are legitimate according to Llewenti customs, you cannot count on any Elf in Llymar Forest to lay blame on his conduct. The Council of the Matriarchs would defend him in any case."

Curwë immediately spat back his reply, his eyes filled with rage.

"Is my loyalty to Dyoren not noble? Do we not share the same hope?"

"Cil, Cim,Cir! I understand, Curwë! Your views are perfectly defensible from your perspective! They would be legitimate too among the Irawenti clans. Do not misunderstand me, I know what noble ambition is in your heart," Fendrya said as she tried to soothe his anger.

Curwë insisted on making his point. "Among my kin, any Elf is free to give his heirloom to the one he chooses. It is the heir's responsibility to refuse it and no one may interfere with his freedom of choice."

Fendrya warned him. "Siw! Curwë, I know of the Hawenti custom. What I am trying to tell you has nothing to do with good or evil, right or wrong, I am trying to make you see how dangerous your antipathy towards Mynar dyl is. If you pursue this unilateral struggle you started all the way to its conclusion, ignoring your opponent's standpoint, if you deliberatly choose to ignore the context you live in, that your friends live in, you will lead us into a bloodbath, I warn you!"

The bard would not accept any of it. "Mynar dyl is a monster, I am telling you. He is a vile character who relishes making his power felt in perverse and cruel ways. You should know what he did to his own brother! Mynar dyl had Dyoren chased down to the most remote island of the Archipelago so that the Lonsely Seeker could be handed over to his judges."

"I know you will not hear it, Curwë, but trying to capture Dyoren is legitimate, it is what the Council of the Matriarchs ordered. Do not let your friendship for your companion blind you. Stay away from the Llewenti clans. Mingling with their affairs will only bring an ill fate upon you."

For the first time, Curwë appeared to accept the arguments of his friend.

"Perhaps you are right, Fendrya. You know I always praised your wisdom and sought your advice."

Once again, Fendrya tried to use her charm to appease the disillusioned bard. With a knowing smile, she reminded him of better times.

"I remember how, during the days of sunshine, back there in Essawylor, when green-eyed Curwë would stop at nothing to charm any young maiden he came across. He wouldn't be happy until he had conquered the hearts of every female in the assembly!"

Fendrya had an amused yet bashful smile as she remembered this happy time. Despite the mischievous twinkle of the doe-eyed maiden that obessed his mind, in that moment Curwë was captivated by the enigmatic, blue-eyed gaze of this face full of character, with sunkissed features and brooding good looks. The bard concluded their heart-to-heart with a lighter tone, in an attempt to make fun of himself.

"The day I will jump from the top of Gwarystan Rock has not come yet,"

Fendrya nodded and laughed.

"I do feel for you," she said. "I know how much you will miss life in Llafal. Did you think I had not noticed, when we were there together, your frequent reveries and your empty gaze? You can tell me, Curwë. There must be someone. Is she beautiful?"
"... She is!" Curwë sighed.
"And sweet?"
"As Eïwele Llyi herself!"

"And yet she did not come with you, on this day of return to Mentolla."

"Nor does she accompany anyone else," Curwë countered.

"So you are hopeful?" enquired the young lady.

"I would not be able to live differently."

"You must strive to be worthy of her," she replied, speaking now as a priestess of the white temple. "Be brave and pure to be honored with her love. This is the highest reward that a devoted Elf can earn from Eïwele Llyi."

"I am trying, but she is so noble and pure that I am afraid of never being worthy," confided the bard.

Fendrya smiled as she listened to the poet's words.

"On the contrary, if you think this way, you'll eventually become worthy of her. Does she live in Tios Lluin at the court of the house of Dol Etrond?"

"No... of course not." Curwë answered quite bluntly.

"But all the High Elves of Llymar live in Tios Lluin... Is she not Hawenti?" The young lady replied, looking puzzled.

"No in truth, she is not," acknowledged the bard openly.

"Beware Curwë, beware! The Llewenti cannot offer a High Elf the type of love he longs for," opposed Fendrya with a severe tone.

Her mind was racing to identify who the lady who inspired such passion could be. After a while, she thought it through. She knew. The unthinkable had happened.
Fendrya had spoken with gravity, and she now looked Curwë insistently in the eye. The bard remained motionless, pensive. Finally, his lost gaze managed to fix itself on her again. The tension between them rose when she mentioned the legend of Llyoriane, the Llewenti queen, and the sacrifice she made to save her people from the wrath of Eïwal Ffeyn as their naves approached the shores of the Islands. Fendrya spoke prudishly to describe how Llyoriane offered herself to the deity of storms to calm his wrath and save her fleet from perdition.

"Queen Llyoriane willingly agreed to be possessed and bruised by the savage deity of tempests, to allow her people to come to this new promised world. She started her reign with an act of sacrifice. I would even say... by striking a bargain. It should be remembered, for it tells us of the integral values of the matriarchs."

"I do not understand."

"I think you do not want to understand, Curwë... The matriarchs all descend from Queen Llyoriane's bloodline. Believe me, Curwë, they do not give their love without expecting something in return."

This offense against the dignity of his beloved set Curwë's imagination afire. "Then I will offer her the mightiest of gifts, you hear me, Fendrya, I will offer her the mightiest of gifts!"

Sweat was dripping from the bard's forehead. Fendrya almost had to cry to make her point heard.

"Do not misundesrtand me, Curwë, that is not what I meant. The favours of matriarchs cannot be bought with gifts. That is not how they think at all."

"And neither is this my way of making my feelings clear," spat Curwë with pride. "I spent my youth reading the works of literature of my people, the Silver Elves. I know tales of undying love, stories of everlasting commitment. There are some Elves of my kindred who accomplished heroic deeds just for the sake of love. They changed the course of history."

Fendrya was frightened by what she was hearing. Passion was overwhelming Curwë.

"I hope you are not serious. You are saying this to mock me, aren't you?"

"Did you know that the mightiest of the Silver Elves descended to the Halls of the Dead to confront Gweïwal Agadeon?" recalled the bard. His eyes burnt like emeralds, as if he himself was ready to take the path down to the king of the Underworld's domain.

Fendrya was now panicked, as she could perceive madness in his eyes.

"Stop it, Curwë! Stop it!" she cried. "Cil, Cim Cir! You are making me unconfortable with these children's tales. Siw! Stop playing with me. You frighten me. When I looked at you just now, I saw you would indeed be bold enough to take that dark path. Would you really risk your life just to shine before the eyes of a maiden?"

"And what if I would?" said Curwë, defiant as ever.

CHAPTER 3: Gelros

2716, Season of Eïwele Llya, 46th day, Gwa Nyn, Llanoalin

"How much that venison?" the bearded Man asked.

His clothes were expensive looking but too large for him, and his eyes darted about with that sneaky gaze typical of the former barbarians whom King Norelin had recently allowed inside the realm of Gwarystan. His pointed beard clung to his torso, almost covering the scar on his neck.

"Eight copper coins, in lawful currency, cast with the effigy of the king," the Elvin merchant responded after a pause, an indifferent look on his face.

Hard currency was required for any exchange between Elves or Men in the kingdom.

The Elvin Merchant was perched behind his stall on a wooden stool. He extended his long legs like a cat stretching its paws after a nap; with this movement came the muffled scraping of metal on metal. Under his broad, worn cloak, the Elf was armed to the teeth with swords and daggers.
He had positioned his cart in the far corner of the city square, away from the bustle of the market.

There were only a small number of goods for sale, among them pheasants he had probably hunted down himself. The birds he had caught were males, with brightly decorated tail feathers and prominent wattles. They had value as within the kingdom of Gwarystan, Elves never kept herd animals, and Men were not permitted to either. Hunting was the prerogative of nobles or prized fighters, and the only source of meat for the communities.

By the look of his bedraggled traveller's clothes, it appeared that this Elf was more at home tracking and hunting along the woods of Gwa Nyn than trading in the cities of the king.

"I have five coins for your two birds small. What you say?" The bearded Man proposed, depositing the said sum on the table.

His coins came in a variety of sizes. Their actual value depended on the metal they were made of and their weight. At first sight, his money looked lawful given the reddish rune that was engraved on its side. The Ruby College had the monopoly of coin minting in Gwarystan.

Though he relied on lingua Llewenti to communicate, this customer's linguistic prowess, like most Men in the kingdom, left a lot to be desired. His aggressive tone was that of a determined dealmaker. As the excitement of striking a bargain rose within his chest, sweat began to drip from the bearded man's forehead.

"I am not interested," replied the merchant with the same indifferent tone.

The Elf added to his elusive answer a few words in an Elvin tongue unknown to the Man with the beard. The language was coloured with innumerable vowels that intermingled with each other like the undergrowth of a dark forest. Only a few isolated consonants were recognized by their abrupt sound.

Seated in the shade of an oak tree, it was difficult to make out the Elf's features. What the bearded Man did notice was the unusual paleness of his interlocutor. After standing before the stall for a few moments more, he realized that the merchant was hardly paying him any attention. The Elf's gaze was fixed upon one of the second-floor windows of an imposing house that bordered the marketplace. The large edifice was something of a focal point in the city. It dominated the sole wharf of the small port where, along with several fishing boats, a swanship was docked.

The bearded Man, as short and fat and as the Elf was tall and thin, interpreted this inattention as an insult to his honour. Sweating more profusely than ever, he stood up as tall as he could. He would not tolerate another insult to his dignity. The Man made an aggressive gesture with his hands to remind the merchant of his duties towards his customers.
This move offended the Elf.
Suddenly, he stood up from his seat and stared at the bold customer.

"Never do that again!" the Elf whispered as their eyes met.

The bearded Man stood frozen. He could not help but wonder how so much violence and pride could be found in just one set of eyes. He felt like he was confronting someone who had returned from the dead, someone whose soul had haunted the Three Dragons' Lair before being sent back to walk the earth. But religion had never interested the short, fat Man. He decided to explore this matter no further and fled like a coward. He even left behind the five copper coins that, just a moment before, he had been ready to defend with his life.
Seeing his customer bolt like a frightened hare, the merchant muttered a few words in his mysterious Elvin language.

"E ow tumat sur ywlo."[13]

The Elf was momentarily distracted from the window he had, until then, been observing so carefully. When his gaze returned to the façade of the great building, he shivered.

'Serog Agadeon![14] She has closed the curtains. Something is wrong...'
His heartbeat suddenly accelerated.

★

---

13   E ow tumat sur ywlo: 'I will kill you for this ignominy' in lingua Morawenti

14   Serog Agadeon: 'Blood of Gweïwal Agadeon' in lingua Morawenti

The merchant's cart moved slowly up the street. It paused just before the gate to the imposing building the Elf had been watching. From this new elevated position, he could look out over the city's market square and only dock.

'The city is quiet. I am glad we chose this lost place,' the Elf thought.

Llanoalin[15] was a small port located at the mouth of the Sian Senky[16] in the north-eastern parts of Gwa Nyn. Only fishing boats and flat-bottomed vessels could be found along its only wharf, for the harbour's waters were not deep enough to host the great merchant ships of Gwarystan guilds. Elvin vessels and Westerners' galleys had to unload their heavy cargo at Ystanoalin. The high towers of Lord Dol Oalin's city could be seen on the other bank of the wide river, a few leagues to the west.

The merchant spun the cart around with difficulty. He then heaved it up the final few feet of the street's slope, finally propping his cargo against the gate. The Elf then fell back against the cart, breathing heavily after the tremendous effort. A sleeping sentry, wrapped in fine chain mail and holding a long spear, was awoken by the din. The guard left his post in front of the locked compound gates to confront the newcomer.

"What's your business here?" he asked, looking suspicious and annoyed. Two bronze Dragons upon an amber backdrop, the insignia of House Dol Oalin, were woven onto his red cloak.
"I come from Ystanalas[17]," panted the newcomer in reply. "I have a special delivery for the steward of the Port."

The sentry looked puzzled and then frowned. Examining the unexpected visitor more closely, he noticed that the merchant's face was incredibly pale, as white as his eyes were black. The guard felt uncomfortable, as he happened to be on duty alone at that late hour. He looked down towards the wharf. The other guards from his unit were supervising the unloading of a small

---

15   Llanoalin: 'The port of Oalin' in lingua Llewenti

16   Sian Senky: 'Blood river' in lingua Llewenti

17   Ystanalas: 'The Fortress of Talas' in lingua Llewenti. It is one of the major cities in Gwa Nyn. It is ruled by House Dol Talas.

merchant boat flying the flag of Urmilla[18]. The swanship had come from Nyn Llorely with a shipment of fruits and plants. It was not expected and its arrival that afternoon had provoked a certain flurry in the usually quiet port.

At last, after realizing that his colleagues would be of no assistance, the guard looked back to the unexpected visitor who stood before him.

"Show me the seal of those who sent you," he demanded in an authoritative tone.

"Of course," the merchant answered simply, and he drew from the inside pocket of his cloak a scroll carrying the dark Pegasus of House Dol Talas.

The guard removed his helmet to get a better look at the densely written document. The scroll was poorly illuminated, due to a shadow cast by the merchant's cart. The guard did not reach the end of the scroll's title before the sharp blade of a dagger was stabbed upwards into his throat. The lethal weapon finished its course by piercing his brain. Without even a groan, the sentry fell like a disjointed puppet. His body made a dull thud as it hit the ground. A trickle of blood ran from his neck out onto the dusty slabs.

The Elf pulled the sentinel's body up into the back of his cart. This morbid task required an intense and sustained effort, given the weight of the heavily armoured sentry. But the Elf's actions remained unnoticed, as the position of his two-wheeled vehicle hid the scene from any witnesses down the street. The Elf then seized the keys to the house's gate from his victim's belt. An instant later, he entered the compound, pulling his cart inside the courtyard. The steward's property was vast, with many different alleys and groves as befitted the mansion of a Hawenti dignitary.

Wherever they dwelled, the High Elves had come to dominate all others thanks to their abilities as craft masters and merchants. They exceled in pure industry and craftsmanship, but they also

---

18   Urmilla: 'Harbour of Urmil' in lingua Llewenti. It is one of the major cities in Nyn Llorely and a port of Gwarystan Kingdom. It is ruled by House Dol Urmil.

commanded commerce, a different force that was perhaps more powerful still. Their prosperity and influence in the Islands was mainly due to their ability at organizing trade.

Now hidden from public view, the Elf hurried to park his vehicle at the back of the house's garden. He seemed to know the layout of the place already, for he quickly found his way to one of the house's entrances.

The Elf closely studied the runes that were inscribed on the backdoor, but after a time he decided to ignore them.

"These glyphs have been dispelled," he murmured with relief.

The Elf immediately set about picking the lock. It proved easier than he expected; after a few moments, a low click signalled that the first stage was complete.

Llanoalin was a small city in Gwarystan Kingdom, known to be a tranquil place. For decades, King Norelin's peace had prevailed in this small port, and its inhabitants had forgotten the threats of the past. Even Llanoalin's most influential inhabitants were no longer being vigilant.

The door bent under the pressure of the Elf's weight before it sprung open, letting a stream of light inside. He stepped over the threshold while drawing another long dagger from his large green cloak. After crossing the parlour in silence, the intruder climbed the stairs which led to the first floor. He knew he was aiming for the building's second floor, but opposite the next flight of stairs was an open door leading to a vast room, illuminated by the light of the setting sun.

The Elf froze when he heard voices coming from the room, hesitating as to whether he could dart up to the second floor without being seen. As he listened to the voices, he realized it was two scribes enumerating the transactions of the day. One was reading out the trade receipts that had been submitted while the other confirmed that the goods had been stored and accounted for. From their monotone voices, it sounded like this boring task had been going on for some time.

A merchant company bought raw materials and goods at their point of origin, transported them to the markets where they would fetch the best price, and then sold them through its trading posts. The regulations controlling such trade were set out by the king's council, and royal guards were responsible for severely punishing those who would dare break trading laws. Hence the efforts the two scribes were investing in completing their task accurately.

The Elf was still hesitating, his gaze darting from the open office before him to the staircase up to the second floor. After a deep, controlled breath, he decided to sacrifice a few moments to poison the tips of his two daggers. The intruder drew from his cloak a phial containing a viscous ointment, the colour of black berries. He allowed a few drops of the concoction to fall onto the blades, being careful not to spill it on his leather gloves. This done, the Elf listened again to the bored voices of the two scribes as he grasped his long daggers.

He rushed into the room. His movements were rapid. After a brief skirmish, the thuds of two bodies were heard in quick succession.

Now with far less caution, the intruder exited the scribes' office and hastened up the stairs, daggers still in hand. The room corresponding to the window he had been watching was in the central part of the great house. After reaching the second-floor landing, he stalked silently along a corridor and up to a great closed door, which he knew marked the entrance to the steward of Llanoalin's private quarters.

Once he reached the end of the corridor, however, he found that the door to this room was protected by a locking mechanism, made from thick wooden frames and wrought iron grids. The lock was a complex system that, upon closer inspection, he knew would be beyond his skills to break. Suddenly feeling helpless, he remained immobile, like prey caught in a trap.
The Elf resolved to strain his ears and listen carefully to the conversation beyond the fortified door. Its panels were so thick that he could barely hear. Then, all of a sudden, the voice of an arrogant High Elf sounded out.

"Is that a threat, my lady?"

"It is a fact," a feminine Elvin voice responded almost as loudly, as though she wanted to be heard.

"You want me to believe that, all these years I have been collaborating with the clan Myortilys, I have in fact been serving the interest of the dark Elves, my own king's worst enemies?"

"Listen to me, my dear steward! The stakes are now extremely high for you. You have already paved your way to the top of Gwarystan Rock."

"There is a problem with all this. Why ever should I believe you are an envoy of the matriarchs of Mentodarcyl? What I see in front of me is an elegant Elvin lady of the Gwarystan court. I am sure you are no stranger to plotting and scheming; indeed, I do not doubt you consider them a particular talent. You have lived as a courtesan in the web of political deceit that enmeshes Norelin's capital. But I cannot imagine you mingling in the affairs of assassins. You are a lowly schemer, my lady, no more. You are simply attempting to blackmail me to get out of trouble. Allow me to give you some advice. When you lie, at least try to keep your stories within the realms of conceivability."

"I advise you to reconsider your position. If you do me any harm whatsoever, you will face the retaliation of clan Myortilys. You have already gone too far. You have accepted our bribes. We have proof of your corruption. Did you think that the steward of a royal port could take cuts from smuggling and illegal trade without leaving any trace of his guilt?"

"You sound convincing enough, my lady. You are very good at your trade. Someone else would probably have been impressed, perhaps even frightened by the threat I see in your beautiful dark eyes.
But I do not fear the murderous power of your gaze... I am still the steward of this port."

"But for how long? Think carefully now. I am giving you one last chance to save your life. All you need to do is affix your seal onto this scroll and take this charming little box full of precious amethysts. Is that so difficult?"

"It is, my lady. If I let your mysterious companions disembark from that swanship without understanding the nature of the rune which protects them, I would be committing a felony. Believe me; Lord Dol Oalin takes perjuries very seriously.

So, let me ask you one last time. Who are these three strangers you added to the list of passengers without my consent?"

The lady remained silent.

The steward struck her across the face.
His anger had been steadily building throughout their conversation, and this final defiance of his authority tipped him over the edge. He started grabbing and then shoving her repeatedly, and the violence escalated until he was punching and slapping her without restraint. He continued hitting her even after she had fallen to the ground.

"Leosca![19]" She cried in a desperate effort to escape his grasp.

A tiny snake sprung from her wrist and bit the steward's neck. For a moment, his look was one of disbelief; he could not understand how the silver bracelet the lady wore could have transmuted into a serpent. But soon, the pain above his shoulder became intolerable and the steward released his hold on her. The lady wriggled out from under him and rushed towards the door. She opened it and suddenly faced an Elf clad in a dark green cloak.

"Gelros," she cried, her breathing heavily , "kill him! Dispatch that vermin!"

A first dagger flew through the air. It hit the steward just above his heart, piercing into his left shoulder.
The victim turned and rushed to the far side of the room, seizing an ivory staff adorned with two bronze dragons that lay on his desk.
The second dagger caught him in the lower back, burying deeply into his spine. He fell heavily onto the ground, his head striking the corner of his imposing desk with significant force.
In a final, desperate effort, his hand managed to seize the ivory staff, but the dark blade of a short sword severed his forearm just below the elbow. Blood gushed onto the floor. The terrified

---

19 Leosca: 'Snake' in lingua Morawenti

steward simply stared at the fountain of blood, as powerful as a geyser, erupting from his arm. A split second later, and the dark blade had swung back around and sliced his throat.

★

Llanoalin was quiet. Its streets were almost empty that evening and the rare inhabitants enjoying an evening walk remained unaware of the bloody events that had occurred in the steward of the port's mansion. Mainly High Elves dwelled in the small city. They lived in rectangular stone structures, several stories high, the size depending on the wealth of the family. Their buildings' architecture interweaved with natural surroundings, creating beautiful and tranquil environments. The stone houses were organized in parallel alleys around the central square. The port was fortified like any other Hawenti city and served as a defence outpost providing protection to the nearby manors and settlements. A long distance separated the city from the closest fortress.

Inside the steward's house however, the confusion was great.

"What are you doing with him? What is this new horror?" the lady was asking, speaking now in lingua Morawenti, gawping at her protector in disgust. She could not restrain herself from vomiting.

"I am sorry, Lady Drismile, but these are the master's orders," explained Gelros in that same language of the Night Elves.

"What can be the purpose of this atrocity?" she barely managed to reply.

"The acid will burn through his eyes and dissolve his brain. Master Aewöl believes that this prevents sorcerers from questioning the dead. I must warn you, my lady, I had to kill three other Elves within the house and compound. I will need to take the same precautions with them. It is a necessary evil if we wish to leave no tracks," Gelros insisted.

Faced with the horror of the scene, Drismile made a supreme effort to control herself. She knew that time was of essence, and that they had to decide upon their next actions quickly. The lady began to think through their next moves.

"We have little time!" she warned. "I must get back to the swanship before nightfall. The guards of House Dol Oalin are awaiting the steward's permission for the passengers to disembark. Failing to deliver the stamped documents in time would expose us to a thorough search of the boat. I promised I would come back with them."

Her voice had regained its usual calm. As she spoke, she walked up to a mirror to check her appearance. Her face was covered in bruises and her makeup was smudged. The intensely pale colour of her skin was now showing through on her cheeks.

"Gelros, take the ring from that severed hand. The steward utilised it as his seal. Use the red ink on his desk and stamp his hallmark on the scroll I have prepared. Then you are free to do... what you must do... and then leave discreetly. The passengers will join you aboard your canoe just after nightfall. You must then depart immediately up the river."

Drismile had drawn from one of her pockets an elegant box adorned with small gems. In it were a variety of perfumes and make-up ointments. Sitting in front of the mirror, she started to rebuild her appearance, forging afresh her external beauty.

"What will you do, Lady Drismile?" Gelros inquired.
"First, I will take as many of the steward's possessions as I can. I know where he stashed his treasure; the key to his vault is hidden in a secret drawer of his desk. I will retrieve the precious gemstones he has accumulated. The steward kept rubies that will be precious to Master Aewöl. I will also burn the documents detailing his illegal dealings with the Alqualinquë to ashes. I will make the scene look like a robbery. Lord Dol Oalin's guards need to believe it was the work of clan Myortilys' assassins," Drismile explained, coming up with her plan on the spot.
"What I meant, my lady, is what will you do once you leave this house? Many Elves know you in this part of Gwa Nyn. You need to escape unnoticed," recommended Gelros.

For a moment, Drismile wondered whether the merciless scout was concerned about her safety, or whether he was considering silencing her forever. She knew what an asset she might be to their enemies; she was one of the few Elves who could trace their master to wherever he was hidden. Understanding this new danger, she responded immediately, eager to demonstrate her control of the situation.

"Thank you for your concern, Gelros. But I have already made up my mind. Once the passengers are safely with you on the canoe, I will return to the swanship and persuade its captain to leave the shores of Gwa Nyn this very night. We will simply cast off and travel the river at low tide. The current of the Sian Senky will carry us to the open sea. We will not even need to row a single stroke."

"What if the guards who are currently stationed around the swanship return to the steward's house?" questioned Gelros.

"I have thought of that too. It is almost nightfall, and once all the formalities associated with the shipment are fulfilled, I will release the guards from duty. I will say that the steward's house is closed and that he wishes to be left alone for the night."

"Are you sure that will work? Will no one doubt your words? What if they find out what's happened here? If we have the knights of House Dol Oalin on our heels, I doubt we will make it to Nargrond Valley," the scout feared. He seemed to doubt her persuasive capabilities.

"Remember, Gelros, I have spent the last few years by the steward's side. I have represented him as his envoy in Ystanoalin and even in Gwarystan. I have participated in all the celebrations here at Llanoalin and have greatly contributed to his recent prosperity. There are Elves who owe me in this small port. Many here trust me.

I would say I can offer you eight hours before the hunt begins."

Gelros looked at her with scrutiny, like a wild cat stalking a potential prey. After some time, he came to his decision, his tone still cold.

"I do not know when we will see each other again, Lady Drismile... but rest assured I will tell Master Aewöl of how well you have served him."

"Thank you Gelros, I appreciate it. You know..." stressed Drismile , "I am a devoted servant of the Guild of Sana..."

She looked away as Gelros seized the severed forearm of the steward, with no more delicacy than a hunter handling a piece of meat.

★★

Gwa Nyn, Ystanoalin harbour, the same night

The canoe slipped rapidly over the low waves of the Sian Senky, darting between the heavy merchant vessels, the Elvin naves with elegant aft castles, and the frail fishing boats.
It avoided the royal warships like a dolphin fleeing dark-wood leviathans. Their enormous stern castles, with classical sea creatures of ruby and gold carved into them, rose above the surface of the water. Hanging from their masts were heavy, swaying pendulums wavering overhead as if to threaten the frail canoe. Innumerable ropes enveloped these apparitions like nets waiting to capture them.

"See, the port of Ystanoalin hosts many ships," said Gelros as he turned towards his three passengers. "These are naves which sail the Sea of Llyoriane. They can withstand deadly collisions. But there are also larger warships of the royal fleet. Those ships can take on the ocean."

A voice with a foreign accent rose from the back of the boat.

"These marine giants sprung from a Hawenti mind. They carry in their heavy hulls all the violence of the Austral Ocean. But, let me tell you, it takes more than that to confront the infinite sea."

Fractured tree branches, the size of sharks, rose up on the water's surface, almost reaching the canoe's deck, before slipping back down on their tails and gracefully drifting under the small nave. The river was a salty green, and deposits of algae had formed at the base of the small boat. A vague smell of seaweed permeated the air, and the night cries of black seagulls were incessant.
The canoe was progressing upstream. The force of its rowers was such that even the strength of the Sian Senky current could not resist them. A weak wind from the north was filling the boat's frail sail. That gentle breeze, like the friendly breath of Eïwal Ffeyn, helped the canoe on its journey away from the sea. As Gelros heaved the oars, he could not take his eyes off the golden facades of Ystanoalin port, which shimmered upon the mirror of dark liquid behind them.

The ancient palaces of the High Elves appeared one after the other in the gloom, tall and proud. When the rooms were lit within, he could make out the numerous paintings, candelabras and bookshelves, below the richly ornamented ceilings.

"We will soon have left the city of Lord Dol Oalin behind us," announced Gelros between strokes.

Despite the darkness of a starless night, he could just about make out the faces of his companions: the severe features of Roquendagor; the sad look in Curwë's gaze; and the closed face of Feïwal, captain of their small boat.

It had been a few years since Gelros, then with his master, Aewöl, had last visited the great city of Ystanoalin, the rich harbour that connected the prosperous plains along the Sian Senky to the Sea of Llyoriane, the heart of the Lost Islands' trade. Seeing the fief of Lord Dol Oalin again was captivating, even for an Elf like Gelros who valued first and foremost the beauty of natural surroundings.

Ystanoalin was located in north-eastern Gwa Nyn, and the capital of the Sian Senky regions. The city itself was spread out across a group of small islands that were separated by canals and linked by bridges. It had been built by the first Lord Dol Oalin in a shallow lagoon, an enclosed bay that lay at the mouth of the Sian Senky. Its large natural harbour was unique across Gwa Nyn, which was otherwise feared by sailors due to its dangerous rocky shores and treacherous currents.
After being conquered by King Lormelin, the city had become the main port of Gwa Nyn, and had been known ever since as the 'City of Water'.
During the reign of the Conqueror, it had developed into a major maritime power, and one of the major stages upon which the wars against the Dark Elves of clan Myortilys were conducted. Ystanoalin was known also as a very important centre of commerce and art. The silk, grain and spice trades had filled the coffers of its elite class; its guilds had been the richest organizations to emerge from the Elvin Wars of old. This had made the stronghold of House Dol Oalin a wealthy city through the ages, and it was still very much renowned for the beauty of its architecture and artworks.

Gelros proudly recalled the time he spent with his master in the City of Water.

"Aewöl believes that Ystanoalin is the most beautiful Elvin city he has ever visited," he confided to his companions in a low voice.

After a moment's pause, Curwë replied. "Ystanoalin has always been at the forefront of culture and learning; it has inspired many a great author and scholar over the years."

"So, I have heard," replied Roquendagor, remembering a recent conversation with Fendrya. "There are many prized books and rare manuscripts to be found in its libraries. The most celebrated of the city's writers were the city's merchants who recorded their voyages to the many isles of the Archipelago."

"Aewöl acquired many volumes when he travelled here. They contain important information about the islands surrounding Gwa Nyn."

This last comment from Gelros further piqued Curwë's interest.

"It sounds as if Aewöl and I share a similar passion for this place. What fascinated me most in the books I read in Llafal is the City of Water's rich and diverse architecture, most prominently the Vauis[20] style. This trademark style, named after the God of crafts, meant Ystanoalin came to be known as one of the most important centres of creation across the Lost Islands."

"Never before had I seen Aewöl be so loquacious," Gelros recalled. "For hours, he discussed the designs that had come out of Ystanoalin. He kept saying how everything he saw around him was inspiration for what he could achieve in future. He even started drawing up blueprints for a new city."

"You were here without the protection of the royal rune. Were you not worried about being discovered?" wondered Roquendagor.

"Oh no," replied Gelros in a reassuring tone , "We spent many days here, relaxing in some of its most famous venues. Such luxury! Never did anyone question us. Aewöl saw to it." The scout raised a smile, not wanting to say more.

---

20 Leïwal Vauis: Known as God of discernment and master of crafts in the Hawenti mythology.

A dry comment abruptly issued by Feïwal jolted Gelros from his reminiscences.

"I heard at the Council of the Forest that Ystanoalin is in trouble. Since King Norelin forged his alliance with the Westerners, it has lost most of its power as a naval base. In terms of influence, it is now lagging behind its rivals, because of fierce competition with the Sea Hierarchs over maritime trade. Since the advent of King Norelin, his elite circles have become decadent, with nobles wasting their gold through partying and gambling. Though it is still a serious contender to Gwarystan in terms of luxury, it is no longer an important centre of power."

"Unfortunately for Curwë," added Roquendagor with a smile , "we don't have time to sample the city's luxuries on this visit..."

Ignoring the irony, Gelros turned to Feïwal. "Maybe you are right, noble Guide. But there are still many Elves in the service of Lord Dol Oalin. We don't want them to find out that you disembarked in Gwa Nyn."

Looking at the silver feather upon the palm of Feïwal's hand, the scout added , "That's the wrong rune protecting you."

The canoe veered to the right, coming away from the shore and exposing itself to the full force of the river. It felt heavy, and the effort needed to propel the boat almost pushed the four rowers to their limits.

Fortunately, the northern wind soon picked up, bringing unexpected support in their struggle up the Sian Senky. The Elves of Mentollà looked one last time at the high towers of House Dol Oalin's palace as they slowly disappeared into the night.

"Nelwiri must have reached the open sea by now," said Feïwal. "I hope the Alqualinquë is safe. Aewöl was right. King Norelin has the river route to the Nargrond Valley closely watched. I would never have anticipated finding so many royal warships guarding the mouth of the Sian Senky."

The Elves of Mentollà remained quiet thereafter, concentrating on coordinating their efforts to get away from Ystanoalin. They needed to row across a populous region, referred to by the Elves of Gwarystan as the 'Garden of Gwa Nyn' due to the abundance of vineyards and fruit orchards that lined the banks of the river. It was an exceptionally beautiful landscape that comprised of small cities and fortresses of architectural splendour, home to the vassals of Lord Dol Oalin. These lands had been shaped by centuries of interaction between Elves of different kin and the Sian Senky itself.

It was a moonless night. From time to time, however, the silhouette of a fortress would become visible on the hilltops.

"The House Dol Oalin's vassals have dozens of fortresses in these parts," noted Curwë, who had remained silent until then. "When Lormelin the Conqueror began constructing Ystanoalin, they were built up from the riverbed as a representation of the High Elves' power. The Hawenti nobility did not want, or dare, to be far from the seat of power, hence they followed suit."

The Elves of Mentollà could not marvel at the sights around them, however. When dawn came, they had already managed to row upstream as far as a vast swampy area that Elves generally avoided. They remained hidden in their canoe the whole day, concealed behind high plants and long reeds.

Roquendagor, who was sat closest to Gelros, took the opportunity to commemorate their reunion. The tall knight was visibly enjoying himself.

"I am glad we are together again, Gelros. It has already been a few years since you followed Aewöl into exile. I still have dark memories of that sad day."

The stealthy scout raised a smile, vaguely embarrassed. So many events had occurred since then that his time in Mentollà seemed long past.

Roquendagor remembered.

"You made a good choice that day when you followed Aewöl. I am sure you have proven your value at his side many times over. You have always been strong and resilient, probably the best hunt master Ystanlewin has ever seen.

Aewöl's strength probably lay elsewhere... but he always demonstrated a certain weakness when faced with the challenges of living in the wilderness. He is a sensible, fragile character, more skilled with quills and scrolls than with swords and shields. I knew he was in good hands when I learnt that you were at his side. I know him well. His knowledge is vast, and he proved wise on many occasions. But he always showed difficulties controlling his temper. Aewöl exerts so much of his strength hiding his thoughts and planning for the future. I cannot imagine how many times I must have told him, 'Come out into the light, master alchemist! Come riding with me through the woods to the mountains! There is so much to see. Immortality is ours!'"

Recalling the days of his youth in Essawylor, Roquendagor's face brightened. He was becoming increasingly vivacious and outspoken. His blue eyes sparkled, and a broad smile creased his friendly features. His hand stroked his shaven head as he reminded his companion of the old stories: the hunting and warfare back in Ystanlewin.
Gelros remained impassive, listening politely to his former lord without showing any emotions. Roquendagor eventually recalled one particular campaign in the Ivory Mountains, when he had killed a great jaguar with his bare hands.

"Only you were there to see it, Gelros! That glorious day!" boasted Roquendagor. "Without you, no one would have believed me. It's too bad that my only witness was so tight-lipped. My feat against the jaguar would have been known across the whole kingdom of Five Rivers..."
"I died, my lord. I think I died."

This interruption from Gelros was most unexpected.

The bizarre statement took Roquendagor completely off guard. After a time, he decided to shuffle down the canoe and sit closer to his former hunt master. Mosquitoes were flying around him and causing annoyance.

"What do you mean?" the knight finally asked, with a tone of incredulity.

"I was killed in the woods of Mentolewin in Nyn Ernaly, a few years ago, my lord. I think I was poisoned by an arrow."

"That cannot be, Gelros; you would not be here with me, being eaten alive by these damned mosquitoes in this stinking swamp. Those herbal concoctions you drink all the time must have saved you from the poison."

"Perhaps, my lord. Perhaps I only thought I had died. Maybe he managed to save me."

"Now that you mention it," Roquendagor recalled, "in one of his many letters to Curwë, Aewöl did refer to some difficult times you went through in Nyn Ernaly, just after we parted. You were severely injured, and a wild Man saved you. He managed to heal your wounds."

"He was not a wild Man; he was a druid and a shape-shifter, who could transform himself into a brown bear of the forest," Gelros contested.

"What kind of hallucinatory talk is this? Aewöl described him as a mad hermit. The poison must have affected you. After you've looked death in the eye, it is often difficult to get things clear in your head," suggested Roquendagor.

"Did Alef Bronzewood raise me from the dead, or did he save me from a certain death? I do not know. After all, does it really matter? I am alive and at my master's service...

Alef Bronzewood dedicated time to me and eventually healed me. I do remember that he asked me a lot of questions. Never did I listen to someone for so long. Alef Bronzewood wanted to know why Aewöl and I had first entered his forest. He wanted to know if, like the Westerners from Tar-Andevar, we were there to cut down the Paubras[21]. He was obsessed with how the Men of the West were destroying the Islands' forests. He could not understand why anyone would sail their great galleys across the seas and oceans to destroy the Islands' forests and fell the Paubras trees.

'Do they not have wood in their own land?' he would ask again and again. 'Why would they dedicate their lives to travel the world, only to destroy, cut and seize? Are they not rich enough with their flamboyant metal garments? Why do they need to accumulate more useless things, of which they have no need?' he continuously wondered. Despite his origins, Alef Bronzewood declared himself a friend of the Elves and an

---

21 Paubras: 'Wood from the Mother's blood' in lingua Llewenti

enemy of Men, a loyal servant to the Mother of the Islands. He explained to me at great length how all Men are descended from demons, from the fiery creatures born of Gweïwal Narkon.

'A fire burns within them that no other element can extinguish. It's this fire within that compels them to expand and accumulate incessantly. All Men are driven by the fear of their own death. They are obsessed with passing the riches they have gathered on to the next generation.

Did the Mother of the Islands not feed them well? Will she not also take care of their children?' he asked. He insisted that, 'Bears also have children of their own. Bears know that after they are dead, the Mother of the Islands will feed their children well with the fruit and honey she makes.'

Alef Bronzewood talked to me over a long period as I gradually recovered. He also explained to me the many secrets of his order and the reasoning behind them. More than once he said:

'The druids are not waging war because they want to seize land back from Men. The Mother of the Islands provides land for all of us, including for animals, Gnomes, Giants, Elves, and even Men. The true reasons the druids go to war against the evil Men is to take prisoners. This is what drives us,' he confided. Alef Bronzewood taught me that there was only one way to get rid of Men's evil souls if we do not want those demons to multiply and finally destroy all there is on Oron."

"Tell me, what is the fate of the druids' prisoners?" Roquendagor asked: intrigued, though imperceptibly worried.

"The druids eat their human prisoners alive," whispered Gelros. "That is how the souls of evil Men are thereafter confined to the inner core of Oron, from whence they came... never to return to the Islands."

Roquendagor had to restrain himself from gagging at this thought. Looking at Gelros' fixed gaze, the knight thought that exile had changed the former hunt master of Ystanlewin. He was no longer the same.

For three entire days, the Elves of Mentollà rowed against the current of the Sian Senky across more than fifty leagues. They fought their way upstream to the gravelled beds of the river, where other difficulties awaited them. In this section of the Sian

Senky, bordered by rocky hills and covered in dense woodland, a south-easterly current kept nudging the canoe starboard of the range's recommended track.

This current soon became too strong and, without the assistance of the wind that had now waned, it became impossible to row their way upstream.

Defeated by the forces of nature, the Elves of Mentollà abandoned their canoe to continue their journey on foot. They rested for a time along the southern river's bank to simply marvel at the glorious sight of hundreds of thriving salmon swimming upstream to spawn.

★★

Gwa Nyn, East of Nargrond Valley, four days later

The Elves of Mentollà progressed through the woods without talking. Their thoughts were as far away as Oron's poles.
Gelros was focusing on their immediate needs: sourcing water, managing their supplies and finding hideouts. He alone knew, from his friend the druid Alef Bronzewood, the way into Nargrond Valley, and therefore held the keys to their common destiny.
The scout had chosen to head to the southern range of the Arob Nargrond[22], being careful to bypass any deep woodland while keeping the banks of the Sian Senky on their right. He knew the river was rich with fish and game, a land of predilection for hunters of all kinds.
Gelros had been impatient to put as much distance as possible between themselves and Ystanoalin. He was convinced that they were still under threat.

Among all who had travelled in the canoe, he alone knew about the four murders back in Llanoalin. Those grave incidents would without doubt have consequences. The scouts of Lord Dol Oalin may well have already picked up their trail. His instincts were telling him that the hunt had already begun. As they walked through the woods, he had been drawing upon all of his talents and experience to hasten their flight and evade their hunters. Gelros would frequently go ahead to clear the way. Whenever Curwë requested that they pause to rest, Gelros busied himself in covering their tracks, skilfully utilizing everything the woods offered him to mislead any pursuers. His zeal for the task was great, but nevertheless his anxiety was growing. Were Gelros' fears exaggerated, or had these precautions already saved them? None of the Elves of Mentollà would ever know.

Curwë wallowed in silence. The bard was apparently deep in thought, and his companions did not dare disturb him.
Roquendagor had tried to discuss exploring the valley of Nargrond but seeing that his companions were paying little attention to his plans, he had finally fallen quiet too.
Feïwal seemed absorbed in matters spiritual. When he was not deeply engaged in prayer, the guide of the clan of Filweni was muttering words to himself.

---

22 Arob Nargrond: 'Mountains of Nargrond' in lingua Llewenti

Gelros was intrigued. He slackened his pace to walk closer to Feïwal. Though he could not capture the full meaning of his monologues, he could hear the navigator talking to himself, like a worshiper overrun with spiritual fever.

"The wind is always whispering in the ear of all Elves. We must accept the message of freedom it carries and reject all other bonds.

'There is no freedom, but the freedom granted by the wind.'

This is the cornerstone, this is the key, and this is the founding principle at the heart of everything. That proclamation is sacred law. It forbids the Elves of the Islands from submitting to laws enacted by tyrants. 'The seeds of Llyoriane,' that's what the deity of storms called the Elves of the Islands: The seeds of Llyoriane. He made them free in relation to one another..."

Gelros remained puzzled by the troubling behaviour of Feïwal. The scout could not pretend that he knew the guide of the clan of Filweni well, but he had never witnessed him in such mental turmoil.

"Are you well, Feïwal dyn? Perhaps we should stop for a time. Dawn will come soon," suggested Gelros.

The group was progressing into the forest with difficulty, preferring the concealment of the night to the light of the day. Curwë was caught in a languor that became heavier every hour that passed. The bard could not keep up the pace that Gelros was setting.

This was the time to rest, decided the scout. He pointed to a small clearing, through which ran a stream in the shade of ancient chestnut trees. His companions felt relieved to catch their breath and ease their straining muscles.

Curwë quickly lay on the ground without bothering remove his armour, even though the bard was equipped for war. Below his long green cloak, he wore leather armour reinforced by a steel breastplate.

Roquendagor disapproved of this lack of self-discipline and could not resist sharing his views as he proudly began placing his own heavy equipment on the ground.

"This new life in Llafal has not done you any good, Curwë. There was a time you would have offered to take the first watch…"

The bard did not respond to this remonstration from his former lord, so Roquendagor took it as read that the first shift would be his. The commander of Mentollà unburdened himself of his plate mail. Soon, gauntlets, helmet, a gorget and other elements of his heavy armour were piled up by the swollen stream's bank.

Meanwhile, Feïwal approached Gelros as the scout was checking the contents of his quiver.

"I have been watching you, Gelros," said the guide of the clan of Filweni. "You are always on your guard. Of course, the valley of Nargrond is a dangerous place…."
"It is a land of treasures," Gelros quickly replied. "Aewöl says the valley of Nargrond is the heart of the Islands, the place where our predecessors buried all their secrets. Many are those who seek them. It is indeed a perilous territory."
"This is true… but I would add that, more importantly, it is where the Fallen Star hit Gwa Nyn…" replied the guide of the clan of Filweni in a low voice.

"Do you see this stone?" Feïwal asked after a moment's pause, picking a pebble out of the stream. "I will drop it."

Gelros watched the stone fall onto the waterlogged ground of the clearing.

"That stone fell just as deliberately as the meteorite fell upon Gwa Nyn, a long time ago, when the Elves were still young. What this means is that the deity of storms also controls the stars in the heavens. The celestial bodies are within Eïwal Ffeyn's mighty power, for he alone fully understands the fundamental forces, brought into being by Ö, that power the Flow that surrounds Oron."

Gelros remained cautiously silent. Feïwal believed that the scout's attitude demonstrated respect and a thirst for knowledge. The guide of the clan of Filweni resumed.

"The Elves, wherever they were born, are all children of Ö. That is the message delivered by Eïwal Ffeyn when he pulled the Star from the night sky."

There was a strange light burning in Feïwal's eyes. Gelros wandered whether it was a sign of madness or an indication of faith. It made him nervous. He grasped his great black yew bow even more tightly. But the scout was intrigued and wished to ask more.

"Do you mean that there are too many Elves who do not respect the message of Eïwal Ffeyn?"

"That is exactly what I mean," confirmed Feïwal with a foreboding tone. "The clans of Llymar do not submit totally and exclusively to Eïwal Ffeyn. They supposedly worship the deity of freedom as an original member of their pantheon, but they ignore his teachings. The Llewenti clans have replaced the message of Eïwal Ffeyn with the word of their matriarchs and their interpretation of the other Islands deities' signs.

It is no wonder, therefore, that they would never support a mass Irawenti migration from Essawylor that would save our people from destruction. The Llewenti clans secretly wish to deny all other Elvin nations access to these Promised Islands. Eïwal Ffeyn's fundamental message is the opposite.

I have now come to fully understand it.

Eïwal Ffeyn created the Islands as the Promised Land for all free Elves, so that our relationships could be based upon a common liberty. Since the beginning of time, he has rejected all other powers: be that the Giants or even the Greater Gods themselves. He was against the High Elves coming to the Archipelago because their king brought with him the tyranny of his laws and vows. No Elf, even a simple Wenti, can be the servant or slave of another, even an immortal Hawenti. Do you understand? This is one of the core meanings of his message. Eïwal Ffeyn put an end to the coercive justice enacted by the rulers of the Elves, in order to establish the freedom that Ö wished for his children."

Gelros did not understand this last statement.

"But Eïwal Ffeyn was defeated by the High Elves," Gelros wondered aloud. "He was imprisoned forever in the Sea of Cyclones if you believe the scholars."

"They lie, Gelros, they lie because they fear what the deity of storms will do when he returns. Eïwal Ffeyn is the wind... He is freedom... He will return and be freed of his bonds, believe me... and the day of his return will mark the Day of Judgment for all those Elves who imprisoned him and scorned his teachings. Do you not see? It has already begun..."

Sensing that some form of dangerous exaltation was seizing Feïwal, Gelros became worried. He feared what affect such mental exertion might have upon the guide of the clan of Filweni. There was still a long way to go. The scout believed these spiritual vagaries to be useless. Somewhat embarrassed, he tried to bring the discussion to a close.

"I hear you, Feïwal dyn... These are... matters you should discuss with Aewöl. He too has knowledge about these... things.
I must now look for food if we do not want to starve. It is almost dawn."

With that, the quiet scout disappeared beneath the canopy, his great yew bow slung at his back. The deadly weapon hardly ever left his side. His dark green and brown clothes faded quickly into the woods.

★★

Gwa Nyn, Entrance to Nargrond Valley, two days later

After a few quiet days, Gelros was less worried that they were being followed. He gained enough confidence to allow the group to move by daylight. Their progress was nonetheless extremely slow, as they kept well away from the main tracks and clearings. The dense woodland was a constant challenge to Gelros' tracking abilities.

There were periods of rain, others of sunshine, followed by thunderstorms. These were days of overwhelming heat, where they could only ever find a little coolness at the edge of the streams and in the shade of the trees. Summer was demonstrating its full, brilliant force. The Elves of Mentollà continued their march in silence.

The next morning, a faint sun, no bigger and less bright than the moon, finally appeared amid the dark clouds. Gradually it grew until a yellow halo had spilled across the horizon. Then, a single piercing ray was soon followed by abundant golden light. The power of the sun dispelled the remnants of the shadows. Its soft radiance reflected upon the fresh moss that lined the ground.

Moments later, the Elves of Mentollà crossed a mountain pass and discovered a sun-drenched lowland. At the edge of the woods, in the encroaching heat of dawn, they stood motionless for a moment at the entrance to the valley of Nargrond. They listened to the unseen birds singing somewhere ahead in the wilderness. The gentle breeze murmured through the pines. The beauty of the place was breath-taking.

Feïwal, deeply moved by the sight, took a step forward, his gaze rising towards the sky. He waived his hand like a cleric paying homage to the heavens.

The valley ran from east to west along the Sian Senky for more than sixty leagues. Two mountain ranges bordered its northern and southern flanks; some of their peaks reached heights of over six thousand feet. The mightiest mountain of Gwa Nyn, indeed the highest mountain of the Lost Islands, could be seen upon the horizon towards the sunrise. The top of Mount Oryusk, the volcano created by the fall of the meteorite upon

Gwa Nyn, towered over of the surrounding elevations from its ten thousand feet. Its massive silhouette marked the end of the valley to the west.

Mount Oryusk was the most active volcano in the Islands, indeed it appeared to be in an almost constant state of eruption. Its three central craters were spewing forth great plumes of different coloured smoke; sometimes white as ice, then dark as shadows, now red as lava. The mountain's lower slopes spread out across the valley of Nargrond, its fertile soils rich with woods, vineyards and orchards.

Curwë pointed to three giant columns that were positioned at the valley's entrance, where the southern and northern ranges of the Arob Nargrond joined together in what looked like a last attempt to imprison the wild waters of the Sian Senky. The three great pilasters were still hundreds of feet high, though a major disaster had caused their ruin. Damaged elements of the gigantic fluted columns lay half-buried besides their ancient foundations.

With a weak voice, Curwë made a special effort to share his knowledge with his companions. During his time in Llafal, the bard had learnt many legends from Matriarch Nyriele.

"These are the great columns of the Gnomes, the first inhabitants of the Islands who settled in the archipelago long before the coming of the deities, Giants and Elves. They chose to build three monuments, for that number is associated with the triangle.

The triangle is the emblem of Gweïwal Agadeon, the Gnomes' Protective God that, according to their legends, fathered their race.

It is said they received a warning from their divine father of an impending catastrophe. Then, fearing that all knowledge of their arts and crafts would be lost in a gigantic flood, the result of Gweïwal Uleydon's wrath, they built these three great columns upon a high hill. The pilasters were made of brass and granite to resist water. Writing in their indecipherable hieroglyphics, the Gnomes engraved the fundamentals of their arts and crafts upon the pillars. In the end, however, what threatened their civilization was not the tidal wave they had expected.

When the meteorite fell upon Gwa Nyn, the hill of the pillars was destroyed, but ruins of the three great columns endured, though they have lost their initial magnificence. The few surviving Gnomes interpreted this catastrophe as a sign of the coming of the Elves to the Islands."

Curwë's companions remained silent, as if petrified by the grandeur of the spectacle in front of them. Their eyes could not fully capture the vast spectrum of colour or the myriad of beautiful markings. All they could take in was the Sian Senky meandering at the bottom of a strangely shaped vale that extended westward and then south-westward from the high path on which they were standing. The Arob Nargrond was one of the deepest ranges they had ever contemplated. Its peaks would tower above the mountains that rose in Nyn Llyvary or even in distant Essawylor. Nargrond Valley was a geological cleft, rarely more than two leagues in width, boarded by steep limestone precipices. Because the valley was so narrow, numerous waterfalls could be seen above the trees. The streams descending from the adjoining mountains spilled downwards in roaring cascades as they reached the verges of the valley's rocky walls. They fell from such a height that they would almost totally disappear into spray before they reached the level of the river, where the land was heavily forested and covered in clusters of trees and large open meadows.

The view from the eastern end of the valley, where the Elves of Mentollà stood, contained a great granite monolith on the left and rocks as high as Gwarystan's towers on the right. Just past this point, the valley suddenly widened with spires, then with a pointed obelisk that looked like a sentinel's tower to the south. On the northern side were 'the four Greater Gods', rising one above the other like gables built along the same angle. The highest crest was Zenwon; the one below was Narkon, 'the Lower Brother'.

From these towering heights, melting snow became torrents and pools, which then surged downwards into cataracts and waterfalls. Creeks and forks of the different streams took drainage from the Arob Nargrond's crest, eventually disappearing into the canyons.

Gelros pointed westward to rapids that were falling from the valley's rim. They combined at the base of the gorges which contained each stream, and then surged around small isles to meet the Sian Senky at the centre of Nargrond Valley, where it spread into a majestic lake.

"That is where we are going," he indicated.

★

The vale that led to the wider valley of Nargrond started with a dense wood. In this higher part of Gwa Nyn, the chestnut, walnut, and birch trees replaced the pines and cypresses that dominated further down on the plains around Ystanoalin.
At sunset, the Elves of Mentollà climbed a large rock to enjoy the magnificent summer evening. From up there, they could glimpse once again that same shimmer of azure many leagues away: it was the lake of Yslla where the Sian Senky met the Sian Dorg.

"The famed city of Yslla, the centre of Elvin lore on the Islands, was built by Rowë Dol Nargrond on the shores of that lake," advised Feïwal.
"Nowadays the place is in ruins," replied Curwë. "The city was never rebuilt after the clan Myortilys raided it and committed genocide against its inhabitants."

Curwë had seldom talked throughout the journey. This gloomy historical reference subdued his companions into quiet reflection.

The next day, they moved closer to the foothills of the southern mountain range, heading west. They hoped to find the hillsides of O Wiony, a landlocked territory formerly owned by the Morawenti. Gelros had told his companions they would meet with Aewöl in the ruins of that ancient estate. Curwë, in Llafal, had heard of this territory, and he shuddered when Gelros confirmed it was their destination. No one ever ventured to O Wiony. Legend had it that the Gnomes still resided there, and only those possessed by madness would dare provoke their wrath. To reassure himself, the bard thought that they would at least be safe from enemy Elves and Men.

117

Night was coming. Their long day's walk had ended. It had been exhausting. A huge black cloud, coming from the north, was rising in the sky. A few drops of rain fell to the ground, preceding a heavy downpour that soon came to soak the soil and drench the woods. Gelros started to search for shelter. Once again, Curwë remained behind. For several hours, he had been walking in the footsteps of his companions with difficulty. It was obvious that his mind was torturing him. He had difficulty focusing on the tasks that were required of him, and barely said a word of apology when he was caught.

By now, however, the bard could no longer control himself. A pain in his cheek was proving overwhelming.

Suddenly, Curwë collapsed onto the ground. He fell heavily, without even a cry.

Gelros, alerted by the sound, hastened back to him. He turned Curwë onto his back to examine his wounds. The scout could only see minor scratches and bruises. But Curwë's eyes, and the drool that flowed from his mouth, worried him greatly. Caught unprepared, Gelros began to lay down his companion on an improvised stretcher that he surrounded with protective runes. Gelros set about burning the magic herbs Drismile had given him in Llanoalin. He was a healer as well as a hunter, well versed in the knowledge of plants and flowers.

Feeling powerless, Roquendagor stood close by, visibly worried and eager to assist.

Meanwhile, Feïwal approached the dying Curwë. He immediately extinguished the small candles that the scout had lit to form a triangle around the bard. Addressing his two valid companions, he ordered.

"Help me! Let us immerse Curwë fully in the water of a mountain stream and pray that Gweïwal Uleydon will restore his vitality."

The three Elves removed Curwë's clothes and armour. They could feel the fever was consuming him. Despite his efforts, Feïwal could not explain his unnaturally high temperature.

They decided to drag Curwë to a small stream which ran down the slope of the hill. There, they immersed his body in the cold water of the mountain. Curwë shivered and his friends began to fear for his survival. But there was such a thirst for life in the bard that, after a time, it looked as if Feïwal's incessant incantations might be having an effect. He regained consciousness, and they decided to pull him out of the stream's cold water.

Feïwal watched over his companion for most of the night but, exhausted from the days of travelling and weakened by their lack of food, he finally sank into a restless reverie.

His surprise was great when Curwë pulled him out of sleep just as dawn appeared. The bard's face was closed and very pale, but he nevertheless made a friendly gesture to each of his companions to thank them for their vital assistance. Curwë still looked weak, but something in his gaze had changed, as if a curse that had been impairing his mind since the beginning of their journey was broken. He kept touching his cheek as if a deadly tumour was gone.

None of them had the heart to question him further. They gathered their belongings, checked their weapons, examined the surrounding country, and then set off on the steep path towards the southwest.

"This stretch will be difficult," warned Gelros.

★

As the day drew on and the Elves of Mentollà made steady progress, they sensed a change in the landscape around them. The further they walked, the more the surrounding wildlife disappeared. No longer was there the unconscious comfort of hares dashing through the meadows, goats chewing on the green buds of virgin vines, or birds fluttering from branch to branch.

They strained their ears, but in the fields and at the edges of the woods around them, there was nothing: no squawking, calling or even rustling.

Feïwal was overcome with an imprecise anxiety. The guide of the clan of Filweni seemed to question the air, the trees, the distant horizons, even the clouds themselves, for an explanation of this sinister phenomenon. They were alone, the only characters animating that magnificent backdrop, their silhouettes standing out against the purple hue of the setting sun. The night went dark and unnaturally warm, and the south wind whistled in the air, filling the lifeless solitudes with a noise even more threatening than silence.

The Elves of Mentollà came across a gorge, through which a tiny stream cut a path down into the foothills. Reeds lined its banks. Despite the early hour of night, they agreed it would be a suitable place to camp. Neither moon, nor any glittering stars, could be seen in the sky.

None of them had the heart to continue their journey in such darkness.

For the first time since setting foot on Gwa Nyn, Curwë offered to take the watch. He seemed to have recouped some of his usual vitality.

While Roquendagor and Feïwal settled down to rest, Gelros joined him by the stream's bank. Without removing his leather gloves, the scout dipped his hands into the cold water and wetted the back of his neck. Though Gelros was undoubtedly suffering from the heat, his face betrayed no signs of tiredness. But in his eye was a form of languor, a sadness in the cautious way he looked at the world around him. Gelros was known for being a solitary and unaffectionate figure. Any rare demonstrations of empathy were strictly reserved for the one he reverently called his master.

On this occasion, however, he could not help but smile at Curwë, visibly proud of what he had accomplished.

"Tomorrow, we will reach O Wiony, where Aewöl is awaiting you. My mission is almost complete. He will be very pleased to see you, though he might not show it. His degradation in Nyn Ernaly has changed him...

But he often talks about you, Curwë, and of the great goals you have both set yourselves..."

"What goals?"

"Why, the Alqualinquë of course!" cried Gelros. "Its growth and prosperity! Though his mind is always busy with many other high preoccupations, that company is always his priority."

The same was not strictly true for Curwë.

"Is it indeed?" the bard replied. "I get regular trade reports from Nelwiri. I can see the pains that Aewöl takes ensuring their accuracy. Though I find it all rather boring, I do sometimes glance at the figures. It's Laeros, of course, the steward I appointed to administer the company, who takes care of those tasks. I am told our profits are growing quickly. We have a monopoly on distribution of those exclusive Irawenti goods, so we accumulate lots of gold. I hear we could even buy a second swanship to increase the volume of transactions. Even I could not fail to be struck by such success!"

This came as no surprise for Gelros. "Aewöl will want to discuss future developments with you," he advised. "He nourishes great ambition for Alqualinquë and will be counting on you more than ever. He has already made new plans." Looking at Feïwal and Roquendagor who rested a dozen yards away, Gelros added , "But what he asked me to tell you is of a different nature. You must keep it secret. It is important you do..."

Curwë looked at his companion, intrigued. Gelros began with a confident tone.

"Aewöl has asked me to inform you of certain secrets before you meet him... Alqualinquë has proven very successful in a relatively short period of time. There are reasons behind our good fortune."

Curwë smiled, but there was still sadness in his eyes. "I thought as much. I noticed we were very quick to establish contacts in many different locations across the Islands. Despite the dangers, dozens of Elves eager to collaborate with us seemed to appear out of nowhere..."

"That is true," confirmed Gelros. "What Aewöl wanted me to reveal you is the existence of a secret guild he controls. Alqualinquë is only the visible part of the edifice, but it is supported by many other Elves across the Islands."

Curwë was surprised. His interest in this discussion suddenly grew.

"How could Aewöl build such an efficient organisation in so little time?"

With a low tone full of deference and respect, Gelros explained. "Aewöl is no common Elf, Curwë. Though coming from far away in Essawylor, his rank is high among the Morawenti."

"I always suspected it back in Ystanlewin, from the haughty manners of his arrogant mother. Aewöl always looked like an over-protected child. But that does not explain how he came to control a secret guild." There was a certain irony in the bard's words.

"The Morawenti were once numerous and influential within the kingdom of Gwarystan," Gelros began.

"I know. It was the genocide committed against them in Yslla, by clan Myortilys, which caused their decline. It started the endless War of Shadows. The history of the Morawenti on the Islands ended abruptly with the murder of King Lormelin by the famed bard, Saeröl. The alleged chief of the Morawenti was then sentenced to death. I read they faced utter ruin after his condemnation," explained Curwë.

"They became leaderless. There are very few of them left, and those who survived have mingled with other Elvin communities and forged new loyalties," Gelros confirmed.

"From what I heard in Llafal, evoking their name is like summoning a ghostly shadow from the past," added Curwë gloomily.

Gelros decided it was time to divulge the facts behind his master's ascent. "A few years ago, in Nyn Ernaly, Aewöl met with Drismile, the Elvin lady you briefly saw on board the swanship in Llanoalin."

Curwë remembered the beautiful lady. "I did notice her; she possessed a certain authority among the community of that small port. She gave the captain of Llanoalin the scroll that allowed us to enter the kingdom of Gwarystan."

"She did. Drismile is an influential Morawenti on the Islands. She met Aewöl in the ruins of Mentolewin when we were still in Nyn Ernaly. They decided to join forces and it has proven very fruitful so far," concluded Gelros.

Curwë frowned. "Indeed, it has... Now tell me, what does Aewöl want me to know?"

Gelros marked another pause, like one readying himself to start a lengthy explanation. He lowered his tone even further so that their companions would not overhear them. Curwë struggled to catch everything Gelros was saying.

"Just beneath Master Aewöl are several Morawenti Alchemists who call themselves the Ol[23]. They are famed blacksmiths who dwelled in Yslla long ago, the depositories of principles that every guild member must respect. After undergoing the initiation rites, important powers have been delegated to them. Their unique heritage gives them the right to grant life or death upon any of the lower members.
Then come the N'ol[24]. They are also all Morawenti. They are initiated into the Guild, but their knowledge is limited. The N'ol were offered a chance to know the truth, and by doing so Aewöl established their loyalty. They coordinate operations and serve as envoys across the Archipelago. They organize and develop trade. Drismile, but also Nuriol, the messenger who frequently has dealings with Nelwiri in the ports of Nyn Llorely, are members of that caste."

Gelros hesitated for a moment, like someone reluctant to say more.

"I also have the honour to be counted among them, so do not be surprised when we reach O Wiony and you hear other Morawenti call me N'ol Gelros."
"On the contrary, I am surprised," Curwë reacted vehemently. "I specifically asked Aewöl to name you as one of the captains of Alqualinquë. We owe you so much, Gelros! You deserve a higher honour!"
"Aewöl was true to his word to you but... I refused."
"You declined our offer? We did it as a mark of friendship. Why would you not accept that position?"
"I know my place. Believe me, Curwë, being counted among the N'ol is already a great honour for me. In truth, I am simply Gelros, servant of my master."
"You are his most trusted companion! That is for sure," Curwë claimed.

---

23 Ol: 'The High ones' in lingua Morawenti

24 N'ol: 'The High ones' servants' in lingua Morawenti

Gelros ignored the praise and chose to finish explaining how the Guild's was organized.

"Finally come the numerous S'in[25], who are the lowest members in the organisation. They were recruited from Elves of all origins, and they can be found everywhere: inside the Llewenti clans, among the circles of the druids, in the entourage of the Dol households and even at the royal court in Gwarystan. Most of them are manipulated and unaware of their role in the Guild. The steward of Llanoalin port... was an example. We bought his services with gems. He had earned a good portion of the gold we were making out of the smuggling."

"He was an example, was he?"

Gelros was not as smart with his words as Curwë was. He realized he had said too much. After giving it some additional thought, he continued.

"I don't think he will wish to do any further trade with Alqualinquë in future. Smuggling goods into the kingdom of Gwarystan is already a dangerous activity. But allowing unknown Elves from Llymar Forest into the realm is an altogether different matter. I believe he frightened himself to death with his own transgression. There is nothing more to be gained from him."

★

The next day, the Elves of Mentollà had already walked for a couple of hours when they decided to stop at the top of a steep hill. The sun was warming the atmosphere, throwing its golden rays over the rocky mountain peaks, and the dew on the bushes was gradually disappearing. Gelros, silent, sniffed the air and turned his gaze frequently towards the great elevations of the Arob Nargrond's southern range. Summer was well advanced, but snow still whitened their tops. Addressing Feïwal, he pointed to the distant slopes of the mountain range. The hillsides could barely be seen in the shadows of the great mountain's silhouette. They resembled the mysterious, abandoned lands of Nyn Llyvary's East, which the Islands' minstrels often evoked in their songs.

---

25 S'in: 'Those without knowledge' in lingua Morawenti

But those darkest places of Nargrond Valley, so imposing to the Irawenti guide for whom the light of the day and the heat of the sun were so important, seemed to mean nothing to Gelros. The scout was accustomed to the density of deep forests and did not fear the shadows.

"We are close!" Gelros said with a steely resolve, pointing to their destination.

It took them a few more hours to reach the lands of O Wiony. The day was in decline when they finally entered the ancient Morawenti estate. A wind from the south swirled the leaves and moved them towards a pond. Lost in the deep gold of the trees, the body of water looked like a dead sea along which the Elves of Mentollà traced their path. Rain had been falling heavily for hours, water-logging the clay soil. No creatures appeared under the dark arches of greenery along the curves of the road.

The plateau where the legendary vineyards of O Wiony could be found stretched along the Sian Dorg, half a dozen leagues south-west of the ruins of Yslla. But the distance through the winding paths of the hills seemed much greater. The road, blooming with yellow, white and mauve, was lined with golden lemon trees, silvery olive trees, and above all with clusters of purple vines, damp with dew. The former estate of Elriöl Dir Sana, one of the legendary smith of Nargrond Valley, was relatively small and seemed to cling to the weight of time as much as to the rocky hills, where its foundations had been established centuries ago.

On the dusty road in front of the ramparts, there were Night Elves, guards clad in dark green cloaks and lightly armoured with silver chain mail. The Morawenti were feared across the Archipelago for they were known to poison their javelins and arrowheads. Harassing their enemies' ranks with harsh attacks followed by quick withdrawals was their favourite tactic, as only few foes could rival the speed of their units.

The guards bowed solemnly when Gelros walked by. They did indeed greet him with the title of 'Nol Gelros' and showed great respect to the scout.

"Loyalty to the community is the most important Morawenti principle," Gelros reminded his companions.

The Elves of Mentollà noted the Night Elves' unusual helmets, shaped in triangles and wrapped in black cloth. It was difficult to see the faces of these guards and it gave them a sinister look. Their tan leather coats, weapons and helmets were all adorned with leaves. They were armed with long swords and javelins of a curved design.

The Morawenti scouts seemed to have been expecting their arrival, and they escorted the newcomers into the ancient compound, past the ruins of the ramparts. The group then continued up a steep street, passing from a faint daylight into shade.

The domain consisted of a main tower, an entrance courtyard, a winery, a cellar, a garden and a large building with six floors. The compound had been left abandoned for centuries, and nature had taken its course. Ivy had overrun the alleyways and scaled the buildings. A heavy, almost frightening silence weighted on these ancient ruins, now home only to shadows. The crumbling walls and broken, mossy stones were covered in wild vegetation. The greenery was so dense that it had even formed a canopy above the courtyard, through which no sunlight could penetrate. The surrounding atmosphere gradually gripped the newcomers' hearts. They were seized with a certain melancholy, a form of sadness, as if they could suddenly trace the sense of all those Elves who had so ignominiously been massacred there. An infinite poetry lay behind it all.

Finally, the Elves of Mentollà reached a small square between the winery and the entrance to the great cellar. In the muted sunset of early evening, just before the sun disappeared over Mount Oryusk, the walls of O Wiony flushed with crimson.

"Wait here," Gelros told them, before disappearing into another narrow passage.

A fountain was flowing in the middle of the square, from a statue made of wood. The sculpture, blackened by time, represented an Elf with his back hunched, wrapped in a black cloak. The artist had given him a threatening countenance, had frozen him in an archetypal gesture of vengeful anger. His right hand wielded a blacksmith's hammer, on which a snake had coiled, and his left hand held a book. Curwë, unconsciously attracted by the statue, came closer to examine it. He could distinguish on the cover of the manuscript a black rune. The bard could not resist shuddering when he saw it. Now on his guard, he decided not to drink from the fountain's water.

The three Elves of Mentollà remained alone for a time, and Gelros' departure filled the courtyard with what seemed like a great silence. Initially, they could not understand the reason for this strange calm. At last, they perceived it. The handful of Morawenti guards and servants around them moved without any noise; like the silence caused by the total absence of birds and animals in that mysterious site.

The Night Elves tended to be thinner and taller in size to any other Elves. Their very pale skin, almost livid, characterised them while their gaze was deep and mysterious. They all had black hair, while their eye colour varied between dark grey and black. Like other High Elves, they had long and pointed ears. They favoured wearing dark coloured tunics with grey or green shades, and robes of fine linens, cottons or silks.

The Night Elves looked distant and uncaring. It was common knowledge in the Islands that Morawenti considered themselves being part of the most unique civilization of all. They viewed with arrogance all others.

Feïwal noted there was no temple, nor any statues of the deities in O Wiony, nothing that signalled any religious allegiance. Curwë explained.

"The Morawenti do not worship any deity. They trust only in their own wisdom and powers and abhor the Gods. Cults and faith are signs of weakness and naivety in their eyes."

The bard knew much about the Night Elves from his discussions with Aewöl.

Meanwhile, Gelros was crossing the estate's cellar, a great underground hall made of stone arches. It used to be a storage room for wines in bottles, barrels and amphorae. It had been built underground to protect the precious nectar of O Wiony. Marks of its former use were still visible.

The ancient wine cellar was made from limestone, a prevalent mineral in the Sian Dorg area. Its columns were monolithic, cut from a single stone from the base to the ceiling. The rounded vaults stood near, with additional pointed arches in the background.

The scout finally reached the innermost area of the cavern, which was located where the great cellar ended. This room must have been the keeper of wines' quarters.

Gelros caught hold of a shrub that grew near, which, not to his surprise, came easily out of the ground. On closer examination of the exposed limestone beneath, he found the hidden locks set into the rock, and quickly succeeded in opening a secret passage. Gelros walked a few steps into the dark hallway that revealed itself before him, and soon reached a door made of worm-eaten wood. That partially destroyed gate opened into a vast underground hall. A glyph, the form of the Morawenti triangle encompassing the rune of Sana, was suspended in the air like a shadowy ray of sun.

Gelros spoke the words , "Curos e Dir Sana."[26]

The glyph momentarily dispelled, and the scout presented himself before his master under the canopy of diverse colours that gleamed in the many gems of the cave's ceilings. Gelros adopted a humble posture, with uplifted palms and a bowed head, betokening at once his humility and dependence. Such was the expressive and contrite form the Morawenti had always shown when presenting to their liege lord. Finally placing his hand on his heart, Gelros completed the ritual salute with this token of submission and obedience.

Aewöl's was seated in the depths of the vast room, facing the entrance. The one-eyed Elf was clothed in a saffron-coloured robe and his head was partly covered by his metal mask, shadowy green in colour. In his right hand he held a rod, its

26 Curos e Dir Sana: 'The heir of Sana is safe' in lingua Morawenti.

handle gilded, and on the top a globe made of Amethysts. His jewel represented a smith's hammer, suspended by a chain of silver. His banner of dark green silk, bearing the rune of Sana surrounded by the black Morawenti triangle, was on his right. In his left hand was an ancient book.

Aewöl was on a long couch, which was surrounded with other marvellous and unique pieces of furniture. The subterranean room had the atmosphere of a rich palace. It was both sumptuous and grand, with damask, velvet, and silk drapery and curtains, and a beautifully carved bed with statues from the Islands' mythology. Mirrors were hanging from two of the walls, giving even more depth to the cavern. There was a strange vibrancy to the place, despite the prevailing shadows. Candlelight emanated from a colourful chandelier made with translucid glass. Precious stones and rare materials adorned many items of the furniture, though silver was the most dominant. The wardrobes were painted with allegories and images of life along the streets of Yslla.

Gelros entered the vast room like a humble fighter reporting in front of his commander. But Aewöl addressed him with passion in his voice.

"Did you know that this cavern's inspired architect was Elriöl, the first master of the Guild of Sana? He took the design from the blacksmiths' guild in Yslla and replicated it here, below O Wiony. This is extraordinary!"
"No, master, I did not know that," Gelros replied laconically, also in the tongue of the Night Elves.

It was considered by all in the Islands as a dead language but nevertheless Gelros and Aewöl, when alone, always exchanged in their mother tongue. Due to the Morawenti isolation during their early history and their frequent dealings with the Gnomes, it had very few similarities with other Elvin languages.

Gelros did not seem surprised by the indifferent way Aewöl had welcomed him, despite how long his dangerous endeavour away had been. Government among the Morawenti had always been dynastic and based upon absolutism. Its principles had been founded long before the Guild of Sana was created, at the time of their first prince when the Night Elves dwelled in the dark forest of Nel Anmöl. Gelros was not one to question usages several millennia old.

Aewöl resumed, clearly excited to have finally found someone to share his findings with.

"In fact, I have come to believe that Elriöl built other secret vaults, here at O Wiony, near the city of Yslla where he dwelled. He must have wanted a location that would not arouse suspicion. You can imagine how many masons there would have been ferrying between the different sites ...

Elriöl must have feared greatly his enemies, that some would slaughter the makers of the Swords of Nargrond Valley, sack their city and its guilds. He must have feared that the treasures of Yslla's library would be lost forever...

To prevent this evil, I believe that Elriöl vowed to construct a secret underground vault, leading out from O Wiony's great cellar and ending deep under the hill...

Now, assuming he did not die before his goal was completed, Elriöl must have protected the passage from the O Wiony cellar to the inner sanctum with other secret vaults, each more difficult to penetrate than the last. My guess is that he created three of these secret vaults, and that this cave is the first of them.

The Gnomes showed me the way into this place after they acknowledged me as the new master of the Sana Guild. Without their ancient knowledge, I would never have found it. Not even the manuscript Saeröl left me gives any hints as to its existence.

I have come to believe that this is the first vault, the one which is most easily accessible from the cellar, where the wise Ol would have gathered around Elriöl, and where they deposited some of their treasures..."

Gelros congratulated his master. "This is very much consistent with some of your earlier findings."

Aewöl ignored this comment. He was operating quite independently of everything around him; only what came into his head dictated the direction of his thoughts.

"I can understand what my forefather Elriöl was thinking. He was fortunate to live in a period of relative peace and prosperity, but he knew that storm clouds were gathering on the horizon. Thus far, the first king of Gwarystan had behaved in a manner that befitted him. Lormelin the Conqueror had submitted almost all the Llewenti clans to his royal authority. He had become the undisputed sovereign of the Islands.

As the centuries passed by, however, Lormelin's judgement became impaired. He grew deaf to the voices of wisdom, and his conduct became irrational and unpredictable. Was it the vengeful Islands' deities who had caused this gradual change? It was the High Elf king, after all, who had discarded those divinities from the very Archipelago they protected. Was his mental decline their divine retribution?

Triumphant after having conquered a realm worthy of his royal lineage, the Conqueror became overly proud after having erected the great city of Gwarystan to the glory of his forefathers. Lormelin became intoxicated with his power. He plunged into all manner of abuse and excess to the point of profaning the old temples of the Llewenti deities, even persecuting their followers...

Elriöl must have seen this coming. Fearful that King Lormelin's apostasy would result in some dreadful consequence, he must have anticipated that it would bring upon them those enemies whom the Islands' deities had constantly kept away.

This dark premonition would explain the genesis of his project... and the existence of this first vault. Look at this achievement! The Morawenti of that time had acquired a greater depth of knowledge than any other Elves, due to their mastery over the Amethyst Flow. Their knowledge of crafts knew no comparison."

Aewöl rose from his long couch. He stood stolid in the middle of the cave; the new guardian of this sanctorum dedicated to the Guild of Sana. The one-eyed Elf proceeded further with his reasoning.

"I did come across something interesting in the Book of Sana, among the old records written by Saeröl during his youth in the valley of Nargrond. After the sack of Ystanargrond by clan Myortilys, Saeröl gathered a council of the surviving Ol. The Morawenti blacksmiths met in a secret underground place of his choosing. His purpose was to form a plan after Elriöl disappeared in the mines of Oryusk. The valley of Nargrond was about to fall. It is my belief that this historic meeting occurred here, in this cave. The council of the remaining Ol feared that the location of the Swords of Nargrond Valley had been lost with the death of Elriöl. What they did not know was that the best-kept secrets of the Guild were lying in other vaults, beneath the very council chamber in which they sat, and over which the young Saeröl, the freshly appointed master, was presiding. And so, did those secrets remain, lost to living memory after O Wiony was plundered by the Dark Elves...

I now believe that only Saeröl knew about the Guild of Sana's inner sanctum. That is where he found Moramsing, which had been safely hidden by the farsighted Elriöl. It proves that the first master of the Guild of Sana was fully awake to the danger he was facing before joining Lon and the smiths of Yslla into the mines of Oryusk.

He knew he might not come back.

If Elriöl was given the task to conceal Moramsing, then it is likely that the other smiths of Yslla would have each been responsible for concealing the other fabled swords.

This is at least true for Rymsing, the Blade of the West. That is surely how it was then passed down to the lines of Dyoreni..."

Aewöl remained thoughtful for some time, as though he had completely forgotten that Gelros was there. At last, his only eye, lost in the dream of unveiling the secrets of his predecessors, fixed upon the scout's silhouette. Only then did Aewöl realize what Gelros' presence's implied.

"Oh, Gelros! If you have returned, our companions must have reached O Wiony..."

"Master, Lord Roquen, Feïwal dyn and Curwë are awaiting you below the great oak," confirmed Gelros. "A meal is ready to be served, and a phial of the finest vintage has been opened. It awaits your approval before it is offered to your guests."

"Did the journey go well? Are our friends pleased that the Sana Guild is helping them with their endeavours? You know I would rather be locked up than betray their trust," declared Aewöl, and there was a hidden threat in his words.

"Master, the journey went well. Your friends all have reasons to be pleased and satisfied with the Guild's involvement. However, that S'in in Llanoalin, the steward of the port, proved to be a scoundrel. He kept demanding explanations from Drismile, he refused to obey orders, and he even threatened her. We jointly decided that death should be the consequence..." confided Gelros.

Aewöl was not perturbed by this news. "To the virtuous Elf, the terror of death is nothing compared to the stain of dishonour."

Gelros did not understand this saying. "Also," he added , "Drismile has served you extremely well. She is now on her way to Mentollà, aboard the swanship of Alqualinquë."

"Good. Very Good! Now let us join our companions! We have missed them so much! There is nothing better than a gathering of old friends. For a second there, I even felt as if the five of us were still those children who dreamed of might and glory in that tiny 'Dragon Cave' below Ystanlewin's dungeons..."

★

Moments later, Gelros returned to the small square, and with him was Aewöl. The one-eyed Elf moved with confidence and vitality and still looked like a young Elf, but he seemed much more seasoned than in the days of Essawylor. He was taller and thinner than his servant, and dressed in elegant clothes, which gave him an undeniable air of power. As he approached, his only eye remained fixed upon Curwë. He stopped in front of his friend when he reached the fountain. Aewöl's cold and grave face could not fail but resemble that of the statue behind him.

"Welcome, my companions! Follow me! I have organized a meal to celebrate our reunion!" Aewöl said with an affable voice.

The Elves of Mentollà rejoiced. They had subsisted during the journey on various fruits and vegetables, but they had a strong preference for delicate foods and wines. Aewöl knew their tastes were extremely discerning.

The one-eyed Elf invited the newcomers to join him in climbing a steep path that led to another of the estate's squares, protected from the sun. From there, one could look out over the hills that ran to the banks of the Sian Dorg. A table had been set

133

up in the shade of a large, ancient oak tree, and they settled down for their meal. Ladies, bowing their heads, approached with warm bread, fresh water from underground springs and honey from the Sian Llewa[27]. They also offered around platters of ripe fruit. The simple scents of the food and drink mingled and counterbalanced each other with delicacy. The travellers savoured this first dish with pleasure, in silence. Once finished, they were given water from large jars. They washed their hands and rinsed their mouths.

Wine, served in the finest of glass, was then offered to them. The Morawenti considered themselves as the most knowledgeable of all Elves in that field.

The colour of the nectar, like a deep red dress, was the first thing they appreciated about the vintage. As it made contact with the air, it then rapidly changed its aroma, flavours and most noticeably its colour. It became as dark as truffles; the dress transformed into a powerful black.

When Aewöl rose to address his companions, it was as if the five Elves had been there, in the shade of that great oak, since the beginning of time, smelling the same delicate aromas and breathing in the same vitalizing air. Aewöl poured himself a little more wine and began.

"As just and virtuous Elves united by unwavering friendship, let us drink this ancient vintage of O Wiony, the prized legacy of this land."

Aewöl did not speak again until he had finished his glass. When he resumed, his tone had changed.

"Feïwal dyn, you will know that sincere words are seldom beautiful, and that beautiful words are seldom sincere. Nevertheless, you will also understand that all of us are filled with gratitude for this second life you have offered us. You strode ahead and led us all beyond the Austral Ocean. That is no small feat.

Over the past few years, I have wondered how I could possibly demonstrate the sincerity of my commitment to you. Indeed, I think I speak for all of us when I say this.

27 Sian Llewa: 'Green river' in lingua Llewenti. It is in Nyn Llyvary close to the Arob Nisty range.

134

Well, the time has now come. The spring of our second lives had not yet begun when you ordered, 'Arise and follow me'. We are now well into its summer, and here are your true friends, gathered around you in the valley of Nargrond to do your biding."

Feïwal responded like a priest addressing his disciples.

"I thank you for honouring your word, my companions. Tonight, we sit together in the valley of Nargrond, the heart of the Promised Islands...
Since we reached the shores of Nyn Llyvary, I dedicated lots of efforts gathering information about that sanctuary of nature and beauty. I spent many days meditating, trying to unveil its mysteries. Throughout the millennia, this land has been the focus of all civilizations.
The first Gnomes erected their three columns of knowledge at its entrance.
Eïwal Ffeyn brought about the fall of a meteorite which formed the final landform of the Valley. With divine runes, the deities of the Archipelago engraved the fate of the free Elves in the Stone, the heart of the meteorite. Then they devoted their care to making it the most beautiful place of the Islands, a beautiful garden promised to the Elves.
Like so many vengeful servants of the Greater Gods, the Giants of Oryusk appeared in the lava of the volcano to drive out the rebellious deities of the Archipelago. These spirits of fire fortunately failed in their work of destruction.
Then, for many centuries, the Elves of all nations, houses and clans fought for its control. Here were forged the fabled Swords of Nargrond Valley by the most renowned blacksmiths of the Elves. They made their weapons with the unique metal from the meteorite. After this feat, the Valley developed into a glorious Elvin civilization under Rowë's rule. Lon the Wise, whose true divine origin is still being discussed, was born in the main city of the Valley. There he demonstrated his capacity to work miracles, by controlling the light of the sun itself. His protector, the lord of the house of Dol Nargrond, gave the Valley its name before his realm was destroyed by the savagery of the Dark Elves, jealous of the loss of clan Myortilys' homeland. Rowë and the other makers of the fabled swords were murdered

in the mines of Oryusk before their corpses were defiled. Lon the Wise was never seen again after that dark day, and a shadow now conceals the entrance to the mines.

Even Men have sought to conquer it. Barbarian tribes from the vast Mainland, blinded by the obscurantism of their evil cult, did not hesitate to cross the dangerous straits and the perilous seas to confront the great Elvin kingdom of Gwarystan. They considered the slopes of Mount Oryusk as the lair of their accursed Three Dragons.

The Nargrond Valley is mentioned in all the sacred texts of the Gnomes, Giants, Men and Elves.

What is the cause of this all-pervading obsession? Can it be anything other than a mighty curse?

These questions will haunt our minds."

After this long preamble, the guide of the clan of Filweni chose not to elaborate further, failing to address the specifics of their situation. This voluntary silence caused certain dismay among his companions, whose impatience was growing. But Feïwal had something else in mind, something he judged more important. Getting up from his seat, he made a request, his tone firm.

"My companions, I invite you to rise. Let us form a circle in the open with only the wind in its centre."

Roquendagor and Curwë immediately stood. After a time, Aewöl obeyed the command too; but Gelros withdrew behind them, simply bowing his head and bending his knee in a demonstration of humility. Seeing this move, Feïwal did not show any irritation. He understood the scout's profound nature.

Solemnly, the guide of clan Filweni performed the ritual.

"The circle is an emblem of friendship. It represents our common virtues. The circle is also an emblem of eternity, having neither beginning nor end. Bonds can be broken by deeds; virtues may be challenged by trials... but friendship will never alter."

Feïwal indicated for the four Elves to gather together and form the circle.

Gelros immediately regretted his withdrawal.

'They will form a square, not a circle!' he thought, suddenly filled with worry.

The sun was setting behind the threatening silhouette of Mount Oryusk. The heat was still overwhelming, though night was approaching. The air felt dry due to the proximity of the volcano. Despite the scorching heat and the thickening of the night's shadows, a sudden breeze ran through the branches of the great oak tree, bringing them unexpected relief. They felt a sense of ease and serenity, suddenly reminded of the Austral Ocean's emerald green waters.

The servants, guards, indeed all the Night Elves present around them, withdrew from the small square as if secretly ordered by the light evening breeze. Only Gelros remained, still kneeling, as the only witness.

Feïwal opened the council with a prayer to Eïwal Ffeyn.

"Eternal spirit of freedom, Protector of the Austral Ocean's seafarers through all dangers, we remain your devoted debtors. Keep us true to our obligations."

He finished with the ritual words of his faith.

"There is no freedom, but the freedom granted by the wind!"

The four Elves looked towards the heavens.

"We, Feïwal, Roquendagor, Curwë and Aewöl," the Irawenti guide proclaimed , "are castaways of the Austral Ocean. We are the survivors that were granted a second life by the mercy of Eïwal Ffeyn.
We solemnly promise we will faithfully serve the true god of Elvin freedom.
We swear."

Like in a dream, a majestic Storm Eagle appeared in the evening clouds. The four Elves contemplated it in all his glory. The great bird flew towards where they stood and landed on a branch of the great oak tree above them.

'DO NOT FAIL THE DEITY OF WINDS!' they heard as fragments of an unknown language reached their mind.

The Storm Eagle vanished, and the four Elves were left astonished and confounded. This vision had made them utterly determined. They stepped forward with their right feet, raised their right hands and displayed their runes to mark their consent. Feeling like they had been transported to the realm of Gods and deities, they cried to the heavens:

"We swear!"

For a long time, well beyond when the sun had completely disappeared behind the western horizon, the four Elves remained silent and motionless.

A few steps behind, Gelros also remained immobile, fully amazed at the scene although he had not seen himself the mighty Storm Eagle. Aewöl and his companions seemed to have made a commitment after experiencing an ecstatic moment, he reckoned.

Gelros understood it was largely the work of Feïwal who had transmitted to his companions his own emotions. The scout wondered if his master had willingly agreed or if his consent had been gained by treachery. Though imperceptibly worried, Gelros concluded that no living Elf could force the master of the Sana Guild against his will.

'Whatever that undertaking is, it has to do with our coming to the valley of Nargrond.' Gelros thought and the fearless Elf shivered.

At last Curwë decided to break the silence. He realised now was the time to reveal what he knew and had kept secret so far. Perhaps his revelations would also press Feïwal to say more of his purpose.

"In truth, we are not the only ones who have journeyed to the valley of the volcano. Dyoren is in Nargrond Valley too. He must be hiding somewhere, perhaps just a few leagues from us...

The Seeker will try to seize one of the legendary swords. He found the trail of Lynsing. Until then, the Blade of the South had remained beyond his reach. Now, he who wields it will come out of his impregnable stronghold and participate in some important gathering summoned by the druids in the grove of Eïwele Llya, on the slopes of Mount Oryusk."

"I learnt from Lord Curubor," Roquendagor intervened , "that druids have the authority to gather all the factions of the Islands, be they Elves or Men. The druids are organized into communities they call Circles. They recruit their members, whatever their kin, from among the priests of the Mother of the Islands. They gained their undisputed power of conciliation after they convinced the belligerents of the Century of War to agree to 'The Pact', a pledge made by all factions to cease the destruction of the Mother's creations. Imagine such a reunion: The kingdom of Gwarystan, the clans and houses of Llymar Forest, the principality of Cumberae, the Ice Elves of clan Llyandy, the Dark Elves of clan Myortilys, and the factions of Men, meaning the Westerners from the great ports of Tar-Andevar and Tar-Miniar, and the multitude of the barbarian chieftains."

For a moment, the five Elves pondered what this new development could imply. Surprisingly, the usually silent Gelros, whom all had almost forgotten, spoke up.

"I know from Alef Bronzewood, the druid who first led us into Nargrond Valley, that only the barbarian tribes who worship the cult of Three Dragons are excluded from the Pact."

"This is true," confirmed Feïwal. "The sayings of Alef Bronzewood can be trusted. I have met that druid on several occasions, and he should be regarded as a close ally. He performed significant services for our cause."

"As far as I am aware," added Roquendagor , "the druid circles have not organized a meeting like this since the battle of Lepsy Peak and the fight for the testament of Rowë. That was four years ago, and the council broke up without any of its members reaching an agreement. I heard rumours that King

Norelin threatened he would never attend a Pact Gathering again. Lord Curubor believed that this reunion in Nyn Ernaly would be the last. He visited me in Mentollà over the winter. I still remember his exact words when he warned me to be prepared: 'Be sure that you retrieve your prodigious armour from that hideout in the wood of Silver Leaves,' he advised 'you are certainly going to need it.'"

Aewöl concurred with what had been said. "There are many signs that another Pact Gathering is being prepared as we speak. My spies have advised me that other Elvin factions are also gathering in the valley of Nargrond, usually the most barren place on the Islands.

As we speak, high-ranking Elves from Llymar are journeying towards the ruins of an ancient shrine dedicated to Eïwal Lon, a few leagues from here, near Yslla. A group of envoys from Cumberae await them in the deserted temple.

My view is that a Pact Gathering will take place this summer in Nargrond Valley. Norelin must have reconsidered his position on the circles of the druids' peace-making initiative. It is in the interest of most of the Islands' factions to promote cooperation and order, and to prevent mutually destructive conflicts. I believe the king has been somewhat forced to the table after the flood that damaged his capital city this spring. An unnatural catastrophe of that magnitude had not happened for a very long time in the Archipelago. To my mind, it represents the culmination of a deep-rooted turmoil.

Look at what has happened these past few years.

Dragon Warriors have come out of the shadows to restore the cult of Three Dragons among barbarian tribes, challenging the influence of the druids. Two of them, Ka-Bloozayar and the dreaded Ka-Blowna, have openly broken the Pact that had guaranteed peace for almost a century. They waged war against the Elves both in the South, where Cumberae is still under attack, and in the North, where they were defeated at Mentollà. The weak response of Norelin to the aggression caused both Llymar and Cumberae to break their vows to Gwarystan. The Llewenti clans and the House of Dol Nos-Loscin eventually denied the leadership of the king, and the factions of Elves are dividing. As a result, a great alliance between the Westerners and Gwarystan, between Men and High Elves, has emerged. More powerful than ever and haunted by a mysterious fear,

Norelin's first decision as ruler of this larger realm was to send his servants after the testament of Rowë. The clans of Llymar intervened and saved Rowë's will.

What fear for the future drove the king to that quest for the Forbidden Will? He must have understood the gravity of the act, utterly sacrilegious in the eyes of the many Elves who still worship the deities of the Islands. Many are those among the seeds of Llyoriane who believe that the catastrophe that partly destroyed Gwarystan was a divine punishment. Norelin must now be pushed to seek the support of the Islands' other powers by an even more potent threat.

Now, Feïwal, I know you have the answers to some of these riddles. What is the part you are playing in all this? Why have you called upon us to gather here, in the valley of Nargrond, where all but the Elves of Mentollà were summoned?"

Gelros nodded, in support of his master's questioning.

CHAPTER 4: Camatael

Camatael Dol Lewin removed his bronze helmet. The polished, sturdy metal was embossed with figures of unicorns, and a crest of white plumes was proudly displayed above. His long black hair was tightly pulled black, clear of his pale face.

The young lord was standing before a precipice. Below him were heavy boulders covered in moss. They had fallen away some millennia ago.
This gorge offered a spectacular demonstration of erosion, a phenomenon characteristic of the Arob Nargrond foothills. The torrent would have originally flowed down through a deep vale before striking a limestone barrier of gigantic boulders.

'The Greater Gods Agadeon and Uleydon must have fought for control of this ford,' Camatael thought to himself, contemplating the geological scars that still bore witness to the chaotic clash of stone and water.

Over time, the fast-flowing stream had eroded the natural limestone barrier, resulting in the gorge he now stood before. The raw power of nature never failed to amaze him. The torrent sprung from ancient, sub-glacial streams, and here it disappeared again into the deep limestone gorges. The lord of House Dol Lewin marvelled at the surrounding cliffs.

The rest of his group, composed of two-dozen clan Llyvary guards, were scaling down into the depths of the gorge, like fearless explorers sinking into the abyss. The Llewenti fighters were protecting Matriarch Myryae dyl Llyvary, ensuring her safety and closely monitoring her progress as she descended the natural steps into the canyon.

Camatael then began his own descent through an impressive beech forest that was anchored into the rock. In order to descend into the canyon, the group had to cross the gorge at several points, down along the various natural stairways forged at various points in this place's violent geological history. Camatael's first crossing was along a set of large boulders wedged between the gorge's walls. It offered him a memorable sight of the torrent below, running almost two hundred feet beneath him at the bottom of the chasm.

Once surrounded on both sides by the naturally excavated gorge, Camatael had the strange sensation that he was walking between two layers of long, ornate curtains. Erosion had revealed many fantastic shapes and brightly coloured mineral deposits. A beautiful palette of greens, ochres and blues were dimly illuminated in the failing sunlight. At one hundred feet above the torrent was a second natural bridge, in the form of a mighty chunk of limestone that arched from one side of the gorge to the other.
The Elves of clan Llyvary ahead of Camatael were crossing that bridge one by one. Their green cloaks seemed to fly hesitantly above the void, like as many small birds caught in a storm.

'This crossing will take some time, given how careful they are being,' thought Camatael.

The air was calm. The silence was deepened by the murmur of insects and the chatter of squirrels playing in the vines which decorated the dense woods along the river. The young lord decided to sit on a rock while he waited for those ahead of him. His silvery chain mail was proving heavier each day. He could barely remember how light the armour had felt the first time he had put it on: a true masterpiece made in the smith guild of Tios Lluin. It was hot. Beads of sweat were collecting on his forehead. Camatael adjusted his long purple cloak and looked towards the Mountain of Oryusk to the west. A plume of steam and black smoke was rising from the summit of the volcano. It kept the ambient temperature constantly high throughout the Nargrond Valley.

A few yards behind, Mynar dyl could see that Camatael was taken aback by the natural spectacle of the gorge. Since the beginning of their journey, Mynar dyl had brought up the rear, voluntarily staying alone.
The Llewenti warlord approached silently, like a cat stalking its prey. His travellers' clothes mingled into the canopy.

"When clan Myortilys' army invaded Nargrond Valley, they desperately needed to cross that gorge. They wanted to launch a surprise attack against the city of Yslla from the north. For no want of trying, however, the bridges they built would systematically collapse. Let down by their own engineers, the Myortilys turned to the Gnomes, who dwelled nearby. The first inhabitants of Nargrond Valley agreed to a pact: a bridge in exchange for the soul of the first Elf to cross. The Gnomes then called upon their divine father, Gweïwal Agadeon, who unleashed a mighty avalanche. The largest boulder became stuck, spanning the torrent. The cunning Myortilys then forced one of their prisoners to cross it first. No one ever found out what became of that High Elf, but the furious Gnomes, feeling cheated, avowed revenge against the clan Myortilys..." Mynar dyl said.

Camatael immediately understood the story's hidden meaning. Of all the Elves who had travelled with them from Llymar, he was the only High Elf. Mynar dyl was secretly delighted at his isolated situation. The warlord of Tios Halabron must have sensed his discomfort.

Before their departure, Camatael had insisted on being escorted by some of his followers. He had suggested Aplor, the steward of House Dol Lewin, and some knights of the temple of light. But the Council of the Forest had decided otherwise. Matriarch

Myryae, the official envoy of Llymar to the Pact Gathering, was to benefit from the protection of an entire unit of clan Llyvary guards, while Mynar dyl and Camatael, the other ambassadors of the Forest, would escort her without their usual retinue. The young lord had therefore felt uncomfortable since their arrival in Gwa Nyn. As fatigue settled in after so many days of traveling, this feeling of unease was evolving into anxiety and annoyance.

Despite Mynar dyl's provocation, Camatael remained largely undaunted. He replied in a haughty tone, his icy blue eyes beaming with intelligence.

"I like the brisk way you tell the old myths, Mynar dyl. You certainly have a talent for relating these gripping tales: like a fireside bard of old, inviting us to chuckle along with you..."

Mynar dyl stood stolid. The irony behind those words made him smile. He was looking at his own javelin with pride. It consisted of a thin shaft, armed with a leaf-shaped head, the colour of emerald, with silvery points at the edges. A long strap was situated at the lower end of the javelin: it allowed him to recover his projectile after throwing it.
Mynar dyl dropped his precious weapon onto the stony ground. He bent down, picked up a handful of sand, and let it fall silently into the void of the chasm.

"Perhaps the fate of the Gnomes' prisoner was not so very different from that handful of sand," the fair Elf suggested, his tone deeply pensive. "Perhaps the hostage followed the same path."

Camatael was shocked by what Mynar dyl's conjecture seemed to imply. As if haunted by an unseen threat, he could not avert his eyes from the mountainous circle surrounding the valley. The unseen swarm of life hidden by the green wall of wild vegetation disturbed him. He felt the presence of countless beings silently encircling their group. Despite his unease, Camatael interpreted his current predicament as a challenge to his courage.

"Don't think I can't see through your innocent little performance," the lord of House Dol Lewin countered, no longer concealing his aggression.

Mynar dyl, calm as ever, swept back a couple of his long blonde hairs that had come loose. Despite the trials of their long journey, he had somehow managed to maintain an impeccable appearance. His shining leather boots hadn't the faintest trace of scuffmarks or dirt, and his long cloak, the colour of leaves, was miraculously free of creases.

After a moment's pause, Mynar dyl responded, acting surprised.

"Please do not misunderstand me! I would not dare offend the lord of House Dol Lewin, high priest of Eïwal Lon, and the Council of the Forest's newest member."

Camatael looked angrily at the warlord. "Watch your words, Mynar dyl! Remember that the council has appointed me ambassador of Llymar. I hold the same rank as you."

"Oh! I am well aware you were honoured with that responsibility. It is the first time, I believe. No doubt the pressure of the position is getting to you. I know how it feels. I have performed the role of ambassador many times. I even played my part at the Pact Gathering which ended the Century of War. That was some time ago and, since then, the Council of the Forest has always sent me as their representative. I think you could treat your peer with a little more respect," Mynar dyl suggested maliciously.

A ray of sunshine pierced the canopy. The emerald stone of his diadem glittered.

Camatael was far from impressed.

"Why don't we step back, look at the points of contention, and work to resolve them. We need to collaborate, after all, and I will be entitled to the same prerogatives as you during this summer's Pact Gathering."

Mynar dyl's tone changed, becoming as sweet as honey, as if he wanted to lull his interlocutor into a false sense of security.

"My lord Dol Lewin, rest assured we are on the same side: that of the Elves of Llymar. Anything else is unimaginable! Our opinions may differ from time to time, no question, but we are fighting under the same banner."

Below, it was taking more time than anticipated to cross the gorge. One of the Elves, struggling with all his equipment, had just slipped on a wet rock and almost fell into the precipice. He had dropped several quivers filled with arrows.

It was subsequently decided that guide ropes would be fixed along either side of the bridge to limit the risks of falling. So far, only half of the clan Llyvary Elves had made it to the other side. The rest of the group were waiting, and these dwindling guards felt anxious about the safety of Matriarch Myryae, who had still not crossed.

Camatael decided that now was the time to clear up the numerous latent conflicts which had accumulated between himself and Mynar dyl since House Dol Lewin had entered the Council of the Forest. A deeply rooted enmity had built up between the High Elf lord and the Llewenti warlord over the last few years. With the tone of a judge pronouncing a sentence, Camatael began.

"You have systematically opposed every single proposal I have made to the assembly. I appreciate that our respective ambitions for Llymar are far from harmonious. But I have come to believe that your antagonism is of a different nature..."

Mynar dyl had a wry smile. "This is pure speculation... though it is true, I did voice my concerns about your recent campaign to bring the House Dol Talas to Llymar. But I had my reasons."

"That was a mistake. The lord of Ystanalas is bravely resisting King Norelin and his alliance with the Westerners. He was ready to abandon his city and join us in Llymar. House Dol Talas have rightfully earned their place among the seeds of Llyoriane. They have faith in the Archipelago's deities and are protectors of the Llewenti cults.

That day, you won the vote at the Council, but the outcome was gloomy. House Dol Talas is still besieged inside its stronghold, at the mercy of the king. We have lost a powerful ally because of you.

In truth, I believe you are afraid of other High Elves coming to Llymar. You wish the ancient clans to retain their dominant influence in the Forest at all costs. Your fundamental vision for the Islands is warped by the wars of Ruby and Birds, when the first Hawenti king subjugated the clans of the Llewenti one after the other. That was long ago, Mynar dyl. Now the Elves of the Islands are confronting the unavoidable rise of Men and their thirst for conquest. Here is our true enemy!" pleaded Camatael.

Mynar dyl nodded. "You speak with conviction, Lord Dol Lewin, for one so young and inexperienced. Indeed, I share some of your views. You know I greatly admire your skills as a speaker.

But surely you can see the reasons behind our current organisation: High Elves should only be granted entry into Llymar once they have proven their value to us. The precedent is that every Hawenti house must demonstrate their fidelity to the Llewenti clans' cause. Look at history! Remember the great feats of House Dol Etrond during the Century of War, and to some extent, those of House Dol Lewin, over the recent years..."

Camatael did not fall into the trap set by Mynar dyl. "What I remember is that you exerted your influence among your allies, trying your very best to prevent my admittance into the Council of the Forest," he recalled, and the young lord's blue eyes were as cold as ice.

Once again Mynar dyl needed to retreat, like a falcon regaining altitude after a failed attempt against its prey.

"That is not untrue. But you will note I failed." The warlord immediately made another attack. "Frankly, I do not believe that House Dol Lewin has any real power, at least not enough to be of significant use to our assembly. How many units can you muster? Barely three would fight for the White Unicorn, no more than seventy fighters in total, by my estimates. I command more than twenty units, made up of the fiercest troops of Llymar Forest. My fighters have proven their worth on many occasions. This is what I call influence. Power without force is barely power at all."

Trying to control his anger, Camatael looked away for a moment. He fixed his gaze upon the eroded limestone rock opposite. Within the stones, mineral rich water circulated under pressure. As it seeped to the surface, the pressure dropped, and thin lines of salt lengthened downwards from the crevices. Then Camatael spotted a chamois in the dim light of early evening. The agile animal crossed the steep rock to lick the salty stones. For some reason, the charming spectacle appeased his wrath. Now master of himself again, Camatael resumed his argument.

"You also argued against welcoming the pilgrims of Eïwele Llyi to Llymar. That was despite them refusing to return to Gwarystan after they heard the knights of the Golden Hand had tried to defile the forbidden will of Rowë. Surely it's in our interests to exploit the malaise that the king has provoked among his subjects with this sacrilegious act."

"Again, I cannot agree with you, my lord Camatael. These Elves can no longer be considered Llewenti. For several generations, they have lived under the yoke of the kings of Gwarystan. After Lormelin's conquests, their forefathers could have joined the ancient clans in the four corners of the Islands. They made a different choice. They kneeled in front of the Conqueror and chose weakness and corruption."

"Those Elves should also be seen as seeds of Llyoriane," Camatael countered , "and they are our natural allies. Despite centuries of persecution, they have remained faithful to the Islands' deities. They were brave enough to start a pilgrimage forbidden by Norelin. They deserve better."

"Your story is always the same. I know what you have in mind. Your goal is to rally as many of these 'would-be allies' as possible under the banner of Llymar. Your ambition is to build a realm that could rival Gwarystan.
Perhaps you secretly seek to re-establish House Dol Lewin in all its splendour and glory. High Elves never change; you are all obsessed with influence, gold, great cities and splendid fortresses... the High Elves are corrupted by their everlasting addiction to the trappings of power. Only your ego can match your lifespan. What you promote with such eloquence is no different from Lord Curubor's ideas. Some see you as his advisor; I say they give you too much credit, for in reality you are only his puppet," concluded Mynar dyl, with a deliberate intent to harm.

Camatael felt deeply offended by this latest insult, which relegated him to the status of a mere hireling. This time, he did not even attempt to conceal his anger.

"I can only imagine what sordid past events must have warped your character into its pitiable current form. What trauma, Mynar dyl, has given you such a miserable, malicious and delusional outlook? Everything you say, everything you think, is utterly devoid of reason and, balance."

"My happiness results from my very misfortune," Mynar dyl replied mysteriously, and not without pride. "I am indeed deeply dissatisfied by the state of the world, and this dissatisfaction shapes my way of thinking. More importantly, it shapes my creations. That is why my art is unique."

The schism between the two Elves was confirmed. Each was the agent of opposing forces: Quartz versus Emerald. Each wished to lead the Council of the Forest.
The two contenders then maintained a stony silence. There was nothing more to be said.

The entire unit had now, at last, made it across the natural bridge. The fighters of clan Llyvary looked to their leader in wonder.
Matriarch Myryae had drawn a pentagram in the soil, with five different runes at its tips. She was now lighting incense, muttering words of elemental power, and conjuring airy spirits to do her bidding. The ceremony took some time, as the matriarch was calling upon the energy of the Sapphire, one of the components of the Islands' Flow. Four little whirlwinds began to appear at her side; they initially took the shape of truncated, inverse cones, before they grew in power and evolved into the shape of fluttering swans. Like a queen during a majestic parade, the high priestess was then transported above the narrow bridge by her four servants of the wind. Everyone else present simply looked on, enthralled by this display of power.

It was now Mynar dyl's turn to cross the dangerous passage above the wild torrent. First, he threw most of his equipment across to the guards on the other side. A leather bag, his long cloak, two quivers full of arrows, his two swords and their scabbards all made it over the chasm. The warlord only kept

151

his javelin with him. Feeling more comfortable with only his leather armour on, Mynar dyl edged outwards onto the narrow bridge. Its surface was slippery because of the spray from the torrent below. Moss and climbing plants had grown all around the stones, presenting even more traps to avoid.

To the surprise of the clan Llyvary Elves who were watching him closely, Mynar dyl was using his javelin as a walking stick. The weapon's tip struck the ground with each of his steps, penetrating the limestone as if it were mud. Feeling more confident with this unusual support, the warlord progressed resolutely across the dangerous passage with his habitual majestic gait.

Then, from the depths of the chasm below, a small stone flew through the air.

The missile hit Mynar dyl square in the forehead.

The shock and force of the blow caused him to lose his footing. He desperately shifted his body weight backwards, to lurch away from the brink. But his efforts were in vain. After one slip more, he fell from the bridge.

In a frantic effort to survive, Mynar dyl, half-conscious, threw his javelin against the rock wall of the cliff. The spear buried deep into limestone. He continued to fall, but the strap soon tightened around his wrist. Mynar dyl swung violently into the rock wall, bouncing twice before finally stabilizing. He was now unconscious, suspended from his javelin's rope above the void.

A cry was heard.

"Look! A small creature is fleeing into the gorge!" alerted one of the Llyvary fighters.

"It is a Gnome!" shouted an archer, as he released a first arrow.

Watching the missile as it flew into the chasm, Camatael suddenly saw the aggressor below him, on his side of the river. The short silhouette was hastening alongside the torrent. He was fleeing with difficulty, struggling over boulders and jumping between rocks. The young lord called upon the protection of his deity.

"Cund o Lon!"[28] he shouted, while tracing a circle of silvery powder around himself.

On the other side of the gorge, Matriarch Myryae came forth and watched the situation from the edge of the precipice. She ordered her fighters to cross the narrow bridge and pursue the attacker. Camatael immediately knew what was expected of him.

Matriarch Myryae's voice was heard, loud and clear. Uttering words in an unknown language, she was summoning to her command the many roots and branches which curved back and forth along the gorge's cliff. The creepers that covered the gorge were responding to her will. The once-motionless plants suddenly animated, and the leafy creatures grasped the suspended Mynar dyl, pulling him back up to the ravine's edge.

Meanwhile, Camatael secured his bronze helmet on his head. The horsehair plume shone in the sunlight. Looking fearlessly at the void before him, he jumped from the cliff's edge without the slightest hesitation, his purple cloak flying in the wind. Crying a word of power, the young lord landed upon a large boulder below, light as a feather. After two more heroic leaps downwards, he had almost reached the torrent's shoreline at the bottom of the chasm. It had taken him but an instant. The Gnome stood merely a dozen yards before him, climbing large boulders which gave access to a wooden walkway that ran along the furious stream.

Camatael drew his long sword and rushed forward. Quick as a snake, the Gnome was already on the footbridge.

The pursuit began, to the deafening noise of the tumultuous waters which reverberated along the rock walls.

The gap between the cliff walls narrowed significantly in this stretch of the gorge, and Camatael found himself enveloped in almost total darkness. He struggled to breathe in the heavy air, as if the humid vapours around him were poisonous fumes released by the rocks. He was seized by a strange kind of dizziness.

---

28 Cund o Lon: 'Protection of Lon' in lingua Hawenti.

The Gnome was about to flee underground through a crack in the rock wall when he chose to turn around and confront his pursuer. He was of small stature, barely three feet high, round-bodied with spindly arms and legs. His face looked ugly, despite the long beard and wild hair that masked his features.

Camatael met his gaze and immediately perceived the anger in this earth-dwelling spirit. It was the first time the young lord had encountered a Gnome, though he had read about them.

The humanoid creature put his hand into a bag and took out a stone. He slung it, aiming at the young lord's forehead.

An Elvin word of power was heard.

The missile flew. It crossed the ten yards that separated the two opponents like lighting. But suddenly, it slowed and finally sank into Camatael's hand. He then let the stone fall to the ground. Its surface was covered in glittering hieroglyphs.

By the time Camatael looked back up to the Gnome, he had disappeared inside a small opening in the bedrock. The young lord approached to check that the gap was too small for him to follow. Soil and vegetation had built-up in the network of fissures across the fragmented bedrock. Cold currents were flowing out of the fissure. There was no way he could continue the chase.

A terrifying underground sound was then heard, like that of an earthquake. Camatael suddenly feared tons of boulders would slide down on top of him. The rock was shaking from the pressure within. The gap widened, and the silhouette of a hulking mass of rock began to emerge from the stone.

Bearing a humanoid torso, a flat head with glowing eyes and two muscular stone arms, the earthy creature finally freed himself from the ancient rock, and immediately used his tremendous strength to batter the Elf lord.

It made several grappling attacks, its monumental strength and size giving it a significant advantage. The creature, however, could not secure a good hold of its far smaller opponent.

A volley of arrows issued from all sides surrounding the gorge. Despite the hardness of Elvin steel, the arrows ricocheted off its stony skin.

At last, the creature tried to bull rush the Elf into a wall. Camatael avoided this attack by leaping to one side while screaming a word of power. There was a flash of dazzling light.

The stone creature lost its balance, tumbled, and came crashing down into the bottom of the chasm, into the tumultuous waters of the torrent. It was smashed into pieces.

Camatael rose and secured a hold on the broken gateway. Elves of clan Llyvary were only just reaching the scene of the battle.

"Are you well, Lord Dol Lewin?" their captain enquired with a voice full of fear. He was amazed by what he had just witnessed.

★

Mynar dyl was sat against a tree truck. Though his forehead displayed a fresh scar, he seemed to be recovering well from his fall into the gorge. From time to time, he brought a crystal vial to his mouth and swallowed a sip of a greenish liquor which Myryae had given him.

"Do not take me for a fool. This sordid creature was waiting for me. It was a deliberate attempt at murder. How else do you explain that wretched Gnome waiting for more than twenty of us to be safely across, before he used his sling against me?" questioned Mynar dyl, enraged by the attack.

The fair warlord's finely drawn mouth and hawk-like eyes expressed hatred. His malevolent gaze hardened his facial expression. The afternoon light illuminated his features in striking detail; a temporary, arresting portrait that seemed to capture his personality.

As soon as Mynar dyl had been lifted onto solid ground, the matriarch had immediately come to his side and provided him with care. Her long, shimmering hair seemed to create a mysterious aura around her. She wore a long green gown with the hood thrown back. A silver necklace, from which hung her emerald rune, adorned her simple and rather severe garb.
With her eyes half-closed; Myryae thought to herself.

"It is said that no movement can escape a Gnome's eyes, and that his slingshot never misses its target."

Camatael was also present by the wounded's side. After returning from the depths of the gorge, he had reported his fight with the Gnome to the two other Llymar ambassadors. The young lord did not sustain serious injuries, but he had still not fully recovered from the encounter. Nevertheless, he felt compelled to react. Somehow, Mynar dyl's complaining irritated him.

"I understand you are angry; I think that is justified... but I fail to see how this attempt on your life could have been premeditated. How could anyone know you would be among this retinue from Llymar? Indeed, Neryn dyl Llyvary was meant to be the captain commanding our units, until the very last moment when you decided to join us."

This last remark drew Myryae's attention. Curious, she asked. "Why did you come with us in the end, Mynar dyl? You came aboard our ship just before we set sail. The hour was growing late."

Sweat still dripping from his brow, the warlord, breathless, hesitated before responding. "I had my reasons..."

The answer proved too vague. "Well, I ask you to share those reasons with us!" urged Myryae with a palpable impatience.

She looked him square in the face, as though the intensity of her gaze could force him to reveal what he was hiding. The secretive Myryae seemed, at first sight, a compassionate priestess, staying silent whenever she could, only ever revealing her thoughts after lengthy observation. Nevertheless, Camatael considered her a powerful, noble lady, whose true nature was concealed behind a tranquil façade.

The silent confrontation lasted a while. Mynar dyl adjusted the three white feathers hanging from a dark green cloth tied around his brown hair.

"I did not want anyone to know in advance that I was heading to the Nargrond Valley," he confided at last. "I wanted my involvement in the Pact Gathering to be kept secret until the very end...

I feared the druids in particular. The Daughter of the Islands warned me against them. Though she is meant to have authority upon them, the Arkylla does not trust most of them, especially

156

those shape-changers coming from the ranks of Men. The cult of Eïwele Llya is organized unlike any other temple. Freedom and independence are the base principles of that faith. Druids do not easily bow before authority."

"That is most true," Myryae agreed. "The cult of Eïwele Llya is home to both Elves and Men of all origins. No one could say for sure that all druids are reliable. They have dealings with almost all of the factions on the Islands, even the Dark Elves..." Seeing that this line of excuse was working, Mynar dyl added insidiously , "They also have dealings with the Gnomes... Oron is filled almost to its centre with the children of Gweïwal Agadeon, the guardians of mines, and of precious stones...

I am sure that druid spies knew of my coming as soon as we penetrated Nargrond Valley. Swarming swallows were flying several days above our trail."

Once again, Myryae seemed convinced. "Indeed. I came to the same conclusions at the time."

Camatael looked around. The Elves of clan Llyvary had been positioned by their captain in a defensive formation around the three ambassadors. Some were hiding in tree branches, bows in hand, while a line of spears and shields had been positioned in a circle close around them. Green cloaks and hoods comingled in the canopy, making their group almost invisible. Tension had eased, and the situation now looked under control.

"This is all nonsense. I believe you give yourself too much importance, Mynar dyl. You are creating this fabulous tale out of fear," Camatael suggested.

'That lonely Gnome was acting on his own,' the young lord thought.

Irritated by what he judged to be an insulting comment, Mynar dyl countered , "I have reason to fear. I have come to the Nargrond Valley for a specific purpose. I wanted my presence to remain secret for that same purpose."

The matriarch rose from her seat; Camatael admired her tall, thin and gracious stature. Myryae was now determined to clear up the concerns and ambiguities which were arising from Mynar dyl's babbling.

"Your words are full of riddles. Don't you think that now is the time to let us know the truth?"

Camatael added insistently, with a clear intent to place the burden of responsibility upon the warlord , "Your secrecy, Mynar dyl, is placing the entire delegation of Llymar and its envoy in danger."

Mynar dyl looked like prey cornered by hounds. He had lost most of his beautiful, steely veneer; his body, covered with bruises and scars, looked weak and vulnerable.

"I have come to Nargrond Valley to see justice done," he admitted at last.

"What do you mean?" questioned Myryae, utterly surprised.

"The Renegade is hiding near us," Mynar dyl explained. "I know from Curwë, who he took as prisoner in Llafal, that his purpose is to interfere with the Pact Gathering. The Renegade might well be within the Nargrond Valley as we speak. Indeed, he could be lurking very close..."

"Surely you have made this all up. It is simply too difficult to believe. Why would Dyoren come to the very place where all those who seek him are gathering? He must have found a much safer hideout."

The matriarch was not convinced.

Mynar dyl sat up, leaning on the tree trunk. Feeling on the defensive, he wanted to reply. The warlord was never as fierce an opponent as when he was under attack.

"He is not hiding at all. Instead, he has come to fulfil his knight's vows: to capture one of the legendary swords, Lynsing. The Renegade believes the bearer of the Blade of the South will be there, at the Pact Gathering. In his troubled mind, he believes that he can seize this moment of vulnerability and recover the sword."

Myryae doubted the rationality of this reasoning. "Assaulting one of the participants during the Pact Gathering, I cannot see anything more dangerous. One might as well sail the Sea of Cyclones in the middle of Eïwele Llyo's season. The circles of druids will guarantee the security of all participants."

Mynar dyl was not short of arguments. "The task looks impossible, I agree. But I have spent a good deal of time thinking like the Renegade does. If he wanted to get close to one of the participants, he would need to infiltrate a delegation. The Renegade has forged many alliances over time, and has bonds with more factions than you would think: wild druids, Elvin outcasts and perhaps also... Gnomes..."

Myryae possessed a deep knowledge of the Islands and its people. Again, she failed to concur.

"It would be unreasonable to assume that Dyoren has enough influence to order the Gnomes of Nargrond Valley to murder you! History has proven, time and again, that they are always reluctant to interact with Elves. The Gnomes are known as crafty and intelligent creatures who do not meddle with the habits of others. The children of Gweïwal Agadeon are reclusive beings, obsessed by their own considerations."

"It is written in the Lonyawelye that Gnomes are not interested in the affairs of Elves," Camatael added, echoing the matriarch's statement.

But Mynar dyl would not relent. "I did not mean to accuse the Gnomes... I rather thought of an assassin, acting on his own... why not? The Renegade knows I am after him, and he will stop at nothing to complete his quest. This is his last opportunity to redeem his honour."

Myryae and Camatael remained silent. Though their doubts still lingered, Mynar dyl's cohesive and sustained arguments concerned them deeply. The warlord observed their silence with keen eyes. The discussion had reinvigorated him. He felt encouraged to say more.

"I have thought hard about this riddle. I have accumulated considerable evidence. And, over the course of researching the numerous manuscripts the Renegade wrote about his quest, I found his writings threw a great deal of light on questions we were originally forced to leave unanswered... And I have reached a conclusion."

At this point, he lowered his voice, forcing his two listeners to lean in closer.

"I believe the Renegade will hide himself among the clan Llorely. Remember, his father was from that bloodline. The Renegade has always enjoyed the support and guidance from the azure seagull of Llorely. Growing up, his father was his only role model, and I do not doubt he has inherited a very similar disposition. Unlike Voryn dyl and me, he never demonstrated the respect he owed to our mother, and to the Ernaly. Personally, I have always considered him a seagull, far more than a hawk of our own."

From the moment that Mynar dyl had evoked Dyoren's name as a potential suspect in the attack they had just endured, Myryae was troubled by a pernicious question looming in her mind.

"You said you were seeking justice, Mynar dyl. Why would that be? Dyoren has not rebelled against you. What he did was deny the authority of the Secret Vale, by keeping hold of the precious blade. He refused to return Rymsing and be stripped of his rank and duties. Though it is a crime according to the laws of the Dyoreni, it has nothing to do with you. I cannot understand why you are so fixated on your half-brother's fate."

With a most stubborn air, Mynar dyl replied. "I have my reasons," and his cold tone implied the worse.

Again, Myryae pressed him. "If you want our support, you must tell us what those reasons are."

"The Renegade killed Voryn dyl," Mynar dyl accused.

"How could that be?" asked Myryae in complete surprise.

Fully releasing the hatred inside him, the warlord poured out a stream of recycled theories , "He killed my brother... and worse still, after cutting the life of his own kin, the Renegade refused to carry out the ritual tributes owed to Eïwele Llyo. Voryn dyl's body was never found in Nyn Ernaly. The matriarchs of my clan looked far and wide for it. Even the Daughter of the Islands became involved. They used their extraordinary divinatory powers to find Voryn dyl's body. And they failed. There can only be one force powerful enough to conceal the fate of a dead Llewenti from those great weavers of the Islands' Flow...

The Swords of Nargrond Valley have this power...

The legendary blades cannot be found, they cannot be detected by any craft that the high mages, the matriarchs or even the Arkys control. The deeds of their wielders remain unknown, protected by the secrecy surrounding the blades and their location.

I owe that knowledge to the Daughter of the Islands herself.

Only one such blade was ever found after the fall of Nargrond Valley; Rymsing, the Blade of the West, and the glaive of the Renegade."

The arguments he just laid out were proving convincing, given the dismay that could be read on his interlocutors' faces. Mynar dyl pushed his advantage further, now using a tone full of sadness and regret.

"Voryn dyl's soul now wanders into the dark tunnels of the underworld and cannot find its way to the halls of Eïwele Llyo. He has been denied any chance of reincarnation. This thought obsesses me... Now, I am the last dyl of clan Ernaly, the last hawk of the forest."

Camatael found Mynar dyl's overly poignant display of mourning for his lost brother hard to believe. Instead, he focused on the events in Nyn Ernaly that had led to Voryn dyl's disappearance. He knew Saeröl, the wielder of Moramsing, could have been involved in the bloodshed that had occurred in the forest of Mentolewin. For some reason, what had happened in Nyn Ernaly made him feel guilty. Wanting to discourage any retaliation against Dyoren, who he intuitively believed was innocent, the young lord tried to instil doubt in Mynar dyl's mind.

"We all came to know that Dyoren fought a duel in Mentolewin, during the pilgrimage of Eïwele Llyi, as her followers were gathered in the ruins of the great fortress of the West. But nobody witnessed that fight. The Seeker was found severely injured inside the ruins of the ancient temple of Eïwele Llyo. Pilgrims tended to his wounds and managed to heal him. The other duellist was never found. It can only mean he fled and managed to hide.

It was also reported by the Council of the Forest's spy that, just before the duel, Dyoren was having words with another bard he confronted in the amphitheatre. All the Elves present that day in Mentolewin attested that never in their lives had they witnessed such an outstanding musical challenge. I believe that this other bard was the duellist."

But there was no way Mynar dyl would change his deeply rooted conviction, given the rage within him.

"Do not muddy the facts, Lord Dol Lewin. Voryn dyl was in Mentolewin Forest at the same time as the Renegade. Voryn dyl never returned, his body was never found. Only the power of the legendary blade that dug his tomb could mask the location of his remains. This, I know. These are the facts."

A long silence followed. It was as if the three Elves needed time to measure the implications of Mynar dyl's accusations. Camatael was puzzled, almost torn apart by the question of what to do next. His natural righteousness forbade him from letting the accusations of Mynar dyl spread further. In the meantime, revealing what he knew about the master of the Guild of Sana and his potential implication in the bloody events of Mentolewin Forest would trigger a series of questions, the extent of which could not be measured. Of course, he felt compelled not to divulgate that secret, which would also compromise Lord Curubor. To tell the truth and be vulnerable, or to hide it and remain safe. It was a most persistent question. Camatael thought of the smiling face of Loriele Dol Etrond, his consort, the mother of his future children. So much was at stake. He was not alone in this.

At last, Myryae expressed what she had in mind. Her recollection of events was also tainted with regret.

"When I learnt that your brother had remained behind in Nyn Ernaly to exact revenge against the outcast Aewöl, I sensed only a great evil could result from that terrible act. Aewöl, whatever his crime, had already been judged. The Protector had sentenced him to exile. It was a wise judgment. Know this! The Council of the Matriarchs never condemned Aewöl to be banished by fire and water. His status was different. None of us could treat him like a criminal, like an Elf without rune. None of us was entitled to chase him and punish him."

"You will recall how I echoed that very sentiment in front of the matriarchs' council when the matter was discussed in Llafal," Mynar dyl reminded her. "I did not support my brother's initiative, nor did help him prepare for it in any way. Overwhelmed by anger at Aewöl's sacrilege, Voryn dyl made an unfortunate choice. But all of us can acknowledge that, whatever his wrongs were, my brother rid us of that despicable Aewöl. The one-eyed Elf was never seen again after he was banished. The matriarchs and the Daughter of the Islands confirmed that he had disappeared without trace. Voryn dyl must have fed his body to the vultures. My brother could prove ruthless at times."

After the sheer violence of Mynar dyl's last words, Camatael had had enough. He would not have any further part in the enmities of these ferocious Elves. Feeling utterly disgusted by what he had just heard, he moved away from the grass and trees and stepped onto the rocks bordering the canyon.

The clan Llyvary fighters were now sitting around, resting. They felt safe under the watchful eyes of their sentries and refreshed themselves among the wild vines and cool fountains. Their long march along rough roads down to the gorge had been hard.

It was now several weeks since the delegation from Llymar had disembarked from Gwarystan. Norelin had granted them special permission to travel across his kingdom. After they had left the great domes and high spires of the majestic city behind them, glittering in the sunlight over the hills of Gwa Nyn, their journey had been long and dreary. They were given no trouble by the royal cavalry units they had occasionally crossed thanks to the royal rune they bore on their hands. It was an odd feeling for those Elves, usually considered rebels by the king, to see High Elf commanders in their shining plate mails and lordly red cloaks, bow before their passage.

Looking at the royal rune glittering upon his palm, a sudden thought crossed Camatael's mind.

'I can barely remember the Elf I was during my time at the royal court, though it was merely a few years ago. Reaching Gwarystan as a fleeing refugee who lost all his wealth during the Century of War, I had to climb the ladder and make many compromises. That young apprentice of the Ruby College, who became a royal steward and eventually the king's envoy, still has reason to be pleased. Becoming a high priest of Eïwal Lon was always, in the end, my fate. In a moment of ire, Norelin banished me from Gwarystan for treason. But now is the time for me to return, proud and tall, to the kingdom that shamed me.'

During the journey, the lord of House Dol Lewin had noticed how, beyond Tios Pasy[29], the kingdom's roadways were less frequented by travellers, owing to the extensive plain that had suffered considerable deforestation. The summer's heat was intense, and the scarcity of provisions and water had proven painful. It was obvious Eïwele Llya had abandoned these lands. Then, pathways had proven rough and dangerous in the wilderness around Tios Senen[30]. They had braved many dangers. Yet they had managed to overcome every obstacle and had finally reached the high passes of the Arob Nargrond's northern range. Despite the difficulty of walking along these mountainous tracks, this part of their journey had been the most pleasant, though also the most time-consuming. Fortunately, plenty of fresh water and fruits were available for walkers along this route.

The descent into the valley of Nargrond had required crossing rough and dangerous terrain, before passages through deep gorges and above wild torrents, not to mention high waterfalls and steep hillsides.

Finally, they had reached the green banks of the ever-running Sian Senky and had been able to progress onwards through the valley to the lake of Yslla. They had circumvented the ancient city of Yslla, keeping a cautious distance. All Elves shun those ruins, for it was said that the ghosts of the dead Morawenti,

29 Tios Pasy: 'City of the flat land' in lingua Llewenti. It is located in Gwa Nyn, in the vast plain south of Gwarystan.

30 Tios Senen: 'City of the hill top' in lingua Llewenti. It is located in Gwa Nyn, north of the Nargrond Valley.

drowned during the genocide perpetrated by the Dark Elves, still haunted the place. The greenery of the Sian Senky valley had been a stark contrast to those vast, deserted ruins. They had passed through many beautiful groves, cool fountains and ancient vineyards that had been long left abandoned.

Now, the Elves of clan Llyvary were enjoying a well-deserved pause after the tumultuous events of the day. The sun was disappearing in the west behind the threatening silhouette of Mount Oryusk. It was generally assumed by the entire party they would be spending the night here. But Myryae felt that they had rested enough already. She seemed impatient to leave the site of the Gnome's attack.

"Arise, Elves of Llymar!" she cried. "Let us move on. We must not tarry longer, for we have only a couple of leagues further to travel before we reach our destination."

The matriarch bid her followers be cheerful, as their long journey was almost at an end. She pointed out the ruins of the ancient temple in the distance, which was their goal. An Elf in her retinue even claimed he could make out the glistening tents of their brethren from Cumberae upon the hilltop.

After a while, the old route they were following diverged, one leading directly north and the other up the banks of the River Sian Senky towards the west, by way of Ystanargrond. Myryae ordered them to follow the latter route. Later, they passed through a deep wood of ancient trees, where long ago the Elves of Nargrond Valley had felled and prepared timbers for the building of Yslla and Ystanargrond.

Eventually, just before nightfall, the group reached a bend in the Sian Senky, which formed a desolate beach. A hill made of tons of gigantic stone blocks acted like reefs and provided a safe harbour, sheltering them from the tumultuous waters of the river. Quantities of quarried stones had been dragged upstream by marine architects of great talent. The Elves of Nargrond Valley had built a lasting bulwark that, centuries later, the Sian Senky's wild current had not yet succeeded in washing away. They must have had plans for a harbour in this desolate place.

The old road went up and the group reached a hillock from which they commanded a dominant view of the entire valley. They could distinguish the ruins to the west. Although wildly degraded, beautiful traces of the original architecture were still visible: the twisted collars, the pure ornamentation of the facades, and the large windows open to light. After this fleeting vision, they felt relieved.

The group continued walking in silence until, after another short climb, the road suddenly revealed the remains of a great temple. Formerly, this place of worship had been famous. It had consisted of high walls, a formidable keep and even a drawbridge. When they approached it, they saw the ditches were without water and the bridge was no longer rising. As for the keep, it had utterly surrendered itself to the bonds of the pervasive ivy. Large blocks weighting several tons had been transported up the slope and lifted on top of one another, forming high walls several dozen feet high. Stones had been cut with precision, and they were still polished, as if the site had only recently been abandoned in the middle of its construction.

From afar, the ruins still possessed a certain ancient majesty. Up close, however, the extent of the desolation afflicted the newcomers.
The known name of the temple was 'Makom co anan vaha'[31], but it was generally simply referred to as 'O Vaha'. The Elves of Nargrond Valley had built it to celebrate light.

★★

---

31 Makom co anan vaha: 'The temple dedicated to the light of the sun' in lingua Llewenti

Gwa Nyn, Nargrond Valley, temple of O Vaha, at night

The sun had already sunk behind Mount Oryusk when the Elves of Llymar finally reached the ruins of the temple. Shadows invaded the surrounding woods and thickets. The fighters of clan Llyvary lit their crystal lamps. They came out into the open and found themselves in front of what used to be the walls surrounding the holy edifice. There was a treeless space before them, which ended in a large ditch. Oaks and pine trees rose above the great stones, like as many unlikely lookout towers. A voice, with a strong southern accent, was heard in the darkness.

"Welcome to O Vaha, Elves of Llymar! We've been expecting you."

A silhouette appeared in the shadows. By his snow-white hair and cold blue eyes, the ambassadors from Llymar knew the sentry as one of the Ice Elves. He looked to be of high rank, given the finesse of his garb and the quality of his equipment. The golden rose of Cumberae adorned his tall helm.

There were old stones running from the brink of the ditch, forming something like a passage into the compound. The gates opened silently, and lights sprang forth until the whole hill top seemed to sparkle with stars. Among the ruins, numerous tents, whose greenly colours comingled with the wild vegetation, were built and hung with many silvery lamps. The travellers were welcomed by a dozen Ice Elves, easily recognizable in their white garments. They were also Llewenti, but from different kin as they hailed from the cold woods of the southern island. The Ice Elves were clad in silvery mail, armed with javelins and oval shields and from their shoulders hung long cloaks made of pelt. The fur was a tawny grey, lighter on the hind part of the back, where the white-tipped hair became wavy.
Many excited voices were heard murmuring about the arrival of the Elves of Llymar. The gates were shut behind them.

When Camatael entered the compound, a light breeze coming from the west carried dark fumes which obscured the atmosphere.

It was an acrid scent; it spread like steam, but its odour was one of ashes. Even if there were a great fire burning nearby, there was no way it could emit a smoke this dense. Only a volcano could throw its poisonous fumes as far away into the valley, just as the ocean can send the scents of salt and kelp far inland.

The fighters of clan Llyvary began to unpack their equipment and goods. The Ice Elves, who formed most of the retinue from Cumberae, came to them, visibly eager to help. They could speak the same tongue, though their southern accent made their interpretation of lingua Llewenti less subtle. The Ice Elves brought many gifts of food and beverages as per the tradition in Nyn Llyandy. These dishes were mostly in the form of cakes and biscuits made of cereals baked in salty cream. The liquors were dry and strong, lacking the sweet complexities of Nyn Llyvary's nectars. At first, the Elves of clan Llyvary looked at these gifts with a doubtful eye but were soon eating and drinking with relish. The food of the Ice Elves was fortifying, and such replenishment was exactly what they needed after their long trek through the wild.

The Elves of clan Llyvary demonstrated their own generosity in return. They offered to their hosts wrapped parcels of clothes they had brought with them from Tios Halabron. There were cloaks, green as oak leaves, with large hoods made of that special silk, only found in Llymar. They also gifted boots, brown as a vivid wood in spring. Each shoe was fastened with a brooch like a swan's feather veined with emerald. All the clothes were made in different sizes, so there were items to fit the Ice Elves and the taller High Elves who made up the knights of the Rose, the personal bodyguards of Cumberae's envoy.

Meanwhile, the group of ambassadors from Llymar went along a narrow path and climbed up a hill across boulders and stones until they reached a dried-up marble fountain, formed of several concentric circles.
To the south-east, beyond the confines of the great temple ruins, stood a great oak. This ancient tree had a massive trunk, and its leaden branches shielded the clearing from high above, like a protective giant with powerful arms.

Below, three Elves, elegantly dressed, were comfortably seated. They sprung from their seats as the ambassadors from Llymar approached.

The Ice Elf captain, who had led them this far, lifted his tall helm to make a ceremonious announcement.

"The envoy of Cumberae dwells here with her ambassadors. The princess wishes to greet you personally," he declared.

The ambassadors from Llymar parted ways with their retinue. Camatael joined Myryae and Mynar dyl, while their personal guards were shown to the quarters that had been prepared for them.

An Elvin lady came forth to greet the three representatives from Llymar. She saluted them with a simple nod. Her arrival made a deep impression on Camatael.

Terela was her name. She was the only child born to the lord of House Dol Nos-Loscin, and heir to the throne of Cumberae. Camatael remembered the words Lord Curubor had spoken about her.

"Terela is the noblest life that was born into the Islands since Lon's disappearance."

Looking at her martial air with amazement, the young lord marvelled at the single fact that made her so unique.

"Since the beginning of the Islands' history, Terela Dol Nos-Loscin is the only Hawenti lady who has ever commanded an army."

Although she was dressed very simply in a white linen dress, from her person emanated an impression of natural majesty. She was as young as Camatael. Barely six feet tall, she could be considered small compared to the standard of her kin. There was an expression of firmness and serenity upon her face. The tense, hard lines of her strained features looked like the scars war sows upon old warriors. Her square-back haircut framed her beautiful face like ramparts protecting a marvellous city.

Her gait looked graceful, and her cold beauty was so extraordinary that Camatael admired her elegant silhouette with relish. Yet, he felt no guilt of going beyond the bonds that

Hawenti conduct dictated. There was in her face serenity and purity that justly reflected her spiritual nature. The princess Terela possessed a serious character and it gave her countenance a certain melancholy. Her great self-confidence made her inwardly strong and superior.

Suddenly, Camatael felt out of place in front of the Elvin princess. The trials of the last few days had made him unrecognizable. The lord of the house of Dol Lewin was emaciated after expending so much energy and burnt by a sun that he had endured with difficulty. All the fatigues of this long journey and the marks of his encounter with the Gnome could be read on his face. He normally relied on his sophisticated and noble appearance to make strong impressions and help him achieve his aims. In that moment, he was a fighter without his armour.

Just as he was trying to rid his mind of this line of thinking, Camatael saw Aertelyr, the guild master of the Breymounarty approaching, as if to reply to his inner monologue. Smiling, the Ice Elf merchant walked towards him, his features pale and his hair snow-white. He was wrapped in a cloak of white lion skin. Aertelyr nodded distantly to greet the lord of House Dol Lewin. His attitude betrayed a kind of haughtiness that Camatael was not used to. The guild master of the Breymounarty said nothing after his slight gesture, but quickly turned aside to salute Mynar dyl.

Camatael remembered a letter that Aertelyr had sent him to complain about the trade competition with Alqualinquë, the new merchant company promoted by the community of Mentollà and protected by the Council of the Forest. Aertelyr had lost the monopoly of trade between Llymar and Cumberae. He felt it unjust how quickly his rivals were gaining influence. Camatael, who was responsible for matters of trade among the Council of the Forest, had judged it sagacious not to dignify what he considered a misplaced request with any kind of reply. To his mind, there was nothing wrong with sharing the profits of maritime trade.

'Master Aertelyr is not wise to show such insolence and spite,' thought the young lord. 'I will remember it.'

Camatael then turned to a High Elf, clad in shadowy-grey robes of rare elegance.

The newcomer welcomed him using the ancient Hawenti tongue. Camatael spoke haltingly in return. The High Elves seldom used their own language, even when dealing with each other. Nowadays, it was only used by a small elite of nobles who, it was widely felt, used it only to demonstrate their superiority.

"Welcome, Alton!" said Camatael, speaking slowly.

"I am glad to see you again, Lord Dol Lewin," responded the young Dol Nos-Loscin, the cousin of princess Terela. "Our last reunion was not long ago, yet so many events have come to pass since then that it feels like an age. I seldom employ the rich and subtle language of our nation, so you will kindly excuse me if I take this opportunity that meeting someone of my kin and rank poses. You see, since House Dol Nos-Loscin left Gwarystan, such occasions have proven rare. We dwell in our city of Ystanloscin now. We mostly deal with the local Wenti. Our kindred in the North are sundered from us. Fortunately, I sometimes go abroad for the gathering of news and the obligations of diplomacy. We need to watch our enemies; you see... My uncle has gathered a rather impressive collection of them lately. It proves... entertaining, to say the least."

The two high-born Elves continued to speak together in soft voices for a time. Then, the princess of Cumberae politely summoned her guests to one of the temple's chambers.

It was not a large room. Nevertheless, the place was still protected by a roof, a rare commodity in these desolated ruins. No luxurious furnishings adorned its walls. Only at the back of the chamber, there was a dais covered with deep green linen, dotted with winged lions, one black and the other white, pinned down at the edges of the platform by heavy strips of gold. The place was filled with a few cushions, a carpet from Ystanloscin and rich furs of Nyn Llyandy. Seats were draped in beautiful tapestries, woven in looms on the Isle of Nyese. A silvery light from two precious chandeliers illuminated an improvised negotiating table, simply made of a wooden plank and two casks.

A bottle of wine, which had escaped the perils of the journey, was brought to the table by Alton. He handled it as if it were a delicate relic. Having carefully removed the cork, he took a set of crystal glasses out of a chest.

Camatael began to drink the nectar with his eyes. He recognized the white liquor as a fabled ice wine from Llacrag. Alton slowly swirled the contents of his glass before putting it down. In an effort to ease the tension that was palpable, he started discussing the merits of the nectar. His delicate voice possessed the unique aristocratic superiority of a noble Dol.

"Do you know what the Ice Elves say about the origin of the Islands' wines? They claim it is the most precious gift that we ever received from the Archipelago's deities. Llyi creates the flowers in the meadows which, infused in good wine, inspire hope. Llya gives the blood of her veins to enrich the soil where the grape vines grow, and Llyo provides the herbs and plants that lift the spirit, nourish the soul, and procure those dreams and visions that transcend our everyday lives."

Myryae looked troubled at this. Among the Llymar priestesses, wine was often associated with the excesses perpetrated by the followers of the dreaded Eïwal Myos, patron deity of the Dark Elves. She disagreed with this interpretation, her tone one of condemnation.

"But, as with all good things in life, there is a price. The matriarchs of Llymar believe the Eïwali of the Islands made their own contribution too, though in a rather different manner. They dreamt up curses to counterbalance the gentle Eïwely's gifts. Eïwal Vars poisons the sap of the vine leaves with a toxic substance that, if absorbed in great quantities, obscures the mind and drives one to violence. Eïwal Ffeyn's winds carries alien pollens that stick to the grapes' skin, provoking dizziness and loss of balance in the eventual wine-drinker. Worse still, Eïwal Myos alters the very seeds of grapes, imbuing them with qualities that alter judgement and encourage recklessness..."

Camatael felt the need to interrupt the matriarch's admonition. "But, despite these perils, Elves have learnt to enjoy the gift of the Islands deities in moderation; if we are deprived of these elixirs, we would surely lose contact with the good things of this world."

The young lord was anxious to preserve the reunion's friendly atmosphere that had so far prevailed. With an exaggerated enthusiasm, he handed his glass to Alton.

"If my eyes do not betray me, what you have so kindly brought to us is one of the fabled ice nectars from Llacrag. I have grown very fond of white wines recently…"

The glasses were filled with the cold beverage and the conversation developed about the qualities of that rare vintage. Though Myryae did not participate in these scholarly exchanges, it was quickly agreed that the complex and elegant Llacrag wine lived up to its reputation.

At last, Terela decided to interrupt the debate. She ate and drank little and already seemed grave.

"Now is the time to begin our discussions…"

The five other Elves looked to her, impressed by her hidden power. The princess was here with them and yet appeared remote, as if her soul had not left the forest of Cumberae where her people suffered.
After they had all drank and eaten, Terela spoke again about the purpose of their meeting. She lifted her white hand and pointed west towards the shadowy form of Mount Oryusk.

"Both Llymar and Cumberae have decided to harden their hearts and respond to the call of the druids' circles. Soon we will meet on the slopes of Mount Oryusk with the other factions of the Lost Islands. Though we do not know what will be discussed during the Pact Gathering, I do not doubt it will be of the uttermost importance. My father has sent me on this errand. He believes the king and the Ruby College must be facing a great peril, for they have not only called upon the aid of their allies, but also that of their adversaries.

173

As envoys of our realms, we will represent the true seeds of Llyoriane and face the lies and manipulations of Norelin's representatives, those traitors who threaten the Islands Elves' legacy.

The clans and houses of Llymar could have chosen not to answer the call, but the Council of the Forest proved wise, and here you are, at our side. None can be sure of peace, nowadays, even those who think themselves safe behind their borders.

As for us, Elves of Cumberae, our war against the Barbarians has brought us to the edge of doom. We have already summoned all available forces to protect our realm in its hour of greatest need. We are ready to fall into battle against the cult of Three Dragons."

Camatael was moved by the princess' words. Back in Llafal, he had pleaded with a certain success the cause of Cumberae before the Llewenti clans. The young lord felt he possessed legitimacy to speak in that moment.

"The Council of the Forest is resolved to go forward. Rest assured, my lady, that Llymar will stand at Cumberae's side."

Mynar dyl said nothing but looked troubled and doubtful. After a lengthy debate about whether to support Cumberae, the warlord of Tios Halabron had lost the vote.

Myryae immediately supported Camatael's sentiment. She felt eager to demonstrate her role as the official envoy of Llymar. The Council of the Forest had empowered her to finalise the negotiations. Thus, she spoke with authority.

"It was decided that Llymar would make its way to the shores of Nyn Llyandy. We will provide you with our assistance."

Despite the kind words of compassion, she was hearing, Terela realized the Elves of Llymar had not yet agreed in detail what they would do. It did not seem like they had a clear purpose, nor had they decided on a specific course of action.
Her cousin, Alton, reached the same conclusion.

"What have you agreed upon, exactly?" he asked with his usual detached air. "We would certainly welcome weapons and supplies. If we wish to turn back the course of history, however, it is fighters we desperately need."

Aertelyr, the only true navigator in the chamber, echoed Alton's request.

"When you leave Llymar, you can no longer cross the Sea of Llyoriane. As you well know, our naves are not tolerated in those waters. The inner sea is the domain of the king's warships and the Westerners' galleys.
On which side of the Islands will you journey? The way to Llacrag and the clan Llyandy's lands lies to the west, but the straight road to Cumberae lies on the other side of the Islands, upon the most dangerous shore. Which way will you choose?"

There was an embarrassed silence.

The two realms had agreed to finalize the terms of their coalition before the Pact Gathering. It was an opportunity to show a unified front before all.
Still the content of their alliance was not obvious as different opinions conflicted within the Council of the Forest as to the scale of its support.

Mynar dyl smiled. Camatael cleared his throat, visibly feeling embarrassed. He looked to the envoy of Llymar.
But Myryae could not commit to anything more at this stage before knowing more of the situation.
Terela understood that further efforts were needed to plead the cause of her realm. She spoke with a tone she tried to make as diplomatic and as gentle as the situation required.

"I see that you do not yet know what to do...
It is not my part to choose for you, but I wish to let you know what my people are living through."

Terela then recounted in length all that had occurred upon the edge of Cumberae Forest during the days of spring. She spoke of her father and his banner, which still rallied all the Elves of the great southern wood. With a voice charged with emotion, she showed her admiration for her father's deeds.

"I always carry in my mind the image of the prince of Cumberae, that formidable knight, his tall helm bent down to the flying horse's neck, charging at the head of the armies of House Dol Nos-Loscin, his silvery plate mail ploughing deeply into the thick of battle. How many times was he drowned from sight by throngs of bucking horses, by swarms of brandished swords, by walls of uplifted shields? Always he reappears, to the joy of his troops, gaining ever more glory in battle."

Mynar dyl felt the need to share his remembrance of his time at the prince's side. He spoke with the compassionate tone of a poet.

"None can doubt how great Garael Dol Nos-Loscin has become; his princely seat and sovereign realm were well earned by his deeds of the past. My own modest contributions to those great events seem barely worth remembering; to compare us would be like holding a mere candle up to the sun."

Aertelyr could not resist mocking him and broke his silence. "I did not know you could be so obsequious, Mynar dyl?"

Looking at princess Terela, the warlord protested. "I stand by what I said. I fought at Lord Dol Nos-Loscin's side through several battles of the Century of War. My lady, your father is the greatest lord I have ever had the honour to meet."

The princess thanked Mynar dyl for his kind words and resumed her story. She told them of the coming of Ka-Blowna.

"A Dragon Warrior then became a chief among the Barbarians, a warrior as had never been seen before," Terela said. "He is both strong and terrible, appearing invincible when wielding his two-handed sword of black iron. Barbarians claim a terror walks with him, a force mighty enough to haunt our darkest dream and deprive us of the Islands' Flow that protects the forest's edge."

The princess bowed her head and she turned her eyes to a small golden brooch upon her breast, wrought in the likeness of a white flying lion with outspread wings.

Camatael saw the brooch's gem flash like the light of the sun. In that instant, he thought Terela royal and holy beyond measure. It seemed to him many years of toil had fallen on her thin and delicate shoulders. The young lord was profoundly moved by the princess' genuine and pure concern for her subjects.
Indifferent to the reaction she had provoked, Terela resumed her plea.

"The druids did not eliminate the faith of Men in the cult of Three Dragons; they barely weakened its evil influence. Its strength will only wane when the lives of Men are severed from the Three Dragons' power. I am telling you; these evil spirits have begun to stir. The barbarians are threatening our lands once again; they are unafraid to unite and launch massive raids, plundering anything they can from us. They have scorned farming in favour of stealing. When their attacks succeed in driving the population from their homes, the wild Men move in and settle, bringing their families and livestock on their long ships.
Llymar must be informed of these events. It is an outrage that such reckless aggression should be tolerated by the Elves of the Islands."

Camatael watched Myryae's reaction to Terela's plea. To see her saddened features, one could have imagined that all the previous hundreds of sackings and burnings in Cumberae had been but fables, and this one the only fact.

'It is always the way,' the young lord thought, 'when danger's in the distance, when the worry remains unseen, you can send words of kindness and feel you've done your part. When you're up close, however, and you see the terror etched across the faces of your friends, the only course of action is to rise up and fight.'

"The Southern Island, then, could be lost," said Myryae unexpectedly. Her voice was low, but Camatael caught it. "Llymar cannot let this happen. We must stand ready."

The matriarch spoke as one talking to herself aloud without knowing it, and none had heard but Camatael. He glanced at her and saw that her oaken staff was idle in her hands, and that her face had a dreamy and absent look to it. There were fleeting movements upon her lips, as if she were witnessing in that moment the horrific scenes of Cumberae's battlefields with her own eyes. But she made no sound, silently suffering with the pain that the Southern Forest's trees had endured at the hands of Men.

"There is one way the ancient Forest of Cumberae can be led to its salvation," Myryae finally said aloud. "Llymar controls fifteen warships. A great swanship now commands our fleet. If the prince of House Dol Nos-Loscin sends for our help, Llymar's army could sweep the barbarian tribes into the sea."

The Elves of Cumberae murmured with content, and Camatael gazed at Alton in wonder. The young Dol Nos-Loscin had turned red with satisfaction and muttered some words of gratification. Aertelyr bowed as well as he could.

Camatael was genuinely seized with emotion. But, at the same time, he was making a quick calculation. With the support of Myryae and her father, the warlord of Penlla, Mynar dyl 's faction would be outnumbered, and the Council of the Forest would most probably decide to muster the full army of Llymar. Camatael saw in that an opportunity.

"If this is to be the Council of the Forest's will," he proposed, his voice well assured , "I will lead the fleet of Llymar across the seas to wage war against the Dragon Warrior's horde. The White Unicorn will come forth."

"Cumberae will be rescued and made great again!" exclaimed Alton. As he said those last words, a sudden deep glow shone in his eyes.

Deeply moved by this generous proposal, Terela rose from her seat. Her breast heaved, and the colour rose in her face. Taking Camatael's glass from the table, she refilled it with the cold liquor that remained, before going around the others until the bottle was empty and the six glasses were served.

"Now is the time to raise a glass to our alliance," she said. "Drink, my friends, and let our hearts know no fear. Daylight will follow the night. But it is high time we rest, for tomorrow and the days to come will be full of new challenges."

She brought the cup to her lips and bade them drink. Terela then arose, and her cousin Alton led her back to her quarters.

The two groups took their leave and returned to their respective meeting areas. The ambassadors of Llymar wished to take counsel together. For some time, they debated how best to fulfil their promise to Cumberae.
But they came to no decision, for Mynar dyl refused to support Camatael's initiatives. Oddly enough, the mysterious matters that would be discussed at the Pact Gathering in the days to come were no longer at the forefront of their minds.

Camatael was weary in body and in heart. He cast himself down upon a bed that had been prepared for him, and fell at once into a deep, restorative reverie. Most of the Elves of Llymar had not waited up for him. Their dreams were undisturbed as they lay calmly on their beds of withered leaves around him. Those still awake could hear nearby voices singing. Outside, the Ice Elves of Cumberae were chanting songs of longing for their southern lands. Their words were sad and gloomy, and told of lament and mourning after the battles of the spring.

At last, their music died down and the starless night became quiet.

★★

Gwa Nyn, Nargrond Valley, temple of O Vaha, middle of the night

A yellow moon played with the clouds in the night. The water of the fountain glittered with silver. Branches of nearby trees were waving and tossing in the wind.

The temple of O Vaha remained frozen inside an ethereal mist, like a lost warship sailing along unknown shores at the edge of a grey world.

A figure came slowly out of the temple's ruins. It was clad in purple, the dark colour absorbing any dim light of the moon. In his hand, the Elf held a golden rod, like those priests of Eïwal Lon wield.

Camatael, like a ghost lost in the night, seemed to be searching his way forwards. He was walking silently along the path that led out of the ancient shrine. The young lord seemed to be floating away from the main ruins. His footsteps left no trace on the humid soil.

As he approached the guards stationed motionless close to the compound's boundaries, he realised they would not see him unless he willed it.

Camatael suddenly noticed a movement to his left. Two figures, faint and small at first, but growing larger and clearer, were approaching. At last, he could see their faces distinctly; Terela and Myryae were speeding towards the wall.

Suddenly, they saw him too.

Visibly surprised by this nocturnal encounter, the princess of Cumberae touched the necklace that hung about her neck with her staff. The figurines of the Two Winged-Lions of House Dol Nos-Loscin adorning the ivory rod came into contact with the crystal upon the chain.

The vision Camatael seemed to experience faded, and he found he was indeed looking at the two Elvin ladies. It was no dream.

The young lord stepped back, surprised by the sudden encounter. Clouds were moving across the night sky. The twinkling of the stars briefly illuminated his gaze, lost in reverie.

"Have you lost your way, Lord Dol Lewin? What has brought you here, when you should be quietly resting with your retinue?" enquired Terela, her voice full of authority.

Seeing his lack of reaction, she lifted her arms and opened her palms towards his face, in a gesture of rejection. Moonlight reflected upon the eyes of the two figurines. The diamonds glittered like gems in sunlight. Camatael gazed at the two-winged lions, as if noticing their black and white colours for the first time. The charm was dispelled. He was released from the strange spell and seemed, at last, to understand fully where he stood.

"What do you wish of me?" Camatael asked in an odd tone. "What are you doing outside the temple in the middle of the night?"

Myryae smiled. Her voice was clear when she returned the question.

"And why do you come to us, uninvited and unwanted?"

The matriarch lifted her hand. From the rune that was marked upon her palm, there issued a greenish light which illuminated the young lord alone, leaving all else around him in darkness. She stood still before Camatael, seeming both powerful and threatening.
Camatael did not step back or resist her. The emerald light faded.

"I had a vision and ... I walked out of the temple," the young lord confided with a gentle voice, both soft and surprised.

The three Elves stood there for a while, unsure of what to do next. At length, Camatael noticed: all was silent around them, all was still, as if the tides of fates had stopped flowing; there was absolutely no noise... no movement...
Terela broke the silence.

"Camatael, I know you are saying the truth. Will you tell us about your dream?"

The young lord did not answer immediately. He was confronting two Elves whose power was greater than his own: a matriarch and a princess who trained their will to the domination of others. Though his sight had grown keener, Camatael could perceive it was of no avail struggling with those that were counted among the wisest of living Elves.

At last, he revealed what he had experienced.

"I saw the face of an ancient, withered Elvin creature. She looked like the statues of the ancient temples in Tios Lluin; like a keeper of souls, or a weaver of prophecies. Ravens were flying around her like messengers, eager to do her bidding. I heard music; some appeasing melody played on a harp. I could also smell orchids... the smell of orchids was all around me."

"Were her robes grey?" asked Myryae.

Camatael did not answer immediately. At last, he said.

"I cannot tell, for I did not wish to look."

"What things were revealed to you? The one you saw has the power to show strange and unbidden events," insisted the matriarch.

The young lord nodded. He realized he was still trembling.

'Am I trembling out of fear or out of curiosity?' he wondered.

But before he could reach a conclusion, what he had seen in his dream came back to him. The vision shifted, and he saw them again. With a voice filled with awe, he told the two Elvin ladies.

"I saw wings greater than those of Storm Eagles... wings waving in the wind, descending slowly... not falling but flying with majesty, until they reached the ground.

I counted five of them: winged horses, their coats all different colours, each with a unique shape and size. There were three smaller steeds, which appeared younger: one steel grey, a palomino, and a silver dapple one. Then came a larger winged horse, the colour of its coat was chestnut. At last, I saw it, a white Winged Stallion, the biggest of all, and it seemed its hoofs were made of gems and its teeth were cut from ivory.

Amazingly, I was not paralysed with panic, simply attracted beyond words by the powerful aura that radiated from the creatures. I looked with all my soul, until I saw the cavaliers riding the Winged Horses..."

The force of the vision was such that Camatael felt the need to sit on the grass. He added, looking at the paths leading to an orchard on a lower level.

"That dream was real. I could swear it. I saw the Winged Horses and their riders landing in this very wood."

Camatael tried to empty his head and let no thoughts enter. The two Elvin ladies looked at each other as though silently consulting one another. At last, they agreed they needed to share the truth with the young lord.

"What you saw in your dream was true, Camatael," said Terela. "The Arkys of the Secret Vale have come to meet us."

These were incredible claims. To the young lord's reason, they sounded utterly impossible. But to the priest of Eïwal Lon's heart, they rang true.

The Arkys were considered the most glorious spiritual order in the Archipelago, though their origin was barely known to the common Elf. Many songs told of their legend, and they continued to fascinate the worshipers of the Islands' deities. Despite their absence, and perhaps also thanks to it, they had become something of a beacon to most Elves in the Archipelago, to those who called themselves the 'seeds of Llyoriane'.
Priests would preach how the Islands' deities had shown their favour to the five high clerics by entrusting them with the location of Llyoriane's tomb in the Secret Vale. There was no concrete evidence of its existence. No Elf had ever entered it and returned. But despite this lack of any witnesses, the Secret Vale remained a major icon in the minds of Elves.
The Arkys had remained hidden for centuries, providing guidance to some and warnings to others, claiming their spiritual superiority as keepers of Queen Llyoriane's tomb.

Always they had relied upon the Daughter of the Islands, the one they named the 'Arkylla', to pass on their message to the Elves.

Myryae knew how to interpret their signs, for she was one of the few matriarchs who could consult omens. She looked at the pale light that reflected on the surface of a small pool nearby.

"Priests of Eïwele Llyo revere the moon; it governs their souls just as it controls the ocean's tides. Their abilities to weave illusions and practice divination are deeply respected by all. Their power must now be at work. They can commune with their deity across the two worlds."

The matriarch further interpreted the vision Camatael had just experienced.

"What you saw in your dream is nothing less than a premonition. The moon is high and the Arkyllyo is near. The high priestess of Eïwele Llyo must have called upon her deity to summon her evocative power and seed that vision in your mind."
Terela concurred. "I see this as a sign... the Arkys wish Lord Dol Lewin to participate in the ceremony. They want him to be initiated into the secret of their return..."

Camatael listened to their words with attention. The veil that obscured his mind had now been lifted, and the discussions between the two ladies had given him enough time to regain his senses.

"I believe your interpretation is true. And now I am glad that I am to march with you. But I will do as you advise. If you judge me worthy of joining you, I will be your most trusted companion. If not, you have my word that I will never speak of this again."

Terela looked surprised but pleased at this answer, full of goodwill. She smiled gently at Camatael and held his hands.

"Your attitude is full of respect, Lord Dol Lewin, and I now understand better why the Arkys wish you to be at our side. Given the scale of the task, there will never be too many of us concerned with defending the Elves of the Islands."

All were agreed. Myryae and Terela turned aside and led him towards the northern slopes of the hilltop. The small group exited the compound by going through a breach in the ruined walls. The guards who were posted nearby ignored their passing. They were taken by a deep slumber, as though time were standing still.

The three Elves came to the edge of the woods, where apple trees grew. Through the canopy they could see the light of Cil, shining with all its brilliance on the western horizon. They descended a grassy slope that led further into the woods before reaching a silvery fountain, fed by an underground source. The murmur of an invisible stream could be heard in the silence of the night. The three Elves were entering a deep hollow.
The place was filled with a soft light. Its walls were ruined stone, and its roof was the glittering stars.
Camatael glanced through the branches to the clearing beyond. He stood in the shelter and concealment of a large beech tree. The young lord took a step backward.

Elvin knights stood in the glade in shining armour, their shields emblazoned with coloured symbols, their lances of an extraordinary length.
At the centre of the parade stood the five Arkys of the Secret Vale. They sat on natural seats formed by the gnarled roots of a great tree. Their heads were bent towards the ground, as if lost in thought or dreams.
Something most strange struck Camatael. A circle of energy was gliding around them, just above the tips of the grass. The whiteness of that field was not like any other whiteness he knew of; almost as intense as that of lightning. Its brilliancy was so blinding that it pained his eyes. In awe, Camatael's breath grew faint.

Suddenly, the white circle vanished.

The wood had been utterly silent until then, as if overwhelmed with the same stillness that comes when a storm cloud darkens a forest. As the circle of energy vanished, the silence burst into the many nightly sounds of the wilderness.

The Arkys rose and stood. They approached the three Elves slowly, clothed in their splendour. Light was somehow dappled across their faces, like rays of the sleeping sun. The Arkys moved forward to meet the envoys of Llymar and Cumberae, like greeting guests visiting their halls. Their refined manners were that of royal sovereigns. Unnaturally tall and slender, they were dressed beautifully with coloured robes cut from the finest silk.

First came the Arkylon, a tall High Elf with long dark hair. Signs of his great age were upon him. It could be read in the depths of his eyes. His great helm had but one opening, which gave him the appearance of having a single eye. His robes were the colour of fiery gold, which any onlooker would immediately associate with the sun. The blade of his lance was made of bronze, and it shone like pure light. The Arkylon appeared like a supreme priest of heaven. He seemed to descend among the Elves to enlighten them with his truth so that they may be imbued with his wisdom.

Then came the Arkyvars, marching at his side, a second in command protecting his lord with the emerald blade of his spear. His eyes were keen as swords in the twilight. Below his greenly robes could be seen an armour made of hide. He had grapes and leaves in his hair, an animal skin draped across his lap, and a soft leather garment to protect his legs.

Three high priestesses followed, walking with grace. A bird was perched on each of their shoulders. With their beauty and nobility, their elegance of movement, adorned with jewels and their hair braided with flowers, they looked like the embodiment of their respective deities.

The Arkyllyi's colour was white, her flower the jasmine and her bird the grand butterfly. She wore golden jewellery. The Llewenti lady was finely dressed in a silk gown enhancing her elegant silhouette. It felt natural for her to display the beauty of her golden hair.

The Arkylla's colour was green, her flower the magnolia and her bird the redbreast. She was shrouded in a long robe made entirely of green feathers and foliage. Upon her head were antlers. Her unnatural eyes were an intense emerald. The ancient matriarch of clan Ernaly, who the Elves called the 'Daughter of the Islands', wielded a long whip of bough and a great wooden staff, shaped like a halberd.

The Arkyllyo's colour was grey, her flower the orchid, and her bird the raven. The Llewenti priestess wore a long silk gown so fine that she appeared to be dressed in a mantle of pure stardust. Her face had a serene glow. Her eyes, like the wells of deep memory, were meant to capture attention and to draw the viewer into her mysterious universe.

The Arkys said not a word but looked long upon the faces of their three guests.

At last, the Arkylon, the Elf known as the first to have discovered the Secret Vale, greeted them personally.

"Rimwë is my name. I was born the second son of Nargrond."

Works of literature had described Rimwë, the younger brother of Rowë Dol Nargrond, as one of the wisest Elves, gifted with a great power to control the Islands' Flow.

The Arkylon blessed each in turn, with a delicate gesture of his hand.

"Welcome Terela, daughter of Prince Garael, it is the first time we meet, and I am glad your father has conveyed you to us. Major threats are still looming, and the Elves of Cumberae need urgent assistance. Lay aside your burden for a while, for the Secret Vale has answered your prayers.

Welcome, Myryae, daughter of the warlord of Penlla, our gathering is another opportunity to renew our vows of friendship with the matriarchs of Llymar.

And welcome to you, Camatael of the house of Dol Lewin, our unexpected guest. May your presence here be a sign of your ever-growing commitment to the cause of the seeds of Llyoriane."

When all the ceremonial salutations were complete, the Arkylon looked at them again. Camatael knew this great Elf was the attributed author of numerous passages from the Lonyawelye, composed by the first followers of Eïwal Lon. His output also included proverbs, songs and odes, which had gradually formed the liturgy of the cult to the deity of Wisdom. Such an orator could influence his audience, even by the tone of his voice.

"We come to you, Elves of Llymar and Cumberae, to answer your call for aid, and to initiate you into the mysteries of our Order. We are the guardians of the tomb of Llyoriane, the Queen who opened the way to the Promised Islands. From the heights of the Secret Vale, may our assembly guide you along the paths of victory against our common enemies. The forces of chaos are gathering and, in these last years, the Elves have wandered according to the tumults of history. But all Elvin races are members of one great kin. The seeds of Llyoriane have the same origin and the same destination. It is by means of this core principle that the Arkys reappear today, after centuries of retreat in the Secret Vale, away from the eyes of the Islands' Elves. We have no fear of terrors and will demonstrate our strength in the struggles to come. Our works will be wrought with justice and balance."

These were noble words that instilled hope. The Arkylon's tone of voice and gestures expressed his loving nature. Camatael and Myryae felt compelled to bend their knees, to demonstrate their adherence and submission. But before they made any movement, Terela spoke. Though respectful and righteous, her tone was one of firmness.

"The Secret Vale is far away, and each year the mists protecting its location have grown thicker. I bring sour tidings, perhaps the evillest that have been spoken since the Century of

War. Spring was full of many grievous deeds in my homeland. The Elves of Cumberae are weary, for danger is closing in around them. Barbarians have entered our borders to wreak havoc within our realm. Our control of the Islands' Flow is waning, as though the sources of its power are in danger of drying up."

Terela talked with a low voice, and a certain blame was burning in her eye. Her accusatory gaze seemed to contain all the complaints she had not yet expressed in words.
Meanwhile, the Arkys looked down in grief. To clear the air, the Arkyllyo spoke for the first time. Her voice was melodious.

"Cumberae's inherent strength has long remained unspoiled. Your lands were filled with the influence of the deities."
"The forest of Cumberae," Terela explained , "has always been a place with a strong potential for the Islands' Flow, rich as it was in natural sources of energy: the ocean's tide, the strong winds, the plentiful streams and the breath of the woods. Throughout this last century, however, these natural powers have been in decline, and the rate of degeneration has worsened over recent years. My family member Miglor, lore master of House Dol Nos-Loscin, believes the coming of Men to our territories is not the cause of this phenomenon, but rather the consequence. Our control over the Islands' Flow has waned. This made us vulnerable, and the barbarian tribes merely exploited that weakness. As our ability to wield the Islands' Flow declined, their campaigns encroached ever deeper into our woods.
According to Miglor's theory, the college of the Ruby is to blame for this spoilage of the Islands' Flow. He thinks that the high mages of Gwarystan wish to deprive us of our access to the forces of nature around us. As for me, I have felt an even mightier power at work, as if the Greater Gods themselves have been influencing our fate."

There was a silence. At length, the Arkylon spoke again.

"I knew of the Elves of Cumberae's perils, but I had not yet grasped the extent of the despair they felt. Let me appease the trouble in your heart with words of wisdom.

Remember the legends of our mythology... After the genesis of Oron, each Gweïwal received his own realm to rule. After millennia of devastation, the chaos was ended. Zenwon received the sky, Agadeon received the underworld, Narkon received the fiery inner core of Oron, and Uleydon received the seas. Since that time, the Greater Gods have avoided openly influencing the fate of the world, because breaking their vows would mean confronting the entire Assembly of the Gods. None of them would dare risk that."

After his pronouncement, the Arkylon looked directly at Terela, as if searching her mind. The princess of Cumberae endured his gaze with stoicism.

Looking back, Camatael now thought she was the strongest Elvin lady he had met during his youth in Gwarystan. He remembered when Terela was the most celebrated maiden of the court, meant one day to become Norelin's bride. Since then, the daughter of Lord Dol Nos-Loscin had continued to think for others, protect others and sometimes sacrifice herself for others. She would have made a glorious queen.

After a pause, the Arkylon continued.

"It is true that, in our current times, great forces are at work. The fight for the control of the Islands' Flow is an unprecedented conflict. For centuries, the college of the Ruby has exerted its considerable power to undermine the influence of the Islands' deities. The College has undoubtedly eroded the power of the matriarchs. It even weakened that of our own Order, until it finally chased us away. The high mages of the Crimson Tower have concentrated the power of the Flow in their hands, and with that power they built the city of Gwarystan up to its current state of magnificence.

But there was a time when things were different. The Islands' Flow used to circulate freely across the Islands. Created by the Gods and the deities, it could be found mostly in gemstones but also in natural surroundings. Its energy was available to all Elves, in accordance with their inherent abilities. The Gods had designed it so.

The College of the Ruby changed the order of things. First, they requested the Elves of the kingdom pay a tribute in exchange for the protection of the king's rune. This tribute was their own just share of the Islands' Flow. Not content with depriving the Gwarystan Elves of the benefits of Oron's forces, the high mages found a way to distort and imprison those forces, to greatly limit its circulation, to the extent that the very source is now threatening to run dry.

Somehow, the college of the Ruby has recently gotten hold of a very rare material that has the unique property of trapping the Flow. A material that can contain it was previously thought inconceivable. Dark must have been the heart of the alchemist who unveiled that mighty secret...

What you are experiencing in Cumberae is the consequence of this most perilous finding."

The Daughter of the Islands intervened. She thrust her antlers into the air. A deep suffering was in her voice and demeanour.

"For our forefathers, the natural world was given and defined. Elves would enjoy its bounties and endure its hardships. Its rhythms and weather cycles changed according to the mood of the deities.

What we are witnessing now is a first; some Elves, blinded by their pride, are actively shaping the world around them according to their will. They are usurping the role of the Gods. In many regions of the Islands, extreme weather patterns are becoming increasingly common, resulting in more floods and droughts, more frequent forest fires and more disturbance of the ocean. This turmoil of the elements reached a peak earlier this year when a tidal wave destroyed the lower boroughs of Gwarystan."

Myryae decided that the time had come for Llymar to express its own voice.

"The matriarchs saw this fearful future coming. We all knew that there was an obvious choice before us when confronting this threat: turn aside from the Elves of the Islands and defend Llymar's borders alone or stand with Cumberae and submit to the Secret Vale.

We have decided to honour our alliance with House Dol Nos-Loscin and seek the Arkys' protection. Our legacy will depend on the choices we are making now. We are willing to pay tribute to the Secret Vale with our share of the Islands' Flow. May the Arkys use that power for the benefit of all."

The Arkyllyi moved forward and gently took the matriarch's hands.

"Have no fear, Myryae, daughter of Leyen dyl. Forget your grief for a while. You have made the right choice by placing your fate in our holy hands. There are many Elves in the Islands who are hoping for the realm that was promised. Wenti and Hawenti, we all are very different, but also very much alike. The seeds of Llyoriane are always bound to each other, sometimes in allegiance, sometimes in conflict. But our future is not finished and done. Every day, with every choice we make, the river of time runs into a delta of possible tomorrows."

The Daughter of the Islands took over. Her deep voice expressed her concern, but also her higher authority among the matriarchs.

"But our support has one condition...
This we know: it was no common tidal wave which ravaged parts of Gwarystan this spring. The hurricane that struck the northern shores of Nyn Llyvary a few years ago was also deeply unnatural. Eïwal Ffeyn is trying to break free from his bonds. The storm deity has become dangerous and uncontrollable. We fear his wrath and his thirst for revenge. If he was freed, if the pearl whose mighty spell imprisoned the deity of Storms was returned to him, his destructive power could severely wound the Lost Islands. Eïwal Ffeyn's retaliation would be blind and could shock the natural balance of the Archipelago forever. The Storm deity shows no mercy. Do you understand what I am saying?"

There was a silence as all imagined the havoc that Eïwal Ffeyn's return would wreak.

At last, the Daughter of the Islands issued her order, her deep voice flooding the night like a waterfall cascading from a cliff.

"Our Order requests that the matriarchs of Llymar renounce the worship of Eïwal Ffeyn."

Myryae had not been expecting such a demand, which sounded rather like an ultimatum to her ears. The Daughter of the Islands had just touched upon a sensitive issue, relating to the concepts of freedom and rebellion. The teachings of Eïwal Ffeyn were central to the Llewenti; the Storm deity's message and role in the history of the Islands was the source of spiritual controversy between the old faiths, defended by the matriarchs, and the new cults which were promoted by the Secret Vale.

After the first years that followed the creation of their Order, the Arkys had used their wealth to develop the cult of the Llewenti deities; but not all the Islands' divinities had found favour with them. The Arkys' chief achievement had been to promote the faith in Lon the wise, whom they worshiped as the deity of Wisdom. The propagation of his teachings had aroused a sense of belonging to the 'seeds of Llyoriane', those Elves who, regardless of their origins, had searched with a true heart the promised Islands. For the first time since the coming of the High Elves, a genuine sense of community had prevailed. Hawenti and Llewenti could share the same pantheon and live in harmony.
The Arkys had managed to establish a new trust among all the Islands' Elves by rejecting all reference to Eïwal Ffeyn, the mortal enemy of the High Elves.

Myryae stood frozen in front of her new masters. She worried that she did not have the authority to accept the Secret Vale's additional condition, which had not been discussed before. It seemed to Camatael that the envoy of Llymar had no other choice but to agree.

Terela saw Myryae's trouble. She must have been waiting for this moment of tension between the participants. When the princess spoke, she had the air of an Elf with a meticulous plan.

"When my father agreed to the alliance with Llymar and decided to call upon the protection of the Secret Vale, he asked me if I could convene a meeting in which the proposals of all parties could be debated."

Camatael noted Terela's carefully chosen words implicitly reminded those present of the collective need to pursue this alliance. He interpreted from her intervention that Cumberae was ready to bow before the Arkys. The young lord listened to what followed with attention. The princess was, without doubt, planning something. Grieving and brooding over the woes of Cumberae had strengthened her mind. Her eye was clear when she detailed her motives further.

"I deliberately chose to hold this meeting here, in these isolated ruins. An old temple dedicated to Eïwal Lon once stood on this spot. What better location, so full of history and symbolism, to celebrate the sealing of our vows? Would it not be like paying homage to those brave Elves who built it?
A few years ago, I conducted an expedition into the valley of Nargrond to discover the ancient site mentioned several times in the Lonyawelye. I wanted to understand why priests of Eïwal Lon had chosen to build a shrine in this location, during such a dangerous period. Why would servants of the deity of Light choose to erect a place of worship in the valley of Nargrond after its fall? The region had been conquered and sacked by the clan Myortilys, who still controlled it at the time of this temple's construction..."

Nobody could fail to notice the change which had come over Terela. She was now speaking with striking resolve, and there was a strange fire in her eyes. The mere expression on her face conveyed the authority and leadership that had been vested in her on the day of her birth.
Camatael remembered that her mother had been the sister of Meoryne, from the House of Dol Valra. This made Terela no less than Eïwal Lon's first cousin.
The princess, it seemed, always operated with the steadiness of one who never doubts her own authority. Without exactly ordering anyone to come with her, Terela departed from the glade with such determination that all followed her footsteps without question.

In the warm night, the group moved along the path which led back to the compound till the clearing was far behind. The knights of the Secret Vale followed them at a distance, their long spears protecting their backs.

Once inside the temple's boundaries again, Terela stopped in a stony area where a grassy ridge diverted a small stream. Amid the numerous boulders and stones, the Elves could see natural stairs covered in mud and weeds. The base of this staircase led to a small stone-paved area opening onto the ruins of a shrine dedicated to the Llewenti deity of war and hunting.

'Ah,' Camatael thought to himself. 'The temple of Eïwal Lon was built on top of the ruins of several shrines, which had been defiled by the Dark Elves during the sack of Nargrond Valley. It explains the presence of Eïwal Vars' symbols on these broken columns: a spear with an emerald blade, and his animal, the stag.'

As they continued towards the south, the main path joined a basalt staircase which led to another area paved with baked bricks. Parallel to the façade of the ruined Eïwal Vars temple, on the other side of the stone alley, stood what looked like a construction site made of wood and bricks. A container full of rubble stood in front.

Terela then turned towards the heart of the site and entered an underground passage which remained unobstructed. The group followed in silence.
They explored the tunnel, taking in the vastness of the hideout. Flickering fires leaped up and shadows danced across the rock. Towards the bottom of the gallery, a trapdoor had been installed quite recently, and around it strong walls had been built, the stones expertly joined. Terela stopped and explained.

"When I last visited the temple of O Vaha, I directed my master builder and his retinue to clean up the ruins' ground before laying the foundations of our camp. During their work, one of my workers, on breaking the ground with his pickaxe, struck upon something which, from the sound, he judged to be hollow underneath. After calling on another companion to clear away the loose earth with his shovel, they found a large brazen ring fixed to a flat stone, with ancient runes engraved thereon."

Camatael came closer to the princess. The beginning of this tale had stimulated his curiosity. Still looking at the Arkylon as though he were the only character of interest, Terela went on with her story.

"The guards who made the discovery were Ice Elves. Their knowledge being limited to their own language; they could not decipher the powerful protecting glyphs. To their minds, the runes simply signified 'the way to hidden treasures'. They started searching the grounds further, in that same area and around it. Their efforts were interrupted by a powerful blast. An intense light was released. The two Ice Elves were instantly killed. We later discovered their eyes had been burnt out, as if from exposure to an intensely powerful sun.
The incident obviously drew my attention and, upon inspecting the ancient runes, I discovered their association with the scriptures of Eïwal Lon.
I spent several long days pondering how to read the protective writings without triggering the explosives runes. At last, whilst praying to the deity of wisdom, I received an answer. I managed to remove the deadly glyphs."

At this, the beautiful Arkyllyi spoke up, her voice soft.
"You are wise in the ways of Eïwal Lon, Princess Terela. That is no small feat you achieved... Your tale is indeed fascinating."
Indifferent to the compliment, Terela resumed. "After my guards removed the fallen columns and the rubble, I conducted a survey of the grounds, where the foundations of an old courthouse lay buried. At this point, I discovered a hollow sound from a stone and, upon lifting it, I could see the secret subterranean passage. More powerful glyphs protected any access. The legendary runes of House Dol Nargrond covered the tunnel's entrance..."
"It must have prevented you from going any further..." guessed the Arkyllyi.
"Surprisingly, it did not," responded Terela with a smile. "Their power had waned. Someone had dispelled it," she declared.

A silence followed. All were curious to know what happened next. The princess resumed.

"I then ordered the flat stone to be raised. Initially, my guards had difficulty finding any way into the hideout, but they eventually discovered a cavity."

"It must have inflamed their desire to know what lay within?" suggested the Arkyllyo.

Her dry, sarcastic tone of voice betrayed her impatience.

"Indeed, they resolved to explore it. A fearless knight of the Rose attached himself to ropes and was lowered down by his companions. He reached the bottom without impediment and found a perfect arch opening into a vault. Broken iron doors lay strewn about the tunnel. They had to remove them and other structures blocking the way. For several days, my guards worked to pull up other stones to admit more light and air," explained Terela.

"May we ask you what discoveries you made?" inquired the Arkyllyo, now failing to mask her impatience.

"Unfortunately, the main finding was simply unveiling the passage to the Vault..." revealed Terela. "We were not, as it turned out, the first to explore it...
Inside, there was nothing, but a few works of art and jewellery which had been ignored by those who had already penetrated the secret dungeon. But on examining the open keystone which used to block the way to the tunnel, I was surprised to find a well-known rune surrounded by ancient scriptures. I concluded that this dungeon was the Secret Vault of Rowë."

The Arkyvars's stolid demeanour began to disappear. Camatael could see it on his face, even by the torchlight. Terela's earnestness was affecting him. He had perceived depths in her he had not suspected before. Indeed, her manifest sincerity and the sheer steadfastness of her attitude seemed to have made all the Arkys thoughtful.

"You will allow us to be the sole judges of this conclusion," instructed the Arkyvars.
Terela ignored the warlike note in his tone. "Indeed, your knowledge in these matters will be valuable. What I saw was the fallen material structures of a construction that was surely meant to be everlasting. For it was obvious, from everything we found, that this Secret Vault had been plundered long ago.

Intruders, in their impatience to access the dungeon, destroyed much of the original masons' labour, and abandoned it to the ravages of time."

"It is indeed a pity that the wisdom of such workmanship and the beauty of the architecture have been so exposed to destruction and decay. Those architects must have taken great pains to build it," regretted the Arkyllyi.

The Arkyllyo was not so accommodating. "Princess Terela, your faithfulness bespeaks your merit, and we do not doubt you are qualified for the highest responsibilities. We are surprised and disappointed, however, that you have instructed your master builder to carry out further works on this sacred site without referring to our higher authority. You will thus obey our injunction: you must report to us anything and everything you have found, or do find, in the original Vault of Rowë."

"Indeed, I would," Terela replied, quite soberly. "Realising that I had made a discovery of considerable importance, I set about sealing the entrance with care, and all my workers swore an oath of secrecy. The Secret Vault of Rowë is now secure, and everything is ready for our ceremony."

The Arkylon concluded , "May the deities of the Islands bless your work, for the benefit of all seeds of Llyoriane!"

The Arkylon was thus expressing his will to proceed with the ceremony which was the original purpose of their gathering. Terela opened the trap door. Camatael concentrated on the descent.

After going down a wrought iron spiral staircase, the group entered a vault with a stone-paved floor. Myryae and Camatael followed her in turn. The Arkys and their escort closed the march. They found, at the bottom of the subterranean complex, a splendid cave supported by six columns; along the architraves were the different hammers of Yslla smith guild, the emblems of the blacksmiths who forged the Swords of Nargrond Valley. The names of the legendary blades were sculpted in regular form into an altar of pure white marble, rich in ornaments.

Standing amazed in front of the carved representations, Camatael read their names with deep respect, almost with faith: Rymsing, the hope, to the West; opposite was Moramsing, the despair, to the East; then Lynsing, the wisdom, to the South;

facing Orsing, the lust, to the North. The names of Aonya and Aksinya completed the list, written in two semi circles, like harmony balancing chaos.

The retinue of the Arkys came into the sanctuary with the solemnity of a royal procession entering a burial place.

As it still stood, the place was a large circular cave with a central crypt, surrounded by six radiating steps. A wonderful marble covering supported by columns stood over in its centre and covered the altar. The architect had marvellously decorated it with gold and gems. He had designed a magnificent mural with golden shields and apples, round and jewelled.

The Arkys and the envoys positioned themselves on the steps of the crypt. A pedestal was carried in procession to the central altar by the knights of the Secret Vale, who held it aloft on their heads.

The Arkylon raised his hands. As he did so, his long golden robes opened, and Camatael caught a glimpse of a cylindrical box attached to his belt. The young lord shivered as he recognized the Testament of Rowë.

The Arkylon opened the ceremony with a ritual prayer to the deity of Wisdom:

"Lon went down into the Mines of Oryusk. The Dark Elves captured him, strung him out upon a rock. On the sixth day, Lon was pierced with an arrow of fire. Lon returned to the light of Ö, leaving us his wisdom as his legacy."

Terela chanted the following verses:

These are the words of the Lonyawelye.
These are the words written after his death.

It was then Myryae who concluded the prayer:

Elves shall learn from the wise priests of light, they shall learn from the Seers of the Sun. For this inheritance we give thanks to Lon, who sacrificed himself to bequeath it unto us. In death, he gained that sacred wisdom known only to the dead.

The Arkylon then ordered that an adamant pedestal be unveiled, at which point the herald of the Secret Vale's knights sought entry into the crypt. The Arkylon ordered him to be admitted, and the herald spoke as he set up the artefact in front of his lord:

Almighty deities of the Islands, Protectors of the seeds of Llyoriane. Keep us faithful to our vows; never may we waver, nor be cast down.

The Arkylon stood and beckoned the assembled Elves to form a circle around him at the altar. He urged the ceremony's participants to proclaim their vows and demonstrate the ties that bind them to the seeds of Llyoriane's fate.

On the eastern side, towards the rising sun, stood the Arkyllyi. On the south side was the Arkyllya and on the west, the Arkyllyo. On the north side the Arkyvars held the standard of Llyoriane in his hands. The envoys of Llymar and Cumberae positioned themselves in between the Arkys to complete the circle, the symbol of Ö.

"Arise, worthy Elves, the Secret Vale has long witnessed the burden of your trials, and we are ready to grant your request in this instant."

Myryae and Terela then advanced towards the pedestal and were addressed by the Arkylon.

"Noble envoys of Llymar and Cumberae, you have presented yourselves to be named 'Followers of the Secret Vale'. The Arkys have deigned to confer that honour upon you. You shall dwell together in unity, for the good of the seeds of Llyoriane."

Then, the story of Eïwal Lon was recounted. They heard how his wisdom was passed to the Elves of the Islands. Myryae and Terela moved inside the crypt and stood to form the two remaining sides of a triangle. Two knights of the Secret Vale approached with rods made of gold. Both were adorned with the eight gemstones of the Greater Gods, positioned according to the divine hierarchy: Sapphire, Amethyst, Aquamarine, Ruby, Diamond, Moonstone, Emerald and Pearl.

The knights were carrying unsheathed, two-handed swords on their backs. They sank to one knee and held the rods horizontally above their heads.

Myryae and Terela then advanced slowly, each taking a golden rod in their right hand. Following a ritual, they must have been taught in advance, they raised the rods slowly and simultaneously above their heads, before quickly bringing them down in a sweeping blow towards the pedestal. The rods did not break when they struck the adamant. Instead, their gold seemed to stick to the pedestal. The shock was so violent that the two envoys had to drop to one knee.

The earth seemed to quake, and the shrine trembled at its base. But the ceremony continued as the force of the Islands' Flow was transferred to the pedestal. The Arkylon placed his hands upon the golden rods and declared.

> *Behold, Llymar and Cumberae dwell together in unity. The luminous ointment is upon their heads and on their garments.*
> *We give you the Sceptre of Lon, symbol of your right to reside within the divine light.*
> *May these rods consecrate your homage to the Secret Vale and be sceptres of righteousness!*
> *May they rise out of our forests and smite the enemies of Llyoriane's seeds!*

Myryae and Terela replied in unison.

> *A star issued forth from heaven*
> *It has split the mountain asunder*
> *We shall know the way by its light*
> *For a light has come to the Elves*
> *That light is the Seeker of Wisdom*
> *And he shall raise up his sceptre*
> *And destroy the sons of our enemies!*

The Arkylon then addressed the Arkyvars.

"Herald of Vars, may you return to the Islands! You have permission to wage war. You have permission to destroy the enemies of Elves.

Now it is time for you to appoint the Defender of Llyoriane's seeds, the chief who will command the armies of Llymar and Cumberae, who will obey the Arkys' commands."

"I have chosen the Defender for his valour and his noble birth," began the Arkyvars. "I appoint the heir of the House of the White Unicorn for he willingly pledged to lead the ships of Llymar against the barbarians. He deserves our trust and support."

He was looking directly at Camatael.

The young lord was seized with shock. Nevertheless, as if bewitched by the honour bestowed upon him, he approached and knelt, as a token of his acceptance.

"I hereby declare you Defender of Llyoriane's seeds," the Arkyvars pronounced solemnly. "Rise, Camatael of House Dol Lewin. I now arm you with this sacred sword; it shall mark you out among the lords and ladies of the Elves. This is Rymsing, the bringer of hope, the same blade that Rowë forged with the blacksmiths of Nargrond Valley. The legendary glaive of the Dyoreni will now be by your side.

Take it, and let it remain in its scabbard until it is drawn to fight for justice. This sword is yours, until that day comes when the army of Llymar have brought freedom to the Elves of Cumberae and delivered them from oppression."

The Arkylon insisted , "You must lead the fleet of Llymar to Nyn Llyandy before the season of Eïwele Llyo comes. What is your purpose?"

Camatael replied with that rare kind of fieriness that reveals so much of a noble Elf's soul.

"To rescue Cumberae. And I will achieve that purpose. For none in these Islands could serve the seeds of Llyoriane with truer heart than the White Unicorn. I will see that the House of Dol Lewin restore its fame."

The words of the young lord, last of his lineage, somewhat faltered towards the end of his reply. There was something pleading in his words. They touched the Arkylon, who lowered his voice before continuing.

"Then go to it, for it is also the Secret Vale's will. Who are your protectors?"

"My Protector is Lon the Wise. But my prayers also go to the deities of the Islands, to Vars the fighter and the hunter, to Llyi the beauty of Spring, to Llya the profusion of Summer and to Llyo the veil of Winter."

Then the Arkylon, in accordance with the ritual of his Order, knelt and laid the rune in his hand upon Camatael's chest as a sign of blessing. He made oath that the Secret Vale's power would follow him until his task was fulfilled. The other Arkys followed in turn, each pledging their oath.

A moment later, a great noise erupted within the Vault of Rowë, as all the knights of the Secret Vale cheered. The entire retinue of proud fighters had been quietly waiting to see this rare ceremony completed, packed inside the small underground hall.

Camatael could feel their support, and it was having a profound affect upon him. He knew in that moment that his honour and esteem had never been higher. The lord of the House of Dol Lewin experienced the thrill of true power flowing through his veins. He felt a great strength, which would allow him to perform his new role with the utmost dedication and passion and lift the hopes and spirits of those Elves who would follow him. He had known for some years that safeguarding the Lost Islands was his one true calling. He now felt confident he would play his part.

CHAPTER 5: Alton

2716, Season of Eïwele Llya, 66th day, Nargrond Valley, temple of O Vaha, before dawn

All the lanterns throughout the temple were extinguished in unison. Once the unseen power had exerted its influence, all became dark and still. The units of Cumberae and Llymar then crept stealthily along the temple's alleys and out through a gap in the western wall. They would disappear into the surrounding woods before daylight to avoid being seen.
It was already warm; the air was thick with the fumes from Mount Oryusk. A noxious stench pervaded the air.

A long column of a hundred Elves were heading north-west into the woods. Scouts were leading the way, with archers close on their heels. The envoys and ambassadors remained safely in the middle, each protected by their guards. The knights of the Two-Winged Lions closed the march, four of them carrying Alton Dol Nos-Loscin's empty sedan chair on their shoulders. Progress was difficult through the wild vegetation of these isolated parts, but all were anxious to travel swiftly. They had received their summons; the Pact Gathering would take place tomorrow.

They wished to get as far away as possible from the king's forces while it was still dark. The units of Cumberae and Llymar knew a royal embassy had been established nearby, in the ruins of

Ystanargrond, and they did not want royal troops on their trail. It seemed, at least, they had so far kept their presence in the valley unnoticed. But Myryae's warning had been firm.

"Every black bird and every vulture you see circling above could be a druid spy. Have no illusions: The priests of Eïwele Llya will be watching all those heading to the Pact Gathering very closely."

"There are other ways information can be obtained," Alton had also insisted. "Everything around us is a threat."

The column marched without stopping for an hour. They had only limited supplies so were progressing efficiently, keeping for the most part to the cover of the trees. Whenever they were forced to cross open meadows, the column would stretch outwards and break into a run, like a herd of deer fleeing predators.

A new wind swept away all last traces of the ash clouds, which retreated west towards the volcano.

Before long, Alton was already showing signs of fatigue. His pace was slow and laboured. The young Dol, at over seven foot, was even taller than most High Elves. He had pale skin and dark hair, and his eyes differed in colour: the right was blue while the left was green. His long, pointed ears were a hallmark of his profile.

Alton wore brightly coloured, elaborately trimmed robes of fine silk. These majestic clothes were making his progress difficult. For reasons unknown, the elegant Elf had opted for stylish, ceremonial garments over more practical traveller's clothes. Only his long ivory staff, beautifully carved at the top into two winged lions, seemed to be of any assistance.

Since leaving the ancient shrine's ruins, Alton had walked alongside the warlord of Tios Halabron, an Elf he had only just met, but whom he had heard much about. Alton was explaining the final leg of their journey to Mynar dyl in some detail. The young Dol knew the Nargrond Valley well from previous expeditions. Wishing to make his point clear, he stopped and started drawing lines in the soil with his staff.

"The upper valley of the Sian Senky is made up of deep gorges, where cliffs and steep banks border the fast-flowing water. Dams built by the High Elves at the time of Rowë Dol Nargrond constrict its flow at several intervals, forming wide lakes. Below the flanks of Mount Oryusk, the valley then widens to contain, on either side of the river, fertile meadows and orchards. Further east, but before the walls of Ystanargrond, lies a wood. It is called the grove of Llya. This is where the Pact Gathering will take place," he explained.

As he spoke, Alton winced and shifted his weight, distracted by a pain in his foot. By the time he had finished his explanation, he was sitting on the ground.

Since their departure earlier that night, his condition had steadily worsened. Alton was continually drinking plant decoctions and bitter potions, but these elixirs did not seem to be easing his pain. He saluted Mynar dyl and declared that he needed to withdraw into his sedan chair. The merchant Aertelyr shot him a knowing glance before helping him to his feet.

Alton and Aertelyr stood for a moment as the march flowed past them. They soon saw the two envoys of Cumberae and Llymar approaching. The princess and the matriarch were engaged in a lively conversation.

Seeing that Alton was hanging back, Terela cut short her heartfelt plea before she reached him. Whatever they were debating, she did not share the same views as the matriarch. She seized this opportunity as a reason to change subject.

"My cousin, you seem to be limping again," she noted.

"I am indeed. The pain comes on so suddenly. I'm suffering with a nasty type of inflammation where the pain keeps hitting in waves. I think the blood is clotting in my tendons; it feels like a demon is eating my foot. I'm afraid it's quite serious, and soon I will no longer be able to walk," the impaired Elf confided, whilst wiping the sweat from his dripping brow.

"Is there anything I can do to relieve this suffering?"

"Oh, no! One might as well try to raise waves in a windless sea. Nobody should touch my injury. It would be too painful."

"This is sad news and I am sorry to hear it. Let Master Aertelyr escort you back to your sedan chair. Our sincere wishes for your speedy recovery go with you, cousin Alton. The Pact Gathering is tomorrow and we need you in a state of good health," Terela reminded him, before adding with a mysterious tone , "Perhaps you can put your period of recovery to good use. We are in dire need of your advice."

"I know what it is you expect. I will not disappoint you," Alton promised.

The princess and the matriarch moved on, closely followed by their guards. Alton and Aertelyr stood to one side of the march. Elvin fighters of the two groups went past them, setting off down the slope with as much haste as the steep terrain allowed. Their long cloaks were billowing in the wind, revealing the long swords and daggers hanging at their belts. Short bows were in their hands and quivers full of arrows were at their backs. In the darkness, members of the two clans could only be differentiated by their armour: for the clan Llyvary fighters, thin chain mail and oval shields emblazoned with the white swan; for the Ice Elves of Cumberae, heavier scale armour and plumed helmets.

Aertelyr beckoned with a quick, subtle flick of his hand. Alton guessed that the navigator wanted to speak to him in private, so he muttered a few strange, indecipherable words, and a sharp hissing sound emanated from his lips.
Instantly, the two Elves were cut off from the noises of the outside world, as if both had suddenly become deaf. But they could listen and speak to one another, confident in the knowledge they would not be overheard.

"What is it you want to tell me?" Alton asked. His tone, so often indifferent and aloof, now expressed undisguised concern.

Aertelyr's answer was direct. "It happened last night."

"You mean the ceremony has already taken place?"

"Yes. The Arkys met in secret with the envoys of Llymar and Cumberae. The celebration of vows was completed, and our principality is now vassal to a new liege. Terela has given up Cumberae to the Arkys."

"Is that so? How could this escape my attention?"

"You were not told, nor was Mynar dyl, whereas Matriarch Myryae and Lord Camatael took part in the ceremony alongside Terela."

"How disappointing!"

"I have discovered that the Arkys wield considerable power. If they do not wish someone to attend their secret meetings, they can ensure his absence."

"Your star must have risen high in the sky! Why would you be invited to such a holy moment when I was not?"

Alton's gaze showed pride. He was an arrogant character with high self-esteem, and haughtily viewed all others as being beneath him.

"No winged horse has ever paid me a visit, noble Dol. I attended without invitation, without being detected."

"I am impressed you managed to elude these mighty guests at their special celebration. You are no ordinary Elf, Master Aertelyr!"

"You pay generously for my skills, noble Dol."

"Now tell me precisely what you saw!"

The guild master of the Breymounarty began to relate what he had witnessed. Of the hundred Elves in the camp that night, only he had been unaffected by the spell that impaired all others. His story was short but detailed. He recounted the events in his usual concise style, sticking to the facts and avoiding dramatic embellishment.

After detailing the number and identity of all the ceremony's participants, Aertelyr's factual account ended with the Arkys and their guests disappearing into the tunnel to Rowë's vault. What Aertelyr said next was pure conjecture: he had felt the passage to the Secret Vault trembling and guessed that the princess and the matriarch had handed over their control of the Flow to the Arkys.

Alton felt the need to sit down, such was his emotion at this revelation.

"So, the commitment has been sealed: both Cumberae and Llymar acknowledge the Secret Vale as their liege!

At last, the Arkys have understood how seriously the world of Elves is under threat: from the factions of Men but also from the king of Gwarystan. It is the first time in history that the Secret Vale has taken a side. Our future suddenly looks less gloomy."

Alton was evidently relieved at the news. It was to his surprise, therefore, when Aertelyr contradicted him with a severe tone.

"The events I witnessed mean nothing of the sort. Can you not see the true purpose of this secret meeting? Your naivety surprises me."

"Is it naïve to watch with delight as a flower bud begins to open?" Alton replied with false candour, and with a quick gesture of the hand the elegant Elf picked a snow-white rose from the wild hedges lining the path.

"You should take these developments seriously, noble Dol," insisted Aertelyr. "That night marked the rise of a new elite class of priests. They have always considered themselves to be wiser than the noblest Elves. The Arkys are merely pretending to protect us from the threat of Men. Their true ambition is to rule the Islands themselves, and it is not hard to imagine how. Llymar and Cumberae will now be required to support the Secret Vale with tributes. For the time being, it is limited to our share of the Islands' Flow, but it will quickly extend to other types of taxes: gold, jewels..."

"Ah, ah!" Alton exclaimed. "You always pay the keenest attention when gold is brought into the equation."

"Gold is everything!" the guild master of the Breymounarty cried, as if he were making a heartfelt appeal.
Alton raised an eyebrow in disgust. "I thought that Ice Elves had cold hearts," he said , "and now I know they do."

The expression on his delicate face suggested he could not disagree more with his master spy.

"Your obsession with riches, Master Aertelyr, is unhealthy. Why not cure yourself of this disease, and donate to the poor Elves of Cumberae after the devastation they have suffered?"
Aertelyr laughed at that. "I did not know you shared your noble cousin's generosity!"

Alton looked offended. "Do not question my commitment to Terela! May the Gods strike me down if I am not her loyal servant and fervent admirer. So beautiful is the princess, I would kiss her feet if only to make her smile..." and to illustrate his lewder meaning, Alton stuck out his tongue obscenely.

Aertelyr smiled a sly grin at this. He came to his point.

"I know Terela did not support this diplomatic initiative in the first place. It must have been the prince, her father, who convinced her to kneel before the Arkys in the end."

"Well, what other choice did he have after this summer's upheavals? A wise daughter always listens to her father," said Alton with a moralizing tone.

"The princess' first instinct was very different, and I agreed with her then. Let me warn you against this Arkylon and his 'holy' companions. Their power is considerable, for they influence the faith of many Elves across the Islands.
My own belief is that they created the cult of Lon out of thin air. They themselves dreamt up this would-be demigod... this so-called 'deity of wisdom'. How convenient it was all his sayings were collected in that supposedly sacred book! They are the only conduits, the only interpreters, the only gatekeepers of those divine teachings. The truth is this: Lon is nothing more than a dead Elf."

Alton brought his hands to his head, as if in peril.

"Oh! My ears are ringing... These are blasphemous words. Your unholy fables remind me of those propagated by the Morawenti when they were led by their chief, the fondly remembered Saeröl. If memory serves, that great artist ended his career at the bottom of Gwarystan Rock...
Beware, Master Aertelyr, of what you are saying! The legacy of Lon the Wise deserves better. I suggest you take up the 'Lonyawelye' again. It is full of good advice. One passage springs to mind at this moment;
    'The original source of all vices is greed. It has an inordinate appetite for suffering.'
You should think upon those words. Who knows? It might benefit you."

Aertelyr was unimpressed by this warning. He pursued his rhetoric with the same conviction.

"The Arkys developed a mythology that differs from the old Llewenti clans, and they claim to enlighten their followers with new truths. The Elves of the Islands were relieved of the 'unworthy' Myos and Ffeyn, vile deities of chaos, incompatible with the Hawenti values. They were given the wise Lon in exchange.

I wonder if the real Lon, who walked alongside Rowë in the valley of Nargrond, even vaguely resembled the divine Eïwal Lon invented by the Arkys. I wonder if he would even recognize his 'teachings' we now live by. I sincerely doubt it.

His sayings were only gathered long after he disappeared. Any witnesses who could have verified them were already buried beneath the ruins of Yslla and Ystanargrond.

If these witnesses could speak, their story would be quite different. The smiths of Yslla never considered their young companion Lon to be a Demigod. They simply called him Lon Dol Valra, took him under their wing and taught him most of what he knew. Why?

Because Lon was simply the son of Meoryne Dol Valra. The fact that his father was unknown is not proof of his own divine essence.

Stitching together disparate fragments of Llewenti superstition, the Arkys invented a new doctrine with its own canon of myths. Its message was unique: that all of us, High and Free Elves alike, are the seeds of Llyoriane, and the promised Islands are our refuge... this is a belief that was deliberately designed to resonate with the greatest possible number of the Archipelago's Elves.

The Arkys' triumph was simply to adapt the old Llewenti beliefs and make them compatible with Hawenti morality. They created a religion for all Elves, regardless of their origin. Their Secret Vale is the imaginary temple towards which all weak, gullible Elves can turn to address their prayers."

For the most part, Aertelyr would only ever discuss business with Alton; indeed, this was the first time Alton had heard him even mention religious matters. The firm conviction Aertelyr was now demonstrating proved that there was more to the guild master of the Breymounarty than first met the eye.

All the same, Alton was growing impatient. The truth was that this conversation, if overheard, could seriously damage him. When he next spoke, it was no longer the habitual babbling of a disillusioned high-born Elf, but the commanding tone of a Dol Nos-Loscin scion.

"I will not hear one word more of these theories. Is that clear?" Aertelyr nodded, but Alton's irritation got the better of him. "In any case, why should we care?" he snapped.

"The answer to that seems obvious to me," replied Aertelyr, unmoved.

"Continue."

"The Arkys' motive is power... Their means are the spiritual force of the Islands' cults...

Noble Dol, the only thing Terela has secured by kneeling before the Secret Vale is more power for the Arkys themselves. Hidden out of harm's way, the Arkys devote all their time to spiritual pursuits and other useless activities. That is all they do. That is all they have ever done. I once read the logbook of a famed navigator from clan Myortilys. This sailor claimed to have entered the Secret Vale and escaped alive."

Alton raised his eyebrows and blinked. "The delirious scribblings of a pathological liar! No common Elf has ever penetrated the Secret Vale and returned. Only the Dyoreni knights have ever been granted that privilege, and they say their memory is altered thereafter. I remember Dyoren the Seventh telling me how, once he had left the Vale, he had been overwhelmed with a strange amnesia and disorientation, so that he could never have found his way back if he tried."

"I do not wish to challenge your core beliefs, noble Dol," conceded Aertelyr, his words like honey. "I know how important it is for you to believe in a higher power."

"I appreciate your sensitivity, master navigator! If only you were this sensitive more often. How painful it is, to be forever bowing before the prince and my cousin! The least I expect by way of compensation is for my subordinates to flatter me in turn. I am, after all, a Dol Nos-Loscin, am I not? Now get to the end of your entertaining story."

"I happen to know this clan Myortilys navigator quite well. I can assure you, he is not one to take accusations of falsehood lightly."

"Oh dear, Master Aertelyr, your Dark Elf fishmonger will have me quaking in my boots…"

The guild master of the Breymounarty remained stolid despite Alton's mockery.

"This sailor," he asserted , "gives us an account quite different from the legends we have come to believe. He reported how the Arkylon rules despotically over the Secret Vale. In his magnificent hall that was built to shelter the tomb of Queen Llyoriane, he feasts without respite. The sixty-six knights of the Secret Vale are his sons and daughters by his couplings with the high priestesses. He chose three concubines, so that there would always be one left over to satisfy him."

Alton stifled a laugh. "I must stop you here, Master Aertelyr. I will no longer take you seriously if you continue to credit such nonsense."

Undeterred by Alton's warning, Aertelyr went on. "Who can tell whether these stories are true or false? Either way, I sense the Arkylon's growing ambition: to be a great lord of Elves, ruling with an iron fist; to be a priest-king, maintaining the supremacy of his order in the name of righteousness; and to be a warlord, willing to sacrifice the lives of his followers in their thousands to defend what he calls truth, and what I call fanaticism."

"Frightening indeed! I think I understand what you are getting at… that our new alliance with the Secret Vale will not be good for the Breymounarty's business," concluded Alton.

This conversation was proving tiring. Alton turned away from Aertelyr, and the sounds of the outside world once again flooded his consciousness.

More than ever, Alton felt his sedan chair calling to him.

He waited for the four knights carrying his personal litter to catch up with him. This sedan chair was more of a portable room, containing a large couch upon which the elegant ambassador could stretch out and rest. It was enclosed by curtains, protecting him from the elements and from the unwanted view of passers-by.

Alton enjoyed the privileges his higher rank procured. Admittedly, he could not claim to belong to a royal Dor household, but nevertheless he felt proud to be a member of the most influential of all Hawenti noble houses: the Dol Nos-Loscin. As the four strongest Elves of his retinue lowered his sedan chair to the ground, Alton issued a stern warning.

"You must be wary, my valiant knights of the Two-Winged Lions. We are walking the paths of the Nargrond Valley at night... a most dangerous place, haunted by the phantoms of our bloody history. Be mindful of your surroundings while I rest," the elegant Elf demanded with his natural authority, knowing his commands would be strictly obeyed.

★★

Same day, Nargrond Valley, Ystanargrond, dawn

It was just before sunrise in Ystanargrond. The moon still shone with a splendid glow over the ruins of the Nargrond Valley's once-great fortress.

The former capital city of Lord Rowë had been built in the westernmost part of the valley, near the slopes of Mount Oryusk. It stood on a spur formed by a lava flow, facing north to the mouth of the Sian Senky. These ruins had suffered from further seismic events after being devastated during the battles between Elvin factions. Various layers of sediment now topped the lava which lay below the city. These layers had been created over the years by large landslides triggered by extended rainfall. Along with many Elvin settlements in the surrounding area, the ancient city was buried under a dozen feet of volcanic ash, carried from the erupting Mount Oryusk by wind from the Sea of Isyl. This land used to be home to sweet-smelling gardens and bounteous orchards, fair houses and tall towers, suspension bridges and paved streets, all the makings of the High Elves who lived there. All that remained now, however, was a faint echo of this past magnificence, like a dream one struggles to remember upon waking. The Elves had long abandoned this place, and the city had been conquered by ashes.

But on that summer's night, a new atmosphere reigned in this usually desolate place. An army of Elves and Men had entered the ruins of Ystanargrond. For a few days now, they had occupied its devastated walls. Servants had toiled tirelessly to erect tents for the troops. Flamboyant banners were billowing out from the top of high poles, as if to pay tribute to the beauty of the starry sky. The soldiers of the king's army were resting, and all was quiet.

Most were Hawenti. There were also some Llewenti, and fewer still Men of the West. All were on their last legs. After the long, forced marches they had endured, their bodies ached with exhaustion and they could barely keep their eyes open.

Every province of the kingdom had sent its representatives. The Dor royal households and the Dol noble houses had come from the farthest corners of the Islands. All, without exception, had been conveyed to the Pact Gathering. Each city had sent its own units. But the druids had restricted each group to fifty guards, the same rule that had been applied to all other participants.

The camp also sheltered the high mages of the Ruby College. In total, more than seven hundred Elves and Men formed the royal contingent. It could have almost been an invading army; such was its might.

It was organised into elite units constituting the core force of each household. High-Elf forces were made up of cavalry commanded by knights and heavy infantry. Long swords and heavy spears were their favoured weapons, and scale armour or plate mail protected the tall, robust Hawenti fighters. The smaller-sized Llewenti filled the ranks of the lighter archers' units.

There were no priests of the Islands' Cults in the royal army. Most of these Elves worshipped neither Gods nor deities, spurning the teachings of all cults, leaving such exaltation to others. The High Elves of Norelin's kingdom only trusted in their own wisdom and generally abhorred the tyrannous side of the Gods' teachings.

Sentries had been positioned at regular interval on the parapet walls. They were surveying their surroundings with constant scrutiny. The tension was palpable. Though this army concentrated many battle-hardened units, it had established its camp behind the walls of Ystanargrond, as though it feared any proximity to the slopes of Mount Oryusk. Dark stories circulated among the soldiers, rumours of mysterious disappearances, of unknown witchcraft and of hidden threats.

*

Outside the royal camp's boundaries, the silhouette of a Llewenti maid was slowly progressing along the edge of a stream. She was looking for rock fish, knowing that, in the early morning, they would be seeking the shelter of stones. The type of fish she was after was called Tyaying[32] because of their small size. They were prized by Elves for their energising properties. To be successful catching these elusive creatures, a spear-fisher had

---

32 Tyaying: 'Small rockfish' in lingua Llewenti.

to be quick and agile. The early dawn was the perfect time to fish for Tyaying; any later, and the fisher's shadow would scare them away.
That morning, the maid was finding it impossible to catch them, so great was their speed and vigilance.

"Damn you!" she cursed. "Cirlaene will not be pleased if I come back empty-handed."

Disappointed and anxious, she turned her attention towards the plants growing in the wet soil nearby. Her mentor had taught her all about medicinal herbs and the art of healing, thanks to which she now earned her living, preparing remedies for her master, a powerful high mage of the Ruby College.
Beneath the trees along the small riverbank, she noticed footprints. Even though they were partly covered by the long, fragrant grass, she could tell these tracks were unusual.

'How strange!' the maid thought as she looked to the heavens. 'What animal these belonged to, I cannot tell.'

Turning her attention back to the task at hand, she wandered further from the camp along a small stream that ran down the nearby vale.
A screeching noise suddenly filled her ears. Some kind of flying creature had brushed past the back of her head. The sheer shock knocked her off-balance and sent her toppling into the stream.

When she stood up in the water moments later, she found herself facing a Dryad. The tree nymph was standing on the bank beneath the green willows.
The unsettling creature was shaped not unlike an Elvin female, but with tiny wings dancing like shadows at her back. Her face seemed to be constantly changing: one moment she would appear young, the next very old, her features apparently morphing at will.
The Dryad offered to help the Elf. When the maid heard her voice, she felt more confident. The Llewenti considered forest spirits to be friendly creatures, protégées of the Mother of the Islands.

After the shock had worn off, the maid allowed the Dryad to join her herb-picking, and they both set off swimming slowly down the stream. In truth, more time was spent splashing each other and playing silly games than collecting medicinal herbs.

The sun, at that early hour of morning, began to peer through the Nargrond Valley from the east, skimming its beam along the plane of the horizon.

The first rays now pierced the trees' canopy. The sky became red. The maid looked at the stones in the stream which had become red too. A strange light seemed to be emanating from the surface of the water around her. She glanced back at her playmate. The vivid sunlight dispelled the Dryad's shape-shifting magic.

'Aye! It's an uncanny place' the maid thought, looking around with an almost fearful expression in her usually bold grey eyes.

The Dryad's true nature was soon revealed as the illusions it had woven began to subside.

The creature now appeared like a grotesque, hellish variant of an Elf, with wings, claws and fangs that left no doubt as to its fiendish origin. Its demonic gaze expressed power and cunning. The maid was struck with panic. She stood still in the water, frozen by terror. Her mind was racing. Like a waking nightmare, she was facing a malicious, otherworldly creature, a demon that surged from the most terrorizing tales of her childhood. Legend had it these Fiends were depraved beings who, after seducing their victims, shape-shifted, and raped them.

She was suddenly blinded by an unnatural darkness. She scrambled up the bank and prepared to defend herself, but an injunction uttered by the creature impeded any further movement.

"Voz razkodur !"

The maid hesitated for a moment, not knowing what she could do, but already the winged creature was on her. It knocked her down, then tied her hands with a thin rope. Overwhelmed with terror, the maid struggled valiantly, but the superior strength of her attacker deprived her of any hope. She was dragged unceremoniously along the banks of the stream. Her terrorized face, dripping and swollen, looked up at her aggressor in horror. The two reached a thick bush, a tangle of thickets and brambles, forming what looked like an impassable barrier. But soon the winged creature had removed the branches that masked the beginning of a path. Even an Elf skilled in the ways of the woods could not have detected this hidden opening. The narrow track went down a hundred feet through the woods before reaching a grove of trees which surrounded a deep chasm.

The Fiend quickly pulled out long ropes that had been hidden in the foliage of the trees, binding its victim further. Firmly tied to the trunks, the ropes facilitated a quick retreat into the chasm. Their descent began, the creature hauling her down like captured prey. Fifty feet below, an underground river bathed the bottom of the chasm, beyond which was only darkness. The Fiend took out a torch, carefully stored in the folds of the rock wall and well protected from the water. It uttered a single incantation and the wooden stick was lit. The sound of the river drowned out the crackling of the torch.

The underground torrent plunged before them towards a large cave in a tumult of bubbling waters. The creature turned its torch towards an opening in the wall a few feet above them. They continued through a narrow tunnel, carved in stone and covered with soot. Smells of smoke reached them. The heat became more intense. More than three hundred paces were thus covered, then the passage widened and led to a vast cavern. The maid could not help but utter an exclamation of terror.

"Eïwal Vars! Save me!" she implored.

In front of them lay a vast hall, more than four hundred feet deep, a hundred feet wide, and whose roof rose in places to the height of a pine tree. The young Elf's eye was drawn by the construction at its centre, an inverted pyramid facing the bowels of the earth. Its tip pointed downwards into a large well of molten lava. Large braziers were arranged at regular intervals on the steps of the pyramid. The light they provided was reflected upon the cave's roof and illuminated the whole cavern.

The desperate Elf understood she was inside an unholy place of worship dedicated to the cult of Gweïwal Narkon, the Greater God of Fire, Father of Dragons and Demons.

The winged creature dragged her down the stairs by her hair. Once at the bottom, it tore the beautiful silk of her robes to shreds. Like an evil spirit of lust, the Fiend seized the maid, its own aggressive nakedness now openly displayed.

It attacked her with brutal force, overpowering her futile defences. Soon it raped the young Elf before howling a hellish cry.

In an instant, the Fiend's carnal body disappeared. A fiery dark smoke dissipated gradually into the victim, penetrating her mouth and nostrils.

After a time, the maid realized she was still alive. Though her body had been severely bruised and the pain in her belly was almost unbearable, she managed to stand up and started retracing her steps. A moment later, she fainted and fell to the ground.

*

When the maid awoke, she felt powerless to speak, like an Elf who awakes from an indescribable dream. She knew what had happened but could not speak it.

Around her, the lively, cold waters of the stream surged along the stones of its bed, and the willows swayed above. Everything was the same as before.

But she sensed something changing within her. Her sense of self had somehow expanded, strengthened; she felt capable of shaking the heavens and moving the earth, like a great warrior with a mystic sword. The maid had always been told to keep quiet. She was forever cooking for her master, washing the dishes, making his bed, cleaning his quarters, tending to his garden, all without a word of gratitude. She had not even begun to learn the art of dancing, to which she wanted to dedicate her life. The years passed, and she felt angry about her lot.

"If Cirlaene stands in my way, I'll cut her down. She has never rewarded my efforts!

If the master tries to impede me, I'll get rid of him too. I hate the filthy looks that eunuch gives me!" she proclaimed.

The young Elf glanced keenly ahead to the distant point which marked the entrance to the army camp. Already, in the first rays of sun, a low hill could be seen, dotted with the ancient ruins of House Dol Nargrond's mansions. Above them shone the brazen roof of the Ruby College's great tent, which capped the entrenched camp, a gleaming dot against the pale morning sky. The maid walked back towards the fortress' ruins and went directly to the two guards who were positioned at the west gate. Their long lances and the swooping griffon on their shields denoted their allegiance to the House of Dol Ogalen. The taller sentry asked her where she was coming from.

"From the small vale where the river runs," she replied.
"Your robes are wet and dirty," the smaller sentry noted.
"I had to swim in the stream."
"You know it is prohibited to go that far?" asked the taller sentry.
"I do," she admitted bluntly, without any sense of guilt.

Neither of the two guards could shake off the strange impression this early encounter left upon them. It was as if some miasma had risen from the dank trenches of the vale and passed into their blood. Finally, the taller sentry recovered and addressed the maid again.

"When did you leave camp?" He was wondering if the young Elf would continue with her brusque answers.
"An hour before dawn. I had tasks to complete for my master. He is one of the high mages," and the maid looked the guard in the eye.

The smaller sentry tried to intervene but was rebuked by his companion, who was visibly unhappy with the maid's discourteous responses.

"Do not wander outside of the camp again or I shall give you three blows with a stick!" he threatened.
"But for now, you are forgiven. Get moving," concluded the smaller sentry.

Since the maid had referred to a member of the Ruby College, he thought it best to err on the side of caution.

For a moment, it seemed as if the sound of the sentry's voice had not reached the maid's ear. She tipped her head forwards, like moving her ear closer to the source of the sound. The two sentries did not understand this odd movement but chose to let her go.

They remained silent and contemplative. They were both preoccupied with the same thought.

A moment later, the young Llewenti was walking through the camp's alleys. Entering this maze was easy enough but finding her way among the many tents and carts required a keen eye. With what looked like sheer indolence, the maid ignored the strange glances of the waking soldiers as she passed them by. She was barely covered by her torn, filthy dress, and this deliberate negligence shocked their sensibilities.

The High Elves sought order and design in all facets of life. The rule of all Hawenti organisations, from the greatest realm to the smallest guild, was extremely hierarchical. The College of the Ruby was no exception. Their need for the strictest order was evidenced by the way they had organised their encampment. Four larger red tents framed the main edifice. Eight other smaller ones formed a second square around it.

The maid was moving towards the far western corner of that symmetrical layout when a Man with dark hair and blue eyes caught her by the arm.

"Why are you not wearing your ceremonial robes? The sun is already high in the sky. You are late, marauding Elf," questioned the Westerner.

"I answer to my master alone," the maid responded defiantly, and she glanced away towards the red tent standing but a dozen yards away.

The young Elf did not so much as shudder, even though she was confronting Turang Mowengot, one of the knights of the Golden Hand, a well-known servant of the king, dreaded for his murderous ways.

A Hawenti lady with a severe-looking face and impeccable dress came out on the steps of the red tent. She called for her attendant to come at once.

"I am here, Cirlaene. I would come if this Man were not delaying me," the maid responded vehemently.

The Westerner hesitated for a moment. He started opening his mouth but thought better of it.

'If she has the nerve to talk to me in that way, this girl cannot present a risk,' thought the knight of the Golden Hand. And he moved away, though his keen eye ogled the young Elf for a good few moments more.

Meanwhile, Cirlaene was looking furious, her eyes bulging and her chest heaving, so enraged was she at her maid's delay. She had always insisted upon impeccable behaviour and rigorous discipline from all her staff. They were both servants of one of the most powerful Elves in the kingdom.

"You have completely disgraced me this morning. The master has been waiting for his rockfish. He told me how disappointed he was. I hope you have a good excuse for this lateness. You owe me an apology."
"Why should I apologise?" the maid asked aggressively, no longer controlling her inner fury.

She looked at Cirlaene with a murderous gaze. This shocked and frightened the lady to such a degree that she fainted, lost her balance and fell from the tent's porch.
She hadn't fallen from so great a height, barely two feet in fact, but Cirlaene was unlucky, striking her head on the cold ground. When the Hawenti lady returned to her senses, the first thing she focussed on was the unpainted wood of the steps she had fallen from. The timber boards were gleaming a fiery yellow where the sun was striking them. Cirlaene soon realized her knee was badly grazed. Both her left shoulder and wrist were sprained. There was no way she could get herself up, so sharp was the pain in her joints. Then, just as would happen in her most worrisome dreams, she heard her master call out from inside the red tent.

"I am ready to be dressed!"

Cirlaene's heart started to beat faster, its rhythm becoming irregular. She was panicking; it felt as if she were trying to straighten a picture frame in a house that was collapsing. Desperate, she called out to her maid.

"Acyle!"

Unexpectedly, however, the young Elf put her fingers to the lips of her mistress, urging her to keep quiet.

"No words are necessary," the maid said. "I know the path I must take. I know the duty I owe the master."

Her eyes blazed with a mysterious fire as she pressed her fingers more firmly and whispered mysterious words.

"Cirlaene! You do not belong to the world of perception, nor do you belong to the invisible world. Cirlaene! Place yourself in the senseless world of dark fires."

The lady fainted again and, before she completely lost consciousness, she felt a hand seizing a paper fan from her silk belt, and heard her attendant calling for aid.

"Guards! Come at once! Come! My mistress is not answering me!"

*

"Are you sure Cirlaene cannot attend to her duties? You know how highly I value her, an excellent servant. We are very few who can enjoy being served by a Hawenti lady," said the high mage as he looked at his novice attendant with regret.
"I am afraid, master, that she is badly injured. The herbs master confirmed she needs rest. It was an unfortunate accident, but be assured I will serve you well," said the Llewenti maid.
"Do not disappoint me, Acyle."

Each day, the high mage had to be dressed. It was an important duty generally reserved for the first maid. It was well known in Gwarystan that 'if a master dressed well, he would act well.'

Acyle set about performing the most delicate part of the dressing process: fitting her master's undergarments and ensuring they were easy to remove. Acyle had seldom enjoyed this privilege whenever it had fallen to her in the past, but she knew how to do it well. She selected the best quality undergarments to ensure his skin would not be irritated.

'The master must have been castrated early in his life,' thought the young Elf as she delicately positioned his undergarments beneath the toga. 'I can only imagine the ambition that must consume those young apprentices of the Ruby College if they are willing to accept this cruel ritual. How could an Elf mutilate himself like this? Is it merely to be close to the king and wield influence?'

It was common knowledge that all members of the Ruby College, whatever their rank or caste, had to be castrated. This was to ensure their fidelity to the royal court; it was thought only eunuchs could live without loyalties to noble houses, guilds and families of their own. With no offspring, they were less interested in building up a legacy, so were seen as more trustworthy.

Despite this unusual condition, Acyle's master was no joyless monk. She knew him to be an insatiable lover of fine food; all his life he had eaten lavishly and at leisure. Indeed, as the maid was making the finishing touches to his official outfit, he was relishing an exquisite dish of trout and honey.

"You were far more prudish whenever you went near my private parts in the past. Today you showed no such confusion," the high mage said unexpectedly, as if reading his servant's superficial thoughts.

Her face showed a mischievous grin. He went on.

"King Lormelin established this tradition within the College just after setting foot on the Archipelago's shores. The Conqueror claimed, 'this bodily impairment will enhance the mind.'

What he really wanted was to deprive us of carnal relationships, what the ancients used to call 'mindless indulgence'. Since the tradition began, members of the College have had a reputation as trustworthy guardian of the royal household.

King Lormelin always insisted that, because we were so close to the supreme power, our minds must be balanced and controlled. He also pretended only this demonstration of loyalty would earn his trust."

Feeling comfortable and relaxed, enjoying this moment of respite before the day began, the high mage began to reflect upon his life in Gwarystan.

"I always was something of a familiar figure at the royal court. I occupied various powerful positions behind the throne during King Lormelin's long reign. The Conqueror even appointed me as regent of his heir's estates when Norelin was underage. But, of course, you were not born at that time. Even most of your forefathers were not.

Times have somewhat changed..." regretted the ancient high mage.

Acyle, now filing her master's nails, ventured something quite out of character for her. She asked him a question.

"Is it true that King Lormelin would be surrounded by members of the College whenever he was bathing or dressing?"

"Indeed, he was. Apprentices would act as a physical shield between the king and his Dol lords, who did not always have his best interests at heart.

The young mages serving him enjoyed great influence, owing to their proximity... But we, the high mages, were only involved in matters of state."

Acyle placed the heavy necklace around her master's neck. Five rubies of significant size were incrusted into gold. A dark vial containing viscous liquid hung from the chain.

"Is it today's unexpected promotion to first maid that has given you so much confidence? I see that you are finally showing some interest in your master's life...

Your positive attitude deserves a reward.

Let me tell you what I needed do to enter the College's final two innermost circles."

"If my master speaks, I am a willing listener."

"This story goes back a long time, to the first years of the kingdom. After the change Lormelin had brought to the Red Law, castration became standard practice, how all apprentices concluded their studies at the Ruby College..."

The mage suddenly laughed, as if he had just remembered an event from long ago.

"Many Elves would have sacrificed their own mothers for a place at our college. But there were a few who ran a mile when they learned what the last stage of their initiation would be. The young lord Dol Lewin is a recent example, as was Almit Dol Etrond before him. Both, it should be remembered, ended up betraying the king..."

It was then that he was struck with an idea. He remained wide-eyed for a time, looking almost naive, as he pondered a possible new method of detecting traitors at the royal court.

'What if refusing castration was an early sign of betrayal?' he thought.

But the mage quickly abandoned the idea. Such a strategy would hardly help birth-rates. He returned to his story.

"To everyone's surprise, the Conqueror also insisted that the existing dignitaries of our caste should all undergo the same emasculation process as the new members now had to. It is important to note that by castration I mean the removal of absolutely everything...
I did it myself, with a blood dagger.
Since then, wherever I go I have carried my severed organs with me, preserved in vinegar. This is what hangs in the glass jar around my neck: the proof of my indefectible loyalty to the line of High Elvin kings."

★

The sun was warm, and the wind was mild when the old mage and his maid exited their tent. Acyle used her recently acquired paper fan to ensure her master stayed cool. She felt proud of performing that task, as it demonstrated her new position to the eyes of all who passed them by.

They did not have far to travel. Barely a few yards away stood another of the Ruby College's red tents. It stood in the far eastern corner of the second square, thus marking the lower rank of its occupant.

The edifice was made of strong canvas. It had been built along the ruins of an ancient house. Certain decorative features of the architecture were still discernible; outside the mansion, there was a limestone wall relief depicting a royal attendant visiting the lord of Nargrond Valley.

Complying with strict college etiquette, Acyle announced the arrival of her master at the tent's entrance, where two young sorcerers were on duty. This morning visit was evidently expected, and one of the eunuchs hurried inside to announce their coming.

A moment later, her master was ushered into the presence of another member of his caste. She recognized him from his red woven toga and his necklace adorned with a dozen small rubies. The only name she knew him by was his rank: The Twelfth Arcane Master[33].

The younger high mage was calmly peeling and picking the seeds out of a piece of fruit and did not trouble to acknowledge his visitor until he had opened his mouth and eaten it.

"Greetings, Cetoron," he said coldly after finishing his food. He then pronounced the ritual words of their caste. "When the world itself is in ruins..."

"...our true selves will remain unscathed," completed Acyle's master.

---

33 Arcane Master: It is used as a title showing their membership in the cast of the Ruby College's high mages.

The two lordly mages stood in front of one another. The difference between them was immediately noticeable. Her master was an old, dark-haired High Elf of weaker build, whereas his interlocutor was tall, far younger, with an aquiline face and the eyes of a serpent.

Acyle knew him well. He was very influential: An Elf who, at no small risk to himself, had answered the call of the Ruby College and rapidly climbed its ranks. The twelve small rubies embedded in his golden necklace denoted his position: the lowest member of the College's highest caste. Hierarchy under Ruby Law was strict and unforgiving; only when promising members performed utterly extraordinary feats could they ever hope of overtaking their elders.

Both sorcerers were equally bald, as the College's tradition required that their heads be shaved every morning. Their long golden staffs were incrusted with rubies.

Again, in the manner of their ancient traditions, they were dressed in the draped red togas of their caste. Since the very earliest times, the high mages of the Ruby College wore red to symbolize the blood they were ready to shed in defence of their liege, the king of the High Elves.

"Well?" asked the younger mage, smiling bitterly.

"Dear Naldaron, I am here on behalf of many of our distinguished fellows. We wish to prepare a petition ahead of today's council. The Pact Gathering is tomorrow, and we still have an opportunity to change the College's plans this afternoon," the older sorcerer answered gravely.

Acyle could sense the tension between the two eunuchs suddenly reach new heights.

"The point of this petition is dull, but I will nevertheless answer it," the younger mage finally agreed. He was making a special effort to control his anger.

"Let me remind you that when you were ordained as the twelfth of our caste, you received this golden necklace and red toga from me. Those were valuable gifts I bestowed upon you," the older sorcerer, Cetoron, reminded him.

"What I sought were the College's teachings, not its material treasures."

"And teach you I did, as was my responsibility as Fifth Arcane Master towards the Twelfth. But when the Elder calls, the Younger must answer. This is the Red Law, that of our predecessors and indeed of our successors. Tomorrow is no ordinary day," stressed the older sorcerer.

He paused, as if expecting some angry outburst in response to his invoking the College's traditions. The high mages had already voted in favour of attending the Pact Gathering. The College's records showed that any agreed motion should be considered its final decision.
But, looking calm and sure of himself, the Twelfth Arcane Master merely nodded his head as a sign his elder fellow should proceed. He did, however, demand the utmost confidentiality for what would be discussed next.

"I will listen to your request, but after that, I will not be drawn into any further attempts to reverse the decision. When a wise Elf is defeated, he should accept it, otherwise he is a fool. The College does not need fools!" he insisted.
"I am the claimant, so I will therefore accept the terms you judge necessary."
"If that be so, then I suggest we withdraw to a more discreet location to continue our talks. One can never be too careful," finally recommended the Twelfth Arcane Master.

A few moments later, the two red mages exited the tent and walked the camp's alleys, closely followed by their respective maids, each fanning her master with an unwavering dedication. They soon discovered there was much confusion around the encampment, as lords and knights, guards and archers exchanged the latest news.

Upon the ancient walls of Ystanargrond, there stood a great concourse of soldiers who had hurried forth from the city ruins upon news that envoys of the druids' circles were in sight. They stood now, Elves and Men, gazing with breathless interest at the coming of the druids. Below, on the other side of the walls, the priests of the woods had drawn so close that the royal troops could make out their poor clothes and long filthy hair.

Meanwhile, the red sorcerers and their servants were heading towards a quieter area of the city's ruins. Indifferent to the birdsong celebrating summer and the innumerable kinds of fragrant flowers around them, they made their way, with firm strides, through the maze of tents.

At last they came up to an ancient mansion, which still had two floors intact. Even more unusually for the ruined city, a balcony running around the building's second floor offered a view over the volcano and the valley.

"Well, for my part, I would be happy to hold our talk inside that building, preferably on the second floor. That terrace offers a commanding view of our surroundings. I am of mind to stop in this impasse and see if we are being followed...

If the fish is too greedy, it will meet the fishhook and will be caught," the Twelfth Arcane Master added with a strange look in his eye.

In a demonstration of sheer paranoia, he began to examine the edges of the ancient mansion. For a moment, Acyle thought she had seen shadowy birds fly out from the sorcerer's staff. It was certainly a sight to behold, watching them dart about among the grey stones of the ancient ruins.

After an extensive search of the surroundings, the shadowy birds returned to their conjurer and whispered to his ear.

The Twelfth Arcane Master had expected to find, in this ruined edifice far from the main camp, a sanctuary of calm, but his hope was in vain.

Purposefully making his way up a grassy knoll which was overhung with olives and myrtles, he came upon a cave, in the entrance of which sat a Llewenti scout, white-haired and wrapped in a long blue cloak. The scout's face was tanned from the many days he had spent outdoors. His gaze was a beautiful clear azure, which expressed both sincerity and disillusion.

The older sorcerer and the two maids followed the younger mage up the slope and were soon standing behind him.

So engaged and deep in contemplation was this lonely Elf that he seemed to have almost forgotten the use of his tongue; but, at last, words returned to him, and he was able to articulate that he belonged to clan Llorely and was a member of the House Dol Urmil's units.

"Little did I think, Elf from Urmilla," said the Twelfth Arcane Master , "I should ever find a true member of clan Llorely so far from his home."

"Nor did I ever expect to meet a high mage of the Ruby College," replied the scout, rather curtly.

The Twelfth Arcane Master ignored this laconic comment but instead closely examined the blue ring on the Elf's little finger. He quickly identified it as a token of clan Llorely's belonging.

It was no everyday occurrence to come across a Llewenti of that kin. These Elves descended from Queen Llyoriane's fifth daughter and dwelled in the northern parts of the island Nyn Llorely, in a tree city called Tios Aelie[34]. That clan had never known much success in war. Ever since its defeat at the Battle of Ruby and Seagulls by the invading armies of Lormelin the Conqueror, it had always bowed before the High Elves. Long ago, they had sworn allegiance to the lord of House Dol Urmil and withdrawn into their woods to continue their traditions. The clan Llorely were known as the most reclusive inhabitants of the Islands.

From their high altitude, the mage and the scout could gaze out at the long valley, covered with waving grass, dense woods and gleaming vivid green in the sun. It stretched away, powerful and unbroken like a great emerald river, towards the three columns of the Gnomes in the east. The sorcerer stared across it with curiosity.

"I understand that, from where you are sitting, you can observe the farther side of the lowland. But I do not believe anything will come across it today. You may see to your other duties. If some traveller comes from this direction, you can rely on us to raise the alarm."

The scout understood it was useless to reason further with a high mage. He withdrew with dignity, probably wondering why, at this far corner of the army's camp, members of the Ruby

34   Tios Aelie: 'City of cedars' in lingua Llewenti. The ancestral home city of clan Llorely. It is located on the north western shores of Nyn Llorely in a forest of giant cedars.

College would break upon his peaceful solitude. With his head held high, he walked in deep thought down the hill towards the camp.

The two red sorcerers watched him until his bronze helmet had disappeared behind the first ruins.

"Well, now we are alone, Naldaron. It is high time we begin our meeting. The council will be held in a few hours, and we still have much to discuss," insisted the older mage.

"I agree, Cetoron, let us enter the room on the second floor. We can place our protective glyphs on its doors," concurred the younger sorcerer, and he reached out a hand of brotherhood to the other.

To the surprise of their maids, the red mages suddenly floated up in the air and reached the terrace a few feet above. They disappeared from the sight of their servants. The maids heard their masters began to murmur their incantations.

Acyle understood the mages must have been drawing pentacles and enchanting glyphs to protect the secrecy of their exchange. As if drawn to them by a mysterious force, Acyle was suddenly overwhelmed with curiosity. She immediately concocted a lie to get her fellow servant out of the way.

"We must remove ourselves immediately," she said. "Our masters demand privacy. They wish for us to wait for them at the tents."

The other maid looked both surprised and intrigued. "I did not hear any such command," she stammered.

"It seems that your master never taught you to anticipate his will. I myself have learnt that lesson well. I am leaving," and Acyle turned on her heels and walked quickly away. "Don't stay!" she called back one last time.

The gazes of the maids crossed. In an instant, and for an unknown reason, the second maid was overwhelmed with anxiety. Dread and anguish were suddenly upon her, pursuing her like savage predators. Unable to control her fear, the young Elvin servant abandoned her lonely post and returned in haste towards the camp.

This was the opportunity Acyle had been waiting for. Still haunted by an obsession to discover what the red mages were discussing, she doubled back towards the ancient mansion, utterly possessed by this unhealthy curiosity. Demonstrating surprising force and dexterity, she easily scaled the rocks to the side of the mansion that almost reached the corner of the terrace. Her hands clung to the stones and weeds like claws, her legs propelled her to the top like wings. After leaping from the top of the outcrop, she landed on the upper floor's parapet and hid behind a broadleaved vine. Now out of sight, she could contemplate the scene before her.

The red mages had entered a deep meditation. Standing still behind a folding screen, they looked absent, as if they had forgotten the great sky and retired from the world.
Their lengthy wait was coming to an end, and they were both about to release their attention when a noise made them turn back. Right before their eyes, a grappling hook had been shot up onto the terrace. The iron hook was dragged backwards before catching onto the stone parapet. The rope tightened under the weight of the climber.

The fierce dark soul of the younger sorcerer glowed as he realised how essential his additional security measures had been.
Acyle had noticed how, all morning, he had been on the defensive. Now she realised he was not paranoid but had good reason to fear spies, or even assassins.

Her gaze moved back to the mysterious grappling hook.
An Elfin hand emerged on the edge of the balcony, clinging onto the stone parapet. A second hand, wearing a blue ring, found another hold on a nearby outcrop.
The spy let out a cry before hauling himself up and leaping to his feet. The cloaked figure of that same clan Llorely scout was now standing on the parapet. He hesitated only for a moment, judging how best to reach a new hideout across the empty terrace.

But the scout then saw the red mages, standing by the door. He shivered, so stunned he could not move.

Too late did the intrusive climber understand the Elves he was confronting. Just as he got footholds to climb back over the terrace's parapet, he felt the stone structure sink and sway beneath him. He tried rushing forward to escape but the crumbling floor pulled him downwards with it.

All the while, the red mages were drawing towards him, and now reached out their arms to send invisible bonds, strong as iron, lashing around him. As the floor continued to cascade downwards, he was reared high in the air, before being flung violently against the second-floor's stone wall.

After a great thud, the scout cried out in pain as bones broke and limbs twisted. At last the helpless creature lay upon what remained of the terrace floor.

The two mages approached him with caution, as if closing in on dangerous prey which, though nearly beaten to death, could still, in desperate act, strike out and harm them.

"So, you hoped to spy on us, lonely Elf?" asked the Twelfth Arcane Master. "How intriguing!"

"I can roam where I please," winced the breathless scout.

"As can I... if indeed it pleased me, I could dance along frozen glaciers or walk a tightrope across a volcano... but in no circumstances would I ever dare eavesdrop on high mages of the Ruby College."

"What are you after?" asked Fifth Arcane Master. He was losing patience.

"Lord Dol Urmil ordered me to watch out for any suspicious behaviour in camp. Before we came, sinister prophecies were told across Nyn Llorely when news of the Pact Gathering reached us. The matriarchs of clan Llorely say that the Flow has been trapped. It no longer circulates around the Islands."

"And you believe these fanciful superstitions?" laughed the Fifth Arcane Master. "Do you really pay those witches any heed?"

The younger sorcerer interrupted the laughter of his peer. He had just become utterly certain the spy was lying.

"You have not uttered a single true word, but your silence speaks volumes. Do you really think you can deceive us?" he threatened, and his voice was deep.

"Ask a stupid question, expect a stupid answer," the scout spat, now on the defensive. He was struggling with great difficulty to fight the intrusive power of the red mages. Already he could sense their mental claws reaching for his brain.

The Twelfth Arcane Master was examining him closely, trying to pierce his disguise. There was a long silence.

"When two thieves meet, they need no introduction," the enigmatic sorcerer said at last , "they recognize each other wordlessly, immediately. Where is your sword, fencer? Where are your poems, poet? You seem to be lost."

The scout remained silent. He did not know what to say, what to do. If he opened his mouth, all was lost. If he kept his mouth shut, he was doomed.

"Give us your name, fool!" ordered the Fifth Arcane Master.

The scout hesitated, as though he had neither the wit nor the memory to tell his own name. Eventually, he uttered a few words, his voice low.

"I am... Neyrod... Neyrod of clan Llorely, I come from the woods of Tios Aelie..."

The forces at work around him were impairing his ability to confront his accusers. His mind felt assaulted by the invisible powers wielded by the high mages.

"You lie, insolent Elf!" responded the younger sorcerer. "You made that name up ... Neyrod does not exist... Is that the only trick you have left to deceive us?
Cetoron, this is no common spy. I can guess who he truly is. This thief has been after me for some time. I demand he be detained."

For a moment, the older mage hesitated. This situation was particularly complex. Although it was plain the scout of clan Llorely was no ordinary spy, it seemed his fate was somehow linked to that of the Twelfth Arcane Master. Acyle's master saw there an opportunity; perhaps this unexpected encounter could give him an advantage over his rival.

Turning to his peer, he vehemently accused him.

"You demand, Naldaron? Have you lost your reason? Would you dare ignore Red Law? Do I need to remind you that members of the College have no coercive power? Our authority comes from the king, but only He can demand justice.

We are no Dragon Warriors, acting unilaterally and despotically. It is not the law of Ka-Blowna which rules our kingdom, but that of Norelin."

"This Elf poses a direct threat to my life," insisted the accused, visibly disturbed by this violent charge.

"From the ring I see upon his finger, this Elf belongs to clan Llorely, and therefore is under the protection of the Dol Urmil, a House that has always served our kings faithfully.

He also is protected by the peace of the druids as one who has been conveyed to the Pact Gathering. I cannot let you take him.

The king cannot afford diplomatic incidents with our allies. Is not the House Dol Talas' rebellion troublesome enough already? Would you also have House Dol Urmil and clan Llorely join forces with Cumberae and Llymar?"

The younger sorcerer seemed to bow down before the force of these words. For a moment, he remained quiet, apparently defeated.

The older mage took advantage of the situation and concluded.

"You may go free, be you scout or spy, but know that your deeds will be reported to the king. Be sure your lord will be visited by the knights of the Golden Hand."

The old mage's priority was to resume his discussion with his younger peer ahead of the afternoon's council. Now that he had managed to outflank his rival, he needed to turn his advantage into success.

The scout disappeared from their sight as quickly as he had come. The red mages remained on the terrace, watching him return to the dwellings of House Dol Urmil.

The presence of Acyle, hidden behind the deciduous vine, still escaped their attention. Despite the risk she was taking, the maid felt safe, almost invulnerable, as if protected by a powerful charm.

After a brief exchange, the sorcerers entered the second-floor room. Acyle watched them concentrating all their whole energy into their hands. Soon, they held a light between them, like a candle burning and illuminating the whole room. The light grew until it formed a translucent and reddish globe around them.

The two mages began. Seen from a distance, their discussion initially looked polite, as though they were engaged in courteous transactions. But the temperature of their exchange was soon heating up.

Without warning, she saw her master raise up his golden staff and draw figures in the air, as if he were explaining unknown realms of the universe and the roads that led to them.

Despite her unnaturally sharp hearing, she could not hear what was said inside the globe of reddish energy. Just from their gestures, however, she could easily tell that the meeting was building to a verbal confrontation of great violence. It was like watching two orators warring like giants. One raved, the other stormed. Each supported his profound sayings with movements of his golden staff. They looked like two wrestlers, neither of whom could overcome the other.

It seemed as if this soundless storm could have lasted for hours but, at last, a distant shout broke in upon the mages' conversation, a low continuous roar like the swelling tumult of a sweeping wave.

Far below, in the dark woods bordering the river, there twinkled many moving lights, tossing and sinking as they advanced. Meanwhile, within the camp, the tumultuous bellowing of the royal troops broke into words of insult, a hundred times repeated.

"Dark Elves be cursed! Dark Elves be cursed!"

The younger sorcerer seized his elder by the wrist and dragged him towards the parapet to observe the scene. In so doing, the mages left their protective globe and their discussion was ended. Their angry faces told no truce had been found.

Acyle looked down into the vale. Creeping through the darkness of the woods, as their brandished torches dimmed and flashed, a warlike procession was passing by. It was the heavily armed silhouettes of the clan Myortilys troops, all clad in black to honour their patron deity, Eïwal Myos.
She realized the Dark Elves' units were proceeding to their own encampment ahead of the Pact Gathering. As a sign of aggression, they were deliberately passing just below the walls of Ystanargrond, provoking the wrath of the royal army.

A moment later, the column of the clan Myortilys troops swept into the undergrowth. The furious shouting from within the camp ceased.
Acyle's gaze returned to the red mages, as her master was raising his head to look his peer in the eye.

"I think you did not quite understand," she now heard him say, emphasising every word.

There was a hush for the answer. The sigh of the wind among the trees and the low lapping of the distant river swelled up ever louder in the silence.
The fiery younger sorcerer looked hard at his elder, ready to spring out.

A great foreboding of evil weighed heavily upon the Fifth Arcane Master, and it was reflected upon his stern face. More than ever, he wanted to bring the truth to light.

"I was part of the College before Lormelin the Conqueror ever set foot on the Islands. You were not even born. Consider this well: you are a child among the high mages, an anomaly. Every single other Arcane Master can trace their own history even further back than that of Gwarystan itself.

I was your teacher, and the first to perceive your rare talent. I know exactly when my disciple lost his way. You have utterly changed this past few years, Naldaron. I no longer recognize you.

Here you are, jeopardizing the future of our ancestral institution with your proposal for this Pact Gathering. How could you enthral even the wisest of our members? I could not believe my eyes. It was like watching a colony of bees argue over the distribution of honey, unaware of the blazing torch looming towards the hive. That was your doing."

The Twelfth Arcane Master remained a haven of calm. In a correct tone, he stressed.

"Just because you are representing 'many' members, Cetoron, does not mean you have obtained a majority of votes... Let me ask you one question. Was my proposal not sanctioned by the vote of the College according to the Red Law?"

The older mage could not care less. He burst with fury.

"One last time, listen to me, Naldaron! We cannot involve the other Islands' factions in the guardianship of the Lenra Pearl, even for the benefits you are hopeful about.

It was foolish enough to extract it from its safe and bring it to the Valley. Someone might use this as an opportunity to seize it. If the Pearl is returned to the Mighty Prisoner and his wrath is unleashed against us, we will all be in grave danger.

I can assure you; he will stop at nothing to destroy all we have built.

The Lenra Pearl should remain in the tower of crimson. Only the Ruby College has the power to protect it."

"I must ask you to stop. You are now violating another of our laws. You are now discussing matters of strategic importance outside the protection of our runes. I am drawing a line under this conversation. I will see you again at the final council this afternoon," replied the younger sorcerer, undaunted.

He turned his back on his interlocutor. The older mage grabbed onto his robes.

"I gave you that staff, I can take it away," he warned his former disciple.

"I worked very hard for this staff. It has served me well: supporting the heavens above my head and making the earth firm beneath my feet."

"Naldaron, I am officially recalling your staff. If you will not hand it over willingly, I will send you to the Halls of Agadeon fast as an arrow," ordered the old mage.

The younger sorcerer gave a shudder. His own savage soul was stirred by the insult, but only his gleaming eyes spoke of the fire within.

He slowly handed his golden staff back to his former teacher with his left hand.

His right hand moved fast. It reached for an invisible scabbard at his back. In a flash, a pommel inlaid with sapphires and a shining blade appeared.

The long scimitar seared through the air.

Letting go his opponent's staff, the older mage raised his own with both hands to meet the challenge, but it was cut in two before his astonished eyes.

The defender seized his former mentor with a silent assault of occult forces. His great will and power seemed inexhaustible. Acyle's master drew back, calling upon all his forces to defend himself.

The clash of energy was great. They were both unleashing everything in their reserves to triumph. Leaves were flying, and wild vines were uprooted. The ruined walls of the edifice shook violently in the struggle.

Acyle fell from her high-up hiding place. By chance, she did not hurt herself when she hit the ground and was quickly back on her feet.

The conflict lasted but a moment. All became quiet. Acyle decided to climb back up the wall. Her hands grasped the creepers on the wall and soon she had returned to her hideout. The scene she discovered froze her.

Her master was on his knees before his victor. She heard the triumphing Twelfth Arcane Master snarling over him.

"It was a grave error you made, attempting to thwart my power, Cetoron. You should have known better."

His teeth were like swords, his mouth dripping in blood. The shining blade of his scimitar was pressing into on her master's throat. The sapphires on the sword's hilt were glittering with rays of the sun.

"Your mind is still stubborn and unbridled. I order you to submit! Don't force me to use my blade!" insisted the Twelfth Arcane Master.

The older mage looked at him, defeated.

'Power lies deeply in the blood of Naldaron,' thought Acyle as she looked at the sorcerer with fascination. 'He may be the most dangerous enemy there is.' She was amazed at his strength of will and steadiness of purpose.

"You will own the Ruby College before you are finished!" her master foresaw aloud.
Sure of his complete victory, the Twelfth Arcane Master's eyes sparkled. "I sincerely doubt it, after the devastation that will be wreaked tomorrow," he mocked. Then, quickly, correcting himself after saying too much, he added , "But for now, I have thought of a way your life can be saved."

There was a moment of silence as the red sorcerer listened with great attention to the noises of his surroundings. He seemed to be interrogating the wind, discovering whether it had brought the rumour of their fight to the camp.
He raised his head and moved sidewise, like a hound attempting to get downwind of an intruder, to smell and identify the source of the danger.

Acyle knew she had to flee before she was discovered. She scrambled down the vine and, without pausing to admire its budding white flowers, ran back towards the ruins of Ystanargrond.

★

In King Norelin's absence, the great tent of the Ruby College stood symbolically at the centre of the camp. The high mages embodied the personal will of the king, while the other Dor and Dol Households represented the varying ambitions of the Hawenti nobles.

The time for the afternoon council had come and the twelve high mages, accompanied by their maids, were arriving in the vast meeting place. It was bright, decorated with rare flowers, and the melodies of strange singing birds hummed through the air.

At the entrance stood two knights of the Ruby, true to their council duties. With blood-red armour and helmets, they had heavy lances in one hand, whilst in the other they held large shields bearing the gemstones of their masters.

Passing before them, the Twelfth Arcane Master nodded unceremoniously, and he entered the great tent with his maid. In an obvious sign of his rising favour, he was saluted respectfully by the four members of the first Square, the greatest of the Ruby College.

Meanwhile, the Fifth Arcane Master was making his own entrance with his new maid.

Immediately Acyle felt deeply troubled at the sight of the pentacles drawn on the canvas of the tent. Overwhelmed with confusion, she shuffled forwards, then back, before standing in a disoriented daze.

Friezes decorated with glyphs boarded the tapestries. Many runes were protecting this place. They could be seen all over the carpets and on the furniture as well.

Acyle seemed to be at a crossroads, with infinite paths leading away from her, but none that would lead her home; fear and pain entangled her.

She refused to follow her master into the tent. The maid paid no heed to his injunctions but remained still, blinking, utterly confused. Her agitation provoked suspicion all around her, as servants and maids were busy preparing the final details for the council. The knights frowned at her.

The four high mages of the First Square, had just completed filling up an aromatic amphora with wine and were about to drink it off. Their hands then froze as they were suddenly arrested by the strong sense that something was amiss.
Acyle began acting erratically.
Her misconduct was clear for all to see and was reflected in the frightened eyes of the servants, the agitated faces of the two knights and in the sudden silence of her master.
The other mages present turned their heads away to avoid the four masters' questioning gaze.

"What in the name of the king is the matter with that lunatic?" cried the First Arcane Master, whose last few days of intensive preparation had left him little patience. "Why do you stand here like a helpless fool, Cetoron? What is wrong with your maid? Are you not her absolute master?"

The old sorcerer's face, still haggard after the degradation that had befallen him just hours earlier, now contorted with fresh anxiety at this latest humiliation.

"I am not responsible for this, Anaron! She deserves punishment!" he said in an attempt at authority, before laying a hand upon his necklace.

A whip of lightning appeared in his hand, and the old mage used it to lash his maid, creating bright sparks at it struck her. But Acyle seemed utterly unharmed by the whipping, as though she were enveloped in some powerful mystery that no blow could break.
Acyle entered a form of deep meditation and refused to move any further but faced the First Arcane Master defiantly.

The most high-ranking member of the Ruby College was a short, thin Elf, with unkempt dark hair and wild eyes, which shone brightly with a strong inner intensity. His hands were concealed behind his back, and over his golden necklace was the largest ruby ever seen in the Islands.
The First mage asked Acyle's master how it was possible for his maid to have reached this unnatural state. His patience was at an end.

"Speak this instant, Cetoron," he shouted angrily. "Another moment and we will have you imprisoned. With your feet in stocks and the chains round your wrists, the view from the top of Gwarystan Rock will teach you obedience.
For the final time, I ask you to speak, and without delay!"

The old mage startled, gave a cry of apprehension and rushed towards his servant, barking incantations at her like orders. But the formula of violent exorcism he shouted did not seem to have power over the bad spirit that possessed his maid.

"Let us bring her in and ask her ourselves!" suggested the Twelfth Arcane Master with a commanding tone.

The First mage walked around the young Elf four times and snapped his fingers while uttering incantations. She remained still, in meditation, like protecting herself in an otherworldly sphere.
So, by his great power, with a single word and a wave of his hand, he transported her through the air and into the great tent. Falling onto the soil, she laid still in the middle of the pentacles. He tried calling to her but in vain.

"If every bell in Gwarystan rang at once it could not disturb this young Llewenti! Her force comes from below this place, from deep underground, where the seeds of delusion dwell. If I cut her bond to them, she will wake and be vulnerable."

The Third Arcane Master approached.

"This maid has two souls inside her, and one is very sick, for it was hurt by the wicked other. I will teach the intruder it is forbidden to come out from one shell and enter another. The time has come for the two elements to separate. Vile demon, I will make you loosen your claws."

No sooner had he spoken, the First mage went in front of the young Elf and sprang her up from the earth and made her bow in front of the northern pentacle, the rune of Water. In that instant, the maid came out her deep meditation.

Holding out a short staff of gold, the Third Arcane Master gave an order of life and death, positive and negative interwoven. The maid could not escape this attack.

First, the three fingers of the maid's gracious hand were struck off. They fell upon the pedestal beside her. Above her delicate breast, a dark mark showed. A blast of energy disfigured her lovely face.

Most servants fled at the scene. The maid of the Twelfth Arcane Master stood paralyzed by horror. Gasping and croaking, her hand covered her mouth as she gazed fixedly on the disfigured face of her fellow servant.
The invisible forces circling around the demoniac maid brutally contorted her body. Now naked, she was fully exposed to the power of the high mages.

The Fourth Arcane Master walked in front of the mutilated young Elf. In a single, sudden movement, he waived his golden staff in the air, leapt upon a nearby pedestal and showered his blows upon her. With a crack and a dull thud, her right leg dropped to the ground. Another fierce blow, and the left followed. Her corpse fell.
But the demoniac maid's brutal laughter echoed through the great tent.

> "Take heed while you have time! For the end of your world is at hand!
And when that day comes, there will be no mercy for those who tried to rise to the level of Gweïwal Narkon!"

The Fourth Arcane Master then wiped the sweat from his brow. "She is yours, Anaron. Do with her as you will," he said.

As the most high-ranking mage of the College moved forward, a smear of blood across his chin showed how hard he had bitten his lip to summon the power he was ready to unleash. He cried a formidable word of power and shouted.

> "Hella Gweïwal tur, Orgo!" [35]

---

35 Hella Gweïwal tur, orgo: 'Go back to your master, demon!' in lingua Hawenti

The soil beneath the maid's corpse opened and her remains were propelled by a mighty force into a dark chasm.

A moment later, all signs of what had happened in the great tent of the Ruby College had disappeared. No blood marks, no severed limbs: it was as if the presence of the demoniac Elf had simply been an illusion.

"The demon's spirit was sent back to the realm of Narkon," proclaimed the First Arcane Master. "We are now in peace and will be able to resume our talks. More than ever, we have a lot to discuss."

★★

Same day, Nargrond Valley, South of Eïwele Llya grove, sunset

It was nightfall in the camp of the Cumberae and Llymar units. Across the moonlit water of the Sian Senky river, amid the thick woods which stretched between the mountains' slopes, lay hidden the encampments of the other factions that would attend the Pact Gathering the next morning.

The air was clear, now fully rid of the clouds and fumes which usually obscured this western part of Nargrond Valley. It was only now, the evening before the Pact Gathering, that Mount Oryusk, like a welcoming host reassuring his guests, had stopped emitting its poisonous smoke and harmful particles into the valley.

The volcano's eastern side, with its greyish soil, its green belt of feathery trees and its background of barren, reddish slopes, shimmered in the dying sun like a dreamscape in the fading light. The occasional buzzard excepted, the sky was empty, stretching out in serene dark blue as far the eye could see. In all its infinite expanse, there was no star but one, Cil, the light of hope, which was slowly making its way across the celestial vault.

The column formed by the troops of Llymar and Cumberae had reached its destination. After journeying southwest, they had crossed the Sian Senky river, and finding there a rocky hill rising from a deep vale, they had settled near its summit.

The fighters were setting up camp for the night, barely two leagues away from the grove of Llya where the Pact Gathering would take place the next day.

There were fish in the stream, the area teemed with game and there was an abundance of wild fruits. The defensive preparations they were carrying out were not unduly interrupted by the search for sustenance.

Seen from afar, the princess of Cumberae's tent appeared like a beautiful vessel, deep green in colour, its broad flapping canvas stained with golden decorative motifs. Its poles were gleaming with brass work. From the single high mast above the large tent streamed the rose-striped flag of Cumberae. That banner, a symbol of purity and of beauty, united House Dol Nos-Loscin and the Ice Elves of the great southern forest.

Inside the command tent, the princess' guards had replaced their weapons with cooking utensils. The delicious smell of dinner being prepared awakened their senses.

Elves subsisted on various fruits and vegetables and their taste was generally extremely discerning. They had strong preferences for delicate dishes, particularly those that possessed a great degree of subtlety when combining sweet and sour flavours.

As for drink, the princess' guards drew water from the cold mountain springs. The woodlands where grapevines grew were now very far away, so they would have to wait for better days to enjoy their most savoured refreshments.

Terela remained alone after Camatael had paid his respects and left for the night. She was praying in the corner of her tent where a little shrine, curtained off by silken drapery, held a precious statue of Eïwal Lon. The beautiful work of art was the greatest treasure of her personal collection. To finish her evening ritual, Terela kissed the beautiful body of glistening marble. The material was as white and fair as sunlight itself, which undoubtedly had been the source of the artist's inspiration.

At the command tent's entrance, a light gleamed upon the knights of the Rose's helmets as they stood guard outside. A red point rose and fell in the darkness. Outside the tent, Alton was approaching, a magical light glittering from his long ivory staff. His six personal knights were marching on his heels.

The elegant Elf had changed much since the early morning when he had retired into his sedan chair. His fresh young face was now hardened with tensed lines, wrought by trouble and anguish. But his eyes were more cunning than ever.

At the entrance, the two knights raised their lances. After a brief hesitation, they let him enter the princess' quarters.

Terela rose, and her fair cheeks flushed with resentment. She looked at her cousin with contempt as he walked in. Though the distance that separated the command tent from his sedan chair was short, he seemed to have been running several leagues. His awkward steps betrayed his weak muscles and low endurance.

"We've not seen you all day, Alton! Your knights protected your litter as if you were at death's door inside. For a while, I thought you had left us forever. Did you think I would not require your services?"

Ignoring both Terela's concerns and her blameful tone, Alton looked at his cousin as though she were the first Elvin face, he had seen in a whole year. His expression demonstrated that his heart was yearning for her.

"Unimaginable, unthinkable, ..." he blurted, his flushed face almost level with that of Terela.
"If you wish to address your princess, it would be well to choose words your lips can frame," she reminded him.

Alton paused for a moment, thinking to himself, totally oblivious to his noble cousin's reactions. It was plain that the elegant Elf was not acting himself in that moment, such was the powerful emotion obscuring his mind. Although he was known as a solitary and peculiar Elf, never before had the princess seen him behave this strangely.

"Have you ever thought, Terela, how that clan Llorely sentry must have felt when he first saw Lormelin the Conqueror's fleet sailing the barren ocean?"
"No," the princess replied simply, though she could not help smiling, so unexpected was her cousin's question.
"Well, I have," Alton answered, deadly earnest. "This question has always remained unasked and unanswered. You will think me foolish, but I have obsessed over it for a long time. I wonder: what would I have done in his position?
Can you imagine that lonely Elf, at his post, at the top of an isolated beacon overlooking the vast expanses of the Austral Ocean? For centuries, that Llewenti and probably his predecessors had remained in that watchtower, exposed to the elements and dying of ennui... until that morning came. The vast sea was filled with the coloured sails of dozens of Irawenti ships, carrying in their bowels the formidable army of the High Elf king. After centuries of performing this duty for nothing, the time had come for that lonely Elf to sound the alarm. What a tragic fate for an insignificant guard!"

"Alton, your story is certainly interesting, but time is of the essence. What are you trying to tell me?" Terela pressed, looking at her cousin with impatience.

"What's important is what I want to confess to you," corrected the elegant Elf.

"I am listening,"

The princess's first impulse was to be severe, to demonstrate her authority, but reflection and doubts followed close upon its heels.

"If I were in that sentry's place, I think I would have fled right away. Perhaps I would have taken the time to raise the alarm and alert my clan companions, but I would have definitely fled to the most remote isle of the Archipelago to hide from the devastation that was approaching the Islands' shores."

"How courageous!" exclaimed Terela. "But that still does not explain what you are trying to convey."

"On the contrary, it does," opposed Alton. "In this very moment, I am deciding to flee this valley. I will not stand by your side one hour longer if you should decide to pursue this path."

"How could you?" Terela asked, astonished by this admission of such weakness.

"I can see it, just as that lonely sentry saw Lormelin's fleet coming 2185 years ago: it is time to flee."

Terela chose to remain silent and stolid. She knew her cousin's taste for theatrics well. Nothing could dissuade him from his drama once he had begun; the best strategy was to let him get to the final act of whatever little play he was performing. The princess folded her arms, looking severe.
Indifferent to the lack of enthusiasm in his audience of one, Alton quickly moved to the conclusion of his tale.

"I have come to know the true purpose of this Pact Gathering."

"Are you sure?"

"As sure as the Two-Winged Lions are the arms of the House of Dol Nos-Loscin," confirmed Alton, now grave.

252

None in Cumberae had ever doubted his ability to foretell events. It was indisputable that Alton often knew things before others. The young Dol's master in the art of divination was none other than Miglor Dol Nos Loscin, the most ancient Elf living in the Islands, and who many thought to be the wisest in the lore of sorcery.

Seeing how certain her cousin was, Terela immediately guessed.

"Is it all a trap? Is that why the Nargrond Valley was chosen as the location for this Pact Gathering?"

Since the beginning of their expedition, the princess had sensed an unknown danger looming above their heads. She now needed her cousin to use his extraordinary augury powers to prove her intuition true.

"It is. The high mages of the Ruby College are plotting a conspiracy. It will happen tomorrow as the Pact Gathering begins, when all its members are present."
"So, the king is seizing his chance to capture me..." Terela murmured.

The last trace of any smile had disappeared from the face of the princess. The immediate future was suddenly very clear before her, and the prospect made her shrink.

Alton noted how his cousin would always reduce matters of great importance to how they would affect her precious self. It was true that, unlike him, Terela descended from the elder branch of the Nos-Loscin family. Her father was a ruling prince, her mother the direct kin of an alleged Demi-god. Her own aunt had been no less than the queen of the Islands, the consort of Lormelin the Conqueror and the mother of Norelin.
Nevertheless, Alton could not resist thinking.

'I did not say her personal safety was at risk. This threat is not only about Terela. The other envoys of the Islands' factions could also be in danger. I am at risk too.'

But seeing he was making good progress with his strategy, he decided to encourage her in this same line of thinking: something his vivid imagination could do only too well.

"Only this afternoon, I looked into the Flow and saw a dozen demonstrations of their sorcerous powers," Alton began with a knowing tone. "This I do not doubt: they will be on us like ravens on a dying horse. It would be futile even for you to resist them. They might try to capture you, or worse. Who knows what fate an heirless king has in mind for a princess next in the line to the throne? He has already refused to marry you, but he may want you close to him still. Perhaps he would prefer to house you in his deepest dungeon, rather than at the top of the high tower of Melindro.

I know many an Elf who would sell his soul just for the pleasure of putting his lips on your delicate skin. The fact that Norelin is your cousin will hardly have stopped his obsessive attraction for the curves of your thin body. It is said the king has developed unusual vices: some even say condemnable practises. With his twisted spirit, perhaps he will try to possess you against your will. The Dark Elves have it that there is no better ecstasy..."

Ignoring her cousin's insinuations, Terela acknowledged , "I've been so naïve... Clearer still grows the future. I can read the fear in your eyes after what you have foreseen."

"We must not take one step further towards that cursed mountain of smoke," insisted Alton.

Like one thinking aloud, Terela carried on , "If Norelin decided to forsake his pledge to the other sworn members of the Pact, no Elf in the Islands will feel safe anymore. Dishonour and shame will be upon the king, and all the High Elves will be disgraced with him."

Alton did not seem so sure of his kin's sense of honour.

"For all the High Elves have achieved since their coming, you cannot deny that the Archipelago is no land of ours, and that we hold it as we won it... by the sword. We have been winning wars though treachery and perjury since time immemorial..." he noted.

But the elegant Elf feared that these wider considerations might steer the princess away from the issue at hand.

"We cannot hesitate to give the necessary instructions," he insisted with all his persuasive power. "Every fighter of ours must come with us at once. Our galleys are awaiting us at Ankalla[36]. Get the order out, your highness. As our units fall back from Nargrond Valley, we can use the scouts we dispatched into the mountains to protect the southern path. Units of sailors can be sent from the galleys to escort us back to the coast. I can see to it all."

"What will be the fate of those Elves who stay? From the Three Columns to Mount Oryusk, old enemies will be at each other's throats, as soon as the factions discover the Pact no longer holds."

"The hounds will tear at each other until the most powerful wins! None will escape save ourselves," said Alton with gloom in his voice and bearing.

As they talked, the two Dol Nos-Loscin cousins kept glancing, with earnest anxious faces, towards the imposing Mount Oryusk. The volcano appeared exceptionally calm, as if it had become totally inoffensive.

"The fallout from this next battle, however, will be much more dramatic," she continued. "After the Elves have drenched themselves in blood, it will be the tribes of fanatic human barbarians from overseas, the savages and the pirates who will succeed the High Elves as rulers. Where we built, they will burn; where we nurtured, they will ravage; where we guaranteed peace, they will wage war."

Seeing Terela still hesitate, Alton pressed her again. "The king is about to break the Pact. Our fate is sealed. We have no choice. Give your instructions, my liege! Please do it, for the sake of Cumberae!"

"I would not dream of running from what is to come if there was a single Elf amongst them worthy of being saved," she said solemnly. "We will warn Llymar and would have alerted others had they helped us in our war against the barbarians. But since they did not so much as raise a fist in solidarity, I will not rescue them now.

You will carry my orders, Alton. We are going back to Cumberae. We shall return home and return at once!

---

36 Ankalla: 'Narrow Port' in lingua Llewenti. It is located on the south-eastern shore of Gwa Nyn.

I will personally inform Lord Dol Lewin and Matriarch Myryae of my decision and strongly recommend they do the same."

The princess of Cumberae rose from her chair and motioned that the audience was at an end. Alton shrugged his shoulders and a satisfied smile broke upon his delicate face.

"I will do as you bid, my liege. Messengers will be sent within an hour. By then, we will be ready to leave, and whatever happens in this cursed valley will concern us no longer."

The elegant Elf saluted with deep respect before turning upon his heels.

'I probably said more than was required to push Terela to that decision. How interesting! It is easier than I thought to play on her fears,' he found.

★

Mynar dyl was sitting quietly at the entrance to his tent when the shout of a frenzied knight of the Rose rung through the darkness. He sprang to his feet and looked about himself. From the tents, from the watch fires, from the sentries, the same order was sounding out:

"We are leaving! We are leaving!"

From all sides, Elves came rushing, half clad, their eyes staring, their mouths agape.

"To Cumberae! To Cumberae!" they yelled.

An archer, with flashing teeth and gleaming eyes, rushed past him, his long arm pointing to the South.

"We leave!" He cried aloud to his companions in arms, who had been looking forward to a restorative night's sleep.

Mynar dyl looked at the rushing Cumberae troops with perplexity. Before him, the same Ice Elves who had finished preparing the camp for the night were now hurrying to ready themselves for another long march, packing and loading, storing and wrapping.

Alton happened to walk by the warlord of Tios Halabron.

"We are leaving!" he urged without stopping. "We are returning home and you should do the same at once!"

Mynar dyl looked at him fixedly, yet he saw him not, so full was his mind of this sudden and unexpected order. It felt as if the solid ground beneath him had given way, as though the work of his life was coming to irremediable ruin. His sharp features were shadowed by anxiety as he looked with questioning eyes at the haggard face of Alton.

"Have you received ill news?" Mynar dyl enquired, barely audibly.

"The worst, it is a question of whether we will be able to escape."

"What are the orders of princess Terela?" asked the warlord of Tios Halabron.

"To withdraw immediately!"

"But why? I heard in Llafal that omens were not favourable, but it was too incredible to believe."

"I heard the same in Ystanloscin. Unfortunately, it was all true!

Here are the princess' orders, as clear as words can be: 'Leave not a scout behind,'" related Alton.

"But what is the cause of this sudden change?"

"It is trap. This Pact Gathering is a vast set-up designed by the Ruby College to capture key hostages from all the Islands' factions. Cumberae cannot afford to lose its princess and heir," Alton confided.

"So you have decided to flee?"

"We have to withdraw, Mynar dyl. Cumberae is letting the limbs wither to make the heart stronger. The horde of Ka-Blowna is about to swarm once more. There are fresh crowds of barbarians from the Mainland approaching our shores as we speak. Every sword is needed to hold the southern forest borders. The two units of Ice Elves you see in this camp are the elite scouts of our army. They will be desperately needed soon."

"Well, I expected better of Hawenti courage. As for me, I am the true representative of the Llewenti clans at the Pact Gathering. I am here to defend the government of our realm after our ancient fashion, and I will not succumb to panic. There are higher powers that protect us," said Mynar dyl boldly.

"Your lack of vision leaves me puzzled. You always reduce everything to the old Llewenti-Hawenti rivalry. But with us, you are confusing sugar with salt."

Alton shook his head to express his disappointment. He understood Mynar dyl could not be convinced. 'An obtuse mind and a stubborn character,' Alton deplored. He felt now was the time to conclude this useless discussion. The knights of the Two-Winged Lions were waiting for him to enter his sedan chair once again.

"If all the Elves in the Islands were of the same mind, our civilization would be lost, much like that of the Gnomes and the Giants. How would the Llewenti fare without their Hawenti allies when confronted with the savage Men who worship the Three Dragons? What would you do against the king, the Ruby College and their Westerners' allies? What would you do against the Dark Elves?

Let me tell you, Mynar dyl; the houses of the Dol Nos-Loscin, Dol Etrond and Dol Lewin are your defenders. You should know better. We, the High Elves, were ever distinguished, both by our knowledge of things and by our desire to know more.

Discipline, the power to command, the quality of our equipment and our knowledge of war: in all these things you fall short. For too long have you depended upon the protection of the High Elves, leaning upon us like a crutch."

Pressed to react after this long diatribe, Mynar dyl showed his unshakable faith.

"Times will be hard, but we Llewenti have deities to protect us. The Islands will be ours once again."

"How touching it is to behold such an idealist who believes in Dryad's tales! Not only are you deaf to the voice of reason but also blind to your own fate. I see the day when the Archipelago may indeed be Elvin again, but only because you and your companions will have been driven into the craters of volcanoes. History is like alchemy; all goes into the melting pot, and if a new Elvin realm should come forth, it will be after eons of strife and war. I fear there will not be any part of that future left for you. You will be long dead.

Do you know the barbarians of Ka-Blowna flail their prisoners alive before nailing their skin upon the doors of our homes? Have you ever seen the Dark Elves tie their captives to a tree and shoot them with their poisoned bolts?"

These were vivid images that Alton was evoking. Mynar dyl's face was shadowed and grave, as if he could see the burnt trees of Tios Halabron and the ashes covering the ruined forest of Llymar. But his resolution remained unaltered. Alton knew this; he could tell from the indefatigable will that was emanating from the warlord's gaze. Mynar dyl did not intend to leave. With an ironic tone, Alton ended their conversation before disappearing into his sedan chair.

"Farewell, Mynar dyl. There are dark days ahead if you choose to stay in Nargrond Valley!"

CHAPTER 6: Dyoren

"Dyoren, wake up! It is time. The sun is rising!"

There was no response. In the darkness of the tent, an inert body was lying still, impervious to the noise. The clan Llorely guard approached, now worried.

"This is no time for morning reveries. The houses are mustering to pay homage to the envoys before their departure to the Pact Gathering," he said, his voice becoming more insistent.

There was still no reaction.

The guard drew near, peering at the pale face of his companion who, he was horrified to discover, had stopped breathing. For an instant, he thought his friend was dead.
He shook the immobile body. To his relief, Dyoren's breathing resumed, though short and shallow.
Dyoren finally woke up, his eyes haggard.
He was then overwhelmed with a wave of intense fear, and began looking around himself for something he could not find.

"Where are you, Rymsing?" he repeated several times. "Have you forsaken me?"

Pain gripped his chest. The Seeker's breathing became frantic, and his whole body began shaking and sweating. The panic attack lasted but a few moments.

Dyoren managed to extract a few leaves from his purse, which he started to chew feverishly. After a time, he calmed.

His face was anxious, worn down by the weight of responsibility. His eyes betrayed the existential despair and spiritual dread that were tormenting him, as if he had just realised, he was doomed to fall short of the deities' expectations. Dyoren's face was marked by hardship, though his appearance remained fair. He had fallen asleep dressed in his dark green clothes. The Seeker had even slept with his traveling satchel and he gripped a long dagger in his hand. Its pommel was shaped in the form of a winged lion. A small lyre struck with the clan Ernaly's emblem lay close.

Despite his efforts to bring himself under control, Dyoren's body began shaking again. Even the muscles in his face were twitching violently. He had trouble standing on his failing legs. A scream of agony seemed to resonate in his mind.

Yet around him, all remained quiet. His companion opened the curtains at the tent's entrance, letting in the fresh morning breeze and revealing a deep blue sky beyond.

Even the clouds that usually hung above Mount Oryusk had vanished. There was no trace of the usual plume of steam rising from its summit. The air was clean, finally free of the volcano's noxious stench.

Dyoren kept chewing on the fresh vine leaves. He concentrated on breathing.

After a while, his limbs started to relax, with each of his trembling inspirations. A gust of wind dried the sweat upon his forehead.

Outside, it was dawn. The ruins of Ystanargrond were emerging gradually from darkness.

"You frightened me! For a moment, I thought you..."

"... had found the way to the hall of Eïwele Llyo," finished Dyoren, his tone grim.

"That is not what I was about to say..." the guard denied, before adding , "The envoys will participate to a ceremony before they leave for the grove of Llya." And he tried his best to cheer his ailing friend. "The weather is beautiful for the coming of the new moon."

Through his grief, Dyoren smiled as best he could. He had been touched so far by the kindness shown by the Elves of clan Llorely and wished to show his gratitude.

"You are more gracious than I deserve, Renlyo. I thank you. I know how dangerous it is for you to harbour me in your ranks. There are many Elves after me."
"Do not be concerned! As long as you are staying with us, you are Aeryos, the greatest artist who ever performed in Urmilla, our true friend like in the days of old. You have nothing to fear under our protection," pledged Renlyo.

Dyoren had to look away. He was deeply moved by this demonstration of true friendship and loyalty.

"I remember those days in Nyn Llorely with great pleasure, when I would walk by my father's side..."
"Aeryos, the fierce hawk, we called you! The bird of prey flying among the gulls. You won all the contests and drew some serious attention..."

But Renlyo's memories were interrupted.
Outside, a trumpet rang as clear as a bell to announce the start of the parade. Its sound grew louder and louder until Dyoren' ear was ringing: the bugle call for his own personal war of truth. The Seeker suddenly stiffened and turned to his friend.

"You called me Aeryos," he said, his voice trembling , "but that Elf is long gone, as is Neyrod, and all the other false names I have used...
I am Dyoren, and I will remain Dyoren until my very last breath. I may have put my sword aside for safekeeping, but there will not be a new Seeker until I renounce my vows..."

There was a long silence. Dyoren's sensitive, passionate soul had retreated far from the pleasures of the world he once loved.

The Seeker focused on the task of painting his face. This was one of the many skills that had so far kept him safe and anonymous during his errands across the Lost Islands.

At last, Dyoren was ready. He looked grave. Renlyo thought now was the time to mention the other reason for his visit.

"Someone came looking for you. It was before dawn, when I was on duty," he said, bearing a serious expression.

"Who was this someone?"

"A Llewenti with a fair face," replied Renlyo. "His hand bore the royal rune that protects foreign ambassadors."

"What did he say?"

"He was asking for information about a fighter who might have joined our clan recently. No one answered him. In the end, Lord Dol Urmil himself sent him away."

"Good! He did well. I am grateful."

Renlyo nodded in agreement. He believed his liege, the lord of Urmilla, had always taken sides with the clan Llorely.

"There is one other thing," he added.

"What?"

"Before he left, that fair Elf said something to Lord Dol Urmil: 'Let it be known, I have found where the Renegade is hiding.' Those were his exact words."

Dyoren turned away, his gaze becoming lost above the decimated rooftops of Ystanargrond, as if his vision were clouded by some insidious mist. His eye scanned the horizon, passing over the profiles of the surrounding hills and mountains, before finally fixing upon the dreaded silhouette of Mount Oryusk.

"I knew I could count on my half-brother to track me down eventually. His hatred for me is profound, far-reaching, unblinking. It isn't just personal rivalry or clan loyalty; this is no mere earthly conflict. Mynar dyl and I are ranged against each other by higher powers: the personal instruments of the quarrelling deities above.

You said this exquisite summer's day would mark the coming of the new moon. Let us enjoy the view before us... while we can," Dyoren concluded as he put on his traditional clan Llorely armour: a flanged cuirass and leg greaves.

He then seized his weapons and put on his bronze helmet, which covered his entire head and neck, with only thin slits for his eyes and mouth. A transverse horsehair crest marked his high rank. Wrapped in his long azure cloak, the unrecognizable Dyoren exited the tent.

★

The army of Gwarystan was gathering on the central square of Ystanargrond, in front of the ruins of Lord Rowë's ancient Halls.

Each unit was marching solemnly. Before the envoys proceeded to the Pact Gathering, a parade of their troops was taking place. The fighters, in full ceremonial garb and with precisely rehearsed movements, were marching to display their commitment to protect their ambassadors.

The soldiers wore weaponry and accoutrements of war. The High Elves' gear was aesthetic as well as functional; their armour was beautifully fashioned from tiny silvery chain mail, making it flexible and light, and each of their weapons was a work of art, finely crafted. The encrusted gems and carved runes of their tall helms glistened in the weak morning sunlight.

Among the oldest of all civilizations, the High Elves were once the greatest and most powerful race in the Islands. Their actions had shaped history. The current reign of Norelin, however, marked the twilight of their kin. Long and bloody wars had ravaged their once-great kingdom, which used to encompass all the Archipelago's isles. Since the Century of War, Hawenti influence had been dwindling. The beautiful cities surrounding the Sea of Llyoriane were becoming quieter each year. Only Gwarystan had not lost its former glory; the capital city still bustled with life, attracting many other Elves and a great number of Men.

As Dyoren passed by the ranks of the soldiers, he saw in their proud gazes that they remained resolute and unbowed. Tall and of slim build, the knights and guards of the noble households were fair to behold in their war dress. They stood a whole head higher than the Seeker and he knew that, in a fight, his own unmatched agility would not keep him safe for long against their strength and valour.

Then, Dyoren joined his fellow guards among the ranks of the House of Dol Urmil. The Elves from Urmilla were unique among the other Households. Half of the troops were composed of Hawenti knights while Llewenti fighters from clan Llorely formed the remaining part. Their home in north-west Nyn Llorely was a land where all Elves lived together under the same basic conditions and rights.

Their lord, Felrian, and his family were themselves characters of note, given their mixed origins. The blood of the Dol Urmil had comingled with that of the first Filweni navigators, the earliest example of the High and Blue Elf races mixing together.

Dyoren had always been welcome in their land, which most Elves called the Irawenti Coast owing to its history. Long ago, the clan of Filweni fleet that transported the High Elves had reached the Archipelago on the shingle beaches of these coastlines. The Seeker had spent his youth in that remote region of Nyn Llorely, along with his father. He returned to Tios Aelie, his home, whenever he had the opportunity.
On that decisive day, Dyoren felt proud to be clad in the azure garments and seagull feathers of his father's clan, the only true family he acknowledged.

Approaching the ancient Halls with his unit, Dyoren could not help but marvel at the beauty of the scene: the colourful garments, the splendid plate mails, the swords set with jewels, and the plumed helmets of the High Elf knights. It seemed the ambassadors of the kingdom had emerged out of the dusty ruined city of Ystanargrond, like lordly apparitions from the greatest Elvin kingdom ever known.

In front walked the heralds with their banners: the three stars of the Dor Inrod and Dor Inras, the two bronze dragons of the Dol Oalin, the white wings of the Dol Urmil, the azure harp of the Dol Braglin and many other proud standards.

'This takes me back to the ceremony at Gwarystan when the Century of War was finally ended. Great lords and knights were assembled that day,' Dyoren recalled.

The accompanying ritual songs drifted along the currents of air that whipped in all directions through the Halls' ruins. The splendidly dressed envoys were crossing the central square, while saluting their assembled troops with fervour. They marched with dignity past the ancient, pink marble seats which decorated the Halls' peristyle. In keeping with tradition, the ambassadors were part of the parade according to the noble houses' ranks; first came the representatives of the Dor households, followed by the Dol houses' delegates.

The morning sun reflected on the fine wool of their togas, the silk of their dresses, the silver and the steel of their armour and arms. The sparkling, colourful procession contrasted sharply with their surroundings: a scattered collection of ruins, exposed to the elements and covered with dust.

Four representatives of the Ruby College brought up the rear of the parade. Dyoren noticed the sinister Anaron, first of his caste, and two other high mages walking at a slower pace behind an older sorcerer, who was surrounded by several knights of the Ruby.

'Why has this lower-ranking high mage been honoured with the preeminent role here?' Dyoren wondered. 'The Fifth Arcane Master is carrying a jewel box. He seems to be the focal point of everybody around.

What could that box contain to be drawing such attention?'

The army formed a corridor on both sides of the majestic procession. The royal troops were vibrant, visibly proud to participate in such an unusual event.

On the Halls' steps stood Ilensar, the king's closest relative. Elder of the royal house of Inrod, this ancient High Elf had crossed the Austral Ocean with the Irawenti fleet. He was a cousin of late King Lormelin.

The prince was splendidly arrayed in the red silken cloak of the royal households and a bejewelled coronet. He was a great lord, known for his boldness, charisma and vision.

Ilensar Dor Inrod emphatically proclaimed the name and titles of each ambassador. He performed his task slowly, savouring every intonation, every stressed syllable used. Proud and noble, the prince-lord of Medystan paraded in front of the elite of Gwarystan's army.

Nine noble houses of the kingdom were represented in the procession beside the Ruby College. Only the House of Dol Talas was missing because of its religious conflict with the king. Its envoy, the Lady Beadiele, had decided to attend the Pact Gathering on her own.

Dyoren was scanning the crowd gathered in front of him when he first spotted the silhouette of Naldaron, the Twelfth Arcane Master, among the group formed by the Ruby College high mages. From that moment on, Dyoren focused his full attention upon his target.

"Today you will not meet with Neyrod... but with Dyoren. One of us, Naldaron, will not see sunset!" he murmured, and his gaze hardened.

The Twelfth Arcane Master seemed totally oblivious to the celebration taking place around him. Lost among the crowd of the high mages and their servants, like someone wishing to remain unseen, his attention was drawn to the group of druids who were welcoming the envoys of the kingdom.

The priests of Eïwele Llya had arrived before dawn to lead the ambassadors towards the grove on Mount Oryusk's slopes, where the Pact Gathering would take place.

Human and Elvin druids, dressed in their traditional brown clothes, walked among the Elves of Gwarystan and used this opportunity to preach the respect of the Mother of the Islands' creations. The brown of their robes represented the essence of fertility their deity granted to all beings.

The Seeker closed his eyes for a moment and uttered.

"Kryd ecsao!"[37]

---

37 Kryd ecsao: 'Detection of the Flow' in lingua Llewenti.

When he opened them again, Dyoren could see the movements of the Flow. Its raw power was borne upon gentle winds. Faint auras glowed around most of the Elves present or upon their belongings, as many of them carried magical protective objects. This ability to probe and detect the Flow around him, he had learnt from his mother, a matriarch of clan Ernaly. It allowed him to identify the source and nature of that essential energy around him.

Just as Dyoren had expected, the air in Ystanargrond was clean of any unnatural influences. The druids had seen to it.
Feeling safer, he could then concentrate his effort on tracking his target's every move.
Naldaron remained calm and focused, not even daring to share a word with his peers. Only he kept looking towards the group of druids on the other side of the esplanade, as if he was trying to identify one of them.

Ilensar Dor Inrod had finished enumerating the many names and titles of the Pact Gathering attendees. A respectful silence spread among the ranks of the assembly. The prince-lord of Medystan addressed the crowd. His tone was solemn.
Ilensar first told of the extreme natural events of the last years, especially of the tidal wave that damaged Gwarystan's harbour. His account echoed more recent news as well, marked by shipwrecks and severe floods.

Dyoren had already heard rumours of these signs of Gweïwal Uleydon's anger. Yet he did not know the reasons for holding this Pact Gathering now, so he listened attentively when the prince-lord of Medystan turned to the matters at hand.

"It is now more than one hundred years," said Ilensar , "since a message of peace between Men and Elves was whispered by the druids to the ears of the belligerents. Word came that the Century of War should be ended, and the factions of the Islands should cease their mutual destruction. Some of us put forth another argument: that greater wealth and prosperity would be found in a world of peace.
For the first time in our long history, the works of the druids proved beneficial to all and the defenders of nature conveyed invitations to the lords of Men and Elves. They spoke of the

grove of Llya on the slopes of Mount Oryusk and asked that all factions gather in that neutral territory to agree the terms of a lasting peace.

Since then, the realms of the Islands have held many such gatherings in the different corners of the Archipelago. Causes of strife are numerous among us: disputed territories, religious struggles, trade wars. Elves and Men will always find reasons to wage war against each other. But since the Pact was agreed, local crises have never degenerated into open conflict. We have also managed to keep the threat of the Three Dragons' Cult at bay. And that was the original goal of our peace treaty.

Today, it is no mistake that we have returned here, to the depths of the valley of Nargrond. Gwarystan and the druids wished to mark the importance of this year's Pact Gathering."

Ilensar was interrupted. A voice rang out among the group of the ambassadors. It was Felrian Dol Urmil; the lord of Urmilla was known to be outspoken.

"Never before have I seen so many units summoned to protect Pact Gathering envoys! Why were such precautions necessary? Some might think war is on our doorstep."

Lord Felrian's intervention triggered a series of queries from the crowd. Others were also anxious about the unprecedented security. Questions filled the air. Most delegations had been kept in the dark as to the purpose of this Pact Gathering.

"Why were we summoned? We want to know!" the herald of House Dol Rondalen asked. His eyes were sparkling like the silver star on his banner.

He was not the only Elf with worries. "If there are rumours of war, can the druids guarantee our safety? Do they have the power to prevent our enemies from attacking us?" cried an ambassador of House Dol Valra.

A voice rose from the assembly's front ranks. "Scouts have reported the representatives of Cumberae and Llymar are leaving the valley. They fled in the middle of the night," advised the envoy of House Dol Warlin.

Out of the confusion came a warlike speech from the knight commander of House Dol Oalin. "The Pact sets out severe sanctions for those refusing to participate in debates. Cumberae

270

and Llymar's cowardice must be met with strength. Ships from these lands will no longer be welcomed in our waters. We ought to consider them our enemies," he argued vehemently.

The steward of the House of Ogalen expressed his anxiety at the news , "If they chose to withdraw the day before the Gathering, they must know something we do not."

This uninterrupted succession of questions and concerns added to the confusion. The tension built up for a while until the prince-lord of Medystan intervened authoritatively.

"Silence! Silence!" cried Ilensar. "Hear me, my lords! You have no reason to prepare for war; none of the factions attending the Gathering would dare break the Pact. In this hour of peril, it is not fear of the druids' retaliation that would hold off our old rivals, but the necessity to unite before the threat which is arising."

The crowd's unrest changed into murmur of collective curiosity. Ilensar was a consummate orator. To captivate throngs of anxious Elves, he used his storytelling skills to recall recent events.

"A few years ago, in the last days of Winter, a messenger came to the gates of Gwarystan. This Elf was a mere fisher, almost naked, barely covered by a cloak made of shellfish. His only weapon was his casting net. Some witnesses in the lower city claimed he had emerged from the harbour's waters. 'Though the sea raged, he walked above it,' reported they.
The messenger called the king to his gate.

At this, the royal guards were greatly troubled, and gave no answer. They immediately alerted the tower of crimson.
After one of the high mages reached the scene, the messenger explained the purpose of his errand.

'A mighty gift was made when the High Elves were in dire need. The time has now come to return it. I speak of a marine pearl coming from the depths of the ocean,' he said.
Those words were bold indeed, for the messenger was referring to the Lenra Pearl, the most precious treasure of the kingdom. The fisher was arrested and taken to the dungeons of the Crimson Tower to be questioned. He was found guilty of demonic witchcraft by the College. Shortly afterwards, the

fisher was thrown to his death from the heights of Gwarystan Rock. His corpse was burnt by the fire of the high mages, and his ashes were returned to the sea."

Thereupon, Ilensar paused a while and sighed.

A long silence followed. Dyoren was hearing this tale for the first time. He wondered if the coming of that 'messenger' to the capital city was the cause of the king's attempt at recovering the Testament of Rowë. The events seem to have occurred consecutively.

'Did Norelin send his Mowengot servants to Nyn Ernaly because he feared divine punishment? The king desired above all else to know the content of Rowë's will, despite the turmoil this sacrilege would cause among his own people. He even fought a battle for it. Was what this 'messenger' said the reason for his anguish?" Dyoren wondered.

After a while, the Seeker made the connection with the tidal wave that destroyed the lower parts of Gwarystan earlier in the year. He came to realize the Cult of Three Dragons was not the only menace threatening the Islands.

Meanwhile, Ilensar resumed his address. He chose to relate events long past that were associated with the Lenra Pearl.

"After the Battle of Ruby and Winds, Ffeyn was diminished and confined, but not destroyed. The Sea of Cyclones became his cage. But the bars of his marine prison can be removed, for they were made with the power of the Lenra Pearl. While it remains in our possession, Ffeyn's destructive influence is restrained, but if that Spirit of Chaos was to recover the Pearl, what then?"

Silence fell. Even looking out upon the sunlit valley of Nargrond with the noise of streams and falls, Dyoren felt a deep shadow in his heart. All the Elves around him were looking at each other in bewilderment. To most of them, Ilensar's tale was wholly new. Of the rumours they had heard before the Pact Gathering, they understood little.

'At last, the things that have been hidden from all, but a few are being openly discussed. I now understand the great peril the Islands face,' thought Dyoren.

Then, all listened attentively while the prince-lord of Medystan spoke in his clear voice once more.

"There can be but one course. The Lenra Pearl should be hidden forever. Those envoys who will sit today in the grove of Llya must now find counsel. We, the inhabitants of the Archipelago, all face the same peril," declared Ilensar, allowing himself a pause before continuing.

"The king has requested this Gathering be summoned so that all parties bound by the Pact can decide the fate of Lenra. The Pearl is no ordinary treasure; it is the one guarantee that the Archipelago is kept safe from the devastation of cyclones and storms. It protects us from the wrath of the Austral Ocean. Losing it would bring about the Lost Islands' doom. Until now, the power of the Ruby College has kept this looming threat at bay. This is how harmony and prosperity have been maintained, within our kingdom, but also beyond our borders.

Yet, Gwarystan cannot keep protecting the weak without compensation. The other realms of the Islands, who shelter comfortably behind us, need to do their part as well.

Today at the Pact Gathering, in this hour of need, our envoys will request their assistance. Only Gwarystan has the power to withstand Ffeyn. What strength remains to counter him lies with us.

Hence, the kingdom will request that the other realms of the Islands give the Ruby College their remaining control of the Flow, to prevent the coming storm from wrecking the Archipelago.

That is the true purpose of the king's initiative to gather the Pact holders once again.

Envoys of Gwarystan, you now know what is expected of you today at the grove of Llya."

The conclusion of Ilensar's speech became the subject of passionate discussions. It made Dyoren react sharply.

'Listen to that doom-monger prophesying imminent disaster! He is stirring up a climate of fear that will only lead to the alienation of all the Islands Elves,' the Seeker thought.

Dyoren could read between the lines of the prince-lord's discourse. Long ago, he had been taught by his mother in the lore of the Flow. Surely, the Seeker did not possess the knowledge and experience of a matriarch, but still he knew enough to understand what was at stake.
The Lost Islands were riven with the energy of the Gods' gemstones, which drifted across the Archipelago. The powerful Flow, like a wind of pure energy, blew across all regions and was available to all those wise enough to control its force.

'Most of the drifting energies have long ago been drawn to the tower of crimson by the high mages, stripping the druids, the matriarchs and other powers of their share. In this way, the Ruby College drains the Flow out of the Islands and prevents the influence of the Gods and deities, overwhelming everything and turning their kingdom into chaos,' remembered Dyoren from his teachings.

'Now, the threat coming from the ocean pushes the high mages one step further to keep their world safe from destruction. By scaring the participants here, their ambition is to concentrate the exhaustive control of the Islands' Flow in their hands, depriving all other powers in the Archipelago of any influence.
For the other Elvin realms, there is a real danger that we will be jumping out of Uleydon's floods and into Narkon's fire,' feared Dyoren.

Ilensar descended the ash-coated steps of the front porch, heaving his high-up position. He crossed the esplanade and came up to the Fifth Arcane Master, who was standing at the heart of the envoys' procession.
A few words were exchanged, and signals were issued for the ambassadors to follow their druid guides. The group of the envoys started heading towards the gates of Ystanargrond, under the watchful eye of the soldiers. The column was made up of three figures of each Household. Only the Ruby College could send a delegation of four of its highest-ranking members.

In the silence of the cobbled laneways, accompanied only by the murmur of the nearby fragrant stream, the kingdom's ambassadors walked with majesty, fully aware of their strength and power, deeply convinced that their cause was right.

At last, the procession disappeared down the hill and into the obscurity of the surrounding woods. The troops began to disperse around the camp, but in a highly disciplined manner, for each unit was to remain on high alert until the ambassadors were safely returned.

Dyoren's heartbeat accelerated. For a moment, his vision blurred, and he could not maintain a clear focus on his target. The tension within him rose to an unparalleled intensity. The Seeker knew that the coming moments would be decisive. He was counting on one last throw of the dice: a momentous act of courage that would either ensure his victory, or kill him, and put an end to his long life of duty.

Dyoren moved forward as the Ruby College's mages went back to their quarters. But before the Seeker had made his first step, he noticed the air change around Naldaron. The sorcerer was using his powers. In the blink of an eye, he had sent forth a wave of energy to one of the human brown-robed priests. In the confusion that followed the end of the ceremony, nobody in the dispersing crowd seemed to notice. Dyoren, alone, glimpsed that brief jet of diamond powder flying like an arrow.

"I am sure he just sent a message to that bearded Man. Curubor once showed me something like it; he has just issued a command with his powers!" Dyoren exclaimed.

Trying to keep his panic at bay, his gaze darted from the druid, who stood several dozen yards downhill, to Naldaron, who had left his group and was now heading towards the maze of ruins in Ystanargrond North.

Dyoren looked back to the druid, trying to discern his features. He had barely seen his face before the bearded Man sharply turned on his heels and walked quickly away, towards the city gates. For a moment, the Seeker thought he recognized the druid from an earlier spying excursion he had made in Gwarystan, close to the tower of crimson. But he could not put a name to that strangely familiar face.

Dyoren immediately drew up a plan of action. Leaving his unit without a word, he rushed back to his tent. Once he made it inside, he went directly to a bird perch, where a hawk was quietly resting. It was a kestrel, a powerful and stocky falcon of brownish colour, which stood apart from the other members of its genus because of the dark slate-grey in its upper plumage.

With the dexterity of habit, Dyoren removed the bird's hood and placed it upon his leather gauntlet.

Exiting the tent, he whispered guttural instructions into the falcon's ear. The Seeker pointed southwest before releasing the bird into the air.

He dropped his helmet, javelin and long azure cloak on the tent's threshold, only keeping hold of his short bow, a quiver full of arrows, his long dagger and his satchel. Dyoren was thus abandoning everything that would connect him to clan Llorely.

A few moments later, the Seeker was running through camp, in the direction just taken by the sorcerer.

"Have you just seen one of the Ruby College high mages pass by?" asked Dyoren to an Elf who was walking across a street of the old warehouse district. "He would have gone through this passage a few moments ago. I bear an urgent message for him," the Seeker added, while displaying the rune of House Dol Urmil upon his hand's palm.

"One of those Eunuchs in red robes?" the knight of House Dol Braglin replied, indifferent. "I saw him, walking around like he was in a dream. Head in the clouds!" he added with a malicious look in the eye, as though the sorcerer's mood might have something to do with his castration. "He made no answer to my greeting and headed to the ruins of the amphitheatre."

Dyoren thanked the knight with a sign of the hand and rushed northwards in the direction the Elf with the Azure Harp emblem had pointed. This area of Ystanargrond was completely desolate and had not been settled by the army of Gwarystan.

In this part of the city, the collapsed warehouses, much larger than many of the city's other former structures, corresponded to far greater piles of rubbles and stones than anywhere else he had so far seen.

After a while, Dyoren entered a network of great standing stones with ancient markings. He eventually came to the remains of a small square. Statues of Lord Rowë and Lon the Wise loomed over the courtyard like ancient marble giants, filigreed with bronze and set with glittering stones. They towered over these ruins, just as their deeds eclipsed those of their followers.

Dyoren could not sense the presence of anyone within range nor within his line of sight. He was convinced, however, that there could be dangerous traps nearby. Just from where he was standing, the Seeker could see several sinkholes, and he did not have much faith in the unstable ceilings of the half-standing buildings that remained.

Dyoren decided to progress more slowly and with great caution, his senses on high alert, straining to detect any glyph of warding or a mechanical pit trap that may be lurking in his way. From inside his satchel, he retrieved a small purse containing powdery gravel. He scattered some of the contents all around him. Soon, traces of recent footsteps appeared before him.

'He must have been in a hurry!' thought Dyoren, surprised at the finding. 'I would have expected Naldaron to cover his tracks with his powers.'

Casting the sandy gravel before him as if he were offering gifts to Eïwal Vars, the deity of hunting, Dyoren followed the trail for more than a hundred yards amid the remnants of the old warehouse district. The trail led him to a small building which, from the solidity of its foundations, looked like an old sentry post. The structure was almost entirely intact, even boasting most of its roof.

Dyoren noticed the doorway was engraved with powerful runes. He understood these markings were channelling the raw power of the Flow, converting it into an elemental, violent kind of explosion. Anyone approaching the entrance would be torn limb from limb, riven by a force powerful enough to pulverise everything in the area.

'He is protecting himself with potent warding spells. He must be inside, designing some new mischief.'

Dyoren did not dare approach any further. Once again, he reached into his satchel and this time extracted a thin rope. He made a quick looping knot at one end.

Dyoren was able to get close enough to throw the rope up to the roof, where it caught on a corner stone. He pulled the rope until it was taut.

The climb began.

More than ever, the Seeker progressed with the utmost caution, knowing all too well that a single dull thud could cost him his life.

After what seemed like an hour, Dyoren reached the roof of the guard post. He noticed the tiling was severely damaged. Some tiles were broken, others had fallen away.

The sound of a loud voice came from within.

Dyoren looked down inside the building through one of the gaps.

The Arcane Master was hovering in the air above a triangular pentacle, while incanting words of power.

Then, all of a sudden, the sorcerer evaporated into a misty cloud, along with everything he was wearing and carrying. The strange mist floated upwards, towards the roof, before passing through a narrow opening. It all happened very quickly.

Dyoren stood still, in awe of the high mage's feat. He watched as the misty cloud drifted away slowly, towards the slopes of Mount Oryusk.

'He is heading to the grove of Llya where the Pact Gathering is held,' understood Dyoren, feeling utterly helpless.

Out of pure rage, the Seeker shot an arrow at the moving target before it disappeared into the woods. To his utter bewilderment, his arrow passed through the incorporeal creature without causing the slightest damage. The cloudy form disappeared into the canopy.

★★

Nargrond Valley, South of Ystanargrond, a few hours later

From his high vantage point, Dyoren caught a glimpse of the bent figure of the druid. Dressed in brown robes, his appearance was unkempt and filthy. Hobbling around, the bearded Man examined the traps he had set, before finally retreating inside a cave.

Dyoren made a high-pitched whistle, which sounded like the squeak of a forest animal sensing danger approaching. His kestrel came flying through the trees' branches, before perching on the Seeker's gloved hand. Like two hunters readying for a charge, bird and Elf turned towards the druid's lair, barely a hundred yards downhill.

"You did well, my friend!" murmured Dyoren in the falcon's ear. "You deserve a reward, one that no bird of clan Ernaly has ever received."

The disappointment of letting the nebulous high mage escape had not been easily put aside, for it had been the closest Dyoren had ever got to his target. But after a moment of furious exasperation, he had remembered the mysterious druid he had seen receive a signal from the sorcerer.

'There is still a way to find his trail,' he had hoped.

Praying that his hawk had been luckier than he, Dyoren had discreetly left the army's encampment by a breach in the southern walls of the ruined city. Lord Rowë's architects had built such imposing ramparts that, to his Llewenti eyes, even the ruins seemed like a formidable barrier.

It had not taken him long to spot his kestrel flying high through the sky above the surrounding woodlands. Following his bird's flight, Dyoren had headed into the wilderness southwest from Ystanargrond, thus moving further away from the location of the Pact Gathering and the army of Gwarystan, but much closer to the volcano's south-eastern slopes and the Mines of Oryusk.

After a couple of hours of intense effort, the Seeker had come within sight of his new prey and could congratulate his hawk companion.

Dyoren now stole down the side of the hill and made his way toward the druid's lair.

'It could be dangerous to approach this wild Man! But do I have a choice? I need to obtain indication of Naldaron's whereabouts by posing as a follower of Eïwele Llya,' Dyoren planned.

There was a heavy silence as he approached the cave's entrance. He had to pass through thorny thickets. His heartbeat accelerated at this deadly stillness. No glimmer of light came from the cleft in the rocks.

Dyoren called. No response came.

So, the Elf decided to enter the cavern. Crossing the opening, he lurked in the shadows within, waiting for his vision to adapt to the surrounding darkness.

The hermit, his uncombed hair dabbled with crimson, was sitting cross-legged on the ground. He was a thick Man, with a grey bearded face and tanned skin, which was gashed with two cuts. His small eyes were sunk deep in his head, like black holes. His legs were strong, giving him the aura of a powerful animal waiting to spring forward.

Crouched in the darkest corner, the druid stood up, revealing a knotted cudgel he gripped in his hand. He moved forward with ferocity, bringing the staff down with all his strength upon the intruder.
Dyoren's dagger deviated the blow.
The druid continued striking madly again and again, like a bear that attacks its prey until it lies limp and still.
But Dyoren's energy came in a flood at this moment of need. He ducked, dived and jumped out of the way, barely managing to avoid the blows. The fight was fierce.

The Elf begged his aggressor to stop, insisting he was there as a friend. Though he was only just avoiding the ferocious blows, Dyoren refused to fight back.

At last, seeing his opponent had no malicious intentions, the druid ceased his attack. He lit a bamboo paper lantern and the shadows of the small cave receded.

"I am sorry, son of the Mother of the Islands," Dyoren apologised. "I come to you in peace. I am a scout from Llymar. My errand is to find our way out of the valley. I thought you could help me."

"*I will not do,*" replied the bearded Man with a harsh tone. He understood the Llewenti language but could not speak it properly. "*What tell you are Elf of Llymar?*" he asked accusingly.

Dyoren showed his small lyre struck with the clan Ernaly's emblem, and he began to sing. His chant told of the forest of Llymar, the beloved woods of Eïwele Llya, of the swift shadows of the Austral Ocean's clouds, the winding blue rivers and the beauty of the pines. It was all simple and melodious, and it seemed to reach the druid's heart, for it spoke of the Archipelago which he loved.

While gently caressing the strings of the musical instrument, Dyoren had time to examine his reluctant host further.

Everything about the Man was strong: his muscular body, thick-set neck and large, powerful hands. Like a wild beast that can withstand the arrows of its hunters, the druid looked capable of holding death at bay. Years of strife had worn his life to the point that his heart and mind were painted clearly upon his wrinkled face. Bitterness and rebuke could be read in his eye now.

The Elf continued playing his instrument. He was a virtuosic player, renowned far and wide for his skills with the lyre. Dyoren preferred sweet and plaintive melodies that rang in harmony with what lay deepest in his heart. His lyricism was beautiful, masterful. The subtle play of his hands upon the airy chords created a melodious language, which echoed memories of the Islands' first days.

Once the music had worked its soothing effect on the druid's aggressive disposition, Dyoren explained the genesis of the lyrics.

"There is great potential in the Mother of the Islands' teachings. Her wisdom is as boundless as heaven and earth, as inexhaustible as rivers and streams, only ending to begin again, like the sun and the moon, dying only to live again like the three seasons of the Islands."

Dyoren understood the human priests of Eïwele Llya, having dealt with them on countless occasions during his journeys across the Archipelago. At first glance, he noticed the druid possessed uncompromising intelligence. It could be seen in the sparkling of his eyes; his mind had been pervaded by the beliefs of an extremist.

'This is a dangerous character: perhaps a visionary or, worse, some kind of fanatic.' Dyoren thought.

The Seeker felt his sudden arrival badly disturbed the hermit's plans. The druid wanted to throw him out of the cave. He knew he had but a few moments to coax his blunt interlocutor into revealing precious information. Like a snake charmer in a taming performance, Dyoren spoke up, with as cheerful a manner as the situation allowed.

"I am no common Elf. I am one of the Llewenti, the kin that discovered the Lost Islands. We are friends of the druids."
"*I not do care*," replied the Man bitterly , "*only the creatures vile believe the Archipelago not exist before they come.*"

Dyoren lowered his gaze, angry at himself for having expressed such an arcing assertion. Naturally, this druid would consider the Gnomes and Giants, or perhaps even animals, as the first inhabitants of the Islands. He needed to do better to earn the hermit's trust.

With a strange look in the eye, almost mystic, the druid declaimed the verses of his cult.

"There are only six colours, but they combine into more variations than could ever be seen. There are only six tastes, but they combine into more flavours than could ever be tasted. Who could ever exhaust the boundless bounty that the Mother of the Islands has laid out for us?"

It was apparent the druid recited those words as a prayer to Eïwele Llya, learnt by heart. Nevertheless, his erratic behaviour betrayed the confusion of his mind.

'This hermit must belong to this faction of dangerous priests who call themselves the 'true druids', extremists who work to restore the Archipelago's original purity. He is visibly mad,' thought Dyoren. 'His anxiety is so intense, someone must have put a spell on him.'

The Elf chose to chant an appeal to Eïwele Llya to calm the Man of the cave.

"And among the four elements none is dominant. Among the three seasons none is ever present. Days can be short and long. The moon waxes and wanes..."

His mother had passed much knowledge about the Islands' deities on to him. Above all else, Eïwele Llya's teachings formed the core of the instruction he had received, for the Mother of the Islands was the main protective divinity of the clan Ernaly matriarchs.

Following this demonstration of faith and gratitude to Eïwele Llya's creations, the druid showed less hostility. It was as if Dyoren's soft music had the ability to appease him.
Then, the hermit spoke with a more serene tone, no longer threatening, but almost confessional.

"I discover the Man is destruction," he confided. *"Me. I find this. My experience. Nobody tell me this. My big mistake? Hope that Man is good. Waste my time, waste my life, to preach to the tribes barbarian."*

The druid was looking at a small pendant, representing his deity, Eïwele Llya, which the artist had portrayed as the embodiment of life and fertility.

'Why is he now sharing his opinion about Men? I did not mention them. This mad hermit acts as if he is expecting imminent divine punishment for all those he cursed,' Dyoren realized.

'To gain his trust, I need to cling on to his crepuscular ode,' he figured out.

Thus, Dyoren immediately agreed with his interlocutor. The Elf's attitude and alertness of expression were striking in that moment. His gentle manners now perfectly masked his intent.

"The truth is Man is defiled and fallen. Few are worth saving; the vast majority are beyond redemption. Man embodies chaos! To submit to Eïwele Llya is to respect her creations. The Llewenti understood that. They do not seek to compete with the Mother of the Islands, they bow before her creations, quite the opposite of Man."

The druid rejoiced at these words and, feeling excited, he added with a vengeful tone:

"*To protect Eïwele Llya creations, I myself teach some Men and I kill all others. I must. If the Man so destructive, let the Man feast on its own blood, destroy itself.*"

The druid had finished his morbid reasoning in a whisper. A silence followed his deadly words.

Throughout his life, Dyoren had defended the causes that were dear to him sincerely, but also with moderation. He had always sought appeasement and compromise over extremism. What he had just heard affected his innermost values. The Seeker had dedicated his life to his quest for these same reasons, as he believed in the importance of his role for the benefit of his kin. Dyoren straightened up and looked at his interlocutor with more intensity. He could feel a deep resentment in his interlocutor's heart.

'It's no coincidence that Mankind has produced an evil such as the Three Dragons Cult,' Dyoren thought. 'Men hate each other deeply.'

The Elf remained quiet, but his irritation made his chin tremble. He wanted nothing more than to leave the cave, suddenly feeling dizzy in the confined, airless space. But he came back to his senses and pursued his strategy. Pretending to agree with the druid was gaining the Man's trust. The hermit would let his guard down and expose himself to Dyoren's scrutiny. Already the Elf could catch the Man's more superficial thoughts. Soon he would learn the purpose of his actions without his interlocutor even knowing it.

"I understand your anger, and I agree with you,' Dyoren continued with a friendly tone. "I feel the same, and my bitterness has only worsened over the years. Living in the forest for the most part, I have learnt a lot; all living things comingled to become fertile, everything that is not devoured... devours."

Dyoren leaned forward and took the druid's hand. The hermit calmed at the contact. Dyoren resumed, his voice as serene as ever.

"When I met the Elves of Eïwele Llya's cult, I finally entered a world delivered from folly, a world founded on respect."

The Elf held his eyes wide open in the shadows, almost as if wanting to enthral his interlocutor with his gaze.

"Everything is sacred to them: the flowers, the rocks and the waters that run the mountain streams. Innumerable spirits live and protect the creatures and creations of Eïwele Llya. If they are harmed, the Mother of the Islands is hurt herself. But Man ...," and here Dyoren took a deep breath, as if trying to control his anger , "Man defiles everything he touches, strips it of its sacredness; nature becomes unprotected, subject to his murderous will. Just look at what Men have done to their homeland in the continent. If they one day become masters of the Archipelago, they will reduce it to an arid waste."

"*Nobody given the Man Archipelago to protect,*" the druid responded. "*But the Man wants to seize Archipelago. Destroy the Mother legacy. Wild beasts, I prefer, much better than Man. But the things will change, the things soon will change. I myself tell you. Every time forest is destroyed by storms, big storms, forest grows again!*"

The bearded Man's eyes were filled with fury. He was now overwhelmed with his hatred for other Men and appeared as if in a trance. It seemed like hidden, unnatural forces were altering his state of consciousness.

'Something is about to happen!' Dyoren read in the gaze of the hermit. 'A mighty disaster will occur today! This raging madman is expecting it with all his soul! That is why he has retreated inside this cave: to avoid being hurt.'

Now deeply worried, Dyoren needed to know more. He decided to pursue his strategy of connivance by agreeing to the hermit's words of doom.

"Something needs to happen, for sure! But how? How can the Mother of the Islands punish those defilers, like they so rightly deserve? The power of Eïwele Llya is in healing and nurturing. She is a divinity of fertility. Who will rise to destroy them?"

"*Greater powers will act. The Seer of Oryusk foretold to me. He look into volcano, saw future,*" the druid answered hypnotically.

Dyoren scrutinized the hermit, overpowering his weak human mind, unleashing all his mental might until he had seized the crucial hidden obsession that had so inflamed the Man's soul.

'He is waiting for this 'Seer of Oryusk' to appear! His mentor will arrive in this very cave, and the promised destruction is about to begin! It explains the state of stasis he is in.'

The Elf froze, terrified by the revelation.
Dyoren then lost all his measured caution, unable to contain the impulse to know everything else immediately.

"Who is coming here? Who is the 'Seer of Oryusk'? Tell me now, I command you!" he yelled, as if his life depended on it.

But the verbal assault broke the spell, and whatever power the Elf had held over the Man was lost in an instant.
A much more present rage was now in the druid's eye. Like a wild animal defending its territory, the stout Man rose to his feet and toppled the small lantern, extinguishing what weak light there was.

"*Go, Stranger! Go now!* "the druid roared, threatening the unwelcome guest with his cudgel.

Despite the sudden darkness, Dyoren saw the hermit's weapon had changed shape; and he realized that a large serpent was entwined around the wood. He heard the snake's hissing as it lashed out.
Dyoren panicked and jumped back. The druid attempted to strike him.

"I am leaving! Spare me!" urged Dyoren, retreating hastily towards the mouth of the cave.

A moment later, and the Elf was outside in the daylight, fleeing through the thorny bushes as quickly as possible. Dyoren did not turn back to check if the druid was following him. He managed to escape and fled like one who never intended to come back.

But his real intentions were quite different.

After running for around a hundred yards, certain that he would now be out of sight, the Elf doubled-back and ducked behind a large boulder, covering himself with a pile of leaves. Soon Dyoren was invisible to the eyes of others. His traveller's clothes blended perfectly with the woodland floor. As he emptied the contents of a small greenish phial on his boots and his hair, he concentrated on his breathing to control its rhythm, so that even the most cunning of animals could not detect his presence. When it came to camouflage, the Elf was as invisible as a spirit of the forest.

The roar of a great bear echoed throughout the surrounded woodland. The powerful animal seemed to be summoning all the beasts of the valley to its side.

Dyoren remained safely hidden. All day, he had found it impossible to step back and think, so focussed had his mind been on the immediate tasks at hand. Now allowing himself a pause, he decided to clarify his thoughts which, until then, had been clouded by the overwhelming odds.

'The mad hermit is definitely the same druid I have seen several times near the Crimson Tower in Gwarystan. If only I could remember his name! It has something to do with the forest... Well, never mind, the two must have been in contact for some time, plotting this day together.

I can't know for sure, but there is a chance that this 'Seer of Oryusk', who the druid seemed to be waiting for, is the Twelfth Arcane Master himself...

And this is all happening during the Pact Gathering, on the slopes of the volcano...

Perhaps, after his mysterious errand, the sorcerer will meet the druid... Yes! That would make sense!

Perhaps luck has not abandoned me. Maybe there is some hope. I just need to stay within reach of the hermit's cave and wait patiently until... until the time comes to reclaim Lynsing,' hoped Dyoren, as his heartbeat accelerated and sweat dripped from his forehead.

After a while, Dyoren heard the heavy steps of a large animal. Without moving an inch from his hideout, Dyoren waited until it walked into his field of vision. It was a large bear, known as a 'Kumol' by the Elves. This rare specimen was an albino, a chance mutation of the black bear genus, unrelated to the sub-arctic white bears that roamed the icy lands of Nyn Llyandy. Dyoren remembered an old tale his mother had told him, in which a great black bear loses its colour after being bewitched by a sorcerer.

The Elf shivered as the Kumol passed a few yards away and failed to smell the Elf's presence. It soon disappeared into the bushes. Dyoren remained hidden, thinking.

'I knew it. I have known it all along, though I failed to see it at the time,' he said in a murmur, as he bitterly looked back on all the hardship he had undergone. At least he was finally being proven right.

'Ironic that the quest for Lynsing should end in that way!' Dyoren deplored, and he had a sad smile. 'The turning point of my life's quest came when I destroyed the six-fingered gauntlet of Eno Mowengot, at the battle of Lepsy Peak. How incredible that I should spend decades roaming the Islands, gathering information for my quest, only to stumble across the one crucial detail by chance!'

The Lonely Seeker tried to trace the events of the last four years, making a special effort to remember all the facts with accuracy. He was trying to find a causal link between his early findings about the Twelfth Arcane Master and what was happening now. Then, a new thought struck him: in case he did not survive, it was crucial that someone else was given the information he had learned. He wondered who he could trust. First, he thought of his bard friend in Llafal.

'But Curwë is far, there is no way I can reach him... On the other hand, my companions of clan Llorely are close. But I would lay a considerable burden on them. They have already taken so many risks for me...'

Suddenly, he hit upon the solution.

'It is in the princess of Cumberae that I must place my hope. She has always proven a loyal ally despite the recent upheavals, one of the very few who did not turn me down after my degradation by the Arkys. She was the only one who believed my findings about Moramsing and Saeröl's survival.
Terela has the power to act. I just need to find a way of getting my message to her... She cannot have gotten far: probably heading now for the southern paths of the Arob Nargrond with her troops...' he remembered from a discussion with Renlyo. 'Perhaps my hawk can find her... But what if it doesn't? What if my message falls into the wrong hands?'

Dyoren was biting his lip in frustration.

Then, an idea came to him. Looking at the pommel of his long dagger, shaped like a winged lion, his face immediately lit up, in a way that would recall a former self from long ago: the young adventurer who used to explore Nyn Llorely's wilderness for the sheer thrill of it.

Crawling forwards with great caution, the Seeker seized a medium-sized stone that was lying in a nearby bramble bush. He used his long dagger to engrave markings upon its surface. The blade of his weapon glowed as he murmured words of power in an ancient tongue. A few moments later, and he looked pleased with his handiwork.

'When Terela offered this enchanted dagger and entrusted me with the secret of her stone runes, I thought she was simply being opportunist. I remember how desperate the princess was for my knowledge about the Blades of Nargrond Valley, especially Aonya, the mightiest of them all.

But whatever her purpose, today I will put her teachings to good use,' he decided, fully determined to make the best out of the situation.

Dyoren knew what power these stone runes held. Somehow, these markings created a mysterious force that would disrupt the Flow in the very place he had engraved them. This disturbance would remain unnoticeable, but Terela would feel it. Even across a long distance, the princess would perceive that someone in the valley of Nargrond was using her stone runes to call to her.

Now convinced that he had chosen the best course of action, Dyoren drew from his bag a scroll, ink and a pen. His first few words were scribbled, almost illegible, such was his excitement. But, gradually, he managed to calm down. The act of writing it all down enabled him to clarify his thoughts.

2716, Season of Eïwele Llya, day of the Pact Gathering, two leagues south of the grove of Llya.

It all began when I destroyed Eno Mowengot's gauntlet four years ago, at the battle of Lepsy Peak.

I took the remains of the evil instrument to Curubor in Tios Lluin. The Blue Mage confirmed the gauntlet had been forged using an extremely rare power: Shadow Fire. Curubor told me Naldaron, one of the young Sorcerers of the Ruby College had earned his seat among the high mages' assembly by crafting dreaded gauntlets such as that one. These devices granted the King's servants with the extraordinary ability to evaporate into a mist, which could escape through the air, only to reappear again in their physical form when they willed it.

As he wrote these lines, Dyoren remembered the extraordinary spell Naldaron had cast that morning, which had enabled him to leave Ystanargrond unseen and, presumably, attend the Pact Gathering. The Seeker feverishly went back to his writing. Despite the stream of words flowing from his pen, he maintained an acute awareness of his surroundings.

Of all the records and documents, I have studied, only the annals of Yslla make any reference to this unique skill being used. The smiths of Nargrond Valley developed Shadow Fire to forge their legendary blades. My instincts have proven true; Naldaron has used Shadow Fire to make those gauntlets, it must mean he has learnt how the fabled smiths made their swords. I know for a fact they destroyed all records of their craft after their masterpieces were completed.

I therefore concluded the Twelfth Arcane Master of the Ruby College must have acquired this secret knowledge by studying one of the legendary blades himself. Since I realised this, I have been obsessed with the idea that one of the Swords may be hidden within my reach.

I spent many long days tracking this eunuch in Gwarystan. I think I came to know every possible hiding place near the tower of crimson, for Naldaron very seldom left it.

But now, my life of wandering finally seems to have served a purpose. It took many thankless miles walking the paths of the Archipelago for this moment of triumph, that day in the streets of Gwarystan when I saw Lynsing for the first time.

Precisely what happened that day is still not clear in my mind. Was it the closeness of her sister blade Rymsing? Was it her power which finally brought the Sword of the South to light? I still see the moment when Naldaron, getting out of his sedan chair outside the tower of crimson, just a few yards in front of me, stumbled. I can still see the knights of the Ruby rushing forward to help him. But most of all, I remember the blade falling from its invisible scabbard. It was there, out in the open for all to see, and Naldaron looked furious. My heart ceased beating, as if time itself had stopped; the shining scimitar with its sapphire-encrusted pommel was there, so close to me, almost within reach, its bare blade shining in the sun. The moment was over almost before it had begun, but it saved my soul. I am the first knight of the Dyoreni to have found any trace of Lynsing. My efforts were finally rewarded.

Then I discovered Naldaron was making excursions into the valley of Nargrond on his own.
Things would be very different now if I had captured him in the first place... but I failed.

I was running after a high mage of the Ruby College, and I found something very unsettling. There is only one Elvin druid who lives at the bottom of the Nargrond Valley in the inhospitable region of the Oryusk Mines. Only that Elvin druid has found ways of surviving near where the Giants dwell.

I now believe the druid of the Mines and the Twelfth Arcane Master are the same Elf, who is also known to his followers as the 'Seer of Oryusk'. How extraordinary to think this sorcerer has found a way to enter the Mines and return alive! It may even be that he dwells in the volcano's depths: the only Elf to know what lurks within!

Today, I am making a decisive effort to recoup the Blade of the South. I am hoping beyond hope I will succeed... but I am afraid... terribly afraid...

This brings me to the present moment. I know my enemy will soon come to one of his followers, a hermit he has most probably enthralled. Their meeting will take place inside a cave on the slopes of Mount Oryusk, near where I will hide this scroll. I need only wait. Today will be a day of reckoning. Lynsing can still be mine. I have the chance to take it back and restore my dignity and honour. For this, I am ready to give my life...

If I fail, it will therefore be your responsibility, my lady, to track down Naldaron. He must be captured and questioned, just as Saeröl must be found as well.

Who is the Twelfth Arcane Master? A sorcerer of doom? A druid of the apocalypse?'

Dyoren finished his account with these questions. He had filled what parchment he had.

"Here lies the last scroll of the Dyoreni," he declared solemnly, while sealing the parchment with his mark and placing it in a small wooden box.

The Seeker buried it in the soil. He placed the engraved stone on the earth above.
Now that his long quest was about to reach its end, Dyoren was overwhelmed with resentment. A powerful feeling of injustice pervaded his mind. He was the first ever of his order to have identified the wielders of two of the Blades of Nargrond Valley. But, the only reward for his sacrifices had been unjust humiliation. Worse still, the Arkys and the matriarchs had responded to his previous revelations about Saeröl and Moramsing with scorn.

Looking to the heavens, his eyes filled with a deep hunger for revenge, he murmured a secret oath.

"I am the knight of the Secret Vale and will remain so; I am the Seeker who was betrayed but who refuses to submit.
I swear before the deities of the Islands, I will not renounce my vows, even in death! No one shall ever succeed me!"

So strong was his conviction as he made this oath, that Dyoren almost fainted. His body started to shake, as though he had lost all command over it.

It took him some time to recover and, once again, he relied on the chewing leaves in his purse to calm his trembling limbs.

At last, Dyoren emerged from his hideout, flask in hand, to draw fresh water from the nearby spring. It was later than he thought, and the sun was far above the horizon. The woodlands had fallen quiet. Dyoren looked across to the peak of Mount Oryusk. It stood there bare and silent under the blue, cloudless sky.

But something strange suddenly startled him. The flask dropped from his hand.

He stood in total amazement.

The air was throbbing with sound.
It came at once and from all sides: rumbling, constant, very deep but incredibly loud, reverberating around the surrounding rocks.

Dyoren climbed the rocky pinnacle above him and stared out to the towering volcano. In his worst nightmares, the Seeker had never imagined such a fearful sight.
The volcano was erupting. A terrifying stream of fire and smoke was pouring in upon the valley. Boulders were pulverized into dust and blasted upwards. Ash was shooting high into the sky as the lava spurted relentlessly up from the earth's core.
Volcanic rock shot up from the peak, and poisonous gas was expelled from a fissure in the mountain's north-eastern slopes. Fragments of fiery earth and rock were shot in all directions in long arcs.
All around the furious mountain, barely a league before him, the air was thick with smoke, ash and cinders. The surrounding air was so hot that these particles were not cooling fast enough, so many had started blazes where they fell.

Dyoren realized that, of all the Elves assembled for the Pact Gathering, he alone was protected from the approach of this dreadful storm of fire, sweeping like a heavy shadow from the unknown depths of Mount Oryusk. He immediately thought of all the participants who would now be in the grove of Llya; those waiting in the ruined walls of Ystanargrond and, beyond them, the scattered, defenceless encampments which stretched down the valley.

This eruption differed from previous ones by its size and its eastward direction.
Mount Oryusk's lava flow had always run westwards towards the sea, through the plain of ashes. But now, for the first time, it was threatening the verdant expanses of Nargrond Valley.

Then something very strange occurred. A purple cloud was slowly invading the limpid sky. In its growing shadow on the ground below, leaves dried on the trees, birds stopped chirping, woodland creatures scattered into the hedges. The shadow then reached Dyoren, whose heart became unbearably heavy. He managed to keep his eyes turned towards the terrifying swarm. He lost himself in prayers, begging for the deities' protection. His hawk had stopped flying. Everything was silent and motionless, except for the vast advancing ash cloud, rolling in immense waves from the volcano. In the valley, towards the east, Dyoren could still see the summer sky, but coming from the west, the heavy mass was progressing relentlessly. The Seeker was weary, full of despair; he began to wonder if the sun would ever shine again on the Nargrond Valley.
The situation was dreamlike in its all-encompassing power, and yet this was no dream, for there was no waking.

At last, in the west, a sickly sun shone down upon the earth, and Dyoren remembered his errand. He stopped lamenting. Leaving his hideout, the Seeker started retracing his steps towards the hermit's cave.

★

Dyoren hid himself long behind a large boulder, a few dozen yards from the cave's entrance. That bare area of white limestone contrasted with the surrounding woodlands, rich with hazel trees and juniper bushes.

A strange, high-pitched wail came from a gap in the rocks close to his hideout, which the wind was blowing through. The mournful sound was like the highest note on an ancient organ. Dyoren froze and watched the strange trail that was now curving among the rocks. The Seeker was straining his ears to catch every single whisper in his surroundings when a dull sound, quite different from the volcano, drew his attention. It was almost imperceptible at first, but soon became persistent, more regular, like the faraway echo of soft drums building to an intense, chaotic symphony.

A moment later and he was convinced.

"It must be him!" Dyoren murmured, leaning on a rock to stop himself from falling.

The revelation that his enemy was approaching struck him with incredible force; it immediately dominated his thinking, as all other thoughts aligned themselves to it. The same noise echoed again, seizing Dyoren with excitement, even though the noise was covered by the rumble of the erupting volcano. An irrepressible shiver ran through his whole body. He listened again. Despite all the noise around him, he could hear his heart beating. The eruption on the slopes of Mount Oryusk seemed to have diminished in intensity. A few moments passed. Dyoren expected with all his being for the sorcerer to appear at any instant, but his eyes told him no one was there. His ears finally picked up the approaching footsteps. He could hear them distinctly: footsteps over rocky soil. Suddenly, just as he was putting his hand to the hilt of his long dagger, the Seeker saw an even darker form in the shadowy landscape before him.

"Here he comes," murmured Dyoren. "He is alone."

The silhouette of a tall Elf was crossing a small ford, faintly illuminated by the weak evening light. There could be no mistake. A deadly cold descended upon Dyoren's heart. The shadow walked quickly but carefully. He was wrapped in the long reddish cloak of the High Mages, pulled up to cover his face. And, under this coat, Dyoren could make out the shape of an invisible sheath. It was Lynsing: The Blade of the South, the bringer of wisdom, and the purpose of his life.

Dyoren made himself as small as possible behind the boulder and waited with strained ears for the moment the sorcerer passed him by.

The moment came.

He sprang from his hideout and lurched forwards, his long dagger raised to stab his foe. The blade cut through the air.
He struck the sorcerer in the back, just below his heart, but it failed to pierce his body.
The bracers around the sorcerer's wrists radiated with a flashing light.
The blade of the Dyoren's dagger slipped and caught the high mage in the arm, burying deeply into his flesh.
Almost by reflex, Dyoren struck out again, slicing at the Elf's left wrist. The long blade cut through his forearm. Blood gushed onto the soil. A jewel box inlaid with silver fell to the ground, a severed hand still gripped around it. It rolled away into a small ditch.

Dyoren stared at the fountain of blood erupting from his enemy's arm. But, despite the wound, the hooded figure quickly reached for an invisible scabbard at his back. A pommel inlaid with sapphires and a shining blade appeared in his remaining hand. But the weakened sorcerer dropped the long scimitar clumsily at his feet.
Seizing the advantage, Dyoren raised his long dagger to deliver the final blow.
The Seeker pierced his opponent's abdomen. But, almost at the same time, the sorcerer hit him in the ribs with a black knife, before he fell heavily to the ground, his head striking a boulder. In a final, desperate effort, the sorcerer's remaining hand managed to seize back his scimitar.

Suddenly, out of the cave's darkness came a thunderous roar. An enormous white bear came charging out into the open. The beast attacked with frenzy, as if protecting its cubs.

Dyoren turned to confront the formidable new opponent. A ferocious close melee began between Elf and beast, between dagger and claw, between proven agility and pure brute force. Having escaped several mortal blows, Dyoren, at last, managed to leap up onto the animal's back. The blade of his dagger pierced the animal's throat, pushed in all the way up to its hilt. The bear made a few staggered steps but did not survive long. The beast looked down in astonishment at the long knife buried in his throat, as though it had been the winged lion carved into the pommel that had killed him.
The bear hit the ground with a loud thud.

The badly injured Dyoren failed to retrieve Terela's weapon from the cold body of the monstrous animal.
He then looked back to where his first victim lay. But the sorcerer was gone.
Despite his many wounds and the dreadful pain in his ribs, Dyoren managed to limp back to the scene of the first fight. Soon, he was following his victim's trail; there was blood all over the ground. But the trail did not lead far. The track ended by the same rock he had been hiding behind. The Seeker used his various tracking skills to detect the presence of the wounded sorcerer. A deep anguish overwhelmed him as he was forced to face the latest setback in his quest.

"He has escaped... he used his powers to escape...
Will I only know defeat?
Am I forever cursed?
Deities of the island, I ask you, am I cursed?" the Seeker shouted to the heavens.

Everything seemed so dark. Before him, the only sight he could contemplate was the disastrous aftermath of the eruption.
Feeling dizzy, and suffering greatly from the pain in his ribs, Dyoren retraced his steps, like a blind Elf who has lost his way.

Then he saw it.

A jewel box inlaid with silver was lying at the bottom of a small pit. Dyoren kneeled and took the treasure.
For a moment, his suffering ceased, as if this finding were the sweetest of remedies for his pains.

Dyoren opened the small box. He was immediately struck by the unique beauty of the jewel inside, a marine pearl made of a crystalline substance, glowing with an unnatural light. The hard-glistening jewel was perfectly round and smooth. It was composed of a nacreous and iridescent material, which was deposited in concentric layers.

Dyoren was deeply moved by the purity of the flawless pearl, its deep azure colour represented the perfect metaphor for the ocean's mystery.

★

A haggard and beaten Dyoren wandered without purpose for almost a league. With the approach of night, the darkness encroached ever further. And still, the same heavy cloud of dust slid from west to east, as the volcano poured out ashes. The smoke was dense, like a curtain being drawn across the sky. Each time Dyoren raised his head hoping to see a lull, his eyes met the same endless cloud. The air was filled with the stench of burning leaves. It was as if the land were covered with pustules. The path sloped upwards as he approached a hilltop when his strength began to give out, and his will began to waver.

'So, all these sacrifices will have been in vain.'

The Seeker tried with all his might to maintain his spiritual balance. But he knew it was in peril. He lurched and stumbled on.

'It is in my nature to fail, I can't escape it,' he deplored.

In his weakened state, he was struggling with the growing doubts that assailed him.

'What more could I have done? Naldaron is behind everything. How could I fight such power? I am sure he has influenced the Ruby College's decision to summon this Pact Gathering. Perhaps he plotted with the druid's circles to organise the Gathering on the slopes of Mount Oryusk. How? How could such a disaster occur? How could the volcano awaken and devastate the valley on the very same day that the Pact Holders are gathering? What mighty forces bring such chaos? It is completely beyond me.'

Still feeling an intense pain in his side, Dyoren looked at the deep wound caused by the sorcerer's black knife. It had been bleeding continuously despite his efforts to stem it. He inspected it again and re-dressed the bandage on the sore. There was no poison inside, but the Seeker feared a powerful witchcraft was at work, preventing the wound from healing as normal. Dark thoughts swelled in his mind.

'His blade must have been forged with Shadow Fire. Its bite will prove fatal.'

Despite the rising desperation, Dyoren could not chase his obsessive thoughts from his mind. He examined the jewel box in his hand once again.

'From the very beginning, Naldaron's purpose must have been to seize the Lenra Pearl. That most prized of all the king's treasures has long remained inaccessible, hidden deep into the dungeons of the Ruby College. But why? What could be his motivation? I cannot believe his plan was to sail the Sea of Cyclones and offer the Lenra Pearl to the Winged Prisoner. Regardless, no ship in the Islands would ever survive such perilous journey.'

Dyoren applied balms upon the numerous wounds inflicted by the bear. These plant decoctions were precious gifts from the matriarchs of clan Llorely that would ease pain but, unfortunately, would not sooth the soul. The deep wound in his ribs continued leaking blood. Beyond his physical pain, Dyoren remained somewhat inert. His will had abandoned him. Languor succeeded pain, as though the sorcerer had managed to reach his innermost passions with his blade. Dyoren's fleeting thoughts and melancholy made images of his memories pass before him, and he painfully relived all his past emotions. His dreams had vanished like light clouds in a dark sky, scattered away by the murderous knife. All the high points of his life were dispelled, his existence changed into a relentless dark journey.

"First, my only companion Rymsing, whom I worshiped as something she could not be. That shining blade, the incarnation of all my hopes, showed me how easily love can be disguised as betrayal, how quickly a luminous glow can disappear into the darkness," Dyoren murmured aloud.

"What a fool have I been! How different did the Arkys prove from what I had hoped! I can still hear their reassuring words, from back in the early days. I can still see their encouraging expressions, safely guiding my perilous quest from afar," he remembered with bitter disgust.

His whole body was exhausted, and his spirit was tormented; he could neither speak nor remain silent.

Dyoren came up to a shelter concealed in the hill's rock wall, and he decided to stop for the night. He would be able to hide there while keeping a panoramic watch over the horizon. This high position commanded a view of the west beyond the volcano, over the green waves of the woods to the distant arid summits of the Arob Far. The great convulsions of that desolate mountain range gave its numerous peaks the appearance of a hound's jaw. It reminded Dyoren that the valley of Nargrond was only a tiny slip in the vast island of Gwa Nyn.

Darkness had almost closed in. The sun was setting, and one last glimmer of reddish light rested upon a rocky peak of the Arob Far.

The beauty of this view eclipsed the desolate spectacle of Mount Oryusk's eastern slopes after the eruption. But when Dyoren's eye returned to that field of ashes, he was struck with astonishment. His falcon was flying in wide circles over the opposite hill, whirling about to let his master know that it had found something.

On the slope opposite from his temporary dwelling, a group of three Elves were progressing with difficulty, their outlines barely visible in the fading light.

It was a strange sight. A tall Elf, assisted by a hooded character clad in an azure cloak, carried a makeshift stretcher. Inside was a wounded Elf. From his bald hair, impressive size and his dark plate mail, Dyoren recognized the leader of the unlikely little company.

It was Roquendagor, the formidable knight, one of the Elves from Essawylor he had met in Mentollà.

Dyoren could barely believe his eyes. He stood there for a long while with his body bent.

Soon, the vision of the three Elves had gone, and the volcano showed up hard and naked against the faint western glimmer. Then night closed in, and all was black once more.

Despite the surrounding darkness and his growing weakness, the Seeker decided to go after the group. But before departing, Dyoren took a potion from his bag.

'The wine of the deities, the blood of the Mother of the Islands. It shall give me the strength that I shall need,' he hoped.

Dyoren slowly drank the precious liquid in long gulps, savouring the full essence of the sweet nectar as if it was his last opportunity to enjoy such pleasure. The wine invigorated him. A strong power flowed through his veins, chasing away, for a moment, the pain harboured in his body.

★

After skirting around the side of a small lake, Dyoren crossed a stream before climbing a long bank and passing through thorny bushes leading up the opposite hill.

Dyoren was cautiously approaching the top when he heard hushed voices. He silently drew closer and discovered a campsite. The Elves of Mentollà were speaking lingua Irawenti to each other, but he managed to roughly understand what they were saying, despite his lack of fluency in that foreign tongue.

A fourth Elf seemed to be back after exploring the surroundings. He was reporting his findings to his companions.

"I could not find him. My birds have fled. There is little more I can do," announced the first voice with its foreign accent.

"Could this all be a trap?" wondered the second voice, whose words were coloured by exotic notes.

"Alef Bronzewood gave me his word. If he did not make it, it means he could not," replied the first voice with conviction.

"He won't have been the only one caught off guard by the eruption," added a third, deeper voice, with a gloomy tone.

Dyoren decided to signal his presence. And so, he walked towards the campfire, strumming at his lyre. He chose a sad and languorous song from the repertoire of the Dyoreni knights, a well-known ode that he used to play in Llafal.

> "When I had lost all which once I held dear,
> With heaviest heart, I fled home in fear,
> Until, far from home, began my true tale,
> Above the mountains in the Secret Vale.
>
> Atop gloomy trees came the creeping dawn,
> Still was I broken, and still did I mourn,
> Then the deities' servants my service sought:
> I must find the blades Lord Dol Nargrond wrought.
>
> I gave solemn vow as the Arkys bade,
> Then one stepped forth, and raised up a blade;
> Gleaming with emeralds was the beautiful sword,
> I held her in my arms: my life was restored.
>
> As Dyoren, the Seeker, was I thereafter known:
> The Secret Vale's knight who must wander alone.
> Yet all across the Islands are a thousand grateful lips
> That whisper of my glory, which no one shall eclipse."

But the linen-haired bard was not in Llymar anymore, and nobody here would applaud his marvellous voice, which rose and fell in perfect counterpoint to his melodious lyre. Instead, a deep commanding voice sounded back from the camp.

"Who goes there? Make yourself known!"

"I am your friend, Roquendagor! I come in peace," answered Dyoren, and his voice was clear. "Do you not recognize my music when you hear it?" he added maliciously.

Emerging from the darkness, the Seeker stepped into the area around the campfire. He threw back the hood of his cloak to salute the four Elves of Mentollà. It took a moment for his eyes to adjust to the light of their blazing log fire.

Roquendagor was standing near his companions, talking to the guide of clan Filweni, Feïwal and to Gelros, the scout. It was difficult to make out the wounded Elf lurking in the shadowy outskirts of their camp.

When Dyoren came further into the light, the Elves of Mentollà stared at him with strange expressions. Although their demeanour was not defensive, they were perplexed, and the Seeker realised he would have to offer some explanation as to what he was doing in such a desolate place. He felt far from comfortable under the stare of their keen eyes.

"These are strange circumstances for a reunion," Dyoren said, watching the Elves of Mentollà's faces, as if their expressions might tell him how best to deal with the situation.

They returned his gaze with the same questioning intensity but said nothing. Dyoren's attention fixed on Feïwal, who stood unmoved, giving no sign of his thoughts. To clear the air, the Seeker came forward, closer to the firelight, with open palms.

"You are wondering why I am here... and so am I," he said, drawing his hand across his brow. "It seems Eïwele Llyo has deigned to wait a little longer before welcoming me to her great hall, for I have been spared today. I was on the other side of Mount Oryusk, away from the grove of Llya. I wonder how many of the participants to the Pact Gathering survived..."

"We were not as fortunate as you," replied Feïwal, finally breaking his silence. "Curwë was badly hurt. He was struck with some fiery debris ejected from the volcano. It is a miracle he was not burnt alive. We've been carrying him ever since."

Dyoren turned to the fourth Elf who was in a corner of the campsite. He was lying down on a blanket with his feet towards the log-fire. The Seeker could not distinguish the wounded Elf's face, but he immediately recognized the voice which answered his unuttered question.

"I am fine, Dyoren. You have not heard the last of my Muswab yet. You'll be covering your ears in agony before you know it."

Grinning rather than smiling, the Seeker looked at his friend with wonder, as Curwë tried to come into the light.

"You have a stout heart," Dyoren said , "but it was foolish to come to the Valley."

There was no further outpouring of emotions between the two friends, for Feïwal interrupted them. His voice was inquisitive and insisting.

"Have you come across any other survivors?" Feïwal asked bluntly.

Dyoren paused. "I did not," he finally answered, but immediately reversed the roles, looking at the three Elves before him. "What are you doing on the slopes of Mount Oryusk? As far as I knew, Mentollà was being represented at the Pact Gathering by the envoy of Llymar."

None of them answered. Dyoren understood the two other Elves would not talk, and that whatever their reasons were for being in the Valley, only Feïwal would tell.

"There have been many druids about, dispatched to various places to serve as guides for the factions participating to the Pact. Have you not seen any? One of them was meant to meet us to show us the way out of Nargrond Valley," insisted the Irawenti guide.

Dyoren thought for a moment, fearing some trap and wondering how this discussion would end. He had known Feïwal during his days in Mentollà. The guide of the clan of Filweni had even provided him with care and advice that had greatly aided his recovery. Yet, he felt in his heart that Feïwal was an Elf more self-regarding than his stern and wise attitude betrayed.

"I cannot help you," Dyoren said at last.

Roquendagor frowned and looked at Feïwal for guidance. But at last, his impatience got the better of him.

"We need to leave the Valley after this disaster," burst the knight. "It is said you know paths that are seldom trodden. Will you not help us?"

There was a heavy silence. Still, Dyoren made no answer.
At this, Roquendagor stepped forward, eager to demonstrate that strength and numbers were on their side. But from the shadows, the voice of Curwë rose.

"Easy, friends! It would be terribly rude to start fighting as I lie here at death's door. I deserve better. Keep your calm! We are allies here. Dyoren is no common Elf, he is the knight of the Secret Vale. I would expect my companions to show him respect..."

Curwë's intervention helped ease the tension. Dyoren immediately understood how necessary it had been, for what he saw in Feïwal's eyes was a more than implacable will. No doubt, the Irawenti guide was after something: and something he direly needed.

"If anyone thinks otherwise, he had better deal with me first!" insisted Curwë, and he made an attempt to get up, only to fall back painfully onto his camp bed.

Roquendagor laughed, Dyoren smiled, Gelros grimaced, but Feïwal remained stolid, his concern sharpened by Dyoren's muted responses.

Seeing he had nothing more to fear, Dyoren made an offer to the company.

"I will soon be on my way. Let me take the watch with Curwë. Take this opportunity to rest. You will need all your strength if you are to return to Mentollà."
"Thank you, Dyoren," said Curwë to mark his confidence in his friend. Turning to his companions, he added , "Now rest, you heard me. We will keep watch. If the mountain gets struck by lightning or the valley gets submerged in a tidal wave, you will be the first to know."

Roquendagor let out a good laugh at this. "Don't wake me up unless Zenwon, Agadeon, Uleydon and Narkon attack the camp. I am tired after carrying you all day, weakling!"

The three Elves of Mentollà withdrew from the two friends. Then, they all fell silent, and one by one dropped off into much-needed slumber. Curwë and Dyoren found themselves alone in the corner of the campsite. First, the two friends sat quietly, as if waiting to see who would take the initiative to speak first.
Finally, Curwë addressed his mentor gravely, anticipating many inevitable questions to come. He bowed his head as he stirred and whispered softly.

"I cannot answer you, Dyoren, even if I wanted to. I am simply following Feïwal dyn in his errand because he asked me to. My friends and I owe him our allegiance, for he saved our lives. Back in Essawylor, we were banished by Queen Aranaele. Feïwal dyn took us beyond the Austral Ocean and offered us a new existence here.
Now, what reasons he had for coming to Nargrond Valley, I sincerely do not know, nor do I want to know. I am simply repaying my debt...
I can guess what you are thinking, what it is you need to ask. Rymsing is safe, Dyoren. I did not take your sword with me. You no longer need worry about it."
Dyoren's answer came almost immediately. "You are being diplomatic in a delicate situation. But your face is telling me more than your words."
"I am not lying, Dyoren, and I have told you as much as I can."

Stepping back a little, the Seeker cast down his piercing eyes.

"I know you would not lie to me, my friend," he muttered. "Now, listen, all of Llymar knows I have no love for my half-brother, Mynar dyl. I know he has had some grievance with you too.
I did not doubt he would gladly avenge the Arkys' honour after my refusal to submit. When I left Llafal after our last encounter, the fiercest of his guards were on my heels. One of them had identified me. It was a lack of vigilance on my part.

Thus, as I sailed my small fishing boat out of the Halwyfal's waters, I wondered if my original mistake might lead Mynar dyl to you. I feared my half-brother would hurt you, and it would all be my fault. That is what concerned me most. As for Rymsing, I did not want to return it to the Arkys after the unjust shame they brought upon me. Nor do I wish to become the first knight of the Secret Vale to lose the Blade of the West. It is a mighty heirloom.

Should that Blade now be the possession of the Arkys, I would consider, just as you have said, that Rymsing is safe, that I no longer need to worry about her.

Have I hit near the mark?"

Curwë did not reply, but his face was filled with relief. To soften the atmosphere and rekindle that precious companionship he had with his mentor, he started playing his own instrument.

The bard from Essawylor did not play one of the cheerful, lively songs his friends so loved, but rather a sweet and plaintive melody that harmonized with the current thoughts of his heart, like the echo of his deepest feelings. It was the strong and unique bond of music which had brought the two Elves together during their time in Llafal.

"I see you have brought your special lyre with you, the famous Ywana," noted Dyoren.

The Irawenti-designed instrument had been saved from the wreck of the Alwïryan. Since then, it had hardly left Curwë's side. Dyoren examined it closely, as if it had the power to recall happier days. He remembered the powerful enchantment that captured his audience when his fingers touched the exotic instrument's chords.

"You carried my guests to unknown lands the nights you played the Irawenti lyre. It was as if a sea spirit was singing for us," Curwë said with admiration.

"The harmonious tones produced by its warm strings has always amazed me. Never in my life had I encountered anything else quite like it," remembered Dyoren. "Do you know, I spent the best days of my life in Llafal, at the House of Essawylor?

That too short period of peace, where we would spend all morning writing music and every night dancing, singing and playing at those famous feasts...

The House of Essawylor was open to all. Naturally, I was curious to experience the culture you had brought with you across the ocean. But what I liked most was the diversity of talent hosted there. Every genre of music in Llymar was represented."

"In a short time, the House of Essawylor became a place for friends of all cultures. I felt a great pride in that," Curwë concurred. "Somehow, those festive nights forged ties between the shipwrecked and our hosts. Back in Essawylor, we had always lived under the absolute authority of Queen Aranaele. When we arrived in Llafal, my friends and I marvelled at the Llewenti customs. Llymar has long refused the rule of tyrants. The clans have always relied on the authority of their matriarchs to guide the community. We admired that."

"Curwë, your House of Essawylor will remain dear to my heart... It was as if, through music, I could smell the fragrances of your homeland, see the colours of the tropical trees and birds, and hear the music of the streams. I felt bewitched by the tales the Irawenti would sing so beautifully. For a few stolen hours, I could escape the burden of my solitary life of wandering," Dyoren confided.

The moon was already beginning its descent when a sudden pain forced him to move from his previously comfortable position. Curwë noticed how his friend's hand would keep reaching down to his ribs, as if a hidden wound were troubling him. He felt the need to demonstrate his support and affection.

"You will return, Dyoren. And I will organise a great party to celebrate your homecoming," he promised, as cheerfully as he could manage.

Dyoren nodded, but in his heart, he knew that joyful reunion would never take place.

After they had eaten and drunk sitting on the grass, the two friends, caught up in their memories, stayed up conversing well into the night. No moonlight bathed the desolate slopes around Mount Oryusk. From time to time, they would blow into the embers of their small fire to keep it from burning out.

At last, the spectacle of the volcano's continued eruption pulled them from their light-hearted discussion. The night was as dark and as gloomy as the bowels of the earth.

Dyoren stared at a fixed point on the ground to overcome his sudden dizziness. The soothing effect of the matriarchs' elixir was starting to wane. Cold sweat trickled down his back, contrasting with the campsite's warm atmosphere. Dyoren suddenly stiffened, as if listening out for nocturnal sounds far away. He knew the time would soon come for him to leave. But first there were important things he wanted to discuss. Changing his attitude, the Seeker turned to his friend, his face grave.

"It is said in ancient songs that Rowë Dol Nargrond was the greatest of the High Elves to set foot on the shores of the Archipelago, surpassing even King Lormelin in his wisdom and lore. According to legends, his father, Nargrond, was one of the fatherless Elves, born from the mind of Ö, the Creator. Rowë had walked alongside the Gods in the early days of the world, benefitting from their teachings, taking advantage of their knowledge. His scholarship and charisma could have allowed him to aspire to the greatest positions among the High Elves. But power was not what he wanted; he preferred to serve others, taking only the title of Dol for himself and his lineage. He became a talented blacksmith and a renowned alchemist, and few among his kin could claim to surpass his talents. For centuries, he served the Hawenti kings and was always at their side. He served them in their conquests, he served them in their wars, he served them in their crimes...

It is written in the annals of those days that Rowë felt deeply troubled by the conditions imposed upon the Llewenti by his liege, King Lormelin, after his conquest of the Archipelago. Many scholars interpreted the Conqueror's deviant behaviour, his thirst for power at all cost, as a sign of the curse laid upon the High Elves by the Gods; like a damnation which would pursue them across whatever seas and mountains they conquered. This was the source of Rowë's profound fear of the future."

"Why are you telling me this? It's not as though the heroes of these legends will spring back to life out of Mount Oryusk," interrupted Curwë, worried by the solemnity of his companion's tone.

"I am telling you this because the hour is late and there is much, I must entrust to you... before we part," replied Dyoren severely.

The Seeker rose with difficulty from the grass and, taking two cups from a small chest that lay on the blanket, he filled them with the content of a potion which he mixed with fresh water.

"This is the last philtre I have. It was prepared by the matriarchs of clan Llorely," he said.

Dyoren gave one cup to Curwë. He bade him drink. Standing before his friend, Dyoren suddenly appeared taller. In his eyes gleamed a new light, prophetic and keen.
At last, once he had drunk his own cup, the Seeker spoke again.

"I believe that Rowë made the legendary blades to shape the Islands' Elves destiny. It became the great work of his life. I believe their forging was a spiritual act, an attempt to fight the curse of the Gods and celebrate the message of the Islands' deities, which was one of hope and independence.
The Blades of Nargrond Valley were made with metal from the meteorite. They were heat-treated on summer solstice. The rituals performed during the process were based upon the movements of the Sun. And Ö, the Creator, has always been associated with natural light. The link between the Sun and the Swords is omnipresent throughout all the smiths of Yslla's rituals. The sunrise signifies revival. I believe the Swords can restore life to the Islands when the time of the great disaster will come."
"So, this is the role you have been playing all along with such blind dedication. It was all because of your everlasting commitment to the Elves of the Islands. What you are saying is that the Swords are not instruments of power, but of salvation."
"This is what I came to believe, and why it is so important to find them. I see the Blades of Nargrond Valley as relics capable of keeping the destructive power of the Greater Gods at bay.
Lon the Wise predicted that a time of great disasters will one day come. Men will be the dominant cause. As human populations continue to grow, the chaos and havoc they wreak will provoke the Greater Gods' wrath. The divine powers of Zenwon, Uleydon, Agadeon and Narkon will summon catastrophes

311

which have not been seen since the War of Elements. Sea levels will rise. Deserts will expand in the warmer regions. Glaciers will conquer new territories and change cold waters into seas of ice. Heat waves, droughts, wildfires, heavy snowfall and rainfall will damage the lands of Men... until... even the last refuge of the Elves will be threatened."

"What we saw today with our own eyes is even more frightening than Lon's prophecy," said Curwë. "I understand why the Swords are so eagerly sought by the Arkys. It also explains the unwavering support the Secret Vale receives from the matriarchs. But what power can the Blades of Nargrond Valley hold to resist such catastrophes?"

"I believe the Swords, when united, can control the Islands' Flow, Curwë. I believe their combined powers could resist the devastation of the Greater Gods."

Curwë hazarded a guess. "But for this to happen, their wielders would have to renounce the power they draw from their mighty weapons."

Dyoren nodded in agreement. "Indeed... I think this was Rowë's purpose from the very beginning; to impose that ultimate test to the Swords' wielders. But before we get to that stage," the Seeker added , "the Swords must be gathered first."

Seeing that his vision and arguments were carrying even more force, Dyoren felt confident to divulge more of what had obsessed him for so long.

"Like some in my clan before me, I chose the path of the Lonely Seekers, although it was the hardest. Neither my strength nor my wisdom has led me far, although hope has never left me... But listen to me attentively, Curwë, and trust my words! These are not the ramblings of a mad Elf."

Curwë seemed to agree, but doubt was now on his face. In that instant, Dyoren's fervour looked very much like insanity. For a while, the Seeker stood with unseeing eyes, as if walking through a distant memory.

"When the four smiths of Yslla entered the mines of Oryusk with Lon the Wise, each wielded a Blade of Nargrond Valley. Only Rymsing was left behind, hidden, and entrusted to Rowë's brother, Rimwë, the future Arkylon.

The smiths of Yslla were killed, Lon never returned and five of the Swords disappeared into the Mines of Oryusk.

After the Valley fell, for centuries, knights of the Secret Vale sought the Swords across the Islands without success. It was therefore commonly believed the Blades of Nargrond Valley were still hidden inside the Mines of Oryusk, guarded by the unknown power that resided there.

And so, the Dyoreni went on their lonely quest; decades and centuries passed until... until I discovered that two of the Swords had been returned to the Elves, to become a great source of chaos and destruction.

Saeröl inherited Moramsing. He used it to murder King Lormelin and to start the long Shadow War against clan Myortilys, the enemies of his people. He changed his guild into a sect for assassins and murderers, leaving a long trail of bloodshed in his wake. Saeröl lives, whatever the learned Elves may believe, and Moramsing still lurks in the dark corners of the Islands."

Curwë interrupted this flow of words, worried about the growing exaltation his friend was showing.

"Dyoren, please calm yourself, you have already told me about Moramsing and Saeröl. You need to rest. I can see you are not well. You are not yourself anymore."

"I will rest when I am dead," countered the Seeker. "You must listen to me now, Curwë. I insist.

The Sword of Despair is not the only one to have been returned to the Elves. There is another Blade that reappeared. The Twelfth Arcane Master of the Ruby College, the 'Seer of Oryusk' as some among the druids call him, possesses Lynsing, the legendary sword which Elrian Dol Urmil wielded in the days of Rowë. I saw his blade. I almost had it by the hilt."

"What do you mean? You are scaring me, Dyoren. You have a fever," warned Curwë once more.

He noticed something strange in Dyoren's gaze. Plainly the Seeker's words did not encompass all he had in mind.

"What I mean is that I am about to make one final attempt to recover Lynsing. Its wielder is close, closer than you could ever imagine. He is gravely wounded. I doubt he will survive long. I will find him, even if I need enter the mines of Oryusk to do so."

"You would deliberately go to your doom?" cut in Curwë.

"It is the doom I choose," replied Dyoren solemnly. "A cruel dilemma lies before me: honour my vows or renounce my life's purpose. I cannot ignore what I have discovered.
Just as I swore, I have kept the secret. Such was the duty of the Seekers as the centuries passed and the rivers poured their streams into the sea. But today the world is changing once more. The volcano has awoken. Unprecedented disasters have followed one another over the past few years, a sign of the ever-growing ire of the Greater Gods.
The new age foretold by Lon the Wise might be coming sooner than we expected. The Swords must be gathered. I must resume my quest. But of these grave matters I will speak no more...
Now, I am in great need, and I ask for your help, or at least your trust."

Dyoren took from his pocket the small box inlaid with gemstones.
Curwë examined it closely.

"It is beautiful," he said. "A masterpiece of ancient craft," he added softly, looking at Dyoren with a new wonder in his eyes.

"No more will I say," answered the Seeker. "My heart is filled with deep concern for what this precious box contains. I will not decide in haste what is to be done with what it holds. In fact, I will not decide at all, and neither should you. Do you hear me? Neither should you. Such decisions are beyond our responsibility."

"Can you not tell me more?" Curwë questioned, feeling disappointed and completely in the dark.

"Listen to me, Green Eyes." It was the first time Dyoren called his friend by the nickname he had chosen for him. "You will do as I say. Take this box, take it out of the Valley and bring it to the purest heart in the Islands: bring it to the princess

Terela of Cumberae on my behalf. She will know what to do. As for me, I must be on my way. My time is precious, and I have already rested for far too long."

"You cannot simply leave us in the middle of the night if that's what you mean. You will not make it far alone. I know you are wounded. Your hand keeps clutching at your ribs. You are weary, and so are we. The Valley is unsafe, and its paths are watched by more than ordinary spies. On our way, we saw Giants coming down the volcano, monstrous creatures with fiery hair, walking in the burning ashes," warned Curwë.

Though it seemed wise for Dyoren to fall in with his friend, the Seeker bluntly refused.

"Leave the Valley and find Terela. Entrust her with the box. Let me go where my fate takes me. This is what I am asking you.
Curwë, you are the son I never had, you are the heir I have entrusted with all the secrets life has taught me. Please do as I say!"

"So, once more, you set off to seek one of the Swords," deplored Curwë.

"I could not be nearer to my goal. I will enter the Oryusk Mines. That is where the answer to all my questions lies."

Curwë's voice now sank to a whisper. "What strength have you left to go into the bowels of Oryusk and confront what lies inside? That is the path of despair...".

"It might be folly, but not despair. I always have hope, even if at this late hour it is a false hope veiling my eyes. Light and shadow are inseparable. They coexist within me, tearing each other apart. So, goes my destiny. Since I uttered my vows, this cursed quest has haunted me every day of my existence.
Whatever happens, I will be free from birth and death. Even when I shut the light from my eyes and become a corpse, I will be free," Dyoren confided.

With no more delay, the Seeker sprang to his feet and bade farewell to his friend, though he was ill at ease. He could not look Curwë in the eye.
Dyoren made a few steps in silence on the floor of dark leaves. Soon he vanished into the shadows of the rocks and trees.

And so, the Seeker went his way into the night, until the woodlands grew thinner and the landscape became scattered with rocks. The slopes of the volcano to the north were dim and smoky.

It was hard, dangerous work, moving in the darkness through this pathless land. Though he stumbled and hesitated, Dyoren managed to progress along the western edge of a stony gorge.

The huge cone of Mount Oryusk rose above him to a great height. Its reddish head stood below a shadowy cloud, suffocated in poisonous fumes.

The ground was becoming steeper. Sweating and suffering, Dyoren needed to turn aside several times before finally reaching a small river in a narrow vale. This stream, which trickled from a larger pool up the volcano's side, was the source of the Sian Dorg, the swift torrent that ran down to the lowlands of Nargrond Valley and ended up in the calm waters of Lake Yslla.

After a while, the steep path he was walking up became so narrow that he started to think he had lost his way. He pushed on, however, and the faint murmur of running water on his left became louder and louder, until he could distinctly hear the stream rushing and splashing between the rocks.

At last, Dyoren reached a wet floor of polished stone. In front of him was the pool of Dorg. It was fed by water cascading from far above. Long ago, the stream had flowed down through the mountain caves and out of the mines' gates. The Elves of House Dol Nargrond had changed its course by creating a fall further up, creating this majestic entrance into the volcano's insides.

The Seeker stood for a moment on the steps of that great gate of rock, which opened into nothing but darkness: the threshold of another life.

His gaze focused on the runes engraved on the gateway. They were badly degraded, as if some wicked spirit had desired to corrupt their power. Still, Dyoren recognized the Swords of Nargrond Valley's symbols. The artist had etched their names using gemstones and metal, diamond for Aonya, black iron for Aksinya, ruby for Orsing, amethyst for Moramsing, sapphire for Lynsing and emerald for Rymsing.

The rising sun appeared above the crest of the mountain, and a faint light broke into flickering beams of gold. The many jewels inlaid into the gates sparkled with a steely glimmer.

A great dread came over Dyoren as he stood before the gates of the mines. A strange thought came upon him: that doom he had long foreseen, he was now imposing upon himself.

An overwhelming sadness filled his heart as images of his long life ran by, accompanied by the music of his songs.

Then, finally, he made a step forward into the mines of Oryusk. It took him no effort to walk towards the darkness; rather, he gave in to it, as if he had no choice.

"I will seek the Swords of Nargrond Valley," he heard himself say. "Such is my vow."

CHAPTER 7: Lynsing

2716, Season of Eïwele Llya, 68th day, Gwa Nyn, Ystanargrond

The night sky turned black as the weak moon succumbed to the grip of a dark, sweeping cloud. Mynar dyl, who had barely moved since the disaster, decided it was finally time to attempt leaving his hideout, the covered terrace of an imposing stone building. He staggered towards its edge, supporting himself on one of the roof's supporting columns. His eyes were still dazed, his ears still ringing.

The warlord of Tios Halabron raised an arm towards the starless sky above to thank the heavens. He looked around himself, weak and aching. It was like he was emerging from the sinister hall where the souls of the Llewenti go after death.

As if struck by the mystery that haunted his life, Mynar dyl let out a loud cry which made his frightened hawk shudder.

"Eïwal Vars has saved me!"

With this effort, he staggered to his feet and climbed down from the stony roof that had protected him during the eruption.

At that very moment, by strange coincidence, the moon reappeared from behind Mount Oryusk's fumes and illuminated the jewel of his diadem. The emerald, impossibly dark only a moment ago, became bright as a star.

All around Mynar dyl were the smoking remains of what had once been the great, ancient ruins of Ystanargrond. It was a spectacular sight: the camp of a vast army transformed into a kingdom of fire.

The extent of the devastation only truly began to sink in when Mynar dyl recognised what had been the greatest edifice in Nargrond Valley's history. Long since abandoned to dust and wild vegetation, the Halls of Rowë were now nothing but a carcass. The blackened columns had toppled into the ash. Its shattered silhouette was barely visible through the fumes and smoke. The structure of the great building was damaged beyond repair. The fires of Mount Oryusk had consumed Lord Dol Nargrond's palace and all the ancient statues that had long embellished its peristyle. Incandescent shards of rock ejected by the volcano were still glowing on the marble steps, like burning salamanders celebrating their conquest.

Life in Ystanargrond had been wiped out with terrible suddenness on the afternoon of the Pact Gathering. Mount Oryusk had released rivers of fire running down from its north-eastern slopes. The grassy land around the grove of Llya had been transformed into an arid waste. But the torrents of lava had stopped at the bottom of the vale. They had been blocked by the Sian Senky; the burning flow had not conquered the slopes of Ystanargrond hill.

Mynar dyl remembered the cry that had come from the western wall.

"Dragons!"

A sentry sounded the alarm, blowing his horn as if the sky was falling around him. The army was alerted as soon as the risk had emerged on the horizon. Terrorized Elves realised that it was not dragons descending upon them, but the wrath of Mount Oryusk.

Fiery debris had shot out from the volcano in all directions, and the extreme heat of the projectiles had created a deadly bombardment upon the army's camp. The loss of life had been appalling. The bombing had devastated a timber warehouse close to where Mynar dyl stood, causing great fires to break out all around.

Before the eruption, the warlord of Tios Halabron had been hiding near Rowë's Halls to watch events unfold from afar. He had avoided drawing attention to himself after exploring the clan Llorely's camp. Although the rune of the druids protected him as a Pact envoy, his isolated position within the army of Gwarystan demanded extreme caution. That caution had saved his life.

From his isolated position, Mynar dyl had witnessed the pandemonium spread among the Gwarystan units. Panic set in as soldiers attempted to evacuate through the eastern gate. The surviving foot soldiers and archers frantically scrambled over the burning corpses of their comrades towards the Sian Senky, seeking the protection of the river's waters.

The mounted Elves had been able to escape much more quickly. Mynar dyl had seen knights riding their horses at full gallop along the streets of Ystanargrond. The cavaliers had not hesitated in knocking their own troops down to save their own skin.

There had then followed a long period of intense fear for Mynar dyl. As the volcanic devastation continued around him, the warlord sat tight in the stone building, singing his prayers to the deities of the Islands and entrusting them with his fate.

In the many hours of surreal chaos which followed, his sense of time and space was distorted. Night seemed to follow day without warning, but still Mount Oryusk was releasing its poisonous fumes and burning missiles, bursting out like dark thoughts of vengeance suppressed for too long.

Eventually, the rain of fire had ceased. His stone hideout had held fast, as if Mynar dyl's prayers had reinforced the roof of the terrace.

But for a long time after, the survivor had remained hidden in his shelter, unable to make the slightest move until it was very late at night.

Mynar dyl decided to survey the deserted Ystanargrond. He felt more confident as calm had now been restored. Moonlight flooded the vast square he crossed, illuminating the many cremated bodies which lay there with a silvery glow. The camp was completely devoid of life. Among the equipment destroyed in the inferno was the great tent of the Ruby College.

Beyond, the ruins of Ystanargrond were a series of blacked, blasted streets, covered with dust, smoke and the foul stench of building materials reduced to ashes.

Mynar dyl had just about concluded he was the only Elf left behind when he saw a single cavalier riding down the river towards the city walls. Weary and haggard, drenched in water and caked in mud, both horse and rider were at the last stages of their endurance. Mynar dyl watched their progress up the hill of Ystanargrond with amazement. He finally recognised the ragged, swaying figure with unkempt hair and wild eyes as Felrian, the lord of Urmilla.

Mynar dyl ran to meet him at the city gates and helped him reel from the saddle. But Felrian Dol Urmil could only point to the volcano.

"The day of wrath has come!" he croaked; his expression filled with terror.
And as Mynar dyl followed his gaze far across the river, he suddenly caught sight of several large silhouettes moving slowly down the vale.
"The Giants of Oryusk!" Felrian cried.

The monstrous creatures, with their stovepipe helms and dragonhide cloaks, were unmistakable even at this distance and under the cover of night. They stood at three times the size of an Elf.

"They have left their caverns inside the volcano."
"We must flee their fury!" Mynar dyl cried.
"Beware! Do not underestimate them like the others did. Giants can be shrewd. It is no accident they are coming from the river. They are expecting survivors to flee that way. We must stay hidden inside the ruins," advised Felrian.
"Do as you wish! I have no intention of confronting them," warned Mynar dyl, almost in panic.

Felrian held the Llewenti warlord by the sleeves of his clothing.

"Don't be a fool! And do as I say if you want to live. We need to hide this horse. It might be our only chance to escape this valley."

Lord Dol Urmil's command did leave an impression on Mynar dyl, and he managed to calm down.

"I will help you," he finally agreed.

Soon, the two Elves were running into the devastated streets of Ystanargrond, the stallion on their heels and Mynar dyl's hawk flying above them. They had to avoid the burning debris and treacherous smoking craters.

As they approached the northern moat and started up the road, they passed a long, rocky wall. There were cracks in the granite from which water vapour sprayed out in misty clouds.
Felrian seemed to know the place. He stepped into a wide crevice in the wall and shouted a word of power. The echo returned from afar. The lord of Urmilla then stepped through a hidden door, looking relieved when his horse also managed to creep into the narrow passage. Mynar dyl, his bird of prey on his arm, followed closely.
Inside, a twinkling colony of golf worms provided a flickering light, which danced upon a pool of glittering water. A natural bridge crossed the room, which had been carved into the rocky hill. Water cascaded from its basalt roof.

'This cavern must have been a shrine long ago,' thought Mynar dyl.

A fresh water spring was gushing further in, almost reaching the heights of the cave's high, domed ceiling.

"I came to pray in this secret temple two days ago. I made offerings to the Lord of all Waters," confided Felrian.
Mynar dyl was astonished by the beauty of the place. "May the deities of the Islands bless you, Lord Dol Urmil," was all he could mutter.

That such a haven of tranquillity could be hidden but a few yards from the chaos outside left him speechless.

The lord of Urmilla sat on a boulder near the pool, wondering aloud.

"When my ancestor transformed this cavern into a shrine dedicated to Gweïwal Uleydon, I doubt he realized what a lifeline it would one day be to his distant heir.
May his faith in the Greater God of all Waters be praised. He was the son of the lady who ruled Urmilla at the time, but his father was an Irawenti shipwright, the second son of Filwen, the navigator. Hence his dedication to Gweïwal Uleydon."

Mynar dyl had always proven interested in genealogy. He could not help but ask.

"Are you referring to Elrian Dol Urmil, the Smith of Nargrond Valley who became one of Lord Rowë's closest companions?"

"I am. In the second part of his life, Elrian lived alongside Rowë in Yslla, but he frequently visited Ystanargrond, which was the main centre of the valley."

"The feats of your forefather are well known in Llymar. Our matriarchs recount he was one of the four smiths who forged the Blades of Nargrond Valley."

"So, it is said. But it did not bring him much luck..."

Seeing an opportunity to demonstrate his value to the lord of Urmilla, Mynar dyl recalled his own participation in recent events on Nyn Ernaly.

"The corpse of your forefather now rests quietly in a safe sanctuary in Llymar Forest. The Llewenti clans kept him safe from the defilement of Norelin's servants. Many paid for the peaceful repose of his remains with their blood."

"I suppose I must thank you, and perhaps also for not mentioning that the sacrilegious king you mention is also my liege...

Anyway, these feats will not recall him to life, nor will they help us save ourselves on our own day of doom."

Their attention was then drawn to the cracks in the outer wall, through which they could hear the rough voices of the Oryusk Giants stomping down a nearby street. The smell of burnt wood started filling the air in the cave. Moments later, smoke was seeping through the gaps in the wall.

"The Giants must be burning the ruins of Ystanargrond to the ground," guessed Mynar dyl.

His hawk was becoming restless, growing anxious at the thickening smoke. Mynar dyl did his best to soothe it, stroking its neck with the back of his hand. Meanwhile, Felrian whispered to his horse in reassuring tones. He then muttered a short incantation, calling upon the forces of the Aquamarine Flow. The smoke of the burning city was held at bay for a moment, while the lord of Urmilla repeated his magic words louder and louder. The dangerous fumes eventually cleared completely, disappearing into the waters of the cavern's pool. Felrian's features became calm again.

"I must have been meant to survive that day," he said, enigmatic.

"You were among the envoys of Gwarystan who attended the Pact Gathering. I saw you in the cortege that left the city walls," remembered Mynar dyl.

"I believe I was the only Dol lord taking part alongside Prince Ilensar. All the other great Elves of the kingdom opted to remain safely in their strongholds, sending their stewards or knights in their stead."

"What happened in the grove of Llya?" Mynar dyl asked feverishly. "From what I saw from afar, it must have been submerged by the burning flow which descended towards the Sian Senky Vale."

"The lava was initially stopped by the stream that borders the sacred glade. As it kept on coming, the slopes of the hill around us collapsed, but the rocks formed a protective boundary around us," explained Felrian, still not believing what he had witnessed.

"A miracle," acknowledged Mynar dyl in awe. "An intervention of the Islands' deities."

"I now know what is meant by the word miracle," agreed Felrian, utterly convinced. "What I saw with my own eyes happened to be just that. But the Grove was far from safe..."

Mynar dyl understood the lord of Urmilla was still suffering. With a gentle tone that Mynar dyl almost managed to make convincing, he invited him to share his story.

A long silence followed. Felrian smiled sadly. Dread could be seen in his eyes.

At last, he stood up, as if he was about to address a crowd. Felrian was known as a bold knight and a charismatic commander. Yet his voice was shaky as he recalled the tragedy he had witnessed first-hand.

"I believe in omens. You might find that surprising coming from a lord of Gwarystan Kingdom...
I regularly visit the matriarchs of clan Llorely in their tree city of Tios Aelie. They had foretold a great disaster. 'The Islands' Flow is trapped', they would tell me. 'We have never sensed this before'
I usually listen to their wise advice, and it has proven useful over the years.
But this time, duty prevailed over wisdom. The prince-lord of Medystan had called upon me, and I would not evade my responsibilities."

"It is said that Eïwele Llyo holds our destiny in her hands, and that escaping our fate is impossible," cut in Mynar dyl.

"The Llewenti deities may well be right..." replied Felrian, thoughtful. "I know fear as well as any Elf. I fought many battles during the Century of War, but this time, the dread within me was different. All through the day, my anxiety grew constantly, to the point of gradually impairing my will. When fear is not properly controlled, it builds its own momentum, and eventually acquires a will of its own...
As I listened to the debates in the grove of Llya, I tried to focus on the Pact Gathering's points of contention.
I remember Cetoron, the Fifth Arcane Master holding the Lenra Pearl out in plain sight. I could see with my own eyes the power of the jewel, whose azure heart blazed so brightly, as

if reflecting the primary force of the grove's well. It possessed a hidden magic of its own nature and was most impressive to behold. I felt hypnotized.

Then, quite suddenly, as if I had awoken from a dream, I understood why the Ruby College had risked bringing the Pearl from the safety of the Crimson Tower to the Pact Gathering. The Lenra Pearl was fashioned with the spells of the Gods, and the high mages were using its power to persuade the other participants to agree to their proposal. Indeed, as all beheld the jewel, the three red sorcerers were speaking eloquently to further their cause.

But there were some who resisted its mighty charm. The clan Myortilys would not accept the Ruby College's proposal. They bluntly refused to bow before the king and surrender their share of the Islands' Flow. With mocking taunts, the Dark Elves managed to rally the clan Llyandy and the barbarian chieftains to their side. The noble houses of Gwarystan and the Westerners sent by the Sea Hierarchs were of no help to the high mages, who were by now calling on deaf ears.

Meanwhile, my attention was concentrated upon the Arkylla who, assisted by a dozen other druids of the first circle, were leading the Gathering. The Daughter of the Islands was tense. I could see she was watchful of any perturbation in the Flow around the grove, as though she had been suddenly made aware of a supernatural phenomenon about to happen."

"A power mighty enough to trigger a volcanic eruption would have been impossible for her to comprehend," speculated Mynar dyl.

"It is completely beyond any of us to understand..." said Felrian, and his gaze seemed lost in that instant.

Seeing the lord of Urmilla losing his train of thought, Mynar dyl pressed him. "But what happened when the eruption began? What was the fate of the other participants? Did they all perish?"

Felrian held his eyes wide open, as if he were reliving what had happened.

"When a catastrophe occurs, time seems to slow down; events unfold in such a way that they look inevitable."

"What did you see, Felrian? Tell me!"

"I saw... everything," the lord of Urmilla replied, standing still in total amazement. "I was in the front row of an impossible spectacle..."

Mynar dyl allowed Felrian to catch his breath. He anticipated what was coming next would be dreadful.

"First, the air all around us filled with rumbling... Then, I smelled sulphurous vapours... I felt an unbearable heat... and I saw...
Yes, I saw Mount Oryusk spewing liquid fire from a fissure in its flank: lava spurting straight from the earth's core.
I saw burning rocks fall from the sky, hitting the barbarian chieftains that stood close to the great stones bordering the Grove.
I saw a huge boulder land right beside me, killing the ambassadors of House Dol Ogalen instantly.
I saw a knight of House Dol Valra fall into a crevasse created by the explosion of a burning boulder.
I was paralysed as I watched the horror unfold.
The high mages managed to form a triangle at the centre of the glade and united their powers to form a powerful shield. A sphere of reddish colour seemed to protect the grove from the constant bombing of fiery debris.
Some of us used that moment of respite to try to escape. The clan Myortilys' envoys attacked the Westerner ambassadors, ruthlessly slaying them and stealing their horses. Meanwhile, the Ice Elves left the glade and disappeared into the surrounding woods.
On the opposite side of the Grove, a barbarian chieftain set himself on fire after he interpreted it all as a sign that the Three Dragons had returned. During his ghastly suicide, he cried that he could see the Fire Drakes flying around the glade.
Following the Daughter of the Islands, many of the other druids suddenly turned into birds. They flew high into the sky. Some were hit by cindery fragments and plummeted into the flowing lava below.
Prince Ilensar gathered his knights around him. They attempted to withdraw in good order towards Ystanargrond, under the protection of their shields. Most of the noble houses'

ambassadors sought his protection and followed his group. But the column was overtaken by a torrent of lava, and they disappeared into its flow. All were killed.

As the eruption intensified, the high mages realised they could not avoid the inexorable destruction of the Grove. One by one, they disappeared into thin air.

One moment they were in front of me, the next they were gone. The three highest ranking mages escaped that way, but Cetoron, the one holding the jewel box with the Lenra Pearl, did not. Before my eyes, as he was unsuccessfully incanting his spell, the sorcerer was attacked from behind by an Elvin druid who had remained behind. The assassin's bright sword beheaded the old Eunuch as cleanly as a scythe cuts wheat...

Finally coming back to my senses after all that horror, I jumped on my terrorized horse, and galloped straight into the torrent which circumvents the Grove. Rushing to certain death, the only word that came to me was: Uleydon!"

A long silence followed Felrian's tale.

"If I make it back to Urmilla," the Dol lord said at last , "I will have a great shrine built to the glory of the Greater God of all Waters. Its columns will be perched upon a cliff above the sea. The hall of worship will look like a mighty vessel with several masts, carved in the white marble quarried at Tios Aelie. Facing the Austral Ocean, at the entrance, a colossal bronze statue of Gweïwal Uleydon will await the Irawenti coming to the Archipelago, as in the prophecy of the clan of Filweni."

Mynar dyl had a disapproving look in his eye, but he did not feel like questioning his unfortunate companion further, who was only just starting to comprehend his situation. His two units from Urmilla were most probably lost. The Dol lord would never again see the knights of the White Wings and the fighters of clan Llorely who had come with him.

Mynar dyl cupped his hands and brought the pool's water the to his lips. The refreshing liquid swelled in his mouth with a burst of delicious flavour.

Encouraged by the taste, he lowered himself slowly into the bath of chilled water. Immersing his entire body in the reviving flow, he felt a great relief, as if this underground source had the power to sooth his soul as well as clean his body. Mynar dyl rested, bathing his spirit in restorative slumber. But the dream hovering at the edges of his mind was soon interrupted.

"May I ask you a question, noble dyl?" enquired Felrian.

"As it stands, I could not very well refuse you anything, noble Dol. My head would be on a Giant's pike if it were not for your wise advice."

As if trying to bring his mind into focus, the lord of Urmilla wondered aloud.

"How is it that you are here in front of me?"
"What do you mean?"

Felrian resumed, his tone now much colder.

"The envoys of Cumberae and Llymar left the valley the day before the carnage. They fled after nightfall, as if they had suddenly learnt about the coming disaster. You did not! What made you stay? And please do not tell me you were still hunting down your brother..."

Mynar dyl hesitated. Until now, he had felt nothing but genuine gratitude. Now the warlord understood that, should he limit his answer here, there would be a lot more Felrian would want to know. The conversation could turn into an interrogation. Hence, after a while, Mynar dyl relented, and told Felrian what happened after Dyoren had visited Curwë in Llafal.

His summary of events was somewhat short and did not shed any light upon his own questionable actions. He concluded by accusing the Seeker, so sure of his ground that he saw no need to offer any rationale with his judgment.

"That is why I came to your tent yesterday morning asking about the Renegade. I suspected he was hiding among the guards of clan Llorely who serve you. I feared he had some new scheme in mind.

Bringing him before the Arkys' justice had become my obsession.

After what happened today, my actions might look insignificant to your eyes," Mynar dyl said as he climbed out of the pool.

"Your initiative was indeed petty. It was also disproportionate and unjust," countered the lord of Urmilla harshly.

Mynar dyl was not ready to be walked over, even by a powerful High Elf lord.

"I know Dyoren was your friend, but the Seeker did what he did. He must answer for his crimes," Mynar dyl insisted with hatred in his eyes.

Felrian Dol Urmil stood up, and in that instant, he was truly a proud lord to behold, despite his filthy blue cloak, burnt boots and damaged plate mail.

"At least you are using his name again! I cannot tell you how my ears hurt when you shame him by calling him the Renegade.
Dyoren is his name.
No pompous cleric, however close to the deities he pretends to be, can make me think otherwise. No unfair judge hiding in his secret vale can make me change my mind.
I have known your brother since he was born.
Never have I met with an Elf so dedicated to protecting his people. Do you hear me? Never!"

The sincerity of this poignant plea made a distinct impression on Mynar dyl. He remained speechless, feeling the pressure mount upon him. Felrian became emotional.

"I want you to know something. When I sent you away from the House Dol Urmil camp, empty-handed, your brother was hiding among us... under my protection and with my blessing.
Many misfortunes have befallen Dyoren, but at least he is still alive.
On my way to the Pact Gathering, I saw his kestrel flying over the south-eastern slopes of Mount Oryusk, leagues away from the grove of Llya and the ruins of Ystanargrond.
I believe your brother found shelter in an area spared by the eruption. I find it a deeply comforting thought, that the Seeker was destined to escape Mount Oryusk's wrath."

Giving into his impulses, Mynar dyl responded with pure bravado.

"Your touching sentimentality for my half-brother does not change the facts. Dyoren is a renegade and a murderer. He killed Voryn dyl. You were protecting a criminal, my lord. That is all there is to say."

The accusation made Felrian's blood boil. Becoming blind with rage, the Dol lord leapt up from where he sat and drew his blade.

"Leave this place immediately! Get out, miserable worm! I will gladly cut your throat if you dare spit one more poisonous word.
I swear before mighty Gweïwal Uleydon himself that Dyoren is no renegade, no murderer and certainly not a brother-slayer. Dyoren was the first knight of the Secret Vale to ever find one of the lost blades. He fought a duel against Saeröl, the wielder of Moramsing. He almost paid for it with his life.
Ask your friend, the Blue Mage Curubor! Ask the young lord of the House of Dol Lewin! They know the truth... for they played a treacherous role in those events. I know exactly what happened in Nyn Ernaly. Dyoren told me.
Now be on your way! Go and face what lurks outside. This holy sanctum is no place for you."

Mynar dyl knew the Dol lord's threats were real. The warlord of Tios Halabron understood he had no choice but to leave. Feeling humiliated, he quickly gathered up his equipment. Soon, Mynar dyl had recovered his precious javelin, his bow, arrows and satchel. An instant later, he was out of the hidden shrine and back on the street.
A quick look behind him confirmed the secret passage was closed again.
All he could think of now was how to escape the ruins of Ystanargrond.

Mynar dyl wrapped his dark hooded mantle about his shoulders. He covered his thin body from head to toe, including gloves and boots. Despite the darkness, his hawk flew above him, scanning the surroundings. Mynar dyl thus managed to remain unseen amid the alleys of the devastated city, until he reached the ruins' limits. There was still a lot of ground to cover between the old walls and the gloomy riverbanks that lay downhill, along the Sian Senky.

Mynar dyl realized how dangerous it would be to cross the open space which separated the two. He feared that, even if he reached the cover of the woods, he could well draw a chase behind him.

Mynar dyl decided to follow a small stream which had formed nearby after the destruction of a marble fountain. At several points along it, its banks were trampled and torn. The waters were fouled, as though some beasts had deliberately polluted it. The night was dark. Only the occasional campfires of the Oryusk Giants were shedding any light.

Mynar dyl's night vision nevertheless enabled him to progress swiftly between the remains of the stone houses and the burning debris. He grew bolder and started retracing his steps towards a breach in the city walls which he had noticed earlier on.

'If I exit through there, I can avoid the main gates,' he thought, hopeful.

But he was soon disenchanted upon discovering the invaders had set up a camp to guard the breach. The monstrous creatures were busy constructing their accommodation.

Mynar dyl knew that, of all the many races of Giants, the Oryusk kin were the greatest crafters. They were famous for being excellent blacksmiths and stonemasons. The quality of their work was evident in the weapons and instruments they were carrying.

Silently, Mynar dyl waited in the shadows until the moon sank again behind the dark clouds.

Then, without warning, a hound, released to sniff out survivors in the surrounding ruins, caught onto the Elf's scent. The watchdog howled. There was suddenly a lot of noise around Mynar dyl: more hounds barking wildly, Giants shouting to each other, and even the neigh of a horse.

Mynar dyl dashed into the maze of ruins behind him, but after turning the first corner he found himself facing two Oryusk Giants armed with huge two-handed swords. They were hauling a freshly captured white stallion back to their camp.

Their shoulders were broad, their skin black as coal and their eyes bright orange. Red flames spurted from their blond hair. They towered over the Elf from a height of twenty feet.

One of the Giants uttered what sounded like a curse in his unintelligible dialect. In a flash, he picked up a rock and hurled it with great strength. The missile came flying towards the Elf as if shot from a catapult.

Mynar dyl dodged the fatal projectile by rolling onto his side. Quickly back on his feet, he launched his javelin at his foe. The spear flew straight into the Giant's head, piercing his left eye. Mynar dyl pulled on the thin, taught rope attached to the javelin; a moment later, he had recovered his precious weapon. Almost simultaneously, his hawk attacked the wounded Giant who was crying out in pain. As the bird of prey spread its wings, it ripped the monster's ear with its beak.

The second Giant rushed forward. In his haste, he let go the reigns holding the horse.

Without thinking, Mynar dyl charged, spear in hand. The Giant swung his great sword, but the heavy weapon was too slow and missed its target. Mynar dyl dived to one side of the monster, rolled, and pierced the Giant's foot with the tip of his javelin. The pain was so bad that his opponent hopped and stumbled backwards.

The hawk attacked again, aiming this time to pierce the monster's eyes. But with a powerful flick of his head, the great Oryusk warrior struck one of the hawk's wings with his helmet. A bloody melee ensued. Yelling and striking, the Giant finally overpowered his aggressor. The hawk fell to the ground at his feet.

Ignoring the fate of his bird, Mynar dyl flung himself upon the horse, getting hold of the reigns. He steered it out of the narrow street and set off at a gallop across the Giants' campsite.

There were fires burning everywhere, but the horse managed to dodge and jump clean over them. The Elvin rider could see, as he passed, groups of astonished Giants along the lines of their pickets. Their encampment stretched for more than a hundred yards. But such was the fear in his horse that it crossed the camp as quickly as an arrow.

Mynar dyl stormed the breach in the wall and reached the open slopes which stretched down to the Sian Senky.
Swift and rugged, his new stallion also had impressive stamina. Soon, the fires of the Oryusk Giants were but a dull smoulder against the black western sky. Heading southeast, ever faster, Mynar dyl sped across the valley, like a fluttering leaf stirred before a storm.
But the warlord of Tios Halabron knew he would not be safe until he had crossed the Sian Senky. There were no bridges over the torrent descending from Mount Oryusk's slopes in these parts.

A league further east, the riverbed widened, and the flow became calmer. There, Mynar dyl found a ford, and led his mount into the Sian Senky. After crossing without difficulty, he turned south and galloped under the light of the moon. He hoped to find cover in the Arob Nargrond southern range.
As the dawn whitened the sky before him, it gleamed upon the waters of the Sian Dorg in the distance.

As morning was coming, Mynar dyl decided to hide for the day. He spotted a thick grove of elms by the riverbank, which would provide shelter for both cavalier and mount. He entered the wood, saw to his horse, and made himself invisible.

★

Late in the afternoon, as he was still resting safely out of sight, Mynar dyl noticed a carrion-bird perched upon a bare tree close to the thicket. He watched with interest as the vulture took flight and headed west towards the volcano.
Upriver, in the direction of the mines of Oryusk, the evening sky was filled with vultures. Flocking in such numbers was unusual; while these scavengers were numerous in the high mountainous parts of Nargrond Valley, they were seldom seen

in the lower hills, the realm of falcons and kestrels. Despite the danger, Mynar dyl's curiosity prevailed. He left his horse safely hidden in the thicket and carefully started walking upriver along the Sian Dorg. Doing his best to remain invisible, he progressed swiftly, keeping a keen eye on the scene above him.

As if responding to a mysterious call, a dozen vultures had descended, darting wildly about the area, all engaged in a violent fight against a lone kestrel flying just above the trees. Undetectable and undetected, Mynar dyl remained seated for a moment in the shade of a tall oak tree, examining the birds' ferocious dance through the air.
Then, as the whirlwind of carrion-birds moved down to the riverbank, Mynar dyl suddenly realized it was no common falcon they were fighting.

"This is Dyoren's kestrel!" Mynar dyl realized, recognizing the bird from its rare plumage.

Now more intrigued than ever, the warlord of Tios Halabron pressed on, sneaking through the reeds with the sun's blinding rays on his back.

After a few hundred yards more, Mynar dyl finally reached a green hollow, where the Sian Dorg river ran. He discovered the vultures' real target, who had been so desperately defended by the great hawk.

An Elf was kneeling on the grass peacefully, his mouth open, his head bare. He seemed to be praying. His eyes were closed, and a sick smile was outlined on his lips. His face was as pale as the white pebbles of the riverbed. He looked cold, despite the ambient morning warmth. His right hand was holding the pommel of a scimitar, its blade thrust into the humid soil, supporting him like a cane. His left hand was pressed into his ribs, in a desperate effort to stop the bleeding from a dark hole in his side.

"Dyoren!" murmured Mynar dyl as he walked up in haste.

From the way he was kneeling, Mynar dyl initially thought his brother was praying to the deities. But something was wrong: the paleness of his face, the utter stillness of his body. Mynar dyl now rushed forward.

"Dyoren?" he called.

Then he saw the sapphires encrusted in the scimitar's pommel, the markings of the smiths of Nargrond Valley on the blade, and the runes of power carved into the sword's hilt. Mynar dyl stood there, amazed.

"This is Lynsing. This is the Sword of the South... How is this possible?" he wondered.

Mynar dyl was in shock. He could not deny the staggering evidence before him.

"Dyoren, you have recovered what was thought lost forever. You have fulfilled your vow," he muttered beneath his breath.

Seeing no reaction, he reached out and shook his brother by the shoulder. Losing the support of the sword, Dyoren collapsed onto the soil, inert. Startled, Mynar dyl tried to wake his brother. He took his pulse, checked his breathing and examined his skull, but found no signs of life.

At last, he saw the deep wounds in the wrists, and he understood. Dyoren's blood had been completely drained from his body.

Mynar dyl became certain his brother was dead. He could not control the powerful emotion which seized him. However strong and insensitive he thought himself, Mynar dyl was now subjected to the full, infinite, irreparable pain that the death of a close relative will cause.

Mynar dyl took the legendary sword in his hands, as if holding a witness that might tell him what had happened. The shining blade glittered like a brilliant ray of sunshine.

Just the day before, Mynar dyl had been going to extraordinary lengths to bring Dyoren, the half-brother he called the 'Renegade', to justice.

All was now changed: after the eruption, the discussion with Felrian, and the countless lives that had been lost all around him. His own life had hung only by a thread. Like the pillars of a weak edifice, the foundations of all his convictions had been shaken.

'If Dyoren recovered Lynsing, if he completed such a deed, it could mean he has been telling the truth from the very beginning. Perhaps his mania was not a symptom of a spirit unbalanced by rebellion,' realised Mynar dyl.
'What if his warnings in the scrolls of the Dyoreni were not insane? What if the Arkys missed what he was doing, and unfairly dismissed him at a crucial moment of his quest?' A multitude of questions were rushing through his mind.

Felrian's faithful defence of Dyoren resonated even louder than before. Memories of his conversation with Camatael on the day of the Gnome's attack also flooded back to him.

'Moramsing and Saeröl; the Twelfth Arcane Master and Lynsing; Mount Oryusk and the threat that lay inside its bowels... we thought these warnings were the last-ditch attempts of a desperate knight to keep his position. The Arkys made me believe it, and the matriarchs of Llymar thought the same.'

After some further thinking, Mynar dyl reached a conclusion.

'Camatael told me of another bard in Mentolewin, of a duel, of mysterious events which had been reported around the pilgrimage. Lord Dol Lewin, too, had never believed in the Renegade's guilt.
If the last entries in the scrolls of the Seekers are now proven true, Dyoren most likely had nothing to do with Voryn dyl's disappearance.'

Mynar dyl needed to express his dismay and his grief. He looked at his brother's cold features. Dyoren's face had been spared and remained shining to the end.

"Truth hurts," Mynar dyl said aloud as he started to understand Dyoren had simply been telling the world what only he could see.

The warlord of Tios Halabron suddenly remembered how he had been deaf to all those around him who had urged measure and caution, so obsessed had he been to capture his elder brother.

A sense of guilt and bitterness now overshadowed the pain of losing another family member. Mynar dyl had behaved disgracefully since Dyoren's degradation. He felt his life tarnished with shame, all the worse because he had not lived up to his high ranking. He did not have the noble spirit to match.

Kneeling before his brother, Lynsing in his hand, he murmured a few words to pay tribute and beg forgiveness.

"Few people have the courage to dedicate their lives to the pursuit of knowledge: because it is painful; because leaving the protection of the forest means danger and misery.

I did not choose that path, you did. You chose the way out of the woods, taking the rocky mountain path. I finally realize your place in our history... But the hour is late... too late... Today, I feel very, very small... I sincerely ask for your forgiveness."

Mynar dyl's hesitating and weak voice had lost its innate self-confidence. Feeling the ground shirking beneath his feet, he tried to find refuge in the teachings of Eïwele Llyo.

"Death is merely a step, a passage. Eïwele Llyo grants us reincarnation within the forest. We return to our origins in nature," he recited, as Llewenti beliefs dictated.

But doubt beset his spirit. The dramatic events of the day sent him back abruptly to his own anguish. His selfishness regained the upper hand.

'What if the High Elves are right, and death is but a single journey after all? If death means entering the Halls of Gweïwal Agadeon, never to return?'

The livid corpse of his brother lying on the ground was the incarnation of this unanswered question. A cold shiver ran through him to find his worst fears thus confirmed.

Dyoren and Voryn dyl had left no heirs. Few survived of all clan Ernaly's noble dyn, born from the blood of Eïwal Vars and Queen Llyoriane. There were only two old matriarchs, dry as dead wood, and him... him alone, without descent.

'It is in the order of things that Elves should die, and no one can escape this fate without threatening the harmony of the world. The tragic history of the immortal High Elves is the perfect illustration of the Gods' irrevocable law. I must therefore accept it. But I desperately need children of my own, otherwise my existence will have had no meaning,' he understood.

Fighting the dizziness which had started to overwhelm him, Mynar dyl set about performing sacred funeral rites. He would not leave his brother's body to the vultures.

"You will find your way to the Hall of Eïwele Llyo, Dyoren. At least I will not fail you now."

Mynar dyl shot arrows at the carrion-birds above him until he had broken up their wretched dance. He then dropped his bow onto the soil and started gathering pieces of wood carried by the river. Using the abundant reeds of the Sian Dorg as ropes, Mynar dyl fashioned a little wooden raft. With his javelin he carved the image of the deity of fate on its surface, before carefully placing Dyoren's body on top.

At last, the warlord put Lynsing in his brother's hand. The idea of doing this had come naturally to him, as it was traditional to leave the deceased Elf's favourite weapon with him on his floating sepulchre. Yet he hesitated for a moment before completing the ritual.

"I suppose Lynsing should now be yours, after all you suffered to seek the Swords of Nargrond Valley. With the Blade of the South in hand, you can present yourself before Eïwele Llyo with dignity," Mynar dyl declared aloud, as if Dyoren could hear him.

But other bitter thoughts came to him, and these, he kept to himself.

'Anyway, I will certainly not be taking Lynsing back to the Arkys, as I did with Rymsing. Let me first find out how deep their hypocrisy and manipulations run. Perhaps these guardians of the Secret Vale are just the blind servants of the ambitious Arkylon. What else can you expect from a High Elf lord? I have been naïve, like so many other Llewenti. It is high time I write my own story. I too can produce myths of my own to make the weak and the stupid bow before me.'

Finally, Mynar dyl lay a traditional necklace across the body, which he fashioned out of a thin rope, oak leaves and the fletching from his arrows. He marked it with Dyoren's personal rune. Then came the most poignant detail of the rite. The warlord of Tios Halabron poured the contents of an oil flask on the body. Tradition required that the body be cremated, so that the soul is released to find its way to Eïwele Llyo's hall.

Then, before setting the improvised coffin alight, Mynar dyl kneeled to pronounce the ritual prayers to the deity of fate. For a long time, he remained immobile, deep in prayer, as if the sincerity of his appeal to Eïwele Llyo might also redeem himself. He had difficulty chasing away the guilt he felt in that moment.

Suddenly, as Mynar dyl was completing his prayer, a terrifying sound rang out from the nearby woodlands, like the howling of ferocious wolves. From the noise they were making, these beasts were drawing near. Listening to the snapping brushwood, Mynar dyl knew they would soon be upon him. Time was scarce; he had only just reached for his javelin when the beasts appeared in sight. Only then did Mynar dyl realise the peril he was confronting.

"Eïwal Vars, help me! These are the watchdogs of the Oryusk Giants!" he cried.

The five approaching hounds looked fearsome. Despite their great size, as large as adult bears, they were moving stealthily, like hunting dogs with keen hearing and sight. Their colour varied from crimson to fiery-brown, while their eyes were glowing red. Small flames covered their sooty black tongues, and fiery spittle was dripping from their jaws.

The ferocious beasts howled, as if seized by a terrible anger. The ghastly, shrill sound echoed throughout the rocky surroundings.

Mynar dyl's face was twisted in sheer terror, and the pale light of despair shone from his eyes. No sooner had he left his position by his brother's corpse; a hound rushed upon him. With a great leap, it sprang with fury against the Elf.

Mynar dyl quickly thrust his javelin upwards at the hound's throat. The tip of the spear pierced the fur and the beast fell like a stone, almost crushing him with its weight. So deep had the Elvin warlord driven his weapon into the creature that he failed to retrieve it.

Now disarmed, Mynar dyl tried to flee, but one of the hounds raced after him, raging like a demon pursued by Gweïwal Narkon.

It released its blazing fire breath. So powerful were the flames that all nearby vegetation became blackened and scorched. But Mynar dyl escaped by diving into the water. He leapt towards the raft on which his brother floated and had just enough time to push the floating coffin into the fast-flowing current of the river.

Scared to death and acting by reflex, he picked up the precious scimitar which lay invisible on Dyoren's chest.

Mynar dyl drew Lynsing from its scabbard and the blade, suddenly revealed, gleamed cold and white like the ice of the Yl Rocks[38]. Grasping the scimitar's hilt even more firmly, he could feel its power surging through his limbs. He became inhabited by a feeling of extreme lucidity, as if the movements of his attackers had become predictable.

Another hound bared its great black teeth and growled wildly. With that, it leapt upon Mynar dyl, who struck him straight between the eyes with the scimitar. The blade pierced the beast's skull with deadly ease. The beast fell.

---

38 Yl rocks: Small icy isles located at the southernmost parts of Nyn Llyandy.

Enraged by this feat, the remaining hellish dogs rode down on Mynar dyl, trying to trample him under their paws. But the Elf made an unexpected leap. He sprang, cat-like, right onto the back of one of the speeding hounds and grasped it about the throat. Both beast and rider fell upon the soil, but Mynar dyl was flung far, and lay dazed for a moment.

His scimitar was still in his hand and the warlord of Tios Halabron rose, fiercer than ever, brandishing his blade high above. Overwhelmed with fury, he felt none could restrain him. His eyes shone with the light of his sword.

The hounds of Oryusk attacked again, charging one after the other, breathing fire. But each time, Mynar dyl would leap out of the way, always one step ahead of the furious beasts.

At last, the three remaining hounds encircled the Elf, denying him any chance of escape. Like a silvery light in a dark sky, Lynsing stabbed and smote, slashed and pierced. The hounds tour into the Elf with their claws and teeth, and several times Mynar dyl cried out in agony.

Twice was Mynar dyl beaten to his knees by the ruthless beasts, twice did he rise to wield his shining scimitar again, fighting like a cornered cat, dealing great, wild blows in all directions. His mantle was torn to shreds, his leather armour mangled, and his helmet sundered when, at last, the Elf delivered the final blow. His feet stumbled. He was spent. Around him lay the corpses of the three hounds of Oryusk. The blade of his scimitar was soaked in black blood up to its hilt.

"Eïwal Vars has saved me!" Mynar dyl cried out, repeating it over and over.

At last, when the last of his fury had left him, he remembered Dyoren, and worried about what had happened to his coffin. The current of the Sian Dorg had pushed it towards the other bank. The raft had become stuck in a swampy area a hundred yards downriver. It was barely visible amid a great entanglement of reeds.

Before the coffin drifted away any further, Mynar dyl decided to act. With a single word of power, he set an arrow aflame. He then retrieved his bow and, with unsteady arms, shot the burning missile towards the other bank of the river. It missed its target. Another five arrows were required before he finally set the raft alight. Relieved, Mynar dyl looked at his quiver. It was empty.

'It is high time I return to Llymar, or this journey to Gwa Nyn will eventually claim my life. What folly took me here!' he thought, looking at the shining blade of Lynsing.

His hands were still shaking.

2716, Season of Eïwele Llyo, 1st day, Nyn Llyvary, Llafal harbour

Blood-red clouds dappled the coast in orange light before, slowly, the flaming globe appeared above the trees, setting the emerald waters of the Halwyfal ablaze. The morning sunlight illuminated the many masts of the naves anchored in Llafal.
The great swanship, like a majestic king among his vassals, towered above the rest of the fleet. It was stripped of its sails and its many oars were lying still, resting quietly in Llafal's waters.

On board, Feïwal and Arwela were walking along the railing. Every day at dawn, the guide of the clan of Filweni would closely examine the ship's deck. But that morning, an unexpected visit had interrupted his routine task. His elder sister was there, wanting to relay in person the long-awaited order from the Council of the Forest. The warships of Llymar would depart for Cumberae the next morning.

"So, Leyen dyl Llyvary finally shares my views," noted Feïwal.

He had difficulty masking his contempt for the warlord of Penlla, the official commander of the fleet. But his mood was unusually good, and his blue gaze filled with excitement and hope. The left half of the navigator's face was tattooed with a runic pentagram. His long, dark azure hair was strewn with silvery feathers, and a diadem of marine pearls adorned his head.

"The swanships will set sail tomorrow at dawn," explained Arwela. "Today we will make all final preparations and load the shipment. The fighters will embark tonight after the feast held in their honour. Orders have been given that they spend the night on board, so that the fleet can depart with the morning tide. This should enable you to cross the passes of the Halwyfal safely."

She climbed the stairs which led to the atfcastle of the ship. Dressed in an azure robe, her long dark hair flowed in the wind, enhancing her natural beauty.

Looking at the dozen Llewenti warships anchored in the harbour, her brother could not resist complaining.

"We have already waited too long. The journey to Cumberae will be dangerous. We will find more than storms in the southern parts of the Archipelago. It will be several weeks by the time we reach Nyn Llyandy. When winter reaches those latitudes, icebergs are said to be the main danger."

Two sailors crossed the deck in silence. The great swanship's crew was composed exclusively of Llewenti from Penlla. They had volunteered to leave their homes behind to accompany their warlord, Leyen dyl, across the seas. Fair to behold, these young Elves did not look like accomplished sailors. They seemed oblivious to what setting out on this journey might imply, beset as it would be by all manner of dangers.

Feïwal was considering them with concern while Arwela resumed her explanation.

"The Council of the Forest wished the fleet to be at full strength before sailing to war. It made sense to have all commanders present," she argued.

"Siw! I do not think one ship will make a difference. I find it incredible that a thousand Elves are risking their lives by waiting for one warlord," Feïwal replied, with the authority of a navigator who has wandered the Sea of Cyclones.

"The swanship bringing Mynar dyl home was last seen south of Nyn Ernaly by the matriarchs' sea birds. It was slowed down by headwinds in the strait of Nyn Avrony."

"Did Mynar dyl really wish to arrive in time to depart with the fleet?" Feïwal wondered. "I doubt it. See how few troops from clan Ernaly have joined us. Most of our units come from Penlla. They are made up of inexperienced sailors who have seldom left this bay. Lord Camatael told me how little Mynar dyl supported the alliance with Cumberae during the negotiations with Princess Terela. I would not be surprised if he had 'arranged' to slow down his journey back. The warlord of Tios Halabron cannot be trusted."

"I think Mynar dyl hates us deeply. I do not know what he abhors most; the Irawenti or the refugees," Arwela agreed.

"It is miraculous enough he survived the devastation of Nargrond Valley. I was at the council when the matriarchs learnt he was still alive. The Llewenti were impressed by his feats; he was the only ambassador of Llymar who remained behind at the Pact Gathering. He could have been killed like so many others, yet he survived. All are feverishly awaiting his return and the news he will bring."

Their conversation was interrupted by an embarkation on the port's waters. This surprising occurrence drew their attention. A small boat had discreetly left the Alcalinquë, another swanship commanded by their brother Nelwiri, and was heading swiftly towards the shore. Two Elves were aboard, rowing without skill but with conviction. The whole situation looked suspect to Feïwal: the timing of the expedition, the behaviour of the two apprentice sailors. It looked like a half-baked attempt at smuggling.
Arwela possessed very good eyesight. She identified one of the rowers, despite her hooded marine cloak.

"What is Fendrya doing on that small boat?" she wondered. "I thought you had commanded Nelwiri to keep an eye on such behaviour. There are passengers on board the Alcalinquë who had better not be seen in Llafal."

Feïwal ignored the criticism veiled in his sister's words. Pretending not to hear was his preferred defence mechanism. Instead, he opted to provide his own interpretation of the situation.

"This afternoon, the Llewenti will celebrate the Day of Myos, which marks the beginning of Autumn. I suppose our lovely cousin wished to participate in the celebrations. I know many departing fighters want to make it a feast to be remembered. Fendrya must have convinced one of the Alcalinquë's sailors to join her. The Llewenti say it is a day for all kinds of sensual pleasure."
"Cil, Cim Cir! Fendrya is definitely a scion of the clan of Feli, always adventurous and often rebellious," smiled Arwela. Yet she was surprised at this news of the celebration. "Myos? I thought that deity was only worshipped by the Dark Elves."

Feïwal concurred with a nod of his head.

"It is true. Myos is the Patron deity of the clan Myortilys and the alleged forefather of their matriarchs. But old superstitions are difficult to eradicate among the clans of Llymar," he noted. "The Day of Myos commemorates an old Llewenti legend. It is thought that Myos made love to Llyo on that night. The deity of disillusions had set himself a challenge: to seduce and corrupt the frigid Eïwele. He fell back on his usual treacherous ways to lure the deity of fate into a feast of debauchery and excess. Llyo was abused that night. Ashamed, she fled into the bowels of the Islands."

"It is another old legend I did not know. Llewenti mythology is undeniably rich, our hosts certainly have some strange beliefs. Did you know their matriarchs believe that Elves with epilepsy hold prophetic powers?" noted Arwela with a mocking air. "And they choose that over observing the night sky to foretell events."

"The matriarchs' teachings cannot be trusted, I agree. What's more, their faith is changing, and this is worrying. They have closed the temple of Eïwal Ffeyn and prohibited worship of the deity of freedom. Rumours have spread among the people of Llymar that Eïwal Ffeyn is a threat, that his wrath is the source of all the disasters which have struck the Archipelago recently. This is heresy. The Llewenti are forsaking their true patron deity."

Arwela knew how angry her brother had been when the matriarchs had announced their decision, which he interpreted as a direct threat to the community of Mentollà. Wishing to prevent another outburst, she changed subject. It was an opportunity to question his latest decision and point out his own contradictions.

"And yet you have decided to sail the high seas again with the army of Llymar.
Siw! Could you not resist commanding the great swanship? Is that it? Or is it rather you could never sit back while another captain takes the helm?" she reproached him with all the spite of someone being left behind.

Feïwal immediately countered her. "I have my reasons to sail to Cumberae with the army of Llymar. Besides, I need you to stay in Mentollà to watch over our community. Luwir will need your wise council more than ever."

"He will not. The only one who needs is you. Yet you no longer listen to me. How many times have I warned you?
It is not wise being so close to Aewöl and his mysterious servants. It is dangerous to involve your family and clan in the dealings of his guild.
It was folly going to Nargrond Valley and it is suicidal going to Nyn Llyandy with the fleet of Llymar.
Cir shines upon your path, Feïwal! The star of degradation watches over you! It is awaiting your fall! And should you continue to approach its deadly light, it will claim your soul," Arwela warned, spelling out quite deliberately the bad omens she had read in the stars to make her point.

Her voice possessed a great power to convince, such was the inner strength of the seer of the clan of Filweni. Feïwal listened to her attentively, but he did not bow to her arguments. His gaze, full of serenity, fixed upon his sister. He wanted her to understand why he had come to these decisions. Brother and sister would not meet for a long time. He needed Arwela strong and confident. She would become the leader of their community if he should fail. So, relying on his usual solemn attitude, he tried to convince her.

"It is true. Recently I have not followed your advice, and on several occasions," he started, still defensive.

"Siw! You have systematically done the opposite of what I have advised, Feïwal! Look at what happened with the mad hermit. I warned you that shape-changer was dangerous. He belonged to a faction of extremists among the druid circles, wild Men and Elves who pray for massive disasters to occur. They are obsessed with destruction. You, we, should have nothing to do with them.
Yet you still met that Alef Bronzewood on several occasions. You believed his tales. And worse, you even crossed a sea and explored the most dangerous valley of the Islands to see if his predictions came true."

"Alef Bronzewood was an ally, a friend of Gelros, whether you like it or not. We need allies... do you understand? Sometimes, you do not choose them."

"I am sure Alef Bronzewood was serving another powerful druid with greater influence," Arwela replied severely. "He was most probably being manipulated. Remember it was he who asked you to meet him in the first place.
You are acting as if this friendship with Gelros aligns him with Mentollà. But that lonely scout is a Morawenti, Feïwal. Night Elves have no friends. That is all there is to say..."

"When I hear your words, it is like I am listening to Mynar dyl at the Council of the Forest. He has often said, 'You are an Irawenti, Feïwal dyn, that is all there is to say!' at the end of his speeches," countered the guide of the clan of Filweni.

"Gelros is the faithful servant of a dangerous master, Feïwal. I have said it from the beginning. I have said it many times, and I will continue to say it. If, in the end, one of the shipwrecked prevails in these lands, I predict it will be Aewöl. Only there will be none of us left to applaud his feat,"

"All I know is: Aewöl brought me Alef Bronzewood, and Alef Bronzewood almost led me to the Lenra Pearl."
Unconvinced, Arwela disagreed. "How can you be sure of that? The reality looks very different to me. You crossed a forbidden sea; you entered a valley where Gnomes and Giants dwell. You risked your supposed friends' lives and your own, just for the sake of meeting with a mad hermit who had promised you the Lenra Pearl. Is that jewel not the most precious in the Islands? Is it not the most guarded treasure?"

"I saw in Alef Bronzewood's eye he was telling the truth. He explained me how to read the revelations his master had experienced. He backed up what he said with evidence.
Siw! The faction of the true druids who supported him, that group of dangerous priests as you called them, wish to free the Mighty Prisoner and clear the Islands of the invaders. They want the Archipelago to be returned to the Free Elves, to become what it was always meant to be, our last refuge. Indirectly these true druids serve our purpose. They pave the way for the migration of our people.
And history has proven Alef Bronzewood right. Survivors of the Pact Gathering confirmed the mages of the Ruby College brought the Lenra Pearl to the grove of Llya.

The Lenra Pearl was very close to me at one point, almost within reach. The great disaster, which was foretold did occur, and the army of Gwarystan was indeed destroyed. Alef Bronzewood came to the meeting as agreed, and I cannot imagine why he would have done so without the prize he had promised. I believe he held the Lenra Pearl in his hand. We came so close to freeing the Mighty Prisoner. Only Alef Bronzewood was murdered before we could reach him."

"I cannot help but worry, Feïwal! Your imagination has got the better of you. The responsibility you feel for the fate of our nation is mutating into a dangerous obsession which makes you see things where there are none."

"Then what about this?" asked Feïwal, challenging as ever.

His eyes became as bright as stars. The guide of the clan of Filweni drew from his cloak a long dagger with a beautifully adorned hilt in the shape of a winged lion.

"What is that?" Arwela asked, surprised. "It looks like a fine weapon indeed."

"Siw! This is the blade which killed Alef Bronzewood," Feïwal triumphantly declared. "I found it buried in his throat the day we were meant to meet. It bears the arms of the House of Dol Nos-Loscin from Cumberae. This is the same house that decided to withdraw its forces the day before the eruption. Matriarch Myryae told the Council of the Forest, for Princess Terela somehow knew what would happen."

All of a sudden, Arwela understood what her brother was trying to do. She knew him well. He was always patient and focussed on the details, but nothing could steer him off course once he had set his mind on something. No wonder it was Feïwal who had led them beyond the Austral Ocean.

"So, you have come to believe the House of Dol Nos-Loscin murdered Alef Bronzewood and took the Lenra Pearl back to Cumberae?" she asked, her voice low, almost defeated.

Arwela now felt her words of caution would make little impact on her brother, obsessed as he was by his quest.

"I cannot know for sure. Everything is so complex. I am still in the dark. The only thing I can do now is find out who owned this dagger. And should he hold the Lenra Pearl, I will take it from him. The Mighty Prisoner must be freed. I owe it to our people.

Think about mother, think about your lover Rogenwë who stayed behind. Would you not prefer to have them safely with us behind the high walls of Mentollà?"

Arwela remained silent for a while, coolly observing the gorgeous hills of Llafal appear in the morning mist as the sun rose above the shoreline.

"Siw!" she said at last. "This is why you are secretly taking your companions to Cumberae. I now understand why Aewöl and his minions are hiding in the bowels of the Alcalinquë. You think you will need them."

"Without their assistance, I would not have made it out of Nargrond Valley. Aewöl's support was invaluable. He has servants to do his bidding and possesses knowledge that no one else has.

Gelros, Roquendagor and Curwë defended me with their lives. One day I will tell you what we went through in the ruins of Yslla. There dwell beings even more evil than the Gnomes or Giants of Nargrond Valley. Elves who survive such perils together forge close ties. That bond cannot be broken, and I am grateful to have them at my side. They have pledged to help me, though they know nothing of my quest. Such loyalty is rare."

Arwela was dispirited by what she was hearing. It seemed as if her brother's ties to his friends were now stronger than those to his family. A deep concern was etched across her face. She made one final attempt to convince him to stay put.

"You do not have to go to Cumberae. You do not need to command the great swanship. No one asked you to participate in this war," were the only words the seer of the clan of Filweni could muster. "There is..." she continued, but suddenly lost confidence.

She did not finish her sentence, knowing it would be of no use. Angry and worried for what the future would hold, Arwela ordered her small boat to fetch her.

"I am returning to shore," Arwela commanded her guards. "There is nothing more I can do here," she added, with a touch of provocation.

The beautiful lady of the clan of Filweni left the deck without a backward glance to her brother.

The tethers and lines of the ship billowed in the light morning wind. Gradually, the Halwyfal's waters were turning blue as the sun climbed in the sky. The northern breeze was driving away the last of the thin clouds.

Llafal, the same evening

The sun faded and sank towards the western shores. Darkness came creeping down from the forest. The daylight was slowly dying.

In the lowest parts of Llafal, by the shores of the Halwyfal, there was a large cedar tree overlooking the great basin. Its long branches kept the isolated beach cool.

Nyriele, the young matriarch of clan Llyvary, was lying down in the shade of the giant tree. Her robe was white as the clouded heavens on a summer's day. Her diadem was sewn with azure flowers, which contrasted beautifully with her blond hair.

She was busy weaving a necklace of Lleùty; the exquisite flower gave off both jasmine and lilac scents. The beach was rich with others like it, which perfumed the air around. As she breathed in the delicate evening scents, it felt like tasting the delights of Eïwele Llyi's gardens.

Night time around the Halwyfal was splendid at this time of year; deep tones from the sky and water would converge as the sun set, creating wonderful colours and moving patterns that even the most skilful illusionist could not hope to recreate. The moon's silvery rays reflected upon the great basin, shading its faint light on a group of swans taking flight.

The ocean breeze shook the branches around Nyriele. It was as if the cedar tree were trembling from its highest leaf to the depths of its roots. The young Elf had been lying silently in this pleasant spot for hours. She was deliberately staying away from Llafal's streets; the crews of departing warships had been invited to take part in the city's celebrations, and she did not feel like joining the festivities.

Nyriele was dreaming, looking at the shores and the sea.

The wild coast extended towards Penlla in the east. It was a vast plateau, with rows of ancient elms, twisted and gnawed by the constant sea wind. The young Elf was staring at the small waves rolling endlessly under the stars, when she saw him, walking under the moon's rays. Nyriele shuddered. The object of her thoughts had materialized before her eyes.

First, she recognized his gait, which expressed his gentle temperament so well, then saw his long curly, light-brown hair. At last, her gaze was drawn in by his green eyes, hopelessly attracted by their unbelievable colour.

"Curwë!" she whispered.

After slipping through the gigantic stones of the deserted beach, the bard came up to Nyriele. He was wearing a long azure cloak, like those worn by Irawenti sailors.

When she rose to her feet to embrace him, every trace of her heartache deserted her, and she fell into a warm trance as memories of their time together flooded back. After a long, much-awaited kiss, their lips parted to catch their breath, and she uttered a few words with a reproachful tone.

"What happened? How could you? You vanished, and I have heard nothing since. All this time you never replied to the letters I sent to Mentollà."

"I have come at last... Fendrya knew you would be here," he murmured back.

But Curwë lowered his eyes, and she understood that he had been helpless. His evident sadness made her care for him even more.

She noticed he was feeling pain in his cheek. When Nyriele examined him more closely, she made out the almost imperceptible red marks left by a rune. Its power was at work even as they spoke, hurting Curwë badly, almost to the point of making him faint. Despite his suffering, the bard apologized as best as he could.

"I regret my absence with all my soul, my lady. I was not well. I was away... I had no choice."

Nyriele could feel his distress. She worried that the great effort Curwë was making to visit her might prove fatal, such was the deadly influence of the rune upon him. Already his gaze was confused, and his spirit appeared troubled. He then murmured what sounded like his last wishes, as if he could drop down dead at any moment.

"When we are apart, I feel a lack, a great emptiness. I feel as if we are two halves of the same being, which fate once deigned to separate. I have fought to come back to you; I have fought with all my heart. But a powerful spell seizes my soul whenever I try to bridge the gap between us. It tortures me. Every time I imagined ways of coming back, it was agony.

But here I am before you, almost dead, but very much your servant."

Nyriele was deeply distressed at this. She also felt guilty for being angry and not enquiring about Curwë's fate with more insistence. Tears of regret and repentance ran down her face. She embraced Curwë again, and wept over his scorching cheek, kissing it with tenderness, until it burnt no more. The young matriarch was graced with special skills. She took her amulet in her hands and invoked her deity.

"May the power of Eïwele Llyi ease your pain. May the mark unjustly laid upon you be removed," she prayed. "I am the high priestess of the deity of love, and I demand that you be healed of your woes."

For some time, the two Elves remained in each other's arms. The young matriarch entered into a struggle against an unknown force, unleashing her innermost power to fight the curse haunting her lover.

At last, Curwë felt relieved, as if he had been touched by divine grace.

"My lady, the pain seems to have left me."

Curwë winked at Nyriele and they hugged each other tight, their bodies trembling with joy. The two Elves let time pass slowly and silently, simply enjoying the deep relief they felt at their reunion. At last, Curwë gathered his thoughts and spoke.

"During my time away from Llafal, I walked the paths of the mountains. I was alone without you but, in truth, I could not have been closer to you. Memories of our time together came back to me constantly. I remembered everything you taught me, everything you gave me. You have such a mind... your knowledge is remarkable, as if you have memorized all you had ever read. You can quote the songs of so many bards. Your great learning has made you a virtuous and spiritual lady. To my mind, you are perfection."

Nyriele blushed with pleasure at these words and, with a mocking air, she immediately replied with a smile , "Are you trying to seduce me with your sweet words, stranger from a distant land?"

Curwë laughed. "I know I could never achieve such a feat. How could a common Elf like me find favour in the eyes of the demigoddess of charm, the descendant of a deity no less?"

Seeing his spirits revived, Nyriele could not resist drawing out this little game of seduction. Assuming the role of the sad and lonely princess, she turned to him with an adorable pout.

"Where do you think my charms have got me with eligible suitors? Nowhere. All contemplate me from afar, and many give me praise, but nobody is bold enough to seduce me. All I can do is stay in the temple of Eïwele Llyi and cry, alone and unloved."

Her charming act triggered an even greater reaction than she had anticipated. Curwë burst into a passionate declaration of love.

"Nyriele, I alone know that your unmatched outer beauty is but the reflection of your soul within."

Visibly enjoying the situation, the young lady improvised further. "In truth, I sometimes hate this beauty you admire so much. You are looking at me now, but all you see is soul. I have a body, too. I must confess, I have prayed to my deity with all my heart to send me a lover, full of desire. And in all my dreams, he had green eyes."

At these words, Curwë lost all measure. He let himself wander into the twisted maze of blind passion.

"At your touch, I forget myself, I no longer worry about my fate, I simply seek your happiness, I seek only to bring you joy. I would give everything for you," he declared breathlessly, and he kissed her with passion.

"You would give me Eawa, that great love the High Elves celebrate in their songs?"

"I came to offer it to you, beloved Nyriele, the flame that warms rather than burns, the everlasting bond which provides more than it consumes. By watching over you, I will sanctify my own existence. I will make us one."

Nyriele shivered, suddenly afraid by the force of her lover's passion.

But Curwë insisted , "I am speaking to you of undying love: a love that changes everything, ignites the hearts, leads the spirit and sometimes demands acting radically."

The young lady felt uncomfortable at these words, intuitively sensing the tragedy such an eternal oath could provoke. For the first time, she understood that, despite his lightness, despite the ease of his manners, despite his charming sense of humour, Curwë was an immortal High Elf. Her lover also was subject to what the Llewenti called the curse of undying love.

Breaking free from Curwë, Nyriele stood like a matriarch before her apprentice. With a tone as soft as she could manage, she started to explain.

"Curwë, life does not work in the way you were taught by Hawenti scholars. It is more complex, subtler, with ever-changing nuance... One cannot simply declare to a lover that one's passion will be eternal."

"I can," he countered boldly. "Do not forget, my lady, you are speaking to the green-eyed Curwë!"

Half-conquered by this impertinent boast, Nyriele could not resist smiling. She nevertheless continued to try reasoning with him.

"Eïwele Llyi told her priestesses: 'when love has taken its course, then comes quiet. The reason is simple: the end of desire'. The deity teaches us pleasure and pain; those seemingly contradictory combinations of emptiness and fullness, want and satisfaction, absence and presence. She talked of how fully satisfying one's desire is very dangerous. It can lead to coldness in the future."

Curwë listened, smiling, but he would not hear nor understand Eïwele Llyi's wisdom. Self-confident as ever, he committed himself further.

"Beyond even the eternity of the High Elves' existence, I promise you the infinity of my love. I believe a single Llewenti life filled with passion will be far nobler than an endless existence without your love."

Curwë had just hit upon one of Nyriele's deepest anxieties about their relationship. Her mother had first warned her about this inescapable bind, and her father had since berated her for ignoring its implications. This question had haunted her since the first time she and Curwë kissed. Anguish was now etched on her delicate features. She could not suppress a shiver. Her voice now less assured, Nyriele explained.

"All Llewenti must accept the condition of our kin: to live a life which has a beginning and an end. Eïwele Llyo alone decides when it begins, and when it ends. Neither I, nor any of my people, can escape that fate. The deity of dreams' decisions are final.
There is no return from that path…
The immortal High Elves want love to prevail over death. They will exchange gold rings and commit themselves to unbreakable bonds which last millennia. Sadly, it is also another sign of their dangerous and arrogant beliefs because death always triumphs in the end.
You must understand that my life will one day have an end and that I will return as a spirit into the forest. The day you lose me, you will be inconsolable. There will be just you and your Irawenti lyre left to mourn the love you have lost. You will cry again and again, until even your marvellous voice will

be inaudible. Your lively, joyous Muswab will transform into a lament. Is that really what you want for yourself? I do not think it is."

At this conclusion, which sounded rather like a condemnation, Curwë felt his tumultuous blood rushing to his heart and to his temples. Without even thinking, he reached into the pocket of his cloak and pulled out a jewel box. The swelling dam of excess love, which had driven him to find Nyriele that evening, was unleashed. In a surge of passion, Curwë kneeled like a knight before his liege.

"I accept this destiny," he solemnly declared. "I'm grateful that fate has chosen this one for me.
I am only a common Elf, but I have a noble heart. When I read about the exploits of ancient heroes in books, I know I could match them all," he claimed, his pale, haggard gaze trying to fix the object of his desire.
"To resist love, when the sky, the stars, the very air, push you to it is like swimming against the rising tide. I understood I would not emerge victorious from that struggle. So, I have decided to love you... while I can.
To my eyes, you are a living and luminous demi-goddess... You are like this jewel I offer you, the symbol of my eternal bond to you...
I give this pearl to you, to the purest heart in the Islands."

Nyriele opened the jewel box to reveal the treasure inside. She almost lost her balance when she saw it, before her gaze fixed steadily on the mysterious crystalline substance, glowing with unnatural light.

"Such absolute purity, such perfection, I have never seen anything more beautiful!" Nyriele exclaimed.

The desire for carnal union rushed through her; she needed them to immortalize this moment of perfect spiritual communion. She came closer to Curwë and embraced him.
Pressed close together, they could hear their hearts beating. She put her arms around him, kissing Curwë passionately. On her lips, she felt the strangest sensation that almost made her faint: as if she had felt the breath of a deity.

A nightingale's song rained down from the heights of the cedar tree. It started out faint, but then grew bolder, vibrant, joyful. Curwë lifted his head and closed his eyes. An intense joy, and infinite awe at the splendour of things, drowned his heart, which seemed suspended in time. It was the beginning of his life, the dawn of all his hopes. Curwë wanted to speak, or even sing to celebrate the sheer beauty of it all, but he could not utter a word. Only then, as he sensed the ephemeral nature of that exquisite moment, did he notice his eyes were full of tears.

Nyn Llyvary, Llafal, five days after the fleet's departure

The nave of Eïwal Vars' temple teemed with many lively conversations. The white swan of clan Llyvary was spreading its wings above the monumental fireplace. Chandeliers sparkled from the ceiling, and the tables were adorned with large candelabra. The large vaulted hall was decorated with colourful tapestries. A crowd of more than two hundred Elves was packed around buffet tables, which were generously laden with fresh fish, smoked eels, sweet-smelling fruits and spicy oysters. Servants were carrying round wooden trays of delicate little appetisers. Young Elves circulated between the tables, refilling the partygoers' glasses with their pots of cider and jugs of wine.

Nyriele made her entrance into the deity of war's temple. A simple, light, white dress with shimmering coloured patterns moulded her slim body, from her bare shoulders to her ankles. Ignoring her admirers' compliments and the wave of praise which accompanied her arrival, the young matriarch of clan Llyvary marched straight through the throng of jubilant Elves.

A moment later, as if he had been waiting for her, the warlord of Tios Halabron appeared below the arches at the other end of the hall. His cloak, green as per clan Ernaly's colours, was a dark stain among the bright party outfits of Llafal's elite class.
A feverish rumour was spreading throughout the temple, rippling through the crowd from the temple's entrance to the besieged buffets, like a gust of wind among the quivering treetops. One name was on everybody's lips:

"Mynar dyl!"

Amazed by such a warm reception, Nyriele tried to get lost in the crowd and make herself invisible. Curiosity had driven her to the temple of Eïwal Vars, but she now regretted following that impulse. The crowd's excitement was making her uncomfortable.

'I do not like the powerful charm that seems to be affecting the audience,' she thought.

The city had brimmed with news of Mynar dyl's return since a swanship arrived at dawn. The wharf of Llafal had been packed by a crowd of Elves, eager to hear the warlord of Tios Halabron's tale. Yet Mynar dyl had been discreet, and few had even seen him. Gossips now whispered that he was there, inside the temple of Eïwal Vars, and some felt sure he would address the selected audience within.

In the absence of a verified story, the most bewildering tales were circulating the streets of Llafal. Some described how Mynar dyl had wandered alone in the plain of ashes after miraculously surviving the volcano's eruption. Others claimed he owed his life to the intervention of an emissary sent by Eïwal Vars.

The fact was, however, that of all those who had journeyed to Gwa Nyn, only Mynar dyl witnessed what had happened at the Pact Gathering. His own story was much anticipated, and his silence since returning was becoming unbearable.

A sense of frightful mystery surrounded the dreadful events of Nargrond Valley, as only bits and pieces of contradictory information had reached Llafal until then.

Nyriele positioned herself behind the statue of Aonyn dyl Llyvary, her forefather and the first Protector of the Islands. From that dark corner of the temple, she could watch the scene without being observed herself. Yet, despite this precaution, Nyriele did not feel at ease, as if some looming threat was hanging over her head.

Five days had passed since Curwë had sailed with the fleet of Llymar towards Cumberae, and to war. She already was feeling profoundly alone. Only Fendrya, who had become her friend and confidant, could now be of any support.

After that marvellous night of pure happiness and pleasure, an insidious sense of foreboding had gradually grown within her. Doubt had followed excitement, and now guilt was replacing fervour. She felt she had acted against Llewenti customs, against what was expected of a matriarch. Her thoughts were confused. Like in a tragedy of old, she was aware higher powers were toying with her destiny, as if Eïwele Llya was furious with the gifts Eïwele Llyi had offered her.

Now, as Nyriele stood in the Hall of Eïwal Vars, surrounded by the statues of her heroic ancestors and mixing with the Llymar elite, she felt strangely out of place.

'How odd I did not dare stand by the matriarchs' side tonight! I have the feeling they are all judging me, accusing me! I know it cannot be so, but I still cannot bear to look any of them in the eye.

It is just Llewenti in the temple tonight, as if the clans needed to gather and unite before the rising dangers. Even Mother and Father have come. I have not seen them standing side by side for a long time; it's like they wanted to show their unity. The situation must be critical,' she thought.

Her gaze turned to Mynar dyl, who was now slowly climbing the stairs to reach the temple's altar. Silence spread throughout the nave. All looked at the warlord of Tios Halabron, who faced the crowd with a proud look. His outfit was simple and plain, but somehow it enhanced his striking beauty. He bent his fair head to salute the matriarchs and the Protector of the Forest, who stood in the front row.

'He is changed,' Nyriele realised, amazed by his charisma and majesty. 'He has been entrusted with new authority,' she understood.

Mynar dyl was holding his usual instrument, a lyre made of silver strings, which legend said had belonged to Queen Llyoriane's brother, a fabled bard of that time.

The warlord of Tios Halabron was adulated in his native land, where some of his verses had even become proverbs. When he started to sing, the Elves of Llafal were hanging on his every word and seemed to be agreeing in advance. His voice rang out, low and wonderful.

Nyriele had never heard this song before and guessed he had written it for the occasion. The composition was perfectly adapted to the grave message the singer wished to convey.

The audience was immediately enthralled, as if by a strange spell. What carried through the nave from the lyre was more than music. It sounded like a timeless ode to the glory of all mythology. It started with a few simple notes. Though delicious, the innocence of this first stanza would not have caught the audience's attention if they had not anticipated what would follow. Then came a sublime torrent of complex composition; stanza after stanza, chorus after chorus, the heroic symphony built to unmatched heights of beauty and audacity.

Mynar dyl's clear voice rose, sounding out under the temple's arches.

"When the Arkys called, I answered them blind;
And the Lonely Seeker was I sent forth to find,
They spoke of a Renegade who no reprieve sought,
Before their high justice, Dyoren must be brought.

I was their Elf in each and every quest,
The Vale valued me as their brightest and best,
But Dyoren had lost any favour he had won,
They spoke only of the evil my brother had done.

Far did I search for his hiding and his hold,
But the rebel escaped, for the rebel was bold,
I heard told he had fled to the Oryusk Mines,
For the darkest places hide the darkest crimes.

The faithful Lonely Seeker had by fortune ill,
Wandered Nargrond Valley: every river, every hill,
To his glorious errand, my brother held steadfast
He had hoped all his life, and he hoped to the last.

Then the proud Dyoren was attacked and slain,
His death, like his life, had been in vain,
In the Sian Dorg, I saw him pale and dead,
Then a sudden fear took me, and I fled.

For the Oryusk Hounds had followed my scent,
My dear dead brother, I could barely lament,
One mighty dog pounced with flaming eyes,
Then amid the snarls, the blows and my cries,

Lordly Eïwal Vars seemed to whisper in my ear,
Half-dead, I reached out, and found his spear.
It was his holy strength that saved me that day;
To his infinite glory shall I ever pray.

Eïwal Vars has given my life back to me,
And whispered a truth that has set me free,
A glorious spell upon me he binds,
To impress upon your faithful minds

That a crown shall be returned, with a green stone,
To the Islands' fair child who shall sit upon a throne,
Vars bids me find a most beautiful bride,
And commands our future daughter be seated by his side."

The bewitched crowd listened, speechless and soundless, until the artist finished his tale and the last echo of his instrument died away.

★

Ignoring the crowd's applause, Mynar dyl left the altar and returned to his quarters inside one of the temple's wings. His personal guards would ensure he was not disturbed after the performance.

He walked into the vaulted room, elegantly furnished with tapestries, carpets and fine woodwork. Hunting weapons, ranging from spears to short bows, decorated the walls, giving the place a rather warlike atmosphere.

Mynar dyl quickly set about preparing the room, as if anticipating the arrival of an important visitor. First, he lit a dozen candles, the wax an unusual yellowy orange. Sensual and passionate smells immediately filled the room.

'Their fragrance captures the fresh, spiced and sensual scents of the Secret Vale. The Arkyllyi described how these smells create the perfect playground for seduction,' he remembered.

He then retrieved a beautifully adorned phial from a locked chest. It was filled with a golden liquid. He looked at the contents for some time, before finally tipping a good portion of it into a jug of wine that sat on the main table alongside two crystal glasses.

As he placed the potion safely back inside the chest, Mynar dyl uttered a few words aloud, as if he was addressing an invisible companion.

"We will soon know whether the gift the Arkys offered me for returning Rymsing is worth a Blade of Nargrond Valley. I am looking forward to seeing the effects that the Daughter of the Islands' elixir will have."

Mynar dyl then caressed a long object, covered in a blanket, and placed it behind his bed, so that no one would see it.

Having finished his preparations, the warlord of Tios Halabron looked at himself in the mirror. Happy with his fair appearance, he decided to allow himself a moment of repose.

He sat on a comfortable chair, filled the two glasses with the wine and marvelled at its yellow colour. Mynar dyl could not resist a taste.

'There is a perfect balance of sweetness and a zest of acidity. There are notes of apricots, honey and peaches. Good! The elixir is perfectly undetectable, as was promised,' he noted with satisfaction.

The warlord of Tios Halabron did not have to wait much longer. Soon, one of his guards introduced a visitor into the small room.

The newcomer was none other than Gal dyl, the Protector of the Forest. The commander of the armies of Llymar looked tense, almost embarrassed. His noble attire and shining jewels could not mask the deep lack of self-esteem he was feeling in that moment.

"I did as we agreed. I spoke to her and she came to visit you. Nyriele is waiting outside," Gal dyl confirmed.

"Has she been informed?"

"I told her the Daughter of the Islands perished during the eruption."

"Does she understand what that means? A new servant will have to be appointed to serve by Eïwele Llya's side," stressed Mynar dyl.

"She does," replied Gal dyl, visibly eager to be finished with the discussion.

"Does she know her duty towards the clans, what is expected of her?" insisted Mynar dyl, not impressed in the least by his visitor's impatience.

The Protector tried to elude the question. "I did not dare remind her, but Matriarch Lyrine has seen to that on many occasions. Nyriele knows that producing a child destined to become the new Daughter of the Islands will be up to her."

Gal dyl shuddered, feeling humiliated by the whole affair. Out of sheer awkwardness, he moved forward, intending to seize the second glass of wine which lay waiting on the table.

But Mynar stopped him with an authoritative gesture of his hand.

"I regret, noble Protector! I have poured that glass for your daughter..."

Gal dyl looked with dismay at his host. Mynar dyl seized the opportunity to exploit his advantageous position further.

"You have done well, Gal dyl," he declared with a lordly tone , "and I am sure that history will remember the part you played in saving our clans.
Indeed, your legacy will be utterly untarnished by the stain of infamy; I know how important that is to you," he added, his sickly-sweet voice full of hidden threat.

But the fair warlord had not finished. "Now comes the time for the most... embarrassing question of the lot. It is no easy thing for me to speak to you about it; after all, you are her dear father, are you not? But I suppose these issues lies at the heart of our agreement. Let me put it bluntly. Did she agree-..."

Gal dyl cut him off, as if more than anything he did not want to hear the humiliating question in its entirety.

"I did... Well, I tried... She is a matriarch of clan Llyvary, sovereign in those matters. I thought it would be wiser to address the matter through parable and metaphor..."
"What clever words did you use, Gal dyl? You are worrying me."
"The best a father can use with his daughter," the Protector claimed. "I told her the story of her birth, what was expected of me, what was expected of Matriarch Lyrine."

This response left Mynar dyl puzzled. He was far from sure about the pertinence of Gal dyl's strategy. Shrugging his shoulders, he ended the conversation abruptly.

"I will see Nyriele now. I thank you for your assistance, Gal dyl. It is important that we, the Llewenti, never forget where our roots lie."

The Protector of the Forest was more than happy to be done with the embarrassing meeting. Without a word, he turned on his heels and disappeared behind the alcove's door.

A moment later, Nyriele entered. She looked extremely nervous. Mynar dyl had never seen her look so defensive. Her keen sense of smell immediately alerted her to the scented candles. Mynar dyl could tell she was trying to identify the nature of the sweet odour in the room. The dubious frown on her face made it very clear to him that, if he wanted to put her at ease, he would have to call upon all his skills in seduction. Feeling under pressure, the warlord of Tios Halabron began.

"Nyriele, your visit honours me greatly. After all the hardships I have been through, this meeting is the best reward I could have dreamed of."

The young matriarch did not respond. Mynar dyl saw she was regretting visiting him as her father had suggested. He decided to act quickly and tried to flood her with information.

Mynar dyl was first and foremost a storyteller, who excelled at captivating his audience. He knew how to adapt to his public and focus on the details that would most pique their interest. Deliberately minimising the part he had played, as though it had been of little importance, he told Nyriele what had happened in the valley of Nargrond. He did not spare her any details about their entrance into the valley, the Pact Gathering or the volcanic eruption.

Nyriele was the first to hear the full tale, and her curiosity gradually grew as the events, vividly described by Mynar dyl, unfolded before her eyes. He had that rare ability to make his listeners feel part of the story he was telling.
She was deeply saddened when she learned the details of Dyoren's death, though Mynar dyl withheld news of the Seeker recovering Lynsing, insisting instead on his efforts to perform funerary rituals in accordance with their faith.
Her initial cold attitude began to soften at this story.

"I am glad Dyoren was sent off properly," she confided.

"He was my elder brother," replied Mynar dyl, and there was a small tremor in his voice.

For a long time then, the warlord of Tios Halabron continued his story. He seldom looked Nyriele in the eye, but rather stared into the middle distance, as though he could actually see what he was so vividly describing.

All the while, Mynar dyl was discreetly observing the effect the candles' fumes were having upon his beautiful interlocutor. Her eyes were widening, her attitude was relaxing, and she was even showing the first signs of empathy towards him.

Mynar dyl felt the time had now come to offer her the drink he had prepared. Eagerly seizing his own glass to quench his thirst after his lengthy recount, he emptied it in a single gulp.

His features froze as he realised how rude he had been not to offer his guest a glass first. Immediately he set about correcting his apparent impoliteness.

Still absorbed by the tale and eager to know how it would end, Nyriele wet her lips and took a sip from her glass. She was not even paying attention to the fine nectar's characteristics, and quickly finished the full contents of her drink. The air was dry due to the candles' fumes, and she felt particularly thirsty.

At this, Mynar dyl inwardly rejoiced. Eager to mask what he was feeling, he turned away, pretending to look for a map which might better illustrate his story.

Fully master of himself again, he laid out a detailed chart of Nargrond Valley on the table and resumed his explanation.

"My journey out of Nargrond Valley was difficult. I had to cross the sheer precipices of the Arob Far. I encountered fell creatures that had lurked there since before the coming of the Elves. There, monsters abide, wandering the mountains' cliffs to snare their prey, hunting silently in the wilderness. There is no food for an Elf in those desolate parts: only death."

The horror of his journey seemed to return to Mynar dyl's mind as he spoke. His features were marked with dread.

"This journey through the Arob Far was the greatest hardship I have ever faced, an unprecedented deed. At times, I was sure I would never get home alive. But finally, I found a way out of the Arob Far and into the plain of ashes, along paths that no Elf has ever dared tread."

Mynar dyl paused. His breath was short, as though he could still feel the pain, he had experienced.

"I then had to pass through the mazes the Dark Elves weave about their realm on the other side of Mount Oryusk, until I finally came stumbling onto the beaches of the Sea of Isyl, exhausted and bowed after so many days of woe.
I wandered for a very long time along those vast expanses, like a solitary outlaw, with only birds and animals for companions. The truth is, I did not fear death itself, but rather being taken captive by the clan Myortilys. I know about their cruel ways. Finally, news of my lonely errand must have reached the Secret Vale, for the Arkys sought me out. A swanship was sent to fetch me."

Nyriele looked at him with intensity, appreciating the full extent of his perilous errand. Mynar dyl could tell she was feeling a certain admiration for his deeds.
He himself was starting to feel the faint exhilaration that the candles' fumes procured. He thought the young matriarch immensely attractive in that moment.
She was dressed in light robes with a rounded collar that plunged towards her breast. A pale light from outside was caressing her face, highlighting her exquisite features. Her blue eyes were wide open and shining.

Mynar Dyl knew he was going through one of those unique moments in life, when prudence and wild emotion jostle for supremacy in the mind.
Nyriele was standing very close to the door. He suddenly found himself in front of her, barring her exit.
So slender was she and so beautifully frail that the overwhelming attraction made him mutter incoherent words of desire into her ear.
Nyriele stood amazed before him; she did not at first understand what he was saying, yet she knew she could not run away.

Mynar dyl felt the sweetness of her breath, and his burning lust overwhelmed him. A split second later and a sensation of exhilarating delight exploded from his lips. For a moment he did not understand that he had kissed Nyriele. Then, deliberately abandoning himself to this sense of feverish pleasure, he devoured her lips. He could not form a coherent thought as chaotic images whirled before his eyes.

At last, so great was the joy in his heart that his courage rose within him. He felt the bold spirit that had brought him out of Ystanargrond rearing up again. Looking Nyriele in the eye, he declared his love.

"I desire you now more than ever. You are Llyoriane's heir, the noblest of all Llewenti maidens.

Come closer to me, beautiful swan, unite with me, let yourself be transformed by me, by the strength of the hawk!

The torrents of love I have for you are the source of Llewenti rebirth.

And from our union, a young Daughter of the Islands will be born, a maiden so fair that Eïwal Vars will cease mourning the loss of Queen Llyoriane and return among his children to request her hand."

Mynar dyl seemed overwhelmed by concupiscence, by a fierce desire to possess her, and it could now be read clearly in his eyes. He was discovering Eïwal Vars' gift, wild desire, inherited from the deity of hunting, who had conquered even Queen Llyoriane.

For a moment, Nyriele was about to yield to his overwhelming will. But looking at the flickering candles, she realised that her mind was feeling weak. Scents of saffron, orange and vanilla were provoking the pleasant dizziness she was feeling.

Nyriele immediately escaped Mynar dyl's embrace and left the room without a word.

Looking at the glass Nyriele had drunk from, the warlord of Tios Halabron smiled.

"How sweet! She ran like a young deer fleeing from a stag...

372

No matter. It is only a question of time before I see you stripped, Nyriele. And then not long after, you will need a new dress: a larger one."

Now alone once more, Mynar dyl could not resist taking out the sword that he had carefully hidden inside the blanket. Examining the reflection of his fair face in the shining blade of Lynsing, Mynar felt dazzled by his own beauty.

"I believe I have discovered what true wisdom is," he concluded. "The answer has been there all along, but I have been too blind to see it. Our daughter is the answer to everything.

ANNEXES

Elvin nations

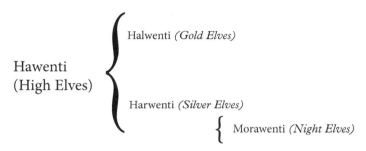

Hawenti
(High Elves)

Halwenti *(Gold Elves)*

Harwenti *(Silver Elves)*

Morawenti *(Night Elves)*

The Hawenti accepted the gift of the Gods and became immortal.

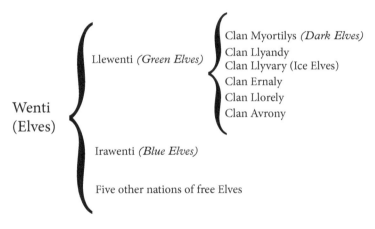

Wenti
(Elves)

Llewenti *(Green Elves)*

Clan Myortilys *(Dark Elves)*
Clan Llyandy
Clan Llyvary (Ice Elves)
Clan Ernaly
Clan Llorely
Clan Avrony

Irawenti *(Blue Elves)*

Five other nations of free Elves

The Wenti refused the gift of the Gods and remained free and mortal.

The Hawenti

The High Elves are called 'Hawenti' in the language of the Llewenti, as opposed to the 'Wenti' who identify as 'free' Elves. The Hawenti accepted the gift of immortality offered by the Gods. They are immortal in the sense that they are immune to disease and do not age, although they can be killed in battle. They are divided into two main nations: The Gold Elves (the most prominent) and the Silver Elves. The Hawenti have a greater depth of knowledge than other Elvin nations, due to their natural inclination for learning as well as their extreme age. Their power and wisdom know no comparison and within their eyes the fire of eternity can be seen. That kindred of the Elves were ever distinguished both by their knowledge of things and by their desire to know more.

The Morawenti

The Night Elves are called 'Morawenti' in the language of the Llewenti. The Morawenti are a subdivision of the Silver Elves, the second of the Hawenti nations. They are therefore counted among the High Elves as they accepted the gift of immortality offered by the Gods. Morawenti are immortal in the sense that they are immune to disease and do not age, although they too can be killed in battle. Morawenti tend to be thinner and taller in size than other Elves. They are characterised by very pale, almost livid skin, and their gaze is deep and mysterious. They all have dark hair, though their eye colour varies between grey and black. They favour wearing dark coloured tunics with grey or green shades and robes of fine linen, cotton or silk.

The Llewenti

One of the seven nations of 'free' Elves, they are called 'Llewenti' in their language, 'Llew' meaning 'Green' and 'Wenti' meaning 'Elves'. They were so named because their first Patriarch's attire was green. They are counted among the nations of Elves who refused the gift of immortality offered by the Gods. Llewenti enjoy much longer lives than Men, living for five to six centuries depending on their bloodline. Their race is similar in appearance to humans, but they are fairer and wiser, with greater spiritual powers, keener senses, and a deeper empathy with nature. They are for the most part a simple, peaceful, and reclusive community, famous for their singing skills. With sharper senses, they are highly skilled at crafts, especially when using natural resources. The Green Elves are wise in the ways of the forest and the natural world.

The Irawenti

One of the seven nations of the 'free' Elves, they are called 'Irawenti' in the language of the Llewenti, 'Ira' meaning 'Blue' and 'Wenti' meaning 'Elves'. They were so named, because their first Guide's eyes had the colour of the tropical seas and azure reflections emanated from his black hair. They are counted among the nations of Elves who refused the gift of immortality offered by the Gods. Irawenti enjoy much longer lives than men, living for four to five centuries depending on their bloodline. Their race is similar in appearance to the Green Elves but darker and wilder, with greater physical powers and a closer empathy with water. They are for the most part a free, joyful and adventurous race, famous for their navigation skills. Having sharper connection with rivers and oceans, they are at their strongest and most knowledgeable when aboard their ships. The Blue Elves are wise in the ways of the sea.
Llewenti clan originating from Nyn Ernaly, member of the Council of Llymar Forest

MAIN ELF FACTIONS AND CHARACTERS

FOREST OF LLYMAR

The clan Llyvary

Llewenti clan, principal and historical members of the Council of Llymar Forest

• **Myryae dyl Llyvary**: Matriarch of the Llewenti, Envoy of Llymar to the Pact Gathering
• **Nyriele dyl Llyvary, 'Llyoriane's Heir'**: Matriarch, High Priestess of Eïwele Llyi in Llafal

The clan Ernaly

Llewenti clan or iginating from Nyn Ernaly, members of the Council of Llymar Forest

• **Mynar dyl Ernaly, 'the Fair'**: Warlord of Tios Halabron

The clan Avrony

Llewenti clan originating from Nyn Avrony, members of the Council of Llymar Forest

• **Gal dyl Avrony**: Protector of the Forest

The House of Dol Lewin- Second branch
Rebel Hawenti house originating from Mentolewin

• **Camatael Dol Lewin**: Lord of House Dol Lewin, High Priest of Eïwal Lon in Tios Lluin

The Community of Mentollà
Group of Irawenti and Hawenti refugees originating from Essawylor across the Austral Ocean, members of the Council of Llymar Forest

• **Feïwal dyn Filweni:** Warlord of Mentollà and High Priest of Eïwal Ffeyn
• **Fendrya dyn Feli**: Keeper of Pearls
• **Roquendagor:** Commander of Mentollà
• **Curwë:** Guild Master of Alqualinquë in Llymar Forest
• **Aewöl:** Guild Master of Alqualinquë in Gwa Nyn
• **Gelros:** Aewöl's servant

PRINCIPALTY OF CUMBERAE

The House of Dol Nos-Loscin
Rebel Hawenti House originating from Cumberae

• **Terela Dol Nos-Loscin:** Princess of Cumberae
• **Alton Dol Nos-Loscin:** Ambassador of Cumberae

Sea of Cyclones

Nyn Llyvary

Nyn Llorely

Nyn Ernaly

Llymar

Main
Land

Sea
of
Llyoriane

Nyn Avrony

Gwarystan

Nargrond

Gwa Nyn

Cumberae

Sea of Isyl

Nyn Llyandy

LLEWENTI ISLANDS

50 Leagues

Marn
Rocks

Llananty

Sea of Isyl

Is Rocks

Llamyos

Nargrond Valley

Arob Nargrond

Ystanargrond

O Vaha

Yslla Lake

Sian Senky

Yssla

Grove of Llya

Mount
Oryusk

Mines of Oryusk

O Wiøny

Sian Dors

Sian Senky

Arob Nargrond

10 Leagues

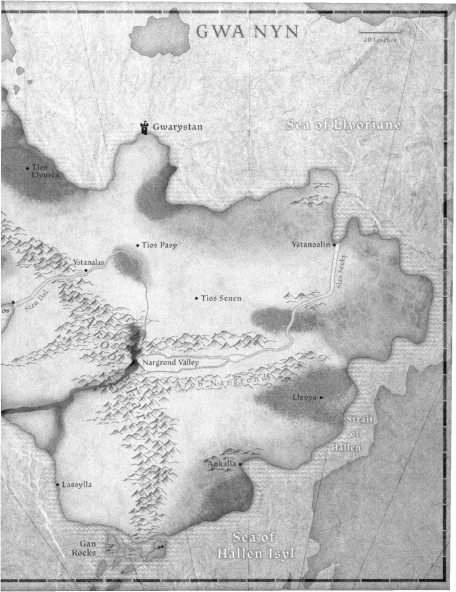

GWA NYN

20 Leagues

Sea of Llyoriane

Gwarystan

Tios Llyurca

Tios Pasy

Ystanalas

Ystanoalin

Sian Senky

Sian Dal

Tios Senen

Nargrond Valley

Afon Nargrond

Llevya

Strait of Hallen

Ankalla

Lassylla

Gan Rocks

Sea of Hallen Isyl

GENEALOGY HAWENTI
ROYAL BLOODLINES

1st Age

Melindro†

Gloren†	Ilorm†	Tircanil†	Inrod†	Inras†

0

Lormelin†

ARANAELE

ILARSIN
ILENSAR
ILENRIS

ORLAS

2nd Age

NORELIN

2700

† Dead

GENEALOGY HAWENTI
DOL NOBLE HOUSES

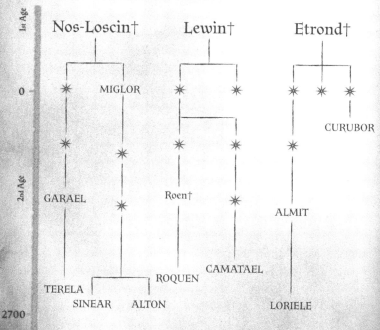

1st Age

Nos-Loscin†   Lewin†   Etrond†

0   MIGLOR   CURUBOR

2nd Age

GARAEL   Roen†   ALMIT

CAMATAEL

ROQUEN

TERELA   ALTON   LORIELE
SINEAR

2700

† Dead
✳ Father

GENEALOGY
LLEWENTI CLANS

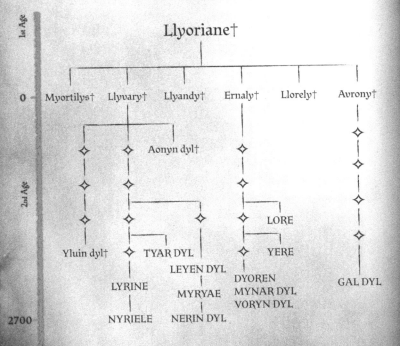

GENEALOGY IRAWENTI
FILWENI CLAN

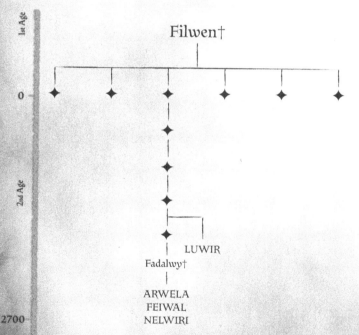

1st Age

Filwen†

0

2nd Age

LUWIR

Fadalwy†

ARWELA
FEIWAL
NELWIRI

2700

† Dead
◆ Father